T.L STURGIS

FLIRTING
WITH
DARKNESS

RAGE AND BLOODTHIRST SERIES BOOK 1

Copyright © 2022
T.L. STURGIS
Flirting with Darkness
All rights reserved.

T.L. STURGIS
www.tyeshiasturgis.com

Printed Worldwide
First Printing 2022
First Edition 2022

10 9 8 7 6 5 4 3 2 1

FLIRTING
WITH
DARKNESS

GLOSSARY OF TERMS AND VAMPIRIC GIFTS/ UNDERSTANDINGS

A Lesser- A term for a vampire weaker than another vampire.

A Warrior- A vampire weaker than the Primus, Omega, And Untouchable. However, they are stronger than a Newborn. They can enter homes without being invited.

Blood Drinkers- Older term for the vampire. Usually used by elder vampires or *Blood drinkers.*

Blood Bond- Passing the memories from one blood drinker to the next. Usually when one is bitten and transformed. If an older vampire such as a Primus, Omega, or Untouchable bites a human and drinks from their blood, it's possible for them to hold memories of the human and sense the human at certain times. They can also know where the human is and feel what they are going through.

Blood Puppets- Minions that follow the *Rulers* out of repayment of debt or as a punishment for breaking a vampiric rule. They are eyes and ears for the Rulers.

Blood-Thirst- Hunger for blood via human or animal. Unstoppable and uncontrollable hunger. Usually, newbies or newborns go through this stage when first transformed. Very hard to resist blood smells and or the sight of blood. Some newbies can resist if they have a particular gift, such as the gift of righteousness.

Comate Stage- A stage where vampires long for a companion. They want someone by their side for eternity. The feeling of loneliness is intense. This is the stage where most transformations happen.

Companions- Vampire partners. Life partners are not necessarily sexual or a lover. Someone to be by their side.

Compulsion- The ability to hypnotize a human into doing whatever is told of them. Usually happens when a vampire gazes into their eyes and gives them a demand. Not all humans are susceptible to compulsion. Only the Primus can use compulsion on another vampire.

Creator- Same as *sire* or *maker*. Newer Blood Drinkers use the term.

Daywalker- Blood Drinkers or vampires that can walk in sunlight. Sunlight can be an irritation but will not kill them like a newbie or newborn.

Fascination Stage- A stage where a vampire thinks they are in love. Usually becomes fascinated with a human but sometimes becomes infatuated with a vampire. Some newborns become fascinated and attached to their maker.

Feeders- Humans that offer themselves to be fed upon by vampires. Most feeders hoped to be transformed because of this act.

Glyphs- A *symbol* on a building to mark a vampire's safe space or location where vampires hang out. Sometimes vampires mark their lair.

Lairs- A secret area where vampires sleep in coffins. Usually surrounded by stone. Dungeon-like with no window and pitch black. *Blood puppets* usually guard this area. Older *Blood drinkers* have lairs.

Maker- Same as a *sire.* Older *Blood Drinkers use the term.*

Newbies- Same as newborns. Newer vampires use the term. Most Newbies hide behind technology and conform to the new century.

Newborns- Newly transferred vampires. Not as strong as the *Primus, Omegas, or Untouchables.* Further down the bloodline and cannot walk in the sunlight, fly, feed off another vampire, or enter homes uninvited. Elder vampires use this term.

Omega- Blood drinkers directly transformed by the *Primus.* These vampires have a *Blood Bond,* and strength, and are just as powerful as the *Primus.* Can walk in sunlight, enter homes unlimited, and can float. Some can feed on other vampires. Weaker than the Primus but are powerful. Can read other vampire minds.

Primus- The original vampires. The first vampires created. All vampires' bloodlines lead to them. They can walk in sunlight, enter homes uninvited, and fly. The strongest of all vampires. They can also feed on other vampires, use compulsion, and read their thoughts.

Royal Blood- The blood of the Primus or Omega. Their direct bloodline. One being transformed directly from one of these vampires is considered having the *Royal Blood* running through them.

Rulers- Omegas or Untouchables appointed as guardians over the Primus. Not to be confused with *The Order, not all Rulers are part of The Order.* Rulers usually have two or more blood puppets that follow them or obey them. *Rulers* report back to the *Primus* of vampiric misdeeds.

Seeker- A human that hunts vampires and other supernatural beings.

Shifter Hybrid- A werewolf that has transformed into a vampire. They cannot form into a wolf. They do not have any vampiric abilities other than strength and speed.

Sire- When a human is transformed by a vampire, the vampire that transforms the human becomes its father of darkness or mother of darkness to the *newbie.* Most vampires are connected and have a desire to please their sire.

Telepathy- The ability to read one's thoughts and/or how one's body senses. Some *Blood Drinkers* can read other vampires' thoughts. Usually older ones. Not all vampires can read each other's minds, but all can read the thoughts of humans.

The Coat of Arms- Similar to *The Order.* A council of vampire hunters or slayers that specializes in hunting down vampires or other supernatural entities. Human counterparts that destroy the undead, etc.

The Gift of Aura- This gift gives a vampire premonitions about the future and sees the unseen spiritual energy around supernaturals and humans—good or bad vibe—as their true character, not what they are feeling at the moment. A vampire with this gift can also sense what type of supernatural being one is.

The Gift of Allies- Both humans and vampires can't resist the vampire that processes this power. They instantly indulge them and put them on a pedestal. Attracted to or fascinated with. Can be angry or even rage towards a vampire with this ability. However, it is hard to dislike them and easy to become attached to them. Other vampires can't read their minds. Their strength and speed are remarkable.

The Gift of Debility- Can look a vampire or a human in the eyes and temporarily paralyze them, freezing them in place.

The Gift of Perception- Can project visions into others' minds. With and without touching them. They can manipulate what others see and can even blind them temporarily. Both humans and vampires. Also, is faster than normal vampires. Strength is slightly above average than a newbie or newborn, but not against an Untouchable, Omega, *a Warrior,* or Primus.

The Gift of Righteousness- being able to control oneself and urges beyond a normal vampire. Some vampires can control their urges without this gift, and it's very rare. It gives them the ability to have clarity during the blood-thirst stage and when they see human blood at a close range.

The Gift of Transference - Can transfer any gift to themselves by grabbing or touching another vampire. Also carries the Vision of Transference.

The Gift of Truth- the ability to sense other vampires or humans lie. If a vampire has the gift of allies, they cannot sense how they are feeling nor read that vampire's mind.

The Order- A council of vampires that make sure newbies or newborns follow all vampiric rules. For example, no human-vampire relationships.

The Vision of Transference- is also known as the *Blood bond*. Being able to see the memories of older vampires. Usually, Older *Blood Drinkers* such as *Omegas* and *Untouchables* can see the visions from *Primus's* past life.

Transformation- When a vampire turns a human or a supernatural human into a blood drinker. This is done by feeding their blood to the other party.

Untouchables - Transformed by an *Omega*. Cannot be harmed or killed by any other vampire. They wear a rare tanzanite stone ring for all vampires to identify them. *The Order* cannot punish them for breaking any vampiric rules. They can also walk in the daylight, enter homes uninvited, and float. Cannot feed on other vampires.

Uproar Stage- a stage where a vampire is angry. It can be an unresolved issue before the transition or after. They live to seek revenge against whatever indiscretion they felt was against them. Emotions of various feelings are heightened.

Depression, anger, sexual tensions, etc. Some newborns experience this stage immediately.

Vampire- an undead creature of the night that feeds off the blood of humans and animals. Usually noticeable by their long canine teeth and pale skin. They are cold to the touch and have various abilities and supernatural strengths.

Vampire Slayer- same as a *seeker*. Older *Vampire Hunters or Vampires use this term.*

Vampire Symbol- An engraved ouroboros. A Celtic dragon eating its tail. It represents a unity of all things human and supernatural. A cycle of destruction and recreation.

Wiccan- Another word for a witch.

Wiccan Hybrid- Witches that have transformed into a vampire making them half-mortal and half immortal. They carry no Wiccan abilities from their past life as a human. May possess a vampiric ability.

Wolf Shifter- also known as a werewolf. Half man and half wolf. Can change into wolf form. Their bite can be deadly to a vampire. They were born and are supernatural humans.

Younglings- also known as a youngins', are child vampires. Usually, these vampires are younger than the age of seventeen. A vampire that was created too young in its youth. Does not carry any abilities and is always in the stage of *Blood-thirst*, making them uncontrollable and murderous.

CHAPTER ONE

S avage. This was the only word that Amara was thinking as her fist throbbed. She watched the man quickly grab his face. Bright red blood profusely spurted out of his nose and between his fingers as he held it. And it was already swelling.

"Have you lost your damn mind!" the man screamed out in agony. "I think you broke my nose, you crazy bitch!"

"I hope I did. Asshole," Amara snapped back. The anger in her voice had elevated to a new height, but she didn't care who heard her yelling. He had deserved the sucker punch dead in the face.

She eyed him as he stormed off, then quickly rushed over to Mariam's side, visibly shaken, and placed her arm around her.

"It's okay," she said as she consoled her. "I got you."

Amara had been a powerhouse at that moment in protecting her friend. They had been through so many ups and downs. But they had each other's backs one hundred and ten percent. In New York City, there were plenty of men just like that lurking around, and it was Amara's turn to have Mariam's back this time.

"Thanks," Mariam said as she adjusted her clothing. "He just came out of nowhere and when he grabbed me… I froze."

"I know. I saw the whole thing, and that asshole got what he deserved. Bestie to the rescue," Amara said, trying to lighten up the mood.

The mysterious man in question had been eyeing Mariam all night. Amara and she had stepped out for the night and gone to a local bar for a girl's night out. All had been going well and Amara was glad to see that her best friend was out and about, attempting to crack open her shell and enjoying herself.

But as Mariam attempted to go to the restroom, the man had cornered her up against the wall in the hallway. As she tried avoiding his advances, the drunken man became aggressive, and as she tried to move away from him, he grabbed her arm and jerked her back.

When Amara looked over and saw the man not only putting his hands on her but also pinning her up against the wall with both his hands, she immediately sprang into action and went over to her friend's side. She tapped the man on the back and, needless to say, the man and his smart mouth ended up eating a knuckle sandwich for his disrespect.

Mariam wasn't weak by all means, but because of her past trauma with aggressive men, she was still working through her issues. It ate Amara up to see her friend resort to such a vulnerable state. She still felt guilty about the past. And that Mariam even wanted to step out tonight, was her trying to move forward from her past. Amara wasn't about to let anyone stop the process of her overcoming it.

"I'll be alright, let's not let that asshole ruin our night," Mariam said while forcing a grin across her face.

"Are you sure? We can leave?"

"Yes, I'm sure and no," Mariam replied. "You still haven't told me about Mr. Right yet and I have a surprise for you."

"A surprise? Oh lord, what are you up to?"

"For me to know and for you to find out."

"Well, I'll wait outside the door until you finish and then I will tell you about Mr. Right."

Amara watched as Mariam entered the restroom and shook her head. As the door shut behind her, she took a deep breath and looked down at her hand. It was red and sore to the touch; however, it hadn't swollen, and she shook off the pain.

Deep down she knew that the incident that just took place shook Mariam and Mariam was good at playing things off and hiding her true feelings. But if Mariam wanted to stay, then that's what they would do, even though Amara was just ready to call it a night for the sake of her friend.

After a couple of minutes, a bright-eyed Mariam appeared from the door. Amara once again smiled at her as she secretly tried to read her face. But Mariam was back to herself as if nothing had even happened. They headed back toward their table and had a seat.

"So, what's his name? And what is he like? And how did you all meet?" Mariam's questions came out of her mouth like a wrecking ball.

"Aaron. He's nice and respectful. Someone I can see being long term," Amara said, smiling. "And we met at my job."

Amara had been waiting for the right guy to come around. Here lately, the men that she had been dating ended up being jerks that only wanted to get in her pants. But Aaron was different, and she could tell.

"Are you serious right now? Your job? What happened to not dating men at your place of work?"

"I know what I said, but trust me, he isn't like the rest and when you meet him, you will see. He's just busy with his job, but whenever he's in town, we spend most of our time together and I love the attention he gives me."

"So let me get this straight. You met him at the night-club, and you barely see him." Mariam's voice trailed off as if her thinking while talking froze her brain. And Amara could see the skepticism all over her face.

After all, Amara's quest for the perfect boyfriend had seemed to fail time and time again. And Mariam knew that this was already sounding like a referee blowing a whistle while waving a big red flag.

"I know what you're thinking… But this is different… I feel it," Amara stated.

"I just don't want you to get hurt again," Mariam said after taking a sip of her water. "You were there for me when Bobby and I broke up and I'm just trying to be there for you. Just take your time with this one."

Plenty of nights Amara yearned for human touch. She hated the sense of loneliness. All the women her age, including Mariam, had at least experienced a boyfriend for longer than six months. However, her luck with a man usually ended up being a one-night stand and a no-call afterward. She was thinking something was wrong with her.

"Anyway, what's your surprise?"

"Guess who's in town?" Mariam sarcastically said.

"Who?"

"Noah and he is looking rather nice these days."

Amara could hear the teasing in Mariam's voice. Mariam had always wanted her and Noah to get together and be a couple, but she didn't know where her feelings lay with him.

Sure, they had had their moments of intense connections and flirting, but it went no farther than that.

The last time didn't end too well for them and even though she had talked to him on the phone from time to time, it had been over two years since either of them had seen him. All of them were childhood friends and Noah, by all means, wasn't a bad guy, but for Amara, she had always felt that she was too wild for him and if she risked dating him, then they would end up breaking up. She didn't want to risk a lifelong friendship over a what-if and felt that it was best if she stayed away from him and let him move on with someone that was better suited for him.

"You know I can't be around Noah. It's weird now."

"For god's sake, you two shared a kiss. So what? Isn't that a good thing?"

"I have someone now," Amara snarkily replied.

"Yeah. Red flag Aaron." Mariam rolled her eyes, dismissing him. "You and Noah have a connection and he not only likes you, but the man is seriously in love with you and… he is single."

"In love?" Amara laughed. "Don't you think that's a stretch? He has a childhood crush on me, but that's it."

"You have a crush on him as well. And I don't think it's a stretch. I'm just stating the obvious."

"I think you need to put down the romance novels."

"I'm just saying." Mariam grinned.

Amara picked up her mimosa and slowly sipped it. She pondered on what Mariam had just said. It would be nice to see Noah again. Even if it was just catching up. But she also knew the crush he had on her. And rejection was not fun. She had plenty of that and she didn't want his feelings hurt as hers had been. She cared for him too much to disappoint him again.

"No… it's just best that Noah doesn't see me," she reiterated.

"Well… it's too late."

CHAPTER TWO

"What! What did you do?" Amara's voice rang with signs of frustration and annoyance.

"I invited him over."

"When?"

"Tonight."

For a split second, Amara's face flushed with anger, but she quickly got over it. After all, Mariam was only trying to help her. And she knew this much for sure. As they hopped in the car and headed towards her apartment, her hand became sweaty with the idea of even seeing Noah again. She didn't know why he made her so nervous. It's not like she hadn't known him for all of her life. And as much shit as she had put Mariam through when it came to her various dating episodes, at least she could make her friend happy and meet up with him.

"I'm not making any promises," Amara said, looking over at Mariam. "We are strictly friends."

"Of course," Mariam said, glancing over at her. "Strictly friends."

This always seemed to happen whenever Amara thought she had found the right person. Another guy stepped in and distracted her, and then she questioned if guy number one was better than guy number two.

They pulled up in front of Amara's apartment building. After getting out of the car, they hadn't walked five feet before she heard a familiar voice coming from behind them. Noah. He rushed over to them, putting one arm around Mariam and the other around Amara.

"Ladies, it's been a long time."

"I'm so glad to see you, Noah," Mariam said.

"What about you?" he teased Amara.

"It's always good to see you," she replied. Her heart was already beating out of her chest. His touch and his smell were enticing enough.

As they reached the front door of her apartment, Mariam quickly rushed past both of them, turning and giving a wink to Amara as she shut the door for the two to have their privacy. She left both Amara and Noah out in the hallway to catch up.

"Listen," he said. "I don't like how things ended last time."

She watched as he moved closer to her, where there was little space between them. "I didn't either," she said, looking towards the ground, trying not to make eye contact with him.

"You running off like that? What was that about?"

As he leaned in, she tensed up, thinking that he was about to kiss her. But to her surprise, he took his finger and gently lifted her chin. She had no choice but to look him dead in the eyes.

"I just didn't want to cross a line with you. Our friendship means too much to me."

He removed his hand from her face and just glared at her. "Remember, I am not like those other guys. My intentions are pure and always will be."

"I appreciate you. But friends is where I think we should stay and besides, I'm seeing someone at the moment."

She looked Noah in the face and could see the disappointment in his eyes. With him and her, he was always the groomsman and never the groom. Amara was the woman of his dreams, but clearly, the feeling was not mutual.

Their friendship was the classic scene out of a movie where a girl meets the guy next door. The boy has a crush on the girl, but in this situation, the boy hadn't quite landed the girl, and the girl seemed to be focused on every other guy besides him. But the boy wasn't about to give up on the girl, no matter how long it took.

"Okay," he said. "I'll back down… for now." He shot her a mischievous grin.

Noah stepped back from her and opened the door. Amara's heart was racing as she entered behind him. They had chemistry. And every time Noah was close to her, she felt butterflies in her stomach. But his friendship was more important than a trial run with him. She had always been hot and cold with guys and dating.

The last time she had seen Noah, they were hanging out, drinking shots of tequila right before Noah was to take off and start his new job out of state. Amara was dancing and almost tripped, leading to him catching her and once they gazed into each other's eyes, Noah moved in closer, and they shared a passionate kiss.

Her phone rang breaking that special moment they were sharing. It was a guy that she had been seeing at the time and she ran off, leaving Noah hurt and confused about where they stood. She had vowed never to hurt him again.

That kiss was a mixture of being drunk and acting in the heat of the moment. Nothing more in her book.

Mariam and Noah were undeniably her true best friends and even though she could be off-putting and hard to deal with, she had their backs as much as they had hers. And that was just another reason she felt that Noah and she would never work out. It was just best if they stayed friends.

As they walked over to the couch where Mariam was sitting, her eyes were wide with a goofy smile that was plastered on her face. "Another passionate kiss?" she questioned them as she giggled. Both of them took their seats.

"Not this time," Noah said, glancing at Amara and then back at Mariam. Amara, however, didn't say a word and secretly wished she had never told Mariam about what happened. But then again, if she didn't, Noah would've. "She is already taken."

"I'm not taken… Just dating someone at the moment."

Mariam rolled her eyes. "The guy is a walking red flag," she mumbled underneath her breath, but loud enough for Amara to hear her sly comment.

"Can we please not talk about my personal life at the moment?"

Amara shot Mariam a look. The look one girlfriend gives her other girlfriend with wide eyes meaning for her to "shut up. You're talking too much." Mariam pinched her lips and leaned back on the couch, ending that conversation.

"Well, ladies," Noah spoke up, trying to break the awkwardness. "How've things been?"

"Same old, same old," Mariam replied, looking directly at Amara.

"Just working and paying bills," Amara responded as well.

She thought of her response. Such a lame answer considering five minutes ago she'd told him she was talking to someone else. She knew that he indeed wanted to know more about that situation and about the new guy in her life.

"What about you?" Mariam eagerly questioned. "What made you want to come to the city?"

"To see my friends, of course." He smiled.

"No way. After two years? I don't believe it," Amara sarcastically joked. She was loosening up, and the awkwardness faded away. Noah was just an old friend catching up and once she had shaken off every thought other than that one, she could just be his friend.

"I have a secret, but I will tell you guys later once everything is certain," Noah said.

Three hours passed, and they talked about life and reminisced about old times. Noah told the story of him and Amara racing on their bikes when they were little. And how they went down a hill heading towards a lake only for him to hit a rock underneath his tire, launching him headfirst in the water.

They all giggled at the stories that he told. Amara gazed at him while he talked and giggled alongside Mariam. Her breathing accelerated and she felt butterflies in her stomach. He was like a breath of fresh air. Noah being in her presence felt like a warm sunny day after a long and miserable winter. She couldn't help but notice how much he had changed since their last encounter. Noah was way better looking, and she couldn't help but think that maybe she should give him a chance. But she quickly shrugged those thoughts off and focused on the fact that Aaron seemed promising. She glanced at Mariam then back at Noah. Just friends.

CHAPTER THREE

Amara tapped her finger on the menu. She wasn't focused and hadn't been for three nights. Noah was still on her mind, but here she was with Aaron at a restaurant called Paterra's kitchen on the outskirts of the city.

"Are you alright?" he questioned. "You seem a little distracted."

"Yeah, I'm fine. Just thinking about an old friend."

"Anyone I need to be worried about?" he said jokingly.

"No… not at all."

Amara had been seeing Aaron for almost three months now. They communicated frequently on the phone and through email when he was at work. And their relationship was developing. They had been on six dates, including this one. He was a big-time sales representative for a marketing company that required him to travel a lot. He was in town for two days and then he had to take off again.

She had feelings for him and probably would be in love by now if he wasn't traveling all over the state and country. From what he told her, he had even made two trips to Japan. And now that Noah was in town, it made things complicated. She understood the position that Aaron had with his company and for now, they would have to make the best out of the cards they were dealt.

He promised her if he landed this deal, then he would be promoted and have a permanent office here in New York City. But until that time came, she would have to share him with his job. She wanted this relationship to work out. There were too many failed attempts at having someone for her and she couldn't bear another heartbreak.

They hadn't moved past the kissing and minor groping stage. But he was coming to her job tonight and this would be the first time that he would spend the night in her apartment.

The vibrating sound of his cell phone broke her attention, and she watched as he quickly glanced at his phone and then back at her. Aaron seemed to be a great guy. Not like any of her past relationships—if that's what they could be called. He had no "baby mama drama." No weird fetishes. He was well-groomed and mature. And he wasn't some narcissistic asshole like the list of men she had previously dated.

The phone buzzed loudly against the table, startling Amara. After a couple more rounds of buzzing, she gazed at Aaron. "Are you going to answer that?"

"Umm, yeah," he said hesitantly. "Just give me a second."

She watched as he hurriedly got up from their table and headed towards the outside doors. She couldn't help but notice his "deer in the headlights" look on his face. Whoever it was on the other end clearly made him feel uneasy.

After about fifteen minutes, he returned. His face was back to being relaxed and everything seemed to be normal.

"Sorry, love," he said as he sat back down. "When the boss calls, I have to answer."

"I understand," she replied, giving him a friendly smile.

She watched as the waitress headed over to the table. "Are you all ready to place your orders?" the woman asked.

Aaron's phone began buzzing again.

"I'm sorry, but I have to take this call," he said, and off he went again.

※

Lou nursed his glass full of dark liquor while tapping the side of it with one finger. He occasionally looked down at his gold and black Rolex watch, feeling a little overdressed in a place like this.

Even though Platinum was an upscale nightclub in uptown Manhattan, it still didn't warrant the attire of a suit and tie. He looked down at his watch once more. Victoria was running late as usual. He was used to it by now, but it didn't make it any less annoying.

He glanced around the club as the collection of hip hop, R&B, and rock music blazed through the speakers. He took in the scents of sex and desperation that were coming off the various men and women that paraded and danced around the club.

As packed as the place was, he was lucky enough to find an isolated corner table overlooking the entire area, including the dance floor, bar, and entrance. Even if the seat was taken, he would've just compelled that party to leave.

In the dim lighting, he watched as the various attractive servers wearing the same V-neck white shirt and tight biker shorts walked past him. Most of them glanced his way, batting their eyes and flashing a flirtatious smile. A few of them—at least four since he had sat down—asked him if he needed a drink, while purposely bending over and flashing their breasts at him. As tempting as they were, he passed on their advances, and when the last one approached him, he had placed a drink order. Tonight, he wasn't interested in any of them. They were not the reason he was here. He had someone else arriving, and her name was Victoria.

He questioned why Victoria picked these types of places for them to meet up–knowing it would get under his skin. She was the one who loved sleazy nightclubs. Not him. But as distasteful as he may have found this place, he still showed up strictly for her.

He was delighted because she differed from all the other blood-drinkers that he knew. She was lively and had a bubbly personality. But she was also strong and ruthless–when she needed to be. She loved being a blood drinker and her lifestyle reflected it. Part of him wished he had been the one that changed her. After all, she was a brilliant vampire with an amazing gift.

That fact was only one of the reasons he had to get her far away from Silas's reach and why he had lied to him about being her *creator*. But now wasn't the time to dwell on the past. He brought his focus back to the present moment and the only thing he wanted to know was where Victoria was?

It had been an hour and a half since he had arrived, and he had been ready to leave the moment he'd walked in the door. He looked down, digging in his pocket, and pulling out his wallet, when he immediately felt a strong sense of eagerness and excitement. He immediately knew who it was. Victoria.

"You're leaving already?" she questioned while chuckling and taking a seat beside him.

"Victoria, why must you always be late?" A look of frustration painted his face.

"I wanted you to enjoy the scenery," she let out as she grabbed the arm of one server walking past. She caught her eyes. "Get me a double shot of whiskey," she told her. She gazed into the woman's eyes, compelling her to do as she asked.

"You know you don't have to do that," Lou said, then tossed back the last sip of his drink and set his glass back down on the table. "That's their job."

"I know, but it's more fun this way." Victoria pulled the woman closer to her. "And bring my friend another whiskey and coke, hon."

She released her arm, and the server nodded yes, then walked off in a trance-like state to go fetch their drinks.

"Why are we here?" Lou questioned her as he shook his head. "We could have met at your place."

Victoria heard the annoyance coming through his voice, but she paid it no mind. "Sheesh, Lou… you're a two-hun-dred-year-old vampire and still uptight."

"I'm not uptight," he mumbled.

"Then what would you call it?" She giggled.

As they felt their server approaching the table, their conversation halted. Once she arrived, they intensely watched as she placed both drinks down in front of them. Then she stood there as if she didn't know what to do next.

"See, *compulsion* makes them move faster," Victoria said, winking at Lou. Then she turned towards the server and locked eyes with her once more. "You are free to go. But stay close, we might need you again." Victoria gave her a rewarding grin as the server walked away.

Lou grabbed his drink. "Are you going to answer my question?"

"About what? Why are you so uptight? Well, love… I can't answer that one." A small smirk came across her face. She placed the tiny straw that was in her drink between her red-colored lips and sipped, still chuckling underneath her breath.

"As much as I love your cunning humor, I will leave this table and we can meet up in another five to ten years," he smugly said as he pierced his lips together.

"Okay… okay," she replied, turning her cheek up in contempt. "I'm lonely… I want a *companion*."

He looked at her in confusion. "But you have me, the uptight one, remember?"

"You know what I mean—" Her brows furrowed. "And I only see you every decade."

"I thought you enjoyed being on your own. Aren't you the one who said a *companion* would slow you down?" he noted. "Besides, you're strong enough to change a human. You don't need me."

Her sudden change of heart did not confuse him. All *blood drinkers* went through the *comate stage*—the stage in which a vampire has an irresistible urge of wanting a *companion* to roam eternity with. It could be a love interest or as simple as a partner in crime.

Lou once had a *companion* in Silas known to be the one other *blood drinkers* feared more than death and even though it was hard for a vampire to leave his or her *companion*, sometimes they had no choice. He had been alone ever since.

"Oh, but yes I do… I need you," she said, breaking his thoughts. She lowered her eyes and glanced down at the ring on his finger. "I need you to change her. You know I'm just a *Daywalker*, but you, sir… You are… *untouchable*."

Lou quickly put his hand over the top of the ancient tanzanite ring and squeezed his hand. They only gave this ring to a blood drinker of a certain caliber—an *untouchable*.

He understood the feeling that Victoria was experiencing. No vampire wanted to live eternity alone. Most *blood drinkers* had companions or love partners before they even hit the *comate stage*. It was only a matter of time before Victoria got swept away by it. Regardless of how tough she portrayed herself to be, all vampires went through this stage of loneliness—even him.

"You know I care about you Victoria but changing a human... is out of the question for me." He grabbed Victoria's hand and placed it in his. "I will not be responsible for a *newbie*. They are unpredictable."

"I know, but I will teach her. I know how *The Order* is... and just in case, that's where you come in." She stared directly into his eyes. "Do you not trust me?"

"Of course, I trust you, and I know how you feel... I've been there," he replied. "But there are rules. If the *newbie* gets out of control, she will be beheaded... Do you want to risk an innocent life... your life as well?"

Victoria sighed. "You can be my shield... if I break a rule. It would be a win-win situation. An *Untouchable* can't be executed... no matter what."

She was right. An *Untouchable* couldn't be executed for breaking any form of vampiric laws. And *The Order* was forbidden to touch any of them by any means. *Untouchables* had the *royal blood* of the *Primus* running through their veins. And to make sure the vampire race was preserved, they were to be left alone.

It was better to let them do as they pleased than to kill them. The *Primus* royal bloodline made the *Untouchables* extremely strong. Some of them even carried memories of *Primus'* and *Omega's* past lives when they were transformed.

Most of them became *Rulers*, and they protected the secrecy of *The Order*. They often spied on other vampires and reported vampiric misdeeds to them. They usually had two or more minions to follow their decrees and to do their bidding for them—something Lou had turned down.

Of course, the Untouchables rarely broke any vampiric rules—knowing how important they were to be followed. The laws hid their existence from the outside world, keeping all *blood drinkers* safe.

Victoria leaned forward looking towards the dance floor. The strobe light caught her face from time to time, illuminating her sun-kissed blonde hair and her fascinating beauty. She didn't look at Lou but pointed at a brunette with long wavy hair that was serving a male guest next to the dance floor.

"Before you turn me completely down... look," she said, still pointing towards the woman. "Just see what I see and sense what I sense."

Lou narrowed his eyes, homing in on the woman. Even with his vampiric eyes, it was hard to capture what Victoria was talking about. The light only showed her silhouette. Without her being closer, he couldn't completely see her face.

Even if the woman's features were attractive, that wasn't enough to put her through the *transformation*. He wasn't the one to take human life nor put a human in a situation that may lead to their death. He respected the sanctity of life.

"No, I won't," he sternly said. "And I prefer you not change her yourself… she's not worth the risk."

Amara's feet were throbbing like they had a tiny heartbeat of their own. With each throb, pain shot through them. She had picked up some extra hours leading into working a double shift. She loved her job working at Platinum, and as much as she loved the party scene and nightlife, tonight had her feeling a little burnt out.

She left the table by the dance floor and headed towards the bar to put in a request for the two gentlemen's drink orders. She had been eyeing Aaron all night and secretly wondered if he was boyfriend material.

"Lacy, I have another drink order, and take your time, please," she called out to the bartender, placing her order sheet down.

Amara turned and leaned her shoulders against the bar, trying to take some of the pressure off her feet. She figured she would have at least a good five to ten-minute break before heading back to the table.

The place was extremely busy and, by looking at the size of the crowd, she figured there must've been a big game or event going on where people flocked to the club to celebrate afterward. At least it would mean good tip money tonight, she thought as she watched another server by the name of Kat heading towards her.

"Did you see the hot guy over at the corner table with the suit... and the nice Rolex watch he's wearing?" she questioned as she whispered to Amara, removing a brown strand of hair from her face and placing it behind her ear.

Amara glanced over at the table and barely saw the face of the man but noticed that a woman with blonde hair was sitting beside him. She took a mental note of that fact.

"Yeah," she replied. "I don't see that happening."

"Are you serious right now? He is gorgeous and has some money."

Amara wondered if Kat had gone blind. Whether she was close enough to see his face, clearly there was a woman already there occupying his time.

"And a girlfriend too." Amara rolled her eyes while shaking her head as she turned towards the bar and collected her drinks. "Besides, I have my eyes on the guy at my table. His name is Aaron, and we have been talking for three months now."

Kat looked towards Amara's table with the two men. "Are you serious right now? I swear you have the worst taste in men."

"I beg to differ… And you're judging my taste? Coming from the girl that wants me to hit on a man with a girlfriend," she sarcastically replied. She lifted her serving tray. "I think I'll take my chances on my guy." She smiled at Kat and then walked away.

"Okay, but I think you're making a mistake," Kat yelled as her voice faded in the distance.

While Amara approached the table with Aaron and the other man, she thought about what Kat had said. Of course, she wanted a good man and yes, she secretly wished she had a boyfriend. And lately, she hadn't been lucky in the dating department, but she wasn't that desperate to go after another woman's man. And besides, hopefully her and Aaron's relationship would work out. She didn't see any red flags in him.

Sure, she'd had a couple of one-night stands that she thought could be more but left her crying in the heartache of rejections and the arms of her best friend, Mariam. Regardless of all that, she was no home wrecker. There were some lines that she wouldn't cross.

"Hey, guys… I've got your drinks," Amara said as she moved toward them. "Two boilermakers." She smiled as she placed the first glass down in front of the man with the slick back hair and wearing a leather jacket. He sized her up, undressing her with his eyes and flashing parts of his teeth as he gave her a sleazy grin.

Then she placed the second glass down in front of Aaron. His sandy brown hair, dreamy green eyes, and clean-cut beard glistened in the nightclub lights. He's gorgeous, she thought as she noticed his smile. How was she so lucky to be involved with him? His looks were the reason she had first noticed him.

"That will be twelve dollars and fifty cents," she said.

Aaron reached into his pocket and pulled out a fifty-dollar bill, then placed it on her tray. Most men in the club tried to put the money in between her cleavage–the reason for them wearing the low-cut shirt as part of their uniform–but not him.

Keep the change… that's for you." Aaron winked. "By the way, I can't wait to see you later on."

"I can't either," she replied, blushing. And I'm also a sucker for a man with a beard and a pleasant smile. She tried to hide the fact that she was blushing.

"Well, Amara—" his friend spoke up and said. "How long have you and my friend been seeing each other?" His giggle seemed to sour the mood around the table.

"Three months," she replied as she leaned over and planted a kiss on Aaron's lips. But his friend just sat there gazing at the two. By his look, she didn't know if he was jealous or if he was one of those annoying friends that liked to tease all the time. He looked over at Aaron with a questioning look, then spoke once more.

"You sir, are a player."

CHAPTER FIVE

L ou closely watched the brunette woman that Victoria had picked out. She walked through the crowd at Platinum, balancing her serving tray above her head and dodging the guest that almost bumped into her. If only she would turn towards them for him to see her face.

He took several sips of his liquor until he realized that his glass was empty. He needed another one dealing with the thoughts about Victoria's request. He was sensing her feelings of loneliness and sadness. And It was making him uneasy. Not only did the request itself feel awkward but also the emotions coming off of her.

Victoria sat there, gazing at the woman. As bad as she wanted the woman, she had no choice but to respect Lou's decision. But she didn't regret the fact that she had asked him. At least she tried, and that was all she could've done. She had broken no rules with *The Order* but if she was to change this woman and the woman broke any vampiric rules, then both of them would have to face the consequences and that was the risk of changing someone into a *newbie*.

"I won't ask again." She sighed. She wasn't happy with Lou's answer, but what else could she do? Lou had advised her not to change the woman herself and she heeded his advice.

He had been the sole reason she had broken no vampire rules and reaped any form of punishment–in one hundred years of her immortal life. He had protected her and guided her. She was beyond loyal to him and his word.

Lou felt guilty. Saying no to Victoria was something he'd never done. After all, she didn't ask for much. But he had his justifications for rejecting her request. Maybe he could make Victoria feel a little better if he agreed to monitor the woman–checking her out. But deep down, his answer would be the same. He cared for Victoria's ego and didn't want to hurt her.

Victoria looked over at Lou, who seemed to be in deep thought. She watched as he analyzed the woman and wondered what he was thinking about. Even though her gift gave her the ability to read other vampires' minds, she wouldn't dare invade him. After a couple of minutes of silence between the two of them, Lou shifted in his seat and spoke.

"She is attractive, but why her?" he questioned as he leaned back in his seat, placing both of his arms across the back of the booth. "What makes her so special?"

Victoria's eyes perked up and glistened. She had believed this conversation was over, but apparently not. She smiled.

Lou sensed the feelings of hopefulness coming off of her and instantly noticed that her mood had shifted. This pleased him.

"She's bold and flamboyant... sometimes outspoken and exquisite, and beautiful," Victoria replied, emphasizing the word beautiful. "And of course my favorite... She loves to party... She is my twin."

"Victoria, give yourself more credit than that. You are exquisite. There is only one you." Lou beamed. "And how long have you been watching this woman?"

"Just for a couple of days and only here," she quickly replied. "I haven't followed her around… A woman like me has other things to do." She flipped a piece of her hair as Lou shook his head and laughed.

"Well, before changing anyone, you know you at least need to check them out," he said.

Victoria never could sit still. She had to be all over the city–a little busybody. Whenever there was a party, she would more than likely be present. She loved New York, the big apple. But Lou secretly wished she would explore other territories like him.

"I know, and I will."

"How can you be so sure that she is the one to be a *companion* for you? You have only seen her in this setting?"

"Because I sensed her fiery side, her urge to want more, and I have been watching her inside this club. I just haven't had the time to follow her around town. But that shouldn't change her attitude that much."

Lou took a deep breath. "You need to be following her before you make such a decision. Even if I were to change her, put her through the *transformation,* you know I could never be by her side... and you know how *newbies* are when they're first created," he intoned, then let out a heavy sigh. "Let's get another drink."

"I understand, I'll be there...is that a yes?" she excitedly asked.

"No, I'm just stating facts." His eyebrows furrowed.

"Okay, Mr. Uptight, I'll take that and another drink."

Victoria was back to herself as she clapped in excitement. Lou wanting another drink and asking more questions was hopeful. "Do you want me to call her over?"

"No," he said. "Not here, not yet."

"Very well." Victoria held her hand out, flagging down Kat, who was walking past their table at the moment.

Kat stopped, delighted to serve this table. "What can I get you, handsome?" Her eyes fixated on Lou, not even acknowledging the person who had called her over in the first place–Victoria.

Victoria, tempted to take her to the bathroom and drink the blood from her carotid for the pure disrespect, refrained. Instead, she loudly cleared her throat to cause the woman's infatuation with Lou to break. And now the woman focused on her.

"We would like two more whiskeys... and make both a double."

"Will that be all?" Kat questioned.

"What is your friend's name?" Lou interrupted.

Kat was confused about who he was asking about until he nodded towards the brunette server, making her bouts through the crowd once more. Almost immediately, he sensed curiosity and jealousy coming from Kat.

"That's Amara." She gave a slight eye roll as she spoke. "And she's taken... sorry," she added.

Thinking that Lou was more interested in Amara than herself, she lied. Lou was reading her thoughts, and they said otherwise. But he didn't react.

"Well... just two rum and cokes," he said as Kat nodded yes and walked away, hoping she still had a shot with Lou.

"Always the ladies' man," Victoria chuckled. "They all love you."

Not interested, he thought.

Victoria veered around in her seat impatiently. She was eager to see whatever he was considering doing. But she didn't rush his thought process and instead stayed silent until he spoke.

He crossed his arms over his chest, still occasionally glancing over at Amara. Still trying to see her face. But her head stayed turned to the side. Even when she was serving a table close enough to theirs, her head tilted, blocking her features. He stopped trying to see her detailed face and homed in on his hearing abilities, isolating the sound of the club music and meaningless chattering. He focused only on Amara's conversation that she was having with her customer.

Lou watched as she stood over the top of a man with groggy eyes and a square jaw. He kept making advances at her and trying to grab her leg. And each time Amara would step backward. He could tell the man was getting on her nerves.

"Do you want to place a drink order or not, sir?" her voice rang out with agitation.

"What I want is a piece of you," he responded, still groping her leg.

With a hard roll of the eyes, she turned to walk away when the man clasped a handful of her butt.

"You son of a bitch," she yelled. She grabbed his wrist, twisting his arm around his back. She forced the man to lay his chest and face on the table, holding him there. He wailed out in pain.

"Let me go, you crazy bitch!"

Amara twisted his arm even harder, causing the man to scream out in agony. "Don't you ever touch me," she said. Then she released him and angrily stomped away.

Her reaction impressed Lou. Victoria was right, the woman was bold. Victoria's response would have been just like Amara's—other than Victoria would've ripped his arm off.

This indeed piqued his interest.

He looked over at Victoria, who had also been watching what just took place. She looked proudly at Amara.

"I'll follow her for a couple of days," Lou said. "And see what we are dealing with."

CHAPTER SIX

Another hour and a half went by, as well as a ton of drinks, waiting for Amara to get off work. Finally, she emerged, holding her head down towards the ground. With her purse over her shoulder, she walked towards a well-dressed man and proceeded towards the door of the club.

"Well, I guess that's my cue," Lou said to Victoria. He stood up and fixed his shirt underneath his suit jacket, which had become wrinkled from sitting so long.

"Go get 'em, tiger." She laughed.

"Don't get your hopes up, Victoria." He gave her a cross-eye. "I'm only following her… nothing more."

"Well, don't make her a meal," Victoria called out as he headed toward the front entrance of Platinum.

Once he was outside, the loud sounds of the city pierced his ears. The sounds of car horns blowing, flashing siren lights, and the chatter of several pedestrians arguing with one another from a drunken night of partying collided. With all the noise surrounding him, it reminded him why he hated being in New York.

He looked around beyond the various people that occupied the sidewalks, but Amara and her companion were nowhere in sight... He picked up senses of anxiety, fear, and sexual desire as the people strolled past him. Each one of them had an agenda in mind.

Some people were getting off work and thinking about resting in their beds. Some were going to work and thinking about when they'd get off and others thought about the next strip club or bar they could go to intending to get laid.

As Lou looked down at his watch, it reflected the time of 1 am, and he soon remembered that he was in the city that never stopped nor slept. Something was always going on at all hours of the day and night.

Older vampires such as himself and Victoria had the luxury of roaming around during the daylight hours. The sun didn't burn them up into a pillar of dust like it would if the *newbies* were to be exposed to direct sunlight. It forced all *newbies* to live in the shadows of the night.

The older vampires had more of the *Primus'* blood running through them, giving them abilities like walking in the sun. Even though all vampires were connected to the *Primus*, not all of them like Lou had been transformed directly by one of them, but his creator was an *Omega*, making Lou a descendant of the *Primus* royal bloodline–an *untouchable*.

But with each *transformation* that a vampire performed, the bloodline of the newer vampire was weakened. This was the very reason a *newbie* wouldn't dare challenge a *Primus*, *Omega, an Untouchable*, or a *Daywalker*—they would annihilate them. Any *blood drinkers* created after the *Daywalkers* were considered *newbies*.

Lou continued reading the thoughts of humans, as he tried to locate the direction Amara had gone. He hadn't been a human for two hundred years, and their senseless thoughts reminded him of the trivial things that humans focused on.

He kept walking towards the parking garage, relying heavily on his vampiric hearing when someone rapidly grabbed him by the collar of his jacket, pulling him into a dark alley and pushing him up against a brick wall.

The hooded man pushed a black and silver blade against his throat. "Slowly reach into your pocket and give me your wallet," he frantically demanded.

Lou laughed. "I suggest you walk away," he told the man.

The man's face grew irritated as he pushed the sharp blade harder up against Lou's throat and instantly sliced it open.

Lou gasped as the man backed up, still holding the blade in his hand, watching him as he dropped to the ground. His blood poured out of his wound.

Had he not been drinking and had fed properly, the man wouldn't have stood a chance against him.

The man quickly rushed over and ransacked his pockets, grabbing his wallet and fleeing into the night. Lou stayed scrunched over. He was too weak to go after him and waited less than a minute till his wound completely healed. Once it did, he stood up as if nothing had happened. If he didn't have to follow Amara, he would hunt him down and rip him to shreds, but there was no time for that. Amara had too big of a head start on him and he needed to find her.

He angrily walked out of the alley, now wearing a blood-stained suit. He pulled his jacket together, covering his blood. His pace sped up as he still focused on finding Amara. Finally, he caught wind of Amara and the man's faint voices. With one simple gesture, he used his vampiric speed to catch up to them.

One thing about being in the city—no one paid attention to the actions of others, not even what was going on around them. No one noticed the blood on his clothes, and no one noticed when he vanished in a flash, disappearing from them.

Amara and the man's voices grew stronger. Lou was close, and he finally spotted them walking in the parking garage. He stayed back a couple of feet, darting in behind the concrete pillars while he stayed out of sight.

At one point, Amara halfway turned her head, thinking that she had heard someone walking behind them. But she didn't turn entirely around and instead shrugged it off.

Her intuition had been right, but Lou was too quick for her human eyes and hid when he accidentally made a noise that caught her attention.

He still watched as they approached what seemed to be the man's gray-tinted BMW. Lou quickly looked around and on the far end of the parking garage, opposite of Amara, a maintenance man was putting his key into a white utility van.

At vampiric speed, Lou met the clueless man, in an instant spinning him around and compelling him to hand over his keys.

"Now leave and call a cab home… Remember, your van broke down and forget about ever seeing me," Lou slowly said to him as he gazed into his eyes. In a hypnotic state, the man turned and walked away.

Lou hopped in the van and put the key in the ignition switch. He turned it over and waited for Amara and her male friend to back out of their parking spot and drive off as he pursued them.

His nose hairs burned as the smell of body odor, stale cigarettes, and bad cologne invaded his nostrils. The mixture of smells reeked throughout the van as he cracked the window, trying to air it out. But it didn't help against his sensitive vampiric nose.

Victoria, the lengths I go through for her, he thought to himself as irritation flooded his emotions. He told her he would follow Amara, and he was honoring his word–even if it meant him getting attacked, having to compel a man, and steal a foul-smelling van. This was becoming chaotic, and he wondered if Amara was worth it all.

After driving about twenty minutes through a city of hell, the BMW pulled onto a side street and parked. Lou drove past them and found a vacant spot on the street a couple of feet from them. He turned off the ignition and adjusted the rearview mirror to get a clearer view.

He watched as the man leaped out of the car, shutting his door, and skipping to the passenger side, opening Amara's door. At least the man was a gentleman, Lou thought to himself.

They both walked up a flight of concrete stairs leading into a brown brick apartment building with several floors. The man held open the front door and Amara smiled as she walked through.

Lou knew he needed to get out of the van to see exactly which apartment number she lived in, but as he opened the door, he sensed a feeling of hopelessness and despair. He spun around as a scrubby-looking male with a dirty jacket and stained blue jeans approached him.

"Hey, man," the staggering homeless man spoke. "Do you have a cigarette?"

Lou paused and exposed his fangs as he grinned at him. He eyed him while the man's face turned into pure shock. Lou was feeling a little famished from the attack and losing his blood. As the man attempted to flee, he caught up to him, grabbing his shoulder.

"I'm sorry, my friend," he said while sinking his teeth into his neck.

CHAPTER SEVEN

Amara wasn't thinking about a damn thing but what had just taken place with Aaron—something that put her in a state of despair and depression. It had been two hours since he had abruptly left, and she had been crying her eyes out for at least forty-five minutes.

She had worked a double shift, invited Aaron home, and still ended up in her porcelain tub—only wishing to drown in it. But she wasn't a damn fish and could only hold her breath underwater for so long. Finally, she pulled her head up and took a deep breath of the stale air.

As her face emerged, she pulled the stopper, draining the bath water and standing up to turn on the shower. She pressed the palms of her hands against her eye sockets. The scorching water poured down her naked back in a single stream and while keeping her eyes closed, she listened to the sound of the water as it sprayed against the tub. She replayed Aaron's exact words, trying to figure out where it all went wrong.

She's so beautiful… He would never leave her… She's the woman of his dreams. But that was a lie… All of it had been a lie. And her dumbass believed it, she thought to herself. All she wanted was a good guy, but maybe Kat and Mariam had been right–she didn't know how to pick a good man when she saw one.

Three months of dating and finally a night of passion with him, quickly followed by another hard rejection afterward. When she realized Aaron was the sickening type–a man that could manipulate a female with his dreamy eyes, dark hair, and gorgeous smile–it was too late.

She slammed her first down against the tub of water, causing it to splash and spill out onto the tile floor. She could hear her best friend Mariam's voice in her head. Remember... if you're the cow...you can't give the milk up for free. And not so soon.

She frowned in disdain. Ugh! That was the last thing she wanted to hear in her head right now, but she couldn't help herself because Mariam was right–and once again, she had ignored her advice.

After it was all said and done, Aaron had put on his clothes, daring to throw her a twenty- dollar bill and say "thanks" as he rushed out the door. Another asshole had blindsided her.

The steam from the tub filled the air, and the fog covered the walls, causing them to condense. They looked as if they were crying right along with her. The dim light in the bathroom made the scene even more depressing. And she couldn't scrub him off of her fast enough.

"I can't take this shit anymore," she cried out. She wasn't even sure who she was talking to. The universe? A higher power perhaps? But it didn't matter. She felt betrayed by every man she attempted to invite into her home.

Her face grew flush with anger, and that anger multiplied with her regret. She wished there was a few good men left. A few good men like Noah. She sighed. She was going on twenty-five and still didn't have a boyfriend. She was starting to believe something was wrong with her or maybe an invisible sign seemed to be plastered on her forehead that read: screw me over... please.

Whatever the reason, loneliness was reaping the best of her. She felt like a pit-stop for people to shit on, and the tragedy of it all was the fact that she was allowing it. And that assumption was consuming her life.

OK, Amara, it's time to stop feeling sorry for yourself. She was better than this. But she still couldn't shake the feeling of pain and emptiness that bellowed in her gut. She was lonely, no matter how badly she tried to play it off. And deep down, she didn't want to be.

She grabbed a white towel from off the rack and stepped out of the tub. She couldn't care less about the pool of water that rested on the ground. As she wrapped the oversized towel around her slim waist, she moved toward the mirror, leaving a trail of wet footprints.

As she wiped the glass, she saw her distorted face from the moisture on the surface. She felt as if something was wrong with her. She knew she was a little self-absorbed, but she was working on that. The whole situation didn't sit well with her. Why couldn't these men see the real Amara? She was nice, sometimes kind, and willing to do whatever to please someone. But maybe that was the problem—she was coming off too needy and way too desperate.

She thought about the countless YouTube videos she had watched on HOW TO CATCH A MAN. And none of the suggestions on how to keep one seemed to work for her.

She heard her cell phone vibrating across her nightstand in the next room. It was now 3 am. She gaped and wondered who could be calling her this late? She scooted across the wax floor with her wet feet in an attempt not to slip and fall on her butt. She reached it without incident, then quickly glanced at the screen, only to see that the number was blocked. But she still answered.

"Hello?" she said as she paused and waited until the person on the other end responded.

"I'm sorry I left like that." Aaron's voice came through on the other end of the phone. "I want to see you again."

She was speechless as an awkward silence invaded the conversation. OK, hear him out before going off on him...at least he called, she thought. But she wasn't about to let him off the hook so easily.

"Hello—" he said, breaking the silence.

"Then why did you leave and throw money at me?" she snapped. "Do you know how rude and how disgusting that made me feel?"

"I know... and I'm so sorry, I didn't mean to make you feel like that..." His voice was low, almost sorrowful. "I was just scared and didn't mean to offend you—"

At least he was apologizing, she thought. That was the first step to making it up to her–considering his actions right after they had sex for the first time. Maybe he wasn't so bad after all.

"Then why did you leave?" she questioned him. Her voice was sterner and more confident.

"I didn't want to... but—" he said and then took another long pause.

"But?"

"But I didn't want my wife to become suspicious."

Did she just hear him correctly? Did he just say, wife? "You're married?" she yelled. Her voice echoed throughout her apartment like a wild banshee.

"Yes, I —" he tried to explain, but she quickly hung up the phone before he could say another word. In her eyes, there was no good explanation for a married man to be cheating on his wife.

Goddamned buffoon. If I didn't already feel low enough about myself, he dropped the wife bomb on me. Bastard!

Now she was furious as hell and humiliated. What was she? A desperate side piece? She didn't think so. And instantly, something inside of her flipped like a light switch. She wasn't a wounded helpless bird, nor was her heart something to be played with. Her emotions turned cold and heartless as she lay down in her bed.

She needed some vengeance. This was the last time a man was going to screw her over and get away with it.

She was going to hunt the bastard down like the dog he is and tell his wife all about him.

CHAPTER EIGHT

Mariam sat on the marble island in the kitchen, suspiciously eyeing Amara. The blinds in Amara's studio apartment were still closed, the place was in shambles, and a container of melted chocolate ice cream leaked out onto the floor.

"Are you going to tell me what's going on?" Mariam questioned.

Amara stayed scrunched over while rummaging through her almost bare refrigerator. A half-eaten Chinese container sat on the shelf along with some spoiled yogurt and a half quart of orange juice.

"I prefer not to." She sighed, while grabbing the orange juice and shutting the door.

"But why?" Mariam said. "You know, you can tell me anything."

"Because, Mariam," she asserted. "I don't want to hear... I told you so."

"Just tell me what happened?"

Mariam watched curiously as Amara reached for a glass out of the cupboard and poured some orange juice in it.

She placed her elbows on the surface of the island while placing her fists on each side of her cheeks. This was her go-to position when preparing herself for Amara's rant, usually about some guy that had hurt her–this week.

"Want some?" Amara ignored her question and instead held up the carton with a half-smile.

She felt the pressure of Mariam's eyes burning a hole in the side of her head as she tilted her glass and drank.

And while Mariam impatiently waited for Amara to spill her guts, she noticed Amara was deliberately stalling her storytelling, causing her patience to run thin.

"Fine, I'll just leave," Mariam said as she slightly rose from her seat.

"He was married," Amara spat out. "And I slept with him…" She walked over to her window and opened the curtains to let the sunlight in.

She gazed out as a black cat sat on the windowsill looking at her. It turned its head, jumped down, and disappeared.

"What?!" Mariam said, but deep down she didn't know why she was even surprised.

"You heard me," she said, walking nonchalantly back towards the kitchen as if it didn't bother her. "Don't worry… I plan on telling his wife."

"And how are you going to do that? You barely know him," Mariam said, shrugging her shoulders. "I think you're being a little irrational right now."

"Irrational? He lied to me!"

"That's why I tell you to take your time. " Mariam barked back. "Before you invite them to your bed."

"See… And there it is," Amara snapped. "The… I told you so…and I waited three months.. Are you happy now?"

"What?! No… not at all," Mariam replied. "I want the best for you…"

"I know," Amara sighed. "I dont mean to be so snappy with you, I'm just upset."

Amara and Mariam were very close, best friends, to be exact. From elementary school to adulthood, they had always stuck by one another's side. When people saw Amara, they saw Mariam as well. Two peas in one pod, their parents would say.

People always believed that they were biological sisters and they let them believe just that. Amara's parents had been killed in a tragic car accident when she was five years old. So people automatically assumed they were.

And it was Mariam's family that took her in. Amara suffered abandonment issues and separation anxiety after the death of her parents. But Mariam's parents did everything they could to help her–even putting her through the best therapy money could buy.

Once she was older, Amara ditched the therapist because she felt like she had outgrown her issues. Mariam disagreed.

"You will find someone... just be patient and he will come," Mariam expressed.

"I'm only getting older…" Amara gazed at her. "I'm almost halfway to thirty and don't have a boyfriend."

"So what? I don't either," Mariam protested. "I'm single and I'm satisfied… You can be too."

Amara was a year older than Mariam, but people believed Mariam was the oldest by the way she carried herself—mature, book smart, well put together, and always had a plan.

Amara was a little immature and pretentious. But yet, they were the yin and yang to each other–somehow they balanced out.

"Oh, I'm not waiting... I have plans... And I want to be successful with a handsome man by my side."

"And you can't do that without a man?"

"I can... but I don't want to."

Mariam took a deep breath of exhaustion. Amara was hard-headed as hell, and she wasn't about to go down an endless road with her.

"Well, there's always Noah…" Mariam said, breaking the tension in the room.

Amara leaned on the kitchen island and rolled her eyes. Noah was a childhood friend. He was a very good-looking man and a good catch for someone, but not her. He was too nice for her, and she preferred her men a little edgier.

"No."

"But he is a great guy… he would be perfect for you." Mariam smiled as Amara shook her head. "I think you should at least give him a chance. He likes you, always has… And if he breaks your heart … Well, I will have your back."

They both laughed as Mariam acted like a boxer, swaying back and forth while making two fist jabs in the air.

Mariam always had her back, no matter what it was. She remembered the time when they were in the cafeteria at school.

Her theme song was "Girls Just Wanna Have Fun" by Cyndi Lauper.

While singing the lyrics and prancing over to her lunch table, she tripped over her own two feet–causing the square pizza, loose corn, and, of course, an open milk container to land on the most popular girl in school. Tracy Cain.

She laughed out of pure enjoyment, but she was the only one laughing. Not Tracy. And as the other spectators in the cafeteria instigated with their oohs and ahs, Tracy angrily stood up and slapped her dead in the face.

Mariam instantly jumped up and decked Tracy right in the left eye. It was such a powerful sucker punch Tracy wore a black eye for a week. Mariam took the fall and got suspended.

"Let's go out tonight!" Amara said. Her face changed from loathing to animation.

"What?" Mariam frowned. This was not at all what she had expected. "Tonight?.... Even after the married man?"

"Yes, tonight!" Amara felt the warmth in her face as it lit up. "Hear me out before you say anything."

"Oh, God." Mariam put her hand on her forehead.

She knew whatever Amara was cooking up in that brain of hers was about to be a horrible idea. And that idea was going to lead to another letdown.

She knew Amara well enough to know that was her pattern. Amara was always doing more harm than good to herself and dragging her along for the disastrous ride.

"I don't think finding another man to replace the last one...is a good idea."

"Okay, I won't.... but you have to go with me if I'm to stick to that promise." Amara grinned, playing on Mariam's empathy. "I just need to let loose right now."

"Where are we going?" Mariam threw her hands halfway in the air as a gesture of giving up. Instead of an hour of Amara trying to convince her, she opted to give in.

"Inferno!" she shouted, clapping her hands.

"Oh, hell no." Mariam shook her head firmly. "Absolutely not!"

With Lou's vampiric sense of hearing, he pried from beyond Amara's front door. He had been there throughout the night. He'd noticed when Aaron left, he stayed while Amara slept, and even saw when Mariam arrived–and was still there currently while they talked.

He darted in and out of the shadows of the apartment hallways as people came and went. But he had heard enough when Amara stated that she and Mariam were going to Inferno. Even though he cringed at the idea of spending another night in a dreadful nightclub and secretly agreed with Mariam about the place, he would be there when they arrived tonight.

With one gesture, Lou was out of the building and beside the van that he so desperately wanted to ditch. He opened the door and sat there for a moment to collect his thoughts. He couldn't believe what he had seen earlier. A face that he only saw in his memories. A face that prompted him of pain, suffering, and death.

At one point, he had left the complex and headed outside to find a snack before resuming his surveillance. He leaned on the back of the van as an attractive blonde-haired woman headed his way. She dropped one of the three shopping bags she held in her hands onto the ground.

He had glanced around and noticed that no one was on the street, which seemed odd for the city, considering someone was always around. Regardless, he took advantage of this opportunity to feed.

He approached her. "May I help you, ma'am?" he said, flashing a friendly grin.

"Sure," she said, glancing up at him. But it turned her smile upside down when she saw the blood on his shirt. "Is that blood?"

He sensed fear and panic as the woman stood up. He moved towards her and immediately clasped her mouth right before she screamed out.

"I'm sorry, ma'am," he said and quickly sunk his sharp fangs into her neck, quenching his thirst.

He embraced her in a way that looked as if they were just hugging. A maneuver he took centuries in perfecting–just in case someone passing by noticed them. He listened to her groans as he grabbed her tighter. And as he bit deeper into the woman's flesh, he glimpsed upward to see Amara standing in her apartment window.

This was the first time he had completely seen her face.

Her presence hypnotized him, forgetting the fact he was still feeding. He directed his vision upon her, feeling like his eyes were playing tricks on him. Katherine? He couldn't turn away, not until he felt the woman go limp in his arms.

He instantly stopped himself, retracting his fangs. He bit his wrist and placed his blood on the wound of her neck, healing her. Realizing that he'd almost drained her to the point of killing her, he shuddered.

Not in two hundred years had he almost made such a dire mistake, but he wouldn't let it happen again. He lightly tapped the woman alongside her pale cheek until she came to.

"Wha–what happened?" Her voice was weak as well as her body, as she slowly blinked her eyes at him.

"I apologize for my mishap… And I'm sorry for what I'm about to do."

He held her cheek, propping her face up. Their eyes met as he compelled her. "Go home, drink plenty of fluids to recover, rest, and forget that you saw me and what happened. All you know is that you woke up feeling sick and dehydrated… Now go."

He watched as the woman stumbled backward, then caught her balance. She weakly walked off without even glimpsing at him. He stared as she headed down the sidewalk, fading in the distance, making a right turn on a side street.

Sighing with relief that he hadn't taken her life, he got back in the van, taking a pause. Amara was becoming more interesting by the moment. He dropped his head back on the seat, shut his eyes, and thought about Katherine… the one woman he couldn't resist.

Lou lifted his head from the head rest of the van. He looked at the world before him now and how much it had changed since Katherine. He started the ignition and drove off. As he did, he saw images of Katherine's frightened face, her helpless eyes, and heard her heart-wrenching screams.

CHAPTER TEN

Mariam continuously shook her head. No reputable woman would ever step foot in a place like Inferno–even the name was too good to be true. Not only the name, but people feared that bar, and rumors of unexplained occurrences circled it.

"No!"

"Please… Nobody will know us, and this will be exciting. Besides, all the men there are no good." Amara giggled. "So it will strictly be another girls' night at a different location. Besides, I barely get a night off."

She was pulling out all her tricks–including poking out her bottom lip and batting her hazel brown puppy dog eyes.

Anything that she could do to persuade Mariam to see things her way she would do. But Mariam let out another harsh "no," and that "no" flowed sternly from her lips.

Amara placed her arms around Mariam's shoulders from behind and leaned in, poking her lip out as far as she could. "I need this. I don't want to sit here all night thinking about Aaron."

Her baby voice was in full effect.

"Aaron?"

"The married man," Amara said.

If her baby actions didn't work, she wasn't sure what would. It was a very tall order. She was asking something that was way out of Mariam's comfort zone.

But she needed to be seen. She needed to be heard, and most of all she needed to be desired–Inferno would guarantee all of that.

Looking at Mariam's worried face, Amara knew she was hesitant. She didn't want to drag her into another dangerous situation and guaranteed this time would be nothing like the last.

She recalled the night they had snuck off to see a band called Snake Eyes. It was Amara's favorite band and even though Mariam would rather have her head buried in a romance novel, hoping that true love would find her, Amara wanted to pick up her comrade and go after him. And his name was Dorian Means, the lead singer.

Being a sixteen-year-old teenager at the time, with a fake id she had gotten for herself and Mariam by flirting with the guy at the quickie mart, she knew it was a stretch to think they might meet him, but she dreamed big then and still did now. Of course, she pleaded and dragged Mariam along with her.

With those two fake IDs, they not only got into the venue, but made it backstage with the band. What happened to Mariam left her in a state of trauma, and she had avoided going to nightclubs and bars since.

She didn't say a word about what had happened, but secretly she disliked Amara for the incident–even though it never came from her mouth. Her selfishness had caused her pain, and she tucked it away for the sake of Amara.

But that was almost nine years ago, and they had gone out before, just not at a place like she was suggesting. Amara watched Mariam in silence as she debated–which seemed like forever–before Mariam finally let out a sigh.

Mariam couldn't say no. Not to Amara, her best friend in the whole wide world, and not in her time of need. And Amara swallowed her pride when she had wanted to step out for a girls' night. The same night they had met up with Noah. The only difference was the place they had gone to had an excellent reputation. This place did not.

She reluctantly nodded her head yes, and as badly as Amara wanted to let out a little chuckle of excitement, she forced herself not to. Yes, once again, she had won her over.

"You did go out the other night when I asked you to. I guess I can do the same for you," Mariam said hesitantly. "The things you get me into…"

Amara tightened her arms around her, giving her a bear hug, along with planting a kiss right on her cheek before releasing her. Once again, Mariam had given into her "crazy friends" demands.

"Thank you. Thank you!"

"How can I say no?"

"I know this is hard, but I'll be with you… side by side. And my fist."

Mariam slightly giggled as Amara shook her fist in the air. After about an hour and a half of chitchat, and her trying to distract Mariam from tonight's adventure in case she changed her mind, Mariam left to go get ready for the night.

The sun had set, and nighttime had crept in. Amara caught herself constantly thinking about the primary focus for tonight. Conquer and destroy.

She wanted to be her old self. The version of herself when she had men eating out her palm, not the other way around. The woman that didn't give a damn about their feelings and would dispose of them like trash–moving on to the next without a care in the world.

She had watched how Noah's dad cheated on and mentally abused his mother. That was the moment that she'd decided–no man would ever treat her that way. She would beat them to the punch.

She had always felt that men couldn't be trusted after witnessing Noah's parents. She just couldn't understand how she went from that version of herself to the one that needed or felt like she needed a man. Maybe she shouldn't have ditched her therapist.

She looked in the long black mirror at the outfit she had picked out. It was a tight-fitting little black dress with a slit on the side, showing just enough skin. It hugged her figure perfectly, exposing every curve. Her breasts looked quite perky in it and her butt looked even better. Damn girl, she thought to herself.

Clothes, hair, and makeup were never her thing. That was a Mariam thing. She didn't care too much for high heels either, and it was rare that she even wore them. But tonight she was. It was Mariam that always tried to dress her up like a life-size Barbie doll, but she didn't mind.

The dress that now hugged her slim body was one Mariam had picked out for her. She chose it specifically for Mariam because she knew if she wore it tonight, it would please her.

This was the first time she had felt good about herself in a long time. Her old self would have owned this dress even though it was risqué, and she wanted all eyes on her tonight.

She remembered when Mariam had selected this dress for a date she had planned a while ago. Even though he ended up being a jerk and canceling at the last minute, she never had time to wear it until now.

She let her long jet-black hair down from the bun that she always wore. The waves in her hair seemed to flow perfectly over her exposed shoulders.

Mariam had always praised her for being tall and slender, with a perfect skin tone, along with having the figure any woman would die for. She would say that her skin was like a warm ivory color even though she thought it was paler. And that her eyes were a perfect shade of light almond brown. To her, just hazel.

She put on her black eyeliner, trying to go with a darker look to fit her new mood. It surprised her how it brought the color of her eyes out. Maybe Mariam had been right with her, wearing more makeup. She chuckled at that thought, as she took off the lid of the lipstick, twisted it, and aligned her lips with a bright red color. Perfect, she thought. Just a hint of seduction.

Two and a half hours had passed, as she looked once more in a mirror, turning from side to side. She bent down and put on one red stiletto as she heard a slight knock on the door. Must be Mariam. She rushed to put on her other heel, then headed towards the door to open it.

There stood Mariam, all dressed up from head to toe.

She was exquisite. Tall, fair-skinned, and slender. The only flaw that she claimed to possess was her freckles. But Amara always thought that they complemented her face. Perfection of beauty, with curly hair that flowed effortlessly. And being a fiery redhead, she had a mean streak that came out now and then–but rarely.

The green dress she wore went well with her skin tone. It made her red hair and sparkling green eyes look radiant. She wore gold earrings, a gold necklace, and a matching gold belt.

Her makeup was flawless, as usual, and when Amara glanced down at her feet, it surprised her to see heels. She looked great, but then again, when didn't she? Fashion was her strong suit, and she wore it well.

"Are you ready to—" She paused as she glared at Amara with approval. "Nice." She smiled.

"Like I said earlier, I'm a new woman." Amara said fiercely. "And yes, I'm ready to go."

She paused for a second as Mariam headed back out the door and towards the hallway. When she wasn't looking, she turned back around. Part of her knew she was dragging her friend into possibly another dangerous situation again—for her gratification. Part of her felt guilty. She knew this was way out of Mariam's comfort zone.

"Maybe this isn't a good idea," she said, feeling some type of way for dragging Mariam along.

"No," Mariam replied. "If this will make you feel better, then I'm all for it."

Amara looked over at Mariam, scanning her face for any signs to just turn around, but Mariam had insisted. As much as Mariam had protected her, it was time for her to return the favor. She quickly grabbed her purse, sliding a twelve-inch switchblade—with skulls on it—inside it.

Tonight would be different.

CHAPTER ELEVEN

There was a dead silence lingering in the air, even though the night was beautiful. Springtime in New York, especially at this time of year, was a perfect mix of warmth and coolness.

The city was brighter, smelled cleaner, and the energy or mood around the city was palpable. The parks were now beautiful green spaces, the flower shows were going on, and the best part was no snow.

But the farther they went from their part of the city, the scenery drastically changed. It went from nice studio apartments with perfect lawns to no green grass and abandoned buildings. No friendly neighbors waved at them as they drove past. The people looked like lost souls just scattered around. It gave them a sense that danger surrounded them and lurked in every corner.

But monsters were everywhere, even in their backyard. They had to be prepared for anything in the city.

It was like an awful scene out of *The Walking Dead.* Prostitutes and druggies were hiding in the alleys and the dark shadows of the night, as both of them remained silent, in their own thoughts.

It was funny how New York had two different sides to it, and if someone never ventured out, then they wouldn't even notice how bad people were living. Amara's eyes peered over the people, the empty lots, and buildings as they drove past.

"I don't want to get into any trouble tonight," Mariam said. The nervousness in her tone was recognizable. The same tone she'd used years ago.

"We won't," Amara said. "Besides, we can't live our lives in a sheltered box. Sometimes It's good to conquer your fears and come out of your shell."

But it wasn't her that had been escorted years ago into a private room and almost assaulted. It was Mariam. Had she not kicked him in his crotch when he grabbed her and ran out of the room, no telling what would have happened. That was the most fearful time in her life, and Amara knew this.

"I understand what happened in the past, and if you dont want to go, I completely understand." Amara said. "I want to make sure that you're okay with this?"

Mariam frowned to herself as she thought back on that night. She didn't want to be put in another dangerous situation and her anxiety was on high. So she justified what went on by reminding herself that they were teenagers then.

"I'll be fine," she smiled. "Let's just have some fun."

Amara once again scanned her friend. Making sure that she was okay with the decision on continuing to go. She didnt see any hesitation from Mariam at the moment and turned her head, gazing out the window.

The closer they got, the more her gut was screaming to turn around and go home. But Amara's stubbornness and determination drowned that little voice out.

"I can't wait to get there. It's going to be epic."

Amara glanced over at Mariam, who didn't respond. Her eyes were still focused on the road, but she could tell that she was nervous. She felt some hints of remorse for dragging her friend out.

Mariam was willing to go down if she did. She was safe this time, and that's all Amara wanted her to know. If the last time had taught her anything, it had taught her to be prepared. She looked down and slightly patted her purse. Nothing was going to happen to Mariam or her.

They pulled up beside a small, red pickup truck. Sitting inside were too rough hard-core men. Both men were wearing black bandanas that were tied around their foreheads and a black leather vest.

The driver had long gray hair, almost white with a matching goatee, and the passenger had black spiked hair, also with a matching goatee. Both men's eyes were stone cold black and lifeless.

The men fixed their eyes on them and watched closely until they parked. The man on the passenger side spit out some brown chewing tobacco from his window and onto the ground. It made her skin crawl.

But if they tried anything, they would get a little surprise. She looked down at her purse once more and pulled it close to her–ready for whatever may go down.

"You girls lost?" They heard the passenger's raspy voice.

He smirked at them as they got out of the car and ignored him. He looked them up and down as if they were a meal that he wanted to devour.

Amara eyed him for a second. Her face turned up and projected a look of disgust, but it didn't deter the man. His eyes didn't budge. The only thing she could think about was the switchblade in her purse. She was ready to use it if she had to–it would've been an invitation for her to unleash it.

"I don't think this is your type of place," the driver shouted, then creepily laughed. His friend followed his lead.

They both looked at the men cross-eyed as they continued making lewd noises and catcalls. And as they listened to the nonsense coming from the men's mouths, they turned their heads toward each other without saying a word.

When they locked eyes, it was like they read each other's thoughts. Assholes. They turned their faces up simultaneously. Glancing back at the men once more and then growing disgusted by the tobacco stuck in between the passenger's crooked teeth.

"Stuck up bitches!" the driver shouted.

Amara immediately held up her middle finger and snarled at them.

"Don't," Mariam said, grabbing her arm, shaking her head, and letting it go. "Let us not get into trouble before we get into the place."

"I guess you're right... but I can't stand assholes like that!"

She wanted so badly to turn around and give them a piece of her mind. Idiots, she thought, but she wasn't about to let them mess up their night.

They continued to ignore the obscenities that faded into the background as they rushed towards the entrance. Heavy-metal music blazed from the inside, and they could smell the stale cigarette smoke that floated from the inside to the outside. This was a downgrade from Platinum.

Mariam gave her a long, hard, worried look. Her face screamed "help me" as she hesitated. She drew her hand backward when she almost touched the sticky doorknob.

"God help me," she whispered from underneath her breath.

She wavered at her question and tried not to second-guess herself. Then mustered out, "It's going to be OK," and reassuring Mariam with a confident, "Yes!"

She knew Mariam wanted to trust her but wasn't sure. She just had to prove that she had her back.

"Let's go."

CHAPTER TWELVE

As they walked inside, the smell of sweat, booze, and smoke almost threw them back instantly. The inside of the establishment looked like an old 1960s bar with ashtrays sitting on the various chipped wooden tables. The siding on the wall had large cracks running down it, and the floor felt like they were walking on a sticky pad.

The outside looked more inviting than the inside, even with its caved-in roof looking like it was going to fall and crush everybody at any moment. Describing the outside of the small building nicely was difficult, considering it was a beastly sight.

The lights were dim like a nightclub setting but she could still see the broken pieces of wood lying on the floor, she assumed from bar fights, and silhouettes of people walking about, only seeing their faces when a glimpse of the light hit them.

The actual bar area itself was small, dingy, and looked rotted. It had lines of empty beer bottles that sat on top that no one had bothered to pick up or throw away. Cigarette burn marks were ingrained in the wood, along with more broken glass scattered everywhere.

Amara wanted to come here. She figured it was far enough away from her side of the city where no one would know her, but she didn't want to come alone. Secretly, she was glad that she had talked Mariam into coming along with her.

She saw two empty bar seats and motioned to Mariam for them to have a seat. Once reaching them, they paused, making sure that the bar stools were halfway decent enough to sit down upon.

"And this is the place you dragged me to?" Mariam said. She wanted to support her friend by joining her. After all, she felt like it was too dangerous for Amara to go alone. "I think we could've picked someplace different."

"We're here now… just try to relax."

They looked like two fish out of water in a place like this, and overdressed. The place was well known. However this was the first time they had been here, so they weren't sure of the dress code. A plain t-shirt and blue jeans would have sufficed.

Finally, after a couple of minutes, a stocky female bartender with spiked hair approached them dressed in the same leather vest the men were dressed in outside. She could tell that the woman's ghastly tattoos and her scarred face made Mariam nervous, but not her.

Like the two men outside, the bartender looked them up and down, judging them, and assuming they were just some privileged brats that wandered in. Not even ten minutes at this establishment, and they were already being evaluated, but she didn't care. She was tougher than she appeared.

"We don't sell any mimosas or any of those fancy drinks here."

She analyzed the bartender for a second as the bartender chewed on the tobacco hanging from her mouth. She wondered if everybody in this place chewed tobacco? Straightening her posture, she held her head up, pretending that the woman before her wasn't intimidating, but that was a lie. She wasn't about to show her weakness.

"That's fine. I'll take a whiskey on the rocks," she answered, and tried not to laugh. She had stolen that line from an old western movie.

"And for you?" The woman gazed at Mariam impatiently, waiting for her response.

"I'll take water?"

The bartender rolled her eyes, spitting the chewing tobacco on the floor, as she went to prepare their drinks. After watching that, she honestly debated whether she even wanted a drink from this place. It was so unsanitary and disgusting, but they were here now, so they might as well go with the flow–if it didn't kill them first.

As the music blazed in the air, she screamed at Mariam over the loudness. A rush of adrenaline ran through her. "Now this is what it feels like to walk on the wild side."

"I guess so." Mariam gave her a thumbs up with a sarcastic grin. But that feeling subsided when a feeling of insecurity quickly came over her.

What were two beauties doing in the beast's lair? Amara thought. When she realized how many eyes lurked upon them, she questioned if they were even safe. But remembering her knife in her purse made her feel superior and somehow a billy badass.

She felt like she had the upper hand this time and was determined not to let anybody mess with them. If they did, she thought, they would meet their fate and she had that fate in her purse.

As annoying as it was that the people were watching and staring at them, this is exactly what she had wanted—attention. She couldn't lie and say that part of her didn't like them undressing her with their eyes. It made her feel desirable.

She had the mindset that the bad guys got blessed and the good guys got cursed. Why not be the rebellious one tonight? A superficial smile came across her face as she watched the bartender head back with their drinks, sitting them down before them.

"That will be twenty dollars."

She frowned, knowing that she was being overcharged, more than likely because of their appearances. But she wasn't about to let this miserable hag ruin their night. She reached in her purse and pulled out the exact amount–absolutely no tip for her.

"Twenty dollars? Okay, fine," she angrily replied, letting her know she knew what she did while placing the money on the bar top.

She watched as the bartender looked at the money like it was fake and noticed that she hadn't tipped her. Her eyebrows crinkled as she tossed her eyes and hastily walked away. Amara, however, was pleased to know that she had gotten underneath her skin.

"So now that you pissed off the bartender… we're here… what's your plan?" Mariam said and checked the inside of her glass before taking a sip of her water.

"To have a good time." She smiled and nudged her shoulder.

She took a sip of whiskey that burned like a tiny fire as it went down her throat and tried to play off the horrible, robust, oily taste that lingered in her mouth. She tried not to flinch, as she knew various eyes were watching to see if she could handle such a drink. She scanned the room and still didn't mention to Mariam her true intentions of being here.

In Mariam's head, she thought that she just needed to clear her mind and be free. But she was looking for a random guy to use and throw away. To treat them like they had been treating her lately–like disposable cattle.

The main reason she kept her mouth shut about her whole intentions was particularly because of Mariam. She would try to talk her out of it, or it was a possibility that she would just get up and leave. She couldn't have that. So, she just continued to sip her drink and smile.

Suddenly, a crash came from the other side of the room. Then it was followed by two stout men wearing the same vest arguing. This wasn't a normal bar, but a motorcycle club.

The music seemed to stop. All eyes were now on the men. They both were drunk as they quarreled raising from their seats. One man threw a punch, missing the other one and the other guy reacted by doing the same.

Neither one of them could sling a punch because of the toxicity in their system. Just two dumb drunks. It was amusing to watch as they swayed back and forth until both of them got tired and just sat back down. Then the music resumed as if it was normal.

Amara snickered as she glanced over at Mariam to see if she was as well–after all, it was amusing–but her face was plastered with concern. She had been watching, but it wasn't entertaining to her at all.

She wished her friend would relax. She just wanted them to have fun and to give a different place a chance. But regardless of her efforts, Mariam wasn't at all feeling the vibe.

"Relax and enjoy yourself," she pleaded. "They're just having fun."

She nodded towards the two men that were just trying to fight each other, only to see them laughing with one another moments later. Then she gave Mariam another playful nudge.

"At least the music is good," she said, trying to lighten the mood and finally getting a half-smile back.

"Yeah, fun," Mariam sarcastically replied as she took a deep breath and exhaled.

She watched her for a moment and could tell that she was trying to enjoy herself, but she wasn't doing an excellent job of playing off her displeasure. She took another sip of her whiskey, filling the burning sensation in her chest once more.

She glanced over at the other side of the room and immediately paused. Her eyes glazed over the well-formed gentleman sitting along the edge of the room. The corner table he was at was barely lit. He also seemed to be out of place like they were. He was well-groomed, had shoulder-length black hair, and wearing what appeared to be an expensive tailored suit with a tie. She raised one of her eyebrows as he piqued her attention.

She didn't know if it was his looks or his alluring eyes? But when their eyes locked, she glanced away. She knew he was now watching her and turned back towards Mariam, who still had a sour look on her face.

She tried not to be so obvious about the mysterious man and instead let Mariam have her moment of disgust with the place and took another gulp of whiskey and wanted so badly to go meet this man without Mariam stopping her. She felt drawn to him. It felt like an instant connection, and she couldn't even explain why.

The more she drank, the smoother it went down and after a couple more drinks, she had enough liquid courage to go talk to him–something that she would have never done on her own. She was used to men approaching her, not the other way around.

She tilted her glass up, took one last sip, and slammed the glass down on the bar. The crashing sound of it hitting the tabletop startled Mariam as she slightly jumped from her seat.

A look of confusion on her face made her laugh. She stood up and straightened her dress, ready to make her move. She had just chosen her victim for the night.

CHAPTER THIRTEEN

Lou had been watching both of them from the moment they had walked into Inferno. He kept his eyes mainly on Amara as both she and Mariam sat down at the bar. The resemblance to Katherine was uncanny, and he couldn't look away.

Even from far away, he picked up on her scent like a pool of blood in a tank full of sharks. Even her scent was like Katherine's. Of course, even without him sensing them, they stuck out like sore thumbs, making it hard for them to blend in with the crowd. Everything about them screamed outsiders. From their mannerisms, from the clothes they wore, and even the way they walked. But somehow they were confident enough to wander into a place like this—lost bunnies in a pack of wolves.

He narrowed his eyes and homed in on her, analyzing her every look. From her distinct features, her long black hair that flowed perfectly across her shoulder, her hazel yet majestic eyes, and even the way she smiled. He couldn't help but stare. She was exquisite. She was his beloved Katherine.

Her skin was perfect—almost flawless and the red lipstick made a lot of her facial features stand out to him. She was stunning, and something about her was unique. He could tell she had a fire that burned inside of her. Something like himself.

He closely examined how she clenched her purse at the signs of danger and knew that she probably had a weapon hidden in there, just in case someone tried to attack them. He chuckled at the thought.

The sense of rage and self-loathing penetrated the air, and it filled his nostrils, causing chill bumps to run down his ice-cold skin. It had been quite some time since he had that type of feeling that made him react. The last time he could remember was when he was human.

He looked down at his arms, amazed by the minor bumps that had risen from his skin. How she could make him feel this way intrigued him. She was unlike anything he had experienced. But what made her so different? He couldn't figure it out, but whatever it was... was intoxicating, beyond control.

She pulled her hair from one side to the other, exposing her neck. He took another deep breath, filling his nostrils up with the smell of her sweet and fruity perfume mixed with a favorable smell of blood, and even from across the room, she was far more potent than any drug that he'd ever come across. He picked his glass up and took a long, hard drink. Calm down.

The urge of wanting to taste her made his canines come out, and he quickly closed his mouth before anyone noticed. Keep it together, he told himself. In the two hundred years he had been on this earth, controlling himself had never been a problem until he went through his *blood-thirst* stage and even then, he could resist. But it was hard to do now.

His first instinct was just to run away, for him to get up and leave, but he couldn't escape his infatuation. Running would have been easier than staying, but he was paralyzed and could not move–that made him drawn to her.

Taking more sips from his glass full of bourbon, he studied her even more and continued to read her thoughts. He laughed at the fact that she thought she was a badass that could take on anyone that tried to come and attack her. But what about him? Could she stop him? That the bartender made her furious and how she tried to be tough about it all was amusing.

By using his mental telepathic abilities, he could get a sense of her cunning personality and that he liked. He could tell that she had a brief fight with the bartender and that he had seen and also liked.

He could also read her friend's thoughts, sensing her fear and uneasiness—the nervousness and the panic that plagued her and the way her body tensed up once someone would walk behind her. He could tell that she had been through a horrible ordeal in the past.

But there was something else that worried him. Something besides Mariam's feelings, but that of Amara he had picked up on. The feeling of desperation that ran through her veins, her sorrow, and the pain in her heart. Someone had broken her trust. And instantly he knew why she was here.

Her hopelessness pierced through him, and he felt what she felt. One downfall of being immortal was feeling the sensations of humans. But not once had he felt such anguish for a human. Maybe Katherine, but no one since then. What sense does that make? Why should he care for this random human? He still wasn't planning on changing her. Did Victoria know she resembled Katherine, hoping he would? Victoria had seen Kathrine before.

She knew how he had dealt with his feelings towards humans after Katherine and *The Order's* warning and he understood humans were nothing more than food. And Victoria knew that this woman's likeness to all things Katherine would more than likely cause him to go ahead with putting her through the *transformation.*

He couldn't believe he was even feeling this way. The undeniable feeling of wanting to be around her. He knew better… he was an older blood drinker and knew how to shut down emotions placed on him by humans, but with her, he felt alive.

He could also sense the eyes that were following her every move. He quickly scanned the room, reading the other men's thoughts, and their intentions were far from good. Thoughts of sexual assumptions, unspeakable acts, and even murder when it came down to them. But he would allow none of those things to happen.

He cringed at their thoughts and felt like slaughtering them. All of them if need be. The thought of slashing their throats and tearing them limb from limb came across his mind. The more his anger rose, the more it caused his fangs to slightly protrude, but he controlled himself from acts of instant rage…this time.

He knew he was the strongest, the toughest, the most invincible one in the entire establishment. He could sense that much. Had a blood drinker stronger than he been present, he would have instantly known. Even though there was his kind that lingered in the shadows, watching them as well. They stayed out of his reach. Most *newbies* feared older vampires. They wouldn't dare come up against him, knowing he was the oldest and *untouchable.*

For a brief second, he caught her looking at him. He figured that he'd stared at her long enough that she must've felt his gaze. And when their eyes met, she spun away. His eyes lit up as he continued to focus on her thoughts. Thoughts of him being her victim were the funniest by far. Never had he looked at himself as a victim, more like a predator. He smiled because that thought had tickled him. He could live with being her victim for the night...

Despite his irritation at the crowd, he snickered at the mere thought of being someone's victim. But as long as her attention was on him, he didn't have to worry about the other swine in the room.

He knew she was trying to play it cool–as if he didn't catch her looking at him. He knew she was trying to gain the courage to walk over to him, and he patiently waited for her to do so. Come on, come on, my love... come to me. He wanted her closer to him, beside him, maybe even for eternity. No.

Baby steps first. He was only watching her for Victoria, nothing more. He had already warned Victoria that if he changed her, he would have to remove himself from the situation, leaving her to deal with the *newbie*. He knew that if the *newborn* acted up or broke vampire rules, it would not fall back on Victoria but on him. That was the whole reason Victoria had asked him to do it and not her. He would never be punished like she would if the *newborn* broke vampiric rules.

He reminded himself that he hadn't been around a human, which made him feel vulnerable and not let it mess with his judgment. *The Order* might watch his every move. He didn't want to get an innocent human killed over a mere thought.

He quickly cleared his thoughts just in case, thinking of nothing but killing her and draining her blood. After some time, he watched as she got up from her seat, holding her drink in hand. Come on, my love... come to me.

CHAPTER FOURTEEN

Amara quickly grabbed Mariam's arm and pulled her from her seat.

"Where are we going?" Mariam whispered in her ear. She had finally gotten used to sitting at the bar, and now Amara was dragging her off to some place unknown.

"To him…" She nodded towards the mysterious man in the suit across the room.

The whiskey she had drunk crept up on her without warning. But she still headed towards him. She felt weirdly drawn to him, and there was no turning back now. She just hoped he didn't notice how intoxicated she had become. You got this, she told herself as she tried not to trip over her feet.

However, Mariam noticed. She wasn't about to let her friend pull her off towards another random guy that she knew nothing about. She tugged at Amara's arm, pulling her back, trying to stop her before they reached his table.

"Are you sure about this? You're drunk." Mariam frowned. "This is supposed to be a ladies' night, remember?"

"Yes… we're here to have fun." She smiled and began bouncing to the sound of the music. "Isn't he hot?"

In her semi-drunken state, she addressed Mariam. She turned towards her, placed both hands on her shoulders, and looked her in the eyes.

"We are good," she said, trying to reassure her. "Everything will be okay."

"Okay... if you say so," Mariam hesitantly replied. She wanted to say more, but she took a deep breath and followed her into whatever mess she was about to get into, praying it wasn't like before.

It seemed like it took forever for them to reach him. She felt like she was walking down a long runway and the people inside the bar were her audience. When they finally got closer, he smiled at both of them.

She tried to suppress her nerves and, in doing so, it became awkward. She hadn't said a word, nor did he. They were just staring at each other, as if they were old friends that hadn't seen each other in a while. She assumed he realized that the alcohol in her system was causing the delay. And then finally, he was the one that broke the ice.

"Hello, ladies." His tone was semi-stern yet soft, but through her drunkenness, it sounded more sexual and deeper.

He seemed polite in her eyes, but they all did at first. It didn't matter how tipsy she was, she would not fall for any of his bullshit. She shifted and forced herself to stand more confidently. They all start nice and then end up being jerks, she thought to herself.

Especially the good-looking ones. Maybe she was over-thinking it. Maybe she was being too harsh. He had only spoken two words so far. The thought of it all made her blush in embarrassment and fluster.

"Hello," she replied, pulling Mariam from behind her and more towards the front. "Do you mind if we sit?"

"Not at all," he said. "Be my guest."

He watched as they took their seats and then introduced himself.

"My Name is Luciano," he said.

She watched as he weirdly spread out his nostrils, took a deep breath, and then gulped. But then again, it could've been her seeing things in her current state.

"But you can call me Lou." He grinned as he invaded her thoughts.

Without a response, she took a minute to analyze him. She couldn't help but notice his charming smile, his dark dreamy eyes that looked like her own, his chiseled chin, and his perfect white teeth—something she hadn't seen since she walked in the door.

He was well-groomed, different from the rest in here, and the scent of his cologne made her body quiver. Stop it, she thought, blushing, and crossing her legs–trying to stop the throbbing sensations she felt below.

His dark eyes crinkled at the corners as his mouth altered. It was almost like he sensed how her body felt. Of course, that would be impossible. Maybe it was her sexual energy that she was giving off. After all, she was trying to flirt by batting her eyes and twirling her hair like some schoolgirl. Something she seemed to do with a man she liked.

Mariam crossed her eyes at her. She knew what Amara was doing as well and figured that this man would be in her friend's bed by the end of the night.

But Amara paid her no mind. She couldn't help herself. Even in the dim lighting, he was gorgeous, and he instantly turned her on. It had to be the alcohol. Yes, the alcohol!

"I'm Amara and this is Mariam," she said, motioning toward her. Mariam waved her hand slightly and gave him a smug look.

"Well, nice to meet you ladies… again." He chuckled, as if it was an inside joke that only he knew.

She held out her hand to shake his, but he hesitated for a minute. Then finally he reached out and shook it. She quivered when their hands locked. He was ice cold to the touch, but it was a little chilly inside the bar, so she paid it no mind.

She shrugged it off and continued to keep her hand in his until she heard Mariam interrupt the moment by loudly clearing her throat. She had held on a little longer than expected and, thanks to Mariam and her fake cough, she quickly released it.

"So, Lou…" Mariam began speaking as she side-eyed Amara before looking back at him again. "What brings you out tonight?"

"Just having a drink… clearing my head," he replied as he nursed his drink.

"Not looking for women?"

"If I run across one that I like, maybe." He glanced at Amara, giving her a half-smile, then looked back at Mariam.

"How about yourself? What brings you here?"

"I haven't quite figured that one out yet," she said, rolling her eyes. "Why are we here?" She looked at Amara.

"It's a ladies' night," Amara responded.

"I'm assuming that's always fun," Lou said and then took a sip from his glass.

She knew what Mariam was doing. She was acting like an overprotective friend—as always. And she didn't want to be the one picking up the pieces in the morning after this guy hurt her feelings. So this time, she stepped in before anything could happen.

Amara stayed quiet as Mariam gave him the third degree and, as she did, she couldn't help herself from admiring his physique. How his eyes lit up when he smiled, how his voice seemed to make her heart skip a beat, and how his muscles bulged from his tight black shirt.

She drifted off in her thoughts while Mariam and Lou conversed and visualized him picking her up and kissing her as she straddled him. She glanced at him as those thoughts came across her mind and blushed—probably beet red by now.

He turned towards her, gleaming and then winking. Then he turned back toward Mariam and continued answering her questions. Did I say that out loud? Wondering if she had, she promptly looked over at Mariam, but she was still talking. No. I didn't. Thank God.

She slightly put her head down, trying not to show her flushed cheeks, but then she felt dizzy. This damn alcohol. Why did she drink so much? The dizziness was getting worse.

She heard Lou interrupt Mariam to check on her. "Are you okay?" he questioned.

"I'm fine... just had a little too much to drink."

She felt him place his chilly hand on her back as she crouched forward in her seat. His icy touch felt relieving and seemed to soothe her. He gently made circular motions with his hand. She didn't know if she felt sick or aroused—maybe both.

This wasn't supposed to happen. This was not my plan. He was supposed to be my victim for tonight. She slightly glanced up at him only to see him smiling once more. She dropped her head back down and quickly picked it back up.

Lou raised his hand, motioning to a server across the room. She headed towards the table. Mariam turned to look at the woman who was coming towards them—another character that seemed out of place for this establishment.

The woman was well dressed in a red button-down shirt and a high-waisted black pencil skirt. She was very attractive, almost unnatural. Another gorgeous bombshell blonde. At least this woman seemed to be friendlier than the unnerving bartender. Her red bottom heels clinked against the floor as she walked up to the table and addressed him.

"What can I get you, sugar?" she spoke in a flirtatious way. Amara's eyes furrowed out of jealousy when she noticed the woman was flirting with him. The server learned to over-expose her cleavage, but to her surprise, he paid her no mind.

"Victoria, I need a glass of water… for my friend, with some bread." Victoria glanced over at her and glared.

Victoria? Of course, a man like this would know a woman like her. Amara wondered what Victoria was thinking. Probably that she was just another pathetic drunk woman and... nowhere near his type. But Victoria didn't speak a word and didn't acknowledge her current condition. Instead, she turned towards Lou.

"No problem. I'll be right back." She walked away as Lou continued to console her.

"Everything will be okay… I gotcha," he whispered.

Mariam kept a watchful eye on him. It impressed her how well he was taking care of the situation at hand. That was a positive sign, and she was an excellent judge of character. Until this point, Lou had been nothing but a pure gentleman.

Amara knew Mariam hated the fact that she had gotten intoxicated, and this was the very reason her choice of drink was water. Someone had to be the responsible one and unfortunately tonight, it wasn't her.

"I'm fine… I'm fine—" she sputtered out.

Now the room was spinning out of control, and she was fighting to stay focused. She couldn't believe that she had allowed herself to get this way and in front of this man—this very good-looking man. Damn. I'm such an idiot, she thought. Her head dropped two or three more times as she tried balancing it. Finally, she mustered up enough strength to raise it and gaze at Lou.

He leaned in towards her. "You know you can't be like this... if you're planning on killing a man tonight."

CHAPTER FIFTEEN

Amara's face dropped to the floor. How did he know about the knife? And she wasn't intending to use it, not unless she needed to.

"I assure you… you won't need to use it… you're safe with me." He smiled.

"What?" Mariam gasped. Her look was of pure confusion.

"I just had a knife," Amara responded. Oh, why did she say that? Now she would never hear the end of it. She pulled the pocketknife from her purse and placed it on the table. "I would not use it."

"Why do you even have it?" Mariam snapped.

Mariam was right. She felt bad but she just wanted to protect both of them if something went wrong. And she just wanted her head to stop spinning. If she could've kept herself together, she could've asked him how he had known about it. But she couldn't focus on anything at the moment.

"Let's not worry about this," Lou said as he grabbed the knife and placed it in his jacket pocket.

She could feel Mariam's eyes gazing upon her and avoided even looking her way. She knew she thought that she was being reckless, but now wasn't the time to undergo any form of interrogation.

She watched as he gave Mariam a slight grin and caught glimpses of his words; that seemed to reassure Mariam that everything would be okay. It was as if he could read her thoughts, as if he knew everything that she was thinking.

Then she heard him speaking about her drinking. "It happens to the best of us," he said jokingly. He was staring at Mariam, hoping that she would also add an encouraging word.

"Yeah... we have all gone through this," Mariam mumbled.

She had caught onto what he was doing even though deep down she was still concerned about the knife and skeptical of him. Listening to them, she wanted to laugh. She had never gotten so tipsy in her life.

Even working at a nightclub, she was used to the overly drunk people she waited on, but never in her wildest dreams did she think she would be one of them. And it was shocking how well Mariam would go along with a complete stranger.

Victoria, the server, finally returned with a basket full of warm biscuits and a tall glass of water. She sat them down on the table.

"I hope this helps." She gave Lou a little wink and walked off.

"Here… take a bite." His voice was demanding as he grabbed one biscuit and held it up to her mouth. She did as she was told and bit into it.

The alcohol had taken over her taste buds, and she couldn't taste a thing. She felt like she was chewing on dry paste and her mouth seemed to stick together with every bite. But she kept chewing, listening to Lou tell Mariam how she needed to eat to absorb the liquor from her system.

"I think I should get her home," she heard Mariam say.

"I can make sure both of you get home safe." His tone had changed to authoritative.

She knew Mariam didn't like his tone, but in her current state, she couldn't respond, disagree, or do anything. Besides, the biscuit had taken over her mouth. She could barely chew it and keep her head afloat. No response or input from her. This was on them.

"And I think not," Mariam snapped back. I could hear the anger in her voice. "We don't know you."

She watched as he leaned closer to Mariam. He locked eyes with her, and his voice seemed to change. This wasn't up for debate anymore.

"I will take Amara home. She will be safe with me." He looked deeper into her eyes as he repeated himself. "You will leave her with me, go home, go to bed knowing that she is safe and call her in the morning… Now go."

Oh, that would not work, she thought. She needed to get herself together and knew his words were going to ensure a full-blown fight between the two of them. And she would never allow someone to disrespect Mariam. She needed to stop this, to defend her friend, but Mariam didn't say a word. Not even a blink. She looked like she was in a trance.

Without saying a word, she got up from the table, grabbed her purse, and headed toward the door. Wait! What? Amara thought to herself. She's not arguing back? She's not even going to say goodbye? Was she mad? Oh no, she had to stop her.

She staggered while trying to get up. "Maria—stop—" With each word, she felt dizzy and fell back onto the chair. Defeated. What had she done?

"Victoria, follow her," Lou demanded.

"I'm on it," Victoria replied.

Amara could feel her eyes slowly shutting. It felt like she was going to pass out. She couldn't figure out which one it was and felt a little frightened now that she was relying on a stranger. Mariam could have left her, and she had to put all her trust in Lou. She drunkenly watched as Lou reached into his pocket and placed some money on the table.

"Let's go." He chuckled.

He gently grabbed her arm, lifting her, and putting it around his shoulder. There was no resistance from her. She had no choice but to let him lead the way.

"I've got you… don't worry," he whispered.

She gave him a half-smile and then, embarrassingly, one of her legs almost gave out, causing her to stumble to the ground. He lifted her back up like she was weightless and led her out of the bar and to his vehicle. He placed her in the car and shut the door. She was drunk, alone, and now at the mercy of a stranger.

He went to the driver's side, opened the door, and got in while grabbing her small clutch purse and removing her driver's license.

"I've got you… love," he said. "I'm going to take you home now."

His dark eyes crinkled at the corners as he gazed into hers. His face seemed to change before her. The veins in his face had darkened and looked creepy. There was something about that and his grin that made her feel uneasy. But maybe she was seeing things. Reality set in for a moment. She didn't know this man. Was she in danger? Was he a friend trying to help or a foe trying to prey on her? She secretly wished that Mariam hadn't left her alone.

He had been nothing but kind to her in the bar, and she prayed he would still have the same courtesy now that they were alone. He seemed decent, not dangerous, but did she know for sure? She had to rely on him. What more could she do? Mariam had abandoned her.

Her plan of taking back her control and being her old self again had backfired. He was no longer her victim… she was possibly his.

CHAPTER SIXTEEN

During the drive home, Amara had fallen asleep. She woke up in her bed, troubled and uncertain how she had indeed gotten there. Peering to the right of her and noticing that Lou was at her bedside, she gasped and jumped back in fear.

"What are you doing here? How did you get in?" she said as she frantically got out of her bed and grabbed the lamp off the nightstand. Arming herself with it, he stretched out his arms, putting his hands up in self-defense.

"You fainted in the car. I got your address from your license, your keys from your purse, and drove you home... That's it." He lowered his hands and his tone once she lowered the lamp. "Then I laid you in your bed."

Fuck me, she thought. Was she that drunk? That she would allow a stranger to drive her home? Know where she lived? And then wake up next to him in her bed? This was not what she was used to.

"You were that drunk," he said with a mischievous grin.

"Excuse me?" she replied. But before she could say anything more or question how in the hell he knew what she was thinking, he spoke up.

"Nothing..." he replied. "I just wanted to wait until you woke up so I could explain how you ended up in your bed. I'm harmless and nothing happened, but since you're okay... I'll leave you now."

She watched as he turned and headed to leave. A sense of guilt and ungratefulness came over her. "Wait," she softly said. "You don't have to leave."

She flushed as humiliation came over her. She was kicking this man out after he was gracious enough to bring her home, make sure she was safe, and in the process not even take advantage of her or rob her. At least she could thank him. She put the lamp back down on the nightstand and shamelessly sat down on the edge of her bed.

He hesitated. So she repeated, "Don't leave... please."

"Are you sure?"

"Yes."

As he walked toward her, she glanced around the room and became flushed with embarrassment. The empty ice cream containers, her unmade bed, the disarray her apartment was in, and the curtains that were closed screamed loneliness or that she wasn't an excellent housekeeper. Clearly, it showed him she was in a dreary place in her life. She clasped her head downwards in shame as he walked closer to her. Then she felt him sit down beside her.

"Thank you," she said while bending over and putting her elbows on my knees. She covered her face with her hands.

"For what?"

"For being a gentleman."

She looked down, noticing that her clothing was still intact. Clearly, that showed her he had been a gentleman. She tried standing up but started swaying back and forth, still somewhat intoxicated. He helped her keep her balance and not completely fall over.

"The alcohol is not out of my system," she said in a giggly but nervous tone.

"It's fine." His tone was manly and when she looked him in his eyes, she got lost in his gaze. He glanced away, breaking the contact in fear he might compel her.

"Do you mind if I remove your dress for you?"

At first, she was confused, but when she looked at where he was pointing, she saw that she had spilled alcohol and breadcrumbs on the front of her dress. She immediately became red and flushed. But despite her looking an absolute mess, his sex appeal was something that she could not ignore. She caught herself stuttering the word "sure" as it came splattering out of her mouth.

He nodded then bent down and dragged up her alcohol-soaked dress. The smell alone turned her off, and it made her blush once again in embarrassment. He continued pulling it up and exposing her light red thong. Then he reached for her red lace see-through bra, removing her dress and dropping it to the floor. There she was, standing, completely exposed.

Had this been someone else from the bar, she probably would've been in trouble, but he was respectful of his every move. She just wished she had been in a better state of mind and got to know him. When she looked at him, his eyes gazed briefly across her breasts. She couldn't help but smile. After all, a man will be a man.

There was something about his mouth and the way he gazed at her. She knew he wanted to touch her but held back his urge. He gently picked her up and walked her over to her bedside.

She was hoping he wanted to make passionate love, but to her surprise, he laid her down and put a cover over the top of her. She must admit, she was disappointed.

"Don't leave," she said as she grabbed his arm. His skin was still cold to the touch, but she didn't care.

The thought of him holding her and then having sex came across her mind. She pulled him closer to her and tried to place his hand on her breast, but he resisted.

"No, not like this," he said as he moved his hand and instead placed it on top of hers.

"You don't want me?"

"I do." He smiled. "But not like this."

He kissed her on her forehead before he turned and headed towards the door. She couldn't let him leave. She wanted him next to her. It was something about his presence that put her at ease, and she was afraid if she let him walk out the door, she would never see him again.

"Don't leave." She raised slightly on the bed. "Lay with me." Did she just say that out loud? Yes.

He looked at her as she followed his every move. She watched how he stood there debating on her proposal and then placing his head down and taking a deep breath. He bent over and took off his shoes. One by one. Yes… he'll spend the night, she thought, while keeping her face solid and hiding her excitement. She continued staring at him. He didn't take off his clothes, and he didn't say a word either.

Instead, he walked over to the other side of the bed and got underneath the covers. She heard him take another deep breath as she crawled up beside him and placed her head on his chest. His body was frigid, and she shivered as the cold went down her spine, but again she didn't mind. It felt good, considering the alcohol was still heating her body temperature. This was nice. Deep down, she wished this moment would last forever.

As she lay there, she pulled her body closer to his. She inhaled a deep whiff of his lovely cologne and his scent put her at solace. As her ear laid upon his chest, she was hoping to hear a racing heartbeat. Something that would let her know she turned him on.

But nothing. Absolutely nothing, but she didn't read too much into it. She was still tired and was ready to go to sleep. She closed her eyes and began drifting off when she heard his soft voice.

"Do you believe in the supernatural?" he whispered.

"I couldn't care less about it," she sluggishly said as she raised one of her eyebrows and was confused by his question. She could feel a headache coming on and her head began throbbing like a tiny beating drum.

"That's not what I meant," he said as she felt him gently kiss her forehead.

She was exhausted, and he realized that this conversation wouldn't be going much farther as she drifted off into slumber.

"Goodnight, love."

Amara opened her weary eyes, trying to focus on them. Her nostrils filled with the fresh smell of bacon and eggs. It was still dark in the apartment, and she noticed her curtains were still closed, with no light shining through.

Not knowing if it was still night or morning, she rubbed her eyes and looked over at the clock. 10 AM. She couldn't believe that she had slept so long. Her body felt considerably drained from all the alcohol she had binged the night before. She felt a slight headache coming on. But what was even more surprising was the fact that Lou was still there and in her kitchen cooking.

She propped herself up in her bed

Her eyes eventually focused. Her dark hair was all over her face, and she used her hand as a comb to look half-way presentable. As she watched him, she was in disbelief. Nobody ever stayed the night and didn't leave. But she was pleased that he did. She smiled as she took in the moment of him preparing breakfast. He was taller than she had originally thought, with his shiny black hair and well-toned body. She instantly felt a spark.

Her mouth watered at the thought of fresh fruit, bacon, eggs, and muffins. This differed from her normal box of wheat cereal that was set upon her refrigerator and a single glass of orange juice to go along with it. Him... this... all of it was nice.

He slowly turned around, reminding her of the Fabio commercials, with his long hair, perfect skin, and deep-set eyes. He gave her a pleased grin as she fixated on his luscious lips.

"Good morning," he said as he continued fixing the plate of food. "I hope you don't mind that I used your kitchen." He grabbed the tray and began walking toward her.

"No...it's fine," she replied, clearing her throat.

Hell, it was better than fine. It was great. She wasn't used to this treatment. A quick Wham, bam, thank you, ma'am, was all she ever got. She studied him as he set the tray down on her lap.

"Breakfast in bed, my lady," he said. His smile was like a sunbeam of light.

The amount of food he prepared shocked her. Brunch in bed, her kind of man. She looked up at him and he was smiling as if he had heard what she had said. She smiled back.

"You know I'm not gonna eat all this, right?" She giggled while admiring the plate.

"I wasn't sure what you liked… so I made a variety of things."

"I see."

She formed another emotional smile, then looked down at all the food that sat before her. She couldn't remember the last time she had bought groceries and when she did, it was usually something microwavable or some form of a quick snack.

Suddenly, she realized at some point he had gone out and bought these items. She couldn't believe it. All of this was unbelievable. She had fallen into a romance movie where the man was gorgeous, and he did everything in the world to win over the woman he loved. Her eyes met his with a twinkle in them.

"Take these," he said as he handed her two aspirins from the tray.

She did have a slight hangover. She did as she was told, putting the aspirin in her mouth and taking a swig of orange juice. Something that she had been doing a lot of for him—obeying. The darkness of the room grabbed her attention once again.

"Do you want me to open the blinds and let some sunlight through?" She kept her mind focused on anything other than how sexy he was up close. But she also wanted to see him in the light.

"No," he snapped, his stern tone shocking her. Maybe he liked it dark. She just brushed it off. After all, the sunlight wouldn't help her headache, anyway. She didn't want to ruin the moment with an argument about the blinds and instead grabbed a ripe strawberry from her plate.

"I'm sorry. I didn't mean to be so rude… I just want you to enjoy your food."

But deep down, it was never about the sunlight. He was an older vampire, so it only annoyed him, but had it been a blood drinker lesser than him, it would have destroyed them.

He was more worried about *The Order*. He secretly wondered if they had been watching him. Because they were always watching, and he didn't want her to become a target.

Amara didn't verbally respond. Instead, she nodded her head and focused back on the food he had prepared for her. She smiled each time she took a bite.

"You're not eating?" she questioned him.

"No… I ate before you woke," he lied.

"Oh… okay," she replied, taking another bite.

After a long pause of awkward silence and her stuffing the food in her mouth, he finally spoke. "I like you, Amara… you remind me of someone that I knew long ago." He sighed.

"Was it a female?" she said, taking on a sympathetic tone.

"Yes."

"A lover?" she questioned.

"Yes." His tone had softened, and she gazed up at him only to see the sincerity across his face. For some odd reason, he felt the urge to tell her about himself. Maybe it was because of Kathrine. He had told her everything, and if he exposed himself to Amara, then she could watch her back if *The Order* started trailing her because of him.

"Can I tell you something?" he asked her. He was still a little hesitant that she would freak out. And if she did, he could just compel her to forget knowing him or anything he had said.

"Yeah… sure." She picked up another strawberry.

He watched her for a minute as she took a bite. She realized the way her lips must have looked at him as they hugged around the fruit–sucking the juice from it. For a moment he lost all train of thought. He shook his head from side to side, shaking off the brief sexual urge of wanting her.

She must admit, it did kind of tickle her, but she knew he was trying to be serious, so she placed a half-eaten strawberry back down on her plate. This wasn't the time to seduce him, but honestly, the only thing that was on her mind was throwing him across the bed and straddling him.

"Do you remember me asking you last night if you believed in the supernatural?"

"I remember it briefly," she responded, not knowing where this question was going.

"Do you believe in supernatural beings?"

"You mean ghosts… werewolves…?"

"And vampires."

She paused for a second. She was a little confused by the question. What did any of this matter? The thought of him fixing breakfast and staying the night was a cover-up. She had somehow brought home someone crazy.

"I'm not crazy," he said sternly, as if he was replying to what she was thinking.

Did he just read my thoughts? "How did you…." A puzzled look came across her face and before she could finish her sentence, he cut it off.

"I know what you're thinking, Amara," he said, grabbing the tray from her lap and setting it on the edge of the bed. "I know everything you're thinking."

Her body tensed up as he moved closer. He was even sexier than before as his dark brows narrowed and his hypnotic black eyes gazed into hers. Something in her body yearned for him to grab her… kiss her… even if he was a little crazy.

She gazed at his body, wondering what was underneath his shirt. The only thing she could think of was a rock-hard chiseled chest with sweat dripping off of it. She wanted him badly. She wanted to be touched by him and she badly wanted to touch him.

He laughed out loud at her thoughts. She was truly unique in his eyes. And as serious as he wanted this conversation to go, her thought was arousing and amusing.

"Are you still reading my mind?" she teased. Then she took her hand and ran it down his chest. "Do you want me?"

"Yes." He grinned. "And I know you want me. I'll give you what you want… if you promise to listen."

"Then I'm all ears."

CHAPTER EIGHTEEN

Lou leaned in and grabbed the back of her head, pulling her closer to him. With no procrastination, he gave her a heated kiss. Her soft lips caused his manhood to stand rock hard. Usually, he could control this, but it was something about her–maybe her resemblance to the love of his life and her scent that caused him to lose all control.

He had gone against all principles, and they ended up having sex. He couldn't fight his urge in wanting her that way. He had to have her. He hadn't been with a woman since Katherine. But at this moment, he had acted on his selfishness.

"That was amazing," he said, turning towards her with a smile on his face, and satisfaction was all over hers. He could also sense her approval.

"Damn right," she replied with a slight giggle.

He turned and laid on his back, and she followed suit. They sat there in silence, looking at the ceiling. He was just about to speak when her cell phone rang.

He listened in on the conversation with his vampiric hearing. First, it was hello from Amara and then a "Hey, girl… I'm just checking on you." It was Mariam, and it pleased him that Victoria had gotten her home safe–not that he even doubted it for one second.

He read her thoughts while she went on with her conversation. He could tell that part of her believed he was still crazy and that the other part of her questioned if he could read her thoughts. She shifted herself, looking over at him just in case and her face turned beet red as she still conversed with Mariam on the other end of the phone, but he had already heard what Mariam had said.

Mariam had questioned whether he was well endowed. He couldn't stop himself from giggling and continued listening in. They promised each other that they would continue the conversation tomorrow and then hung up.

She set her phone down and grabbed the pink robe that hung on the hook next to her bed, putting it around her petite body. Then she tied it in the front and got back into the bed.

"Listen, Amara… this may have been a mistake." He ran his fingertip up and down her arm.

"What?" Her voice turned angry.

"It's not what you think," he replied.

"Then what is it?" she shouted. "You just wanted to get me in the sack?"

"No! I have other reasons." He gently grabbed her chin and turned her head towards him, staring directly into her eyes.

"I'm not what you think I am… I'm a vampire."

CHAPTER NINETEEN

"And I'm a werewolf... roar," Amara said as she raised her hands mimicking a wolf pawing motion. She laughed out loud when he mentioned he was a vampire. It lightened the mood, but she still didn't like the fact that he expressed he couldn't be with her.

Her teasing him only fed into his frustration. Maybe it wasn't a good idea to have this conversation with her. But he understood why she didn't believe him. What he was telling her was unbelievable. A monster made up for the movie screens, but he wasn't a fictional character and was very real.

"I'm serious, Amara," he said.

"Okay, I'm feeding into it," she sarcastically replied. She rolled her eyes and focused on what was about to come out of his mouth.

But his words meant nothing. He needed to show her. Reveal to her the real him. He got off of the bed and went towards an empty wall in her apartment.

Placing both palms on the wall, He began crawling up it until he reached the ceiling. He heard her gasp and sensed fright and mistrust. But he also felt her sense of curiosity. Which gave him hope she would respond positively. He jumped at lighting speed, swooping her up off the bed, and into his arms, and then gently placed her feet on the ground.

She was silent, and he studied her worries. There's no way. How did he do that? She stepped back, looking at him in disbelief. Could he be? A vampire? They're real? Another set of questions swarmed the inside of her mind.

Her face was blank, with no expression, not knowing whether to run or to stay. The same repetitive notions raced through her thoughts, and he read each one of them. Is this a dream? Is he genuinely a vampire? She questioned herself until he answered it all for her.

"Yes, I am," he repeated.

"Your… really… a…." She couldn't get the words to fall out of her mouth. "Are you going to hurt me?"

"No, that is not my intention," he declared. "I can control my urges."

His urges, she thought. Did it cross his mind to drain her blood? Was she nothing but a mere snack to him? Why would he even tell her any of this? She would have never known about him and what he was. What were his intentions towards her? There was so much she wanted to know.

"No, I will not feed on you… I'm telling you because I dread that I have involved you in something that I never intended to… and I'm informing you so that you can recognize the dangers that unfortunately you may be a part of."

"Stop doing that." Her voice quivered as she rubbed her forehead. She was taken aback because he was indeed reading her and not just magically guessing what she was thinking.

"Doing what?"

"Reading my thoughts," she replied.

"How else am I going to make you believe?"

"I've thought… you have done enough." She paced the floor back and forth. "Just give me a minute to process it all."

He sensed she wasn't afraid of him and that she was worried. He sat back down on the bed, giving her time to gather her thoughts. Knowing how he first felt when being approached by his *maker* and when he first told Katherine about himself, he understood this moment. After all, if she would've run or screamed, it would've forced him to compel her to forget about him and the moment that they had shared. And he didn't want that.

She took a couple more seconds pacing the floor, like a madwoman that was confused. Then finally she stopped. A look of sincerity swept across her face as she sat down alongside him. It took her a moment just to speak, and he waited patiently. She was trying to think of the words she wanted to come out of her mouth.

"Are you afraid of me?" he asked, even though he knew her answer.

"No… somewhat. I don't know…" She paused. "You said that I'm in danger?"

"Yes," he replied as he placed his hand on her shoulder. She slightly jumped, and he removed it. She wasn't quite comfortable with the whole idea of him being a blood drinker. "And I am truly sorry for that… I didn't mean to get this close to you. I was only supposed to watch you, but I got too involved."

"What do you mean, watch me? And in danger from who?" Her voice shook with nervousness.

"It doesn't matter. What I'm more concerned about is *The Order*."

"*The Order?*"

"Yes," he responded. "Vampires are forbidden to have human relationships for various reasons. *The Order* is a group of vampires that make sure that it doesn't happen and I'm afraid that they may have seen me with you. But I'm not sure. Just in case… When they realize I haven't transformed you, they will eliminate any threat that may expose us to the world."

"The threat being me?" she stated.

"Yes," he replied.

"So change me," she demanded.

He never desired to be anyone's *sire*, for being that came with a price. But he had felt her pain. The hurt she felt, the loneliness, and the hopelessness. It brought him back to a place of grief that he knew too well. But in the end, becoming a vampire would solve none of those issues.

"You don't know what you're saying," he said, taking a deep sigh and hanging his head down low.

"You want to change me, don't you?" she repeated. That's what she had been thinking, and she knew he had probably already read her thoughts. "Then I won't be in danger, right?"

"Yes and no," he responded. He didn't know how she was going to be if he transformed her into a *newbie*. Plus, he had vowed not to transform anyone. He'd lost Katherine, and he didn't want to be responsible for another person.

"Why not?" Her tone was soft. "You want me to be with you? Don't you?"

"It can't be both."

"I don't understand then… both what?"

"I can't transform you and be with you… it doesn't work like that… not for me."

"Why not?"

Her eyebrows pieced together, and her mood changed. She scooted back as she now faced him. He sighed, knowing that she wanted to be with him. In a relationship and happily ever after. But he couldn't promise her that, no matter how much she looked like Katherine. That was what had gotten him into this mess. He had made a mistake.

He knew it was not possible. Besides, being her *sire*, he could control her every move. And that was not his desire, and the only way not to do that was to stay away from her. Her choices would not be of her own will. And she would only do as he said. He didn't want that for her. Not for anyone. He had transformed no one since he had been reborn into this darkness. And he already knew she wanted to be like him.

"You're special and you need to know that." He grabbed her small, dainty hand and placed it in his. "I know you don't quite understand what's going on…" He watched as her eyes filled up with tears. "But Victoria will keep you safe… I promise."

"Victoria? the server at the bar?" she cried. "And not you?" A lone tear ran down her rose-colored cheek.

"I'm sorry… I never meant for this to happen, and I never meant for it to go this far." He lifted her head. "You will be safe… I promise you."

The emotions of hurt and betrayal coursed through him. The pain she felt saddened him, and all he wanted to do was make it go away. He was having feelings for her.

She couldn't see beyond the emotional wall she had put up. He was abandoning her, and that's all she felt at the moment. In time, hopefully, she would accept the reason he could not stay. Patience, my love, all the answers that she craved about this vampiric life, Victoria, and *The Order*, would come…but for now, she couldn't see past the hurt he was causing her.

"When I opened up to Katherine, it took her time as well… even when I couldn't see the future and I know the same will happen for you."

She had to process it all and eventually, when she did, a simple thought dawned on her. "So this is all about

Katherine?" she questioned. "I can be your Katherine… if you will allow me."

But he needed her to understand that this lifestyle was not glamorous. He hesitated, wondering if he should just compel her, He immediately sensed desperation. He needed her to understand; he wanted to speak up. Maybe this wasn't a good idea? He was now second-guessing himself.

"I want this life," she said aloud, and when she noticed his hesitation, her thoughts began racing quickly. She frantically looked around the room.

"Amara…" He clenched his hands into fists. "Don't!"

Reaching over and grabbing a safety pin from the nightstand, she swiftly pricked her finger and squeezed a slight amount of blood from it. This has to work, she thought as she placed her finger up to his nose.

The smell of her blood filled his nostrils. He tried turning away, but he couldn't fight off the urges that ran through his body. This was too much for him to resist, and she had put her finger up to his nose to entice him. What had she done? The veins in his face darkened, showing through his pale skin and his eyes turned a dark reddish color.

She gasped having seen nothing like this. She could tell that he was trying to hold back, but his sharp, white fangs emerged with force. He turned, entirely exposing what he truly was–a vampire. And that vampire was panting fiercely, while sinisterly looking at her.

But none of it made her afraid. She was ready. "Do it!" she demanded. She didn't understand how it worked, and he had explained little about being a vampire. Of course, his intention was never to change her, and he still stood by that fact. But she had watched enough movies to grasp the idea. She pulled her hair to one side, exposing her bare neck. "Do it!"

"Stop!" he yelled. He leaped off the bed, avoiding her advances. "You do not realize how serious this is. You see me now? Can you handle being like this? You're lucky… I can control myself. Another blood drinker would've immediately killed you for the move you just pulled."

His eyes bulged, and his upper lip curled up to one side as he snarled at her, then swiftly turned his back to her. She hung her head low in shame. When he turned back around, his face had turned back to normal.

"I'm sorry." She sulked. "I wasn't trying to upset you."

"You're reckless," he snapped. "This is life or death. What I am, what others are, is not something to take lightly."

"I just didn't know what to do."

"I see you weren't trying to cause harm," he said, gently walking back towards her. "But this isn't a life that you want."

She didn't realize how much her impulsive action would upset him. She felt guilty and ashamed and hastily stuck her finger in her mouth, sucking off the drop of blood and placing her hand underneath her leg.

"I'm sorry," she repeated, dropping her head down further. She appeared like a child. First with Mariam, and now with him. She couldn't help but seem like an embarrassment.

"It's okay… don't be so hard on yourself and don't do that again." His voice was soft yet stern.

As he sat down beside her, he placed his hand on her back. He stroked it up and down, consoling her.

"I'm only telling you this because I don't want harm to come to you." She felt him caressing her back, soothing her. "And I don't want to compel you. I want you to go to Victoria if you have any problems and yes, she is a vampire, like me… I'm trusting you with this information."

"She's a vampire?"

"Yes," he said. "But she can protect you if *The Order* comes around."

After seeing him change before her eyes, she was ready to take this situation more seriously. She was jumping the gun. She didn't know what she was thinking. Maybe she hadn't been thinking at all. Realizing this, she needed to know more, so she focused her attention purely on him.

"I want to tell you a story if you don't mind." He took his hand off her back and placed it in his lap. He shifted uncomfortably and she could tell by his body language whatever he was about to tell her, he wasn't comfortable telling it.

"I want to tell you about Katherine…"

"Katherine?" she questioned, trying not to show the jealousy that came across her when she heard her name. The love of his life, apparently. As a woman that wanted him, she didn't know if she cared to hear about their love story, but she didn't say a word and respected the fact that he was willing to open up to her.

"Yes… there was a time I felt like there was no one meant for me and wanted to give up on life," he said in a sunken tone. "I moped around day after day and life became pointless. It had no meaning, and I had lost all faith in love and myself. I wanted to end it all."

She eagerly listened as he told her how this darkness led him into a drunken state, doing anything and everything he could. He no longer wanted to feel the pain he had bottled up inside. But nothing worked. The more he drank, the worse he felt and before long, he was thinking about ending his own life.

He feared the thought of being alone. His first wife, the woman he once cared for and had dedicated his life to, left him for a younger man. She left only a note and no explanation why. Breaking his heart into a million pieces, she had been his everything. Leaving him without a blink of an eye and the rejection had been unbearable for him to take.

Amara looked at Lou with tears in her eyes. She felt every word he spoke. She felt his pain, even through his words. That hopelessness, the loneliness, and she resonated with all of his emotions. She watched as he slowly put his head down. Just by the way he spoke, she could tell that his heart still ached even to this day.

He glanced at her for a moment, then turned his head and stared straight ahead of him. He took a minute to think back on his emotional state. "It wasn't only your physical appearance that attracted me to you but also I sensed your desperation and loneliness when you were inside the bar, and I want you to understand that I've been in your shoes." She could feel the emotions as he was sharing. They were far too familiar as he continued.

In his time of depression, he had gone to a local tavern to drown his sorrows and, when leaving that same tavern, he took a different route home. He was staggering and walked down a dark unfamiliar alley, longing for someone to rob him and put him out of his misery. And his prayers were soon answered as he saw a mysterious man in the distance coming toward him. His angel of light, he thought, but he had been wrong. When the man stood before him, something had been off about his appearance. And that didn't sit well with him.

He remembered him clear as day, with his unnaturally pale skin, and his bright blue eyes that looked into his soul. He knew that this man was not a man at all, but something more sinister and unnatural as fear and panic raced through him.

This man made him feel uneasy. The thought of wanting someone to end his life changed when he had locked eyes with him. The reasons he was fighting were unknown. He had invited death, so why was he fighting against it now? He swung at the man, trying to hit him. The man darted from side to side, dodging each punch at lightning speed.

His devious laugh rang out through the darkness of the night. When he'd had enough dodging punches, he grabbed his arm and threw him up against a brick building. Damn near knocked him out. He remembered he thought every bone in his body had broken. He fell from the wall down into a dirty, wet puddle. Lying there, his body had gone limp.

Before he could collect his thoughts and rise back up, the man swiftly lifted him by his neck with one arm, pulling him closer to him. He was unnaturally strong and couldn't fight him off. In one quick move, the man dropped him back down and grabbed a fist full of hair, then pulled his head back, biting him on his neck. The way he attacked him was unnatural.

"You longed for death and I'm here to grant you what you want," the man said. "Do you still want to die?"

"No," he muttered.

Then he felt the man's teeth pierce his neck and could hear him sucking his blood— draining him of human life, almost to the point of utter death. That was the first time he truly feared death. He felt his life slipping away. When the man had finished, he watched as he lay on the ground, struggling to get up.

"I gave you something better than death," the man said as he backed away from him.

Lou raised his body just enough to watch the man dart down the alley at accelerated speed, only to disappear in the darkness of night. Then he passed out…

"There are so many reasons I crossed the line with you, Amara." He looked at her with compassion, while taking his finger to move a small piece of hair that had fallen in front of her face. "But I never should have. You made me feel vulnerable."

"Did you choose me only because of Katherine?"

"Yes… and no. I do care for you," he said. "As someone like me, we live for eternity. People die and then people are born. Everything else in this world is meaningless… empires rise and then they fall… and new worlds are formed. But having a *companion* to live eternity with is the only consistent thing and Victoria wanting that very thing is why we are at this crossroad."

"So she wanted me as a *companion*?" she confusingly questioned.

"Yes… all vampires go through a *comate stage*, a stage where vampires long for a *companion*. They want someone by their side for eternity and not necessarily romantically. The pain of loneliness is intense."

"So why didn't she change me?" she questioned. "Why send you?"

"Because there are rules in our world and things are not as simple as they may appear. I wanted to make sure Victoria was choosing wisely, so I agreed to follow you and observe you for her."

She couldn't respond. She longed to be like him and like Victoria, and he knew it. Victoria wanting her to be her *companion* made her feel special–as if someone cared for her. Something that she hadn't felt in a long time. It made her mind up and she wanted to go down this journey.

"I'm ready," she told him.

"No, I can't."

"And why not? Victoria wanted this, didn't she?" she asked, trying to convince him as she tilted her neck to the side once again, waiting for him to change her and to give her a new life. She wanted to live forever. Just like him.

"I can't and I won't." He jumped back away from her. "You don't understand what happened with Katherine… I vowed never to transform anyone. I don't want to be responsible for someone I care for."

"You say you care for me, then help me understand. Tell me what happened?" she said.

Lou hesitantly paced the floor before sitting back down on the bed. He took a deep breath. He hadn't told this story in years. But maybe Amara would understand why he thought the way he did.

"I'm not ready," he said. "But I will tell you this… I promised myself that I would never love or be with another woman and I won't. I haven't in one hundred plus years. I'm a loner, Amara. I roam this earth trying to find a meaning to all of this and nothing more. I don't want to hurt you, and I'm not rejecting you because of anything that you did."

"You're just punishing me for what happened in your past!" she shouted.

"I can't make you understand," he replied. "There's more to this life than just becoming what I am or being together.

This is beyond Victoria and yes, my personal feelings play a part, but I have made my decision. I cannot and will not transform you. I'm sorry."

He had failed to explain this. Of course, he didn't want to go into all the details. She would have to work with what she knew and as long as she sought Victoria out, if something were to happen, she would be okay, and he knew this. There were so many reasons for not transforming her. That included not wanting to damn someone for eternity as a vampire or changing her and having her meet sudden death because she failed to follow a vampiric law.

And by the way she was acting, transforming her into a *newbie* would be a mistake. Then there was the fact that she wanted to be with him. There was no way that he could be her *sire* and give her the freedom to live her new life. At least not at first.

With him around, that would be impossible. One mis-understood demand or request and she would be under his control. That was not what he wanted for her. As a newbie, she would be like his prisoner, his servant, doing everything at his beck and call. He was lucky enough for his *creator* not to be around when he was transformed. At first, he didn't understand, but later on, he did.

Amara felt her face flush, and she grew angrier. Without him, she was alone again. She thought they had shared a special moment. Yes, she had just met him, but the things he did for her were like a night on steroids, and she wanted more. More of him. She thought they had a connection, but clearly, she had been wrong.

"I can't be around you and be your creator. It doesn't work like that." He tried explaining, but she wasn't hearing it. In her eyes, regardless of the circumstances, it was another rejection.

"Vampire or not, you're just like all the rest!" she blew up, yelling and jumping up from the bed. "Just leave!"

"Amara…" he cried, trying to calm her down, but she didn't want to hear it. Her rage was in full effect.

"Get out!"

Part of her wanted him to stay, hold her again, and explain his entire story, no matter how long it took. And to make her feel like he wasn't deserting her. But maybe this was for the best. She sobbed. He was just another jerk, an asshole that was leaving her after he had gotten what he wanted.

"Don't shut me out. You can't do this alone."

"Get out!" she yelled again.

"Amara.."

"No," she angrily pointed at the door.

She watched as he held his head down, saddened by her response. But she didn't care. She continued to watch as he turned and, at vampiric speed, he was at her front door.

He sighed, but she turned her head in disgust. Then just as quickly as he had made it to her door, he was gone.

Her survival was now in her own hands. She had rejected him and Victoria. No longer would he physically interact with her. Deep down, she knew he had left in despair, never wanting to hurt her or for her to feel abandoned by him. But sometimes she reacted without thinking things through. Another downfall Mariam would always chastise her about.

Her heart sank… she was alone and loneliness to her was worse than death.

While Lou headed towards Victoria's place, he thought about what had transpired and about Katherine. Why did he lose control? Why didn't he stop himself and just leave Amara alone? But what happened he couldn't take back... not now. He recalled the last night he and Katherine spent together.

Katherine had found him in that alleyway, that night he was born into this life of darkness. 1820. The era when the first *Christmas Carol* was performed and when Beethoven was well known for his magnificent talent. It was so long ago, but he could remember his last night with her as if it was yesterday.

Katherine had just gotten out of their enormous bathtub. During this age, only the wealthy owned tubs in their homes and bathed a few times a month. But with him by her side, Katherine had all the luxuries she wanted. She never asked for much, but she took pride because she could take a bath whenever she wanted to. He dried her off with a large towel and, as he did, he marveled at her naked form. It kick started his heart, and he softly kissed her on her back.

"You know how much I adore you, right?" he whispered in her ear.

"Of course, my love." She smiled as the creases around her eyes formed. She glowed when she smiled, and he loved to see her happy. She turned around and faced him.

"I don't know what I would do without you," he lovingly spoke.

"Ummm… live forever." She giggled as she was referring to his vampiric state.

"Only in this form, but my world would be meaningless."

"Well, you can always transform me," she mumbled.

He soured at that response. He cherished her dearly, and the last thing he preferred to do was change her into the monster he assumed he had become. He knew what he had to do to satisfy his urges, and he couldn't see her being like that. The way she was, he loved her.

"Maybe another day," he said as he kissed her on her forehead. "Let's be merry with the way we are right now."

He noticed her sense of resistance, annoyance, and impatience, and he hated the fact that she felt that way. He recognized she craved to be like him for them to live in eternal bliss together, but he needed her to be human a little while longer—for him.

He grabbed her silk nightgown and draped it over her head as she held up her arms for him. He loved everything about her. To her warm soft skin, the sweet smell of roses that came off her body, and her gorgeous chestnut eyes. Everything. And without being a vampire, she was still flawless in his eyes.

"It's okay," she said. "I love you enough to wait." He met her velvety lips as she planted a kiss on his forehead. "Let's go lie down." Her tone had a slight amusement in it.

They walked over to the French-style mahogany bed. The mattress was made of soft cotton and not with the down or hay that most were made of. He wanted the best for her and had gone to great lengths to get this mattress for her. It was around the same time he was looking for the pendant that they had heard about.

Before she could reach the bed, he used his vampiric speed and strength to swoop her off her feet and lay her down on her side of the bed.

"You're too good to me," she said. "I don't deserve all of this… I don't deserve you."

"I owe you the world and then some," he said. "You saved me."

In the same manner he had picked her up in, he instantly used that same speed to reach the other side of the bed and lie down facing her. But when he looked at her once again, he sensed her resistance.

"What's wrong?" he questioned. He could've read her thoughts, but he refrained from doing so. Her thoughts were private, and he wanted to respect that. She took a deep sigh, her beautiful brown eyes went to his face and stayed there.

"My love, I am bothered. I look at you and you stay the same, but I grow older with each passing day. I am now eight years older than you and people will soon notice. How old do you want me to be when you transform me? When I'm old and gray?"

"When the time is right," he sympathetically responded.

"Please…" She placed her small dainty hand along his cheek and just her simple touch made him melt. "Please make me like you so that we can be together."

He hesitated before speaking. "Would this make you happy?" he said, turning his head in shame. "To be a monster like me?"

"Oh love, you're not a monster," she solemnly replied. "You are the most loving, kind, and handsome man I have ever known and not once have you ever been a monster. Never to me."

"If I do this, will you not hate me for it?"

"How can I ever hate you? I love you regardless, and this is my decision, not yours."

He focused his gaze back on her. He sensed her love and compassion for him, and it warmed his lifeless heart. She truly made him feel alive. Human. Normal. Would it still be the same if he were to change her?

"How about we hold each other tonight… I want to feel your warmth and remember this moment," he told her.

"You're going to do it?" she gleefully questioned. A sparkle came across her eyes.

"Tomorrow, my love… only for you… but tonight we enjoy your last night of… being human."

She smiled and turned her body. He pulled her closer to him, feeling her warmth as she cradled in his arms. A sense of happiness and excitement penetrated her. He kissed the back of her head as he slightly smiled. Maybe it wouldn't be so bad? he thought. As long as she was happy, he could live with whatever came after.

As they both drifted off into slumber, gasses from their old oil lamp accumulated and formed an explosion. The fire ignited quickly and spread rapidly through their wooden home. The fire had blocked all entrances and ways to escape. When he felt the heat, he quickly woke Katherine and looked for a way out. He jumped back towards a window that flames hadn't consumed. Kathrine was still in the bed trying to figure out what was going on.

Lou jumped back as the fire quickly reached their bed. He tried to grab Katherine as she screamed at what was going on. The flames blazed but he couldn't get to her.

When a fire is present, it is in a vampire's nature to cower from it. Fire could kill him and turn him into ash. But through his desperation, he would risk his life for hers. But as soon as he was about to go through the flames that had now surrounded the bed and the ceiling above it, he didn't see the wooden beam that broke off and fell upon her. She was now pinned down and on fire.

She screamed in agony from the pain and as the fire continued to blaze, he couldn't get close enough to her. He put his arm up to shield himself from the flames. Burning himself a time or two and jumping backward. He looked at Katherine in horror, but by now the fire had completely consumed the bed along with her. There was nothing he could do but listen to her screams until there were no more. She had burned to death, and he wasn't able to save her.

That night broke him. It forced him to leave her. The fire had become too much. And till this day, that night pained him. The love of his life was no more, and he felt as if he was to blame. He carried that guilt with him and hadn't forgiven himself since.

From time to time, he could still hear her screaming, like bees buzzing around. He hadn't cared for or loved another woman and vowed never to do so to honor her. Until Amara—he cared about her wellbeing.

He couldn't protect Katherine, but he would do his best to protect Amara.

CHAPTER TWENTY-THREE

A single tear ran down his cheek as he pulled into the driveway of Victoria's place. He kept the ignition running as he closed his eyes and sat there for a moment, trying to block out the horrible memories he had just recalled. But no matter how many decades had passed, it still stayed with him like a dark cloud hovering over his head.

He heard a light tapping on his driver's side window and there stood Victoria in the still of the night. He rolled down his window and gazed at her.

"Are you going to get out, or am I going to have to drag you in?" She chuckled.

The thought of her dragging him anywhere was her way of poking fun at him. After all, he was ten times stronger than her. His mood soured, and she could read it all over his face.

"Well, I'll leave you to yourself… I'll meet you inside." Her voice had softened, and he watched as she slightly nodded her head and headed inside.

He took some air into his lungs as he shut off the ignition to the car. The scent of decaying animals, damp moss, and wet tree trunks filled his sensitive nostrils. Why Victoria wanted to live on the outskirts of the city she claimed to love and find an isolated wooded area to live in still made no sense to him, but then again Victoria had her ways about her that no one could understand—-even if they tried. She was the partier but yet the loner at the same time. That was confusing.

He stepped out of his vehicle and shut the door as he headed towards her front door. Once he was inside, he headed towards her red leather couch and had a seat.

"Want a drink?" she questioned as she poured herself a half glass of dark liquor—her drug of choice. "Looks like you can use one."

"No," he flatly stated.

The sound of his voice snapped her attention towards him. "Uh-oh," she said while grabbing her glass and walking over to him. "What happened?"

She couldn't read his thoughts, but he could read hers. This was because she was *a lesser* vampire than him, but they did not consider her a *newbie*.

"I won't change her," he sternly replied.

"Why? What did you find out?" she questioned as she sat on the smaller couch across from him. He could hear her soft gulp as she took a drink of her whiskey. And she could tell he was in a foul mood. She could even sense that much.

"You knew she resembled Katherine. I would never have expected you to use her image against me," he said. He wanted to be mad at her, angry with her for putting him in a vulnerable situation, but he couldn't, and not because he favored her, but because of her vampiric gift.

Victoria had *the gift of Allies*. A gift where another vampire or human that was in her presence couldn't resist or show outrage towards them. She was likable, even if they disliked her. Her gift annoyed him–this was one of those times.

"I thought you would consider transforming her because she resembled her." She lowered her drink. "I was being selfish. I'm so sorry. She would make you happy and I wanted her as a companion. I was wrong to deceive you."

"Victoria… you should know better than that." He sighed. "She made me feel vulnerable."

Her ears perked up. "How close did you get to her?" she questioned as she took a sip of her drink. Her questioning eyes gazed at him as if she was waiting to hear the latest gossip.

"I spent the night with her." He shook his head.

"You did what?!" Victoria replied. Her voice was a mixture of surprise and curiosity.

"Maybe I need that drink."

"I'm on it." Victoria used her vampiric speed, which was quicker than most, fixed his drink, then she was back on the couch without missing a beat. She handed it to him. "Do tell," she said, trying to suppress her smile, but he could sense her excitement and he rolled his eyes and took a drink before continuing.

"She looked so much like Katherine, and in some ways, she reminded me of her. It was like being with Katherine all over again." He twirled his finger along the rim of the glass. "I felt an attachment… a bond. And one thing led to another." He continued to nurse his drink as if he was reliving the moment.

"You had sex with her?!" Victoria looked shocked. Lou hadn't been with a woman since Katherine and, deep down, she still hoped for him to change her. A moment of guilt came over her as soon as she thought about that. How selfish of her. Lou was her friend, and she had caused him to relive his pain. Damn *comate stage*.

"Can we not be so direct?" he chastised her.

"I'm sorry," she said, lowering her voice. "Did you form a *blood bond?*"

"What? No!" he quickly spat out. "I didn't drink from her."

He could feel the guilt and hopefulness coming off of her. Guilt for hurting her friend and hope that he still may change her. He read her thoughts and knew that she believed there was a chance for him to still transform her.

"I'm not taking her through the change. It's still a no."

"But why? What's done is done. It's okay for you to be happy and me as well. We deserve that much," she pleaded. The comate state was in full effect, and she couldn't help herself. "Clearly you care for her."

"I care for her enough not to get her hurt and thanks to you, I have put her at risk of *The Order*. Is that what you wanted?" he snapped.

"Oh hogwash, we haven't heard about nor seen anyone connected to them in decades. And why would they watch you? You are an *untouchable*… even if you crossed a line, you won't be punished. They're forbidden to touch you, remember?" She took another sip of her drink. "Now, if it was me, it may be a different story."

"That doesn't matter. I told her about me and you. She knows about vampires, and you know *The Order* will eliminate any threat to our race and they do not forgive."

"Well, why did you do that? Why did you tell her?"

"A moment of weakness," he responded, holding his head down. "I'll watch her for a couple of more days, but then it is your responsibility to keep her safe. That was the only reason I had to tell her about you… if she ever needed to come to you."

"Just great," Victoria annoyingly replied. "Now I'm a human babysitter. She would be better off if she was a vampire, don't you think?"

"No," he sternly elevated his tone. "Her emotions are all over the place. Even in the club, I sensed her desperation, hurt, loneliness, and pain from being used by unavailable men. That rage she carries will ensure that as a *newborn* she will be in the *uproar stage.* She is a risk and one neither you nor I will take. I forbid you to even change her."

"Okay… Okay. So now what?" she disappointingly questioned him.

"When I leave this god-forsaken city, you will look after her. Protect her. And keep her safe. Look at it as a human *companion* without being next to her. I want you safe as well."

"I guess." Victoria was not pleased with it, and it clearly showed. "But I put you in this situation, so I'll do it… I know you move around and after all, I have an eternity." She threw her hands in the air and slapped them down on her lap. She watched as Lou raised from his seat and set his glass down on the end table.

"Where are you going?" she asked.

"To check on her."

"Don't end up in her bed this time."

CHAPTER TWENTY-FOUR

I t had been two whole days, and Lou was running on pure exhaustion from lack of sleep. Even a blood drinker needed to rest, but he had to check on Amara one last time.

He pulled up next to the curb where he had parked before, the time when he first started following her. It was about time for her to head to work. He waited patiently as she came out of her building and hopped in a red Volkswagen beetle. He had seen this same car once before when Mariam was driving it and he figured she had borrowed it for the night. This pleased him, knowing that she wouldn't be catching rides home with random strangers.

As it pulled off from the street and headed down the road, he trailed her from a distance, seeing as she would occasionally swerve as she fixed her hair and applied makeup while looking in the rearview mirror. He frowned. She was being reckless by driving and taking her eyes off the road, something that he didn't like.

He paid close attention to the surroundings as he continued driving with his vampiric eyes, looking for anything that may be suspicious or a car that may follow her, but he noticed nothing.

Finally, she had reached her place of employment and pulled around the back of the building, parking her car. She climbed out and proceeded to the back door of Platinum. He waited for her to enter and then he entered through the front of the building, finding a wall to post up against and hide in the shadows. The last thing he wanted was for her to see him. After all, she was still upset with him, and he knew that much.

But her attention was elsewhere. She was talking to a gentleman with brown, shaggy hair. He homed in to listen in on their conversation.

"Noah, what are you doing here?" He picked up her excitement as she placed her arms around the man.

"You know, whenever I'm in town, I have to see my favorite girl. And I have some news to tell you, but not right now. I want it to be a surprise."

A sense of possessiveness and insecurity came over Lou as he eavesdropped. The hug from Noah had pissed him off, but he didn't move. Hopefully, he wasn't one of these assholes she was used to dealing with. She deserved better. He watched intensely as he continued to prey on their conversation. Noah had a surprise for her, that much he heard, and he wondered what it was. But he wasn't close enough to read his thoughts.

At one point she glanced in his direction, and he backed up against the wall, making sure the darkness fell upon his face. It was way better this way, he thought to himself. Watch and not be seen.

However, someone spotted him—Kat. "Hey, handsome. I see you're back." She grinned so hard he could see the chipped tooth that was towards the back of her mouth. "What are you doing hiding over here?"

He immediately locked eyes with her and compelled her to forget seeing him and even knowing him. And as before, she walked away in a trance-like state without saying a word. As bad as he hated the thought of compelling someone, this time it was necessary. He couldn't risk Kat telling Amara that he was there. It had to be done, and he had a feeling it would not be his last.

He studied her as she occasionally flirted with various men at the tables she was attending. Her flirtatious ways pained part of him, but he also understood that this was just part of the job and how she made her tips. That didn't mean he had to like it. He knew she could handle her own—he had witnessed that, but if she couldn't, he would be there to break every bone in their bodies.

Gazing around the nightclub, there was still no sign of *The Order* being there. Everything was how it should be—normal. Just the same drunken men and women partying around the nightclub. Maybe Victoria had been right. *The Order* may not be watching him or even around. At least for the rest of the night, he could relax some. He had watched her until she made it home safely and then left town. The rest was on Victoria.

As he waited, he caught glimpses of her glowing face whenever the light struck it. He took the moment, wanting to remember it. She was the closest thing that reminded him of Katherine, and it was nice to see her face after all these years—even if it wasn't her.

As the night winded down, he felt like she was in no real danger and his guard had been significantly lowered. Noah had been watching over her as well, and she seemed to be okay—no matter how frustrating it was to watch other men gawking and pining over her. But she was undeniably beautiful even with the droplets of sweat forming on her forehead, ruining the makeup she so desperately risked her life trying to apply.

Finally, her shift had ended, and he had compelled at least three servers to dismiss him. He saw Noah waiting on her and then walking her out towards the back and to her car.

He left out the front where he had parked and waited on the little red beetle to appear from around the back. He saw when Noah left the parking area in his golden-colored car, but she hadn't appeared yet and waited a couple more minutes and still nothing. What was taking her so long?

He stepped out of his car and rushed towards the back of the building. He was shocked to see that she was pressed against the car as a man demanded for her to hand over her purse.

"Give it to me now, bitch, or your life will end," the man demanded. He flipped open his sharp silver eighteen-inch switchblade.

Lou instantly recognized the man's voice. It was the same man that robbed him and slit his throat and he knew what he could do. In lightning speed, he was over to the man just as he stuck the blade into Amara's stomach. She gasped as she dropped to the ground. Her head bobbed against the metal frame of the vehicle.

Lou twirled the man around, snatching the blade from his hand and launching it.

"What the fuck? It's you," the man said in a panic. Lou sensed his fear but didn't care as he lifted him from the ground.

"You slit my throat and now I'm going to break yours," Lou said as his face changed before the man's eyes. His darkened veins and demonic eyes exposed a creature that was full of fury.

He snapped his neck with no effort. "Scum," he said aloud as his eyes blazed a bloodshot red color. The man's lifeless body dropped to the ground. This was one kill that he didn't mind cleaning up. The man wasn't worthy to be fed upon. Lou valued human life, but not this type of predator. In his eyes, he saved someone else from ever being harmed by this man again.

He rushed over to Amara's side, who was now clenching her stomach. He could smell the fresh scent of blood that was gushing out of her wound, and when he looked down, he could see it as well. It stained the front of her white shirt as if they had bathed it in blood. The man had cut her deep.

He heard her heartbeat slowing as she was dying—bleeding to death right in front of his very eyes. He couldn't save Katherine, but Amara still had a chance. There was no time to debate. He immediately bit his wrist, causing himself to bleed, and held it up to her mouth.

"Drink!" he shouted. "Drink from me… if you want to live."

CHAPTER TWENTY-FIVE

Amara woke up in her bed, dazed and confused. She immediately sat up and peered towards her stomach. There was nothing. Then she saw a movement in the corner of her room. When she looked over, it was Lou sitting in her overly large chair, eyeing her.

"What happened?" Her head felt clouded.

"You were attacked," he said.

Then the memories of the man's deep-seated eyes and raspy tone demanding her purse appeared, flooding back in. She remembered him stabbing her and then recalled drinking from Lou.

"I drank from you?" she stated. "That's why I'm healed."

"You will also start going through the *transformation* process," he declared. His statement was not pleasing at all, but more of disappointment.

"You didn't prefer this… did you?"

"No," he retorted.

"So why do it at all?" she snapped as her cry became elevated in anger. She studied him with her eyes blazing as if they were on fire. Her current wounds had healed, but the wound he left in her heart hadn't.

"Would you have preferred me to let you die? You were bleeding to death. What else could I do?" His tone matched hers. "You're so stubborn."

"And nothing has changed. I want you to leave!" she shouted. "Now!"

"You can't do this alone. You will need someone to guide you."

"Well, it won't be you," she angrily replied as she pointed toward the door.

And once again she watched as Lou flashed to the front door, gazed back at her, and headed out without saying a word. What was she to do now? Lou was the only vampire that she had ever encountered and, like always, she had reacted based on her emotions–not thinking beforehand, something that Mariam had consistently chastised her about. She quickly opened the door, taking a glance down the hallway–hoping that he hadn't fled. But he had already disappeared, and she had no way of tracking him down.

She slowly shut the door, sliding down it until she was perching on the ground. She bent her knees, drew them close to her chest, put her hands on her face and reflected on the moment at hand. Deep down, she recognized Lou was not like any other guy that she'd ever met. Despite that, she ran him away. She was alone and clueless–that of her own doing.

Now, she would soon transform and be part of a world she knew nothing about. The undead. She only had the story that Lou had told her and because of her selfishness, she had lost the one person who could teach her the ways of this dark life.

She started feeling sorry for herself. The whole reason for her to go to Inferno in the first place was not to be a victim. Even though it failed, somehow she had become one, even after it was all said and done. It was a man that had almost taken her life and it was a vampire that had given it back to her.

She was not about to go back into depression and had to get herself together. She was a vampire now, or at least she was supposed to be one. But she still didn't feel different. Forget it all. She didn't need him. She'd read enough books and concluded that she could teach herself to be a vampire. There's always Google. She needed no man, vampire, or anyone to assist her.

She giggled at the thought of it. Just a day ago, vampires didn't exist, or at least not in her world. Now, she was going to be one and turn to Google for her answers.

She thought about becoming a rebel with her newfound abilities. She was going to be a force to be reckoned with. The more she thought about Lou and the heartache that she had to endure, the more furious she became.

She was bitter. Beyond bitter. And her thoughts proved that. And that bitterness grew deeper inside of her. She wasn't thinking straight. And for some odd reason, her bitterness was boiling over like a hot volcano.

For all the men that had rejected her, hurt her, and abandoned her—she would kill them all. She paused, shocked by her thoughts. Yes, she would say the things that she was now thinking, but this time, her rage was more valid. More assuring. She felt like doing the things she was thinking. She clenched her fist so hard that her nails pierced her hand.

She felt like coming back with a vengeance. Ridding the world of them with their smooth-talking, chauvinistic ways. She was going to take out as many of them as she could. And nothing was going to stop her.

She would now have to live in the dark and wondered if the people that were darting in and out of the shadows of the night were indeed vampires? Realizing she would never feel the warmth of the sunlight on her face anymore was now a reality. She was now an official lady of the night. Fearless, heartless, and bold. Something about that thought made her smile.

Standing up, she dusted herself off and walked over to her full-sized mirror. Still, she noticed no change. But she knew it would happen. She smiled again. The feeling of not believing or feeling unworthy had gone. She believed in her soon-to-be new self, the one that every male suitor would soon fear.

Before she met Lou, she was on a mission and planned to finish it. But this time, she would be unstoppable. Not weak. By using her charm and charisma, she would lure men of evil intent to their death. No longer was she the prey–but the predator.

Her entire existence had meaning now. Being supernatural, her new journey in life started the moment Lou offered his blood to save her. Thank you, Lou. He had no clue he had created a monster.

She became dizzy. Her head felt like the world around her was spinning and headed towards her bed to lie down. She figured the change was taking place. From the story Lou had told her, this was going to be painful, but she was prepared to take on whatever was about to happen next and knew that this was something she had to go through. Alone.

She lay down and stared up at the ceiling waiting for the pain to kick in but before long, she had drifted off into a deep slumber.

It was still dark outside, with a couple of hours left until daylight. She woke up in unbearable pain. Drenched in sweat, she tossed and turned, trying to fight off the agony she was in. Her body was physically dying, and far more painful than when the man had stabbed her. She felt as if she was dying. She cried out for anyone to save her.

For someone to just end her life because the pain seemed unbearable for her to take. Her body felt as if someone was breaking it into a thousand pieces and then putting her back together. There was nothing she could do but accept her fate and what was going on with her.

It seemed like forever for the pain to ease up, but it had only been minutes. Her pain didn't last as long as Lou had explained. Or maybe it did. Once the pain faded, she had a gnawing, indescribable feeling in her stomach and felt hungrier than ever before.

From what she had read about vampires, a *newborn* such as herself would be uncontrollable, and she was believing it as her cravings intensified. As her body called out to be filled, she knew what it wanted—-blood. Regular food was not an option. Blood was the only thing that was going to indulge this craving.

She could only think about feeding. She stumbled towards her front door, opening it like a madwoman, almost flinging it off its hinges, and frantically looking down the hallway. No one was in sight. Was it this easy for her to take a human life? Honestly, the hunger was overwhelming, and she didn't think twice about it.

She was weak, but she walked down the hallway, sliding her body against the wall like a zombie of the undead until she reached the main entrance and left the building entirely. The hunger was intensifying as she stood outside of the building and on the sidewalk full of people.

She could hear each one of their thoughts, and it was overwhelming. She quickly placed her hands over her ears, trying to drown them out, but her throat irritated her, feeling parched and dry. It again intensified her hunger. She could smell the sweet aroma of blood in the air as the wind blew, which made her mouth intensely water, and her canines began emerging. The unwelcomed thought of feeding on them invaded her mind repeatedly.

She lowered her hands and quickly covered her mouth and hurried to get away. If Lou could fight off attacking a human, she could too. She ducked down the closest dark alley to avoid contact with anyone.

She heard a faint rumbling noise as she immediately turned to look behind her. The rats racing behind the dumpster were making a chattering sound. At vampiric speed, she caught one. Then held it up to her mouth. The human side of her felt disgusted by the thought of drinking its blood from it, but the vampire side needed to feed.

She snarled her nose up at it and sank her teeth into the rodent. Once the blood hit her tongue, the thought of fulfillment came across her. The warm, delicious blood pumped through her, and she felt its blood racing through her veins. It renewed her as the feeling of starvation disappeared. Her blurred vision was now cleared, she felt stronger, and could focus again.

She dropped the deflated rat down on the ground, wiped her blood-soaked mouth, and looked around at her surroundings. Everything was beyond beautiful. For the first time, she was seeing the world with *newborn* vampire eyes. And could truly see what was before her.

CHAPTER TWENTY-SIX

She studied the tiniest details of the world. The objects that she would have never discovered with her human eyes.

Everything was more detailed and refined. She could detect the plant's veins. They were vivid green, and their leaves were crying, with small droplets of moisture that formed upon them.

Things progressed slower, making her able to catch every movement that was continuing around. Her eyes followed as the rodents in the alley went into the darkness, scavenging for materials to eat. A simple fly dropped on a woman's head as she strolled past her, a thief shuffling past a man that he pick-pocketed ever so effortlessly, and she watched eagerly from the alley, marveling at everything she saw.

It was truly remarkable what she could see. An entire life of possibilities that she hadn't realized before. She touched the stone building in the alley. And when she did, the heaviness of its structure seemed light. She pushed vigorously against it, crushing the stone as pieces of concrete fell to the ground and removed her hand, gazing at it. It was still small and dainty, but a weapon. Her strength was unreal.

A bunch of loud noises broke from every direction. She heard people's thoughts as they trudged past. She gripped her ears. All of their thoughts came at her like bats in a cave. And each one sounded like nails being scraped against a chalkboard. She focused on only her thoughts and their thoughts did not scramble as each thought sounded clearer.

She swiftly learned that she could focus on an individual and pick up exactly what they were thinking. Some worried about bills, being evicted, lovers, death, and so on. She giggled to herself. This was amazing. Unrealistic. Indescribable. She couldn't understand why Lou wasn't as excited to be immortal as she was. Possessing these types of abilities—one could only dream.

She shuffled out of the alley and once again grew hungry. The rat hadn't been enough. She gazed out the alley, watching as people walked by. With each person, she could smell the distinct scent of blood. Some blood was sweeter than others and some blood smells were sour in her nostrils.

Nevertheless, she knew the rat was only going to do so much. Embarrassed at the fact that she was still in her night robe, she bound it around her waist, keeping her head down and racing back to her apartment. She couldn't use her speed because she didn't want to cause an alarm. But everyone was in their world anyway, as they stepped past. They didn't even notice the way she looked. But she still walked at a human pace.

Noticing that if she concentrated even harder, she could listen to their tiny heartbeats coming through their chest. She was feeling unsure of herself. An immediately intense desire came over her to go on a rampage and feed on each one of them. Her fangs protruded from her mouth and the next person who walked past, she was going to grab and feed.

She heard the distinct footsteps of someone approaching closer to the alley. This was her moment to strike and as she did, a hand grabbed her arm and quickly pulled her back.

"No, you don't," the blonde-haired woman said.

"Let go of me," Amara said angrily, jerking her arm from the woman's grasp. "Who the hell are you?"

"I'm your best friend and savior." The woman smiled. "Here, take this." She tossed her a plastic hospital bag full of blood.

Amara grabbed it, ripped it open, and quickly downed the blood. As the human blood flowed through her, she felt a jolt of energy and not like before when she had drunk from the rat. It was delicious and exhilarating. As if she was tasting her favorite food for the first time. Sweet and succulent. And smooth like a good bottle of brandy. Her body appreciated every sip.

Once she had drunk the bag, she looked back up at the blonde woman, who was now smiling at her. She looked familiar but she just couldn't place where she had seen her before. At that moment, her thirst and everything else that was known to her was her only focus.

"Feel better?" the woman asked.

"Who are you, and what do you want?"

"I'm here to help you," the woman said, sensing aggravation and anger coming from Amara.

"I don't need your help," Amara snapped. She was still mad about how things ended with Lou and was now taking it out on the blonde. It was something about her saying that she was here to help her that reminded her of Lou. "Go away, lady."

The woman pierced her lips together before speaking. "Here is another bag before I go, and if you need me… well, I'll be around."

Amara took the bag of blood without saying a word. The woman smiled once more and shook her head. "Well, stay out of the sun and change your clothes the next time you come out." She hesitated for a moment and then quickly disappeared.

Amara looked down at her clothing. Who was that woman? she thought. It was another supernatural being. But instead of dwelling on it, she quickly rushed out of the alley, keeping her head down and clenching the bag of blood close to her chest.

Five minutes later, she was now closer to her building, barefoot and barely dressed. Looking like a beast. An animal. But for some odd reason, it didn't bother her. Knowing that she was stronger than ever before, that she could take out anyone that posed a threat, caused a God-like mentality. She held her head up confidently as she opened the door and walked down the hallway.

When she reached her front door, she opened it and locked it behind her, thinking that the woman had followed her. But she was alone and there was no knock on her door. And from that moment on, she thought about the mysterious blonde no more. After all, she had more important things to think about, such as her new *transformation.*

She headed straight towards her bathroom and looked in the mirror, not knowing what to expect. From all the vampire stories she had read, they weren't able to see their own reflection. To her surprise, she could and she had changed. No longer was she the girl with the sickening eyes with dark circles. No, she was gorgeous. Perfection. She thought she felt her little heart flutter, amazed at how flawless her skin was and blemish free.

Her eyes weren't just hazel anymore but a beautiful chestnut almond with a reddish tone that seemed to sparkle, and her dark black hair was a bluish black, that was wavier than normal. Healthier. And It laid perfectly down her back and shoulders.

However, she was paler than normal, almost unrealistic, but nothing that she couldn't fix with a little makeup. Her lips were full, luscious, and plump. A perfect shade of soft pink. Even down to her perfectly arched eyebrows. She couldn't find one flaw in her.

She twirled around in excitement. She was beautiful and all-powerful. This felt fascinating. She laughed out loud in hysteria. What could be so horrible about becoming a vampire? Now she was a killer by design and needed blood for her survival, but this was just an occupational hazard to her.

From all the movies and books she'd read, vampires were miserable, not wanting to feed off of humans, or worried about being lonely. But not her. She felt none of that. The only emotion that was heightened was rage. She wanted to kill, and she couldn't seem to shake that.

She wanted to kill dishonest men and anyone that stood in her way. She scoffed at the thought of loneliness. If she chose to be, she had a lifetime to find someone. She was lonely already, but at least she had a reason to live now.

She noticed her curtains were still closed from the way Lou had fixed them. Seeing from the sides, the sun peeked through. And it was rising. She cowardly ran away and felt the urge to sleep. There was nothing to gain by staying up during the day and now was the time to preserve her energy for the night.

She lay and daydreamed about Lou. The way he had made her feel, the breakfast in bed, the sex. It all ran through her head. And then guilt. She hated the fact that she had kicked him out and the way she had treated him when all he wanted to do was help her. But what could she do about it?

She could still smell the Brut cologne that was left on her pillows. She grabbed one and took in the smell, closing her eyes, thinking of what it could've been with him. Did she miss him? Did she feel some type of devastation because he was gone? Until this point, the only emotion she had was rage. Maybe there was hope for her... for them–humans. Smiling, she went to sleep until nightfall.

When she woke, it was night. The sun had gone down, and it was her time to roam. She slept the whole day and felt well rested. She looked around her apartment. Everything seemed still. Silence. Emptiness. She needed to do something other than being confined to these walls.

She decided she wasn't about to spend another second cooped up. Jumping up, she went to take a shower. After all, Lou had given her a gift, and she wasn't even human any-more. Why not enjoy it?

While in the shower, Lou crossed her mind again. She needed to find him. She wanted to apologize for what she had done and even if he couldn't be around her, she would just have to accept it. But she needed to hear his voice and needed him in her life. Her emotions were all over the place, like an overactive child.

The water felt great as it ran down her newly naked and perfect frame. The warmth from the water put her at ease and felt more intense as it trickled on her back. Even things that touched her skin felt different. The sensation felt more intense. Intriguing. And her body became more alive. She was in ecstasy. Just the feeling of the water felt like a soft hand gently gliding its fingers over her.

Once finished, she hopped out, grabbed her towel, and began drying herself. After pondering the situation, she went back to Infernos to find Lou. After all, that's where she'd met him and maybe he would still be there.

She wanted him to see how well she was adapting to her new life and how she could overcome the *transformation* and master her first kill–even if it were nothing more than a mere rodent. She frowned at that notion and also wanted him to see how her appearance had changed. He's going to love it, she thought. And, of course, she wanted to apologize for the way things had played out with them.

After combing her hair and applying makeup, she picked out a skimpy red dress. She wanted to feel like the new vampire she now was — sexy but powerful. She put on a pair of red- bottom spiked heels and applied the finishing touches, wearing the same bright red lipstick that she wore when she had met him.

She was officially a new woman. A woman of the undead, and she was ready to take on the world. And her hunger.

As she headed towards the garage, she wanted to be a little rebellious. Establishing that she would not take her car, she looked over at a van that had a lightning bolt spray-painted on the sides of it.

"Hmm," she mumbled under her breath. She strode over to the van. She glanced to see if anyone was around. When she realized she was alone, she opened the door with her newfound strength and hopped inside.

She knew it was wrong, but she wanted to take it, anyway. Why follow the laws of humans when she wasn't one of them anymore? Besides, who could stop her? She was immortal. A set of keys dropped in her lap as she pulled down the visor. She laughed, something that she had been doing often since her change. It was funny how easy it was for her to take the vehicle. She started it up as she turned down the rock music that blared from it and headed towards Inferno.

After another hour and a half drive, she finally pulled up in the parking lot. This is where it all began, she thought as she hopped out of the vehicle, staring at the van for a brief second. She couldn't believe she had stolen it.

She was loving her new rebellious side and smiled as she shut the door and headed toward the bar. She had the confidence of a bull. And it was way stronger now than before.

She walked inside and the music blazed like once before. There were some familiar faces and some different ones from the last time she was there.

She gazed around the room, taking in the scenery. It was the same. Nothing special. Not even for her vampiric eyes. Drunks arguing, tons of cigarette smokers, even the bartender that overcharged her last time. Her fresh eyes allowed her to see things in more detail, like the scrambling roaches on the half-scuffed up floor, and the small spiders crawling up the wall. Oh, the things she wanted to unsee.

She boldly strutted over to the bar and motioned to the bartender. Watching her as she walked over, she read her thoughts. The bartender noticed something different about her and that she seemed different from Miss Goody Two Shoes that had come in last time with her friend. Still, regardless of how different Amara seemed to be, she figured that she probably wanted some girly drink… Amara even read her thoughts about how the bartender was going to take her money's worth trying to rip her off.

She kept her poker face, regardless of the bartender's thoughts about her, as her thoughts were all about her and how she felt about Amara's type. But Amara knew last time that the bartender was judging her, and instead of ripping her throat out, she shot her a conniving grin as the bartender finally approached.

"I remember you," the bartender grudgingly said.

"Yeah, I remember you too," she grinned. "Get me a rum and coke."

"Okay," the bartender replied, turning to fix her drink.

"And try not to overcharge me this time." Amara invaded her thoughts once more, hearing, "Damn, she's got some balls. Maybe she's not as weak I think," the bartender thought. "Damn right," she said under her breath as she watched the bartender walk away.

She looked towards the table where Lou was sitting when she first met him. He wasn't there; he was not in the bar at all. She hoped he would be there, but a woman sat where he once did.

"Here you go. This one is on me."

She looked at the bartender as she sat her drink down in front of her. After giving her a nod and a wink, she turned around to assist another customer. She assumed her comment about overcharging her let her know she wasn't just some prissy girl. She set up straight on the barstool feeling proud.

She grabbed her drink and took a small sip, glancing at the woman at Lou's table, who was staring at her as well. She had recognized her from the alley and the woman was the waitress that helped her out when she was with Lou. She could sense that the woman wanted her to join her. Curiosity piqued her interest. She tried reading her thoughts but got nothing.

She slowly rose from the barstool and walked toward her. As she approached, she didn't take her eyes off her. She felt drawn to her. What makes this woman so special? She had to find out. She grew frustrated while making it through the crowd that was dancing and the staggering drunks, but finally she reached her table.

"Hey," the woman said.

"You're the woman that stopped me," Amara replied as she pulled out a chair and took a seat.

"My name is Victoria."

"You're Lou's friend. I knew I recognized you," she said as she anxiously looked around, searching for him.

"Yes, and he's not here," Victoria said.

Both of them stared at each other for a brief second, as if they were sizing each other up. How much did she know about her? And what had Lou told her? She waited for her response, seeing if Victoria could read her mind as she took a sip of her drink. And she took a moment to scan the room once again. She secretly still searched for Lou in the crowd.

"He's not here," Victoria said once more, as if she was becoming annoyed, watching as Amara scanned the room various times and looked towards the door whenever someone walked in. "And I know more than you think I know."

Victoria had gotten her attention. She was reading her thoughts, but why couldn't she read hers? She tried focusing harder on Victoria, but she still didn't pick up anything from her.

"And…. you can stop trying to read my thoughts," Victoria added as she took another sip of her drink. "You and I are alike. But you can't read my thoughts because you are *a lesser… a newborn.*"

"I don't know what you're talking about," she harshly responded. Deep down she knew Victoria was different. Even Lou seemed different as a vampire.

They were more put together and a lot more intriguing than she was. She didn't like the thought of being *a lesser* or whatever Victoria was talking about. The only thing on her mind was what Victoria wanted from her? Even though she knew.

"Yes, you do," she grinned.

"Yes, I do what?"

"Know what I want from you." Victoria chuckled.

Amara knew Lou wanted Victoria to protect her and be a companion for her. But she couldn't respond the way she wanted to, by just telling her to fuck off. And as much as she wanted to hate Victoria, she couldn't.

Victoria continued to sip her drink and giggle at her. She knew she was trying to play clueless, but it wasn't working. She grew frustrated at Amara's nonchalant demeanor. Lou was right, her emotions were all over the place and that was an understatement. She was going to have her hands full with her. She spoke up.

"He told me about you and what happened for him to change you," Victoria said as she set her drink down on the table. "Rough."

"Okay, so you know… so what?" she sharply responded.

"I, however, I am glad that you are now part of the team," Victoria responded. "We are going to have so much fun."

CHAPTER TWENTY-EIGHT

Amara curled her lip to one side and scowled at her. Lou must've known that she would eventually show up seeking him at Inferno. But why would he send Victoria? Why didn't he come himself? So many questions ran through her mind.

"You know why he is not here," Victoria replied to her thoughts.

"Why?" she said while crossing her arms and rolling her eyes, acting like a brat. Who is she? His representative? And why her? None of it made any sense. He could have come by himself. He couldn't force her to be somebody's *companion*.

"He can't be around you," she expressed with sincere emotion. "Lou was right when he told me you would come back looking for him…" She shook her head.

"Why can't he? He is my *creator*… my *maker*." She became defensive. This was all ridiculous to her. She tried not to show her anger, but it showed through anyway.

She realized quickly that in her immortal state, whatever emotions she felt seemed to intensify ten times more than normal. But she didn't care. This entire conversation was upsetting.

"He is your *sire* now. A lot of things come with that… things that you don't understand." She leaned in closer. "But I'm here to help you understand."

"Listen, I don't need you, and I don't need him," she scoffed, then stood up and looked her in her eyes. "As you can see, I'm doing just fine on my own."

"Amara, you need to listen. You're a *newborn*… and I'm a lot older than you and even I don't know it all." Victoria was trying to remain calm by keeping her voice down. "Even we have things to be fearful of. And I'm here to teach you… this is what Lou wanted me to do."

"And who is he? A nobleman? He left his *newborn*, remember?" She snatched her drink off the table, tipped it up, and taking in the last sip, she slammed the glass back down. "I don't have time for this. If he wanted to help me, he would be here!" She put both her hands down on the table and frowned at Victoria. "Tell Lou I don't need him or you."

"But all you got is time." Victoria couldn't help but laugh and make a sly remark. Amara needed to calm down. She was losing her shit again and the red flags that Lou warned her about were showing.

Amara grew red as she fixed her dress and turned abruptly to walk away. She was furious at the fact that he would send someone in place of him. And that Victoria was making light of the situation. But she had stood her ground and now, not knowing what to do, she anxiously looked through the crowd to figure out her next move. Lou, Lou, Lou. She wanted to hurt something, attack something. It fueled her body with anger.

Stomping off from the table, she didn't look back. She didn't need her. She noticed a lone man at the bar and headed his way. She needed a victim—someone to take her anger out on. Before approaching him, she stopped to read his thoughts.

She sensed sexual deviance and read thoughts of various women's body parts running through his mind. Women's legs, women's breasts, women's butts. All he could think about was sex, and he wanted to manipulate someone into having sex with him. Then he would find another one and the cycle would continue.

This type of thinking enraged her. She too had been one of those gullible females that this man would attract, and then the next morning, throw her away like a discarded tissue. No more, she thought. This will be his last time. She fixed her hair as she approached him..

His back was turned when she reached him. He was already disgusting to her, but she didn't let it show. Putting on a smile, she tapped the man on his shoulder.

"Hey," she said seductively.

He turned around to see who had tapped him on his back, looked her up and down, and was in awe of what he saw. She was beautiful, almost mesmerizing, and her body was to die for. His thoughts echoed in her head like a bell.

"Well, hey there," he replied in a masculine tone while eyeing her up and down.

"Do you mind if I sat here?" She pointed at the empty barstool beside him. Reading his thoughts, she already knew that he had been saving this seat for his brother, but he didn't even care about him anymore. His focus was on her.

"Not at all." He grinned.

His thoughts invaded her mind once more. The things he wanted to do were unimaginable, but she kept a straight face, trying to focus on the words coming from his mouth. She sat down on the barstool and crossed her legs. He was a dirtbag alright. His eyes were all over her. Undressing her. Showing her no signs of respect.

She thought about how easy it was for this man to pick up women. His looks were quite inviting. He was handsome. The mysterious type–almost like Lou. With his dark black hair and ocean blue eyes. He had all the looks. He had a slick way of talking. It would be so easy for a woman, such as herself, to fall for a man like this.

"What's your name, gorgeous?"

The question threw her off guard. Such a simple question, but she knew she couldn't give him her real name.

She hesitated for a second, trying to figure out what name to give him. "I'm Anna." He didn't seem to notice her hesitation with her name, and she had scanned his thoughts to make sure. Nothing.

"Well, Anna, I'm Roy," he said as he placed his hand without permission on her thigh.

She grimly looked down at his hand. Wanting to rip it off, for even violating her, she remained calm.

You're barking up the wrong tree, she thought as she gave him a phony smile. He had no clue how badly she wanted to crucify him.

Placing her icy hand upon his, she could see that the coldness gave him a chill. But he couldn't care less. His mission was to get inside her pants and nothing more. She leaned over and grabbed his drink, which sat in front of him on the bar.

He watched her as she seductively tipped the glass up, slowly taking a sip and keeping her eyes on him at the same time. Damn, his type of woman, he thought as he began caressing her thigh, and when she didn't stop him, he took it as a proposition to continue. Easy target, he thought.

When she first felt his warm hands touching her body, she wanted to cringe. But her face remained unbothered. She set the glass down and moved in closer to him, uncrossing her legs, making it easier for him to rub her inner thigh.

That action shocked him, but he would not pass up the opportunity. He moved his hand back some and then slid it underneath her dress. Now that she was a vampire, her skin was freezing to the human touch, but he chalked it up as her just being cold-blooded. He didn't care. Wanting her even more now, he continued to rub her inner thigh, hoping he could heat her up but in all the wrong ways.

"I can tell you want me, Roy," she said, placing her hand on his private area. He slightly jumped but did not remove her hand. This excited him, and she could tell by the growing bulge in his pants.

He looked around the bar to make sure no one was looking; everyone was doing their own thing, and it was like they were in a world of their own. The more she caressed him, the more excited he got. He couldn't believe it. It was a win-win for him.

"I gotta van outside… want to go?"

CHAPTER TWENTY-NINE

She craved to devour Roy. The scent of his blood was soothing and inviting, making her want to sink her teeth right into him, but she resisted. Not here, she told herself, as she peered into the crowd. There was no way for her to feed on him in front of all these people and she was hungry like before.

"My van is perfect… and it's a little more private."

"No problem… to the van, it is." His grin was ear to ear.

Before she could respond, a sense of annoyance and curiosity came over her as another man approached from behind. She turned around and noticed he looked exactly like Roy. Twins. She could tell that he was a lot more reserved than his twin just by his appearance. He placed his hand on Roy's shoulder, seeing what was going on.

Both of them swiftly removed their hands from each other, as she blushed at the thought that they'd been caught. She should have known better being a vampire and all, but she still was new to being quicker with her actions. Embarrassed, she turned her head and held up her hand to call the bartender over.

"Another rum and coke?" she said. This time, she was more polite.

She nodded and turned back towards Roy and his twin brother. She needed a drink as she looked at both of them. The twin held out his hand to introduce himself.

"Let me not be rude," he said as he glanced at his brother, then back at her. "My name is Conrad."

She reached out to shake his hand and, as she did, she spotted his reaction when he detected her cold touch. A sense of questioning curiosity grew over him and she speedily pulled her hand back from him out of nervousness.

"I'm Ama—Anna," She almost slipped up on her name because she was more worried about what he assumed about her icy hand.

"She's beautiful, isn't she?" Roy interrupted them. He looked at her like a slab of meat and didn't care about her getting to know his brother. He just wanted to make it to the van.

Unlike his brother, Conrad was not about to be rude, and she could sense all of this. Observing her as he looked at Roy with a smug face, he rolled his eyes at him and smiled back at her. Yeah, he's an asshole. She started reading his thoughts.

"Excuse him, he's rude." Conrad tried to lighten the mood.

The bartender returned with her drink, setting it down. She inhaled a whiff of her blood. Ugh. She didn't know what it was, but she smelt horrid, like someone that had been rolling around in a dumpster, and it instantly turned her off. Why hadn't she spotted this before?

"Is this one on you, too?" she questioned as she smiled at her.

The bartender didn't respond this time. Instead, she just turned around and headed on her way. She took the drink and turned back towards Roy and Conrad, not wanting to end any conversation. She was on a mission, and she looked at Conrad, hoping he would shut up and let her get on with destroying his brother

"Well brother, we are about to head out." Roy stood up, giving his brother his seat.

"You're not leaving, are you?" Conrad questioned.

"Just have to handle some business." He smiled as he grabbed her hand, pulling her from the barstool. "This won't take long... I'll be in her van." He winked.

Finally, she thought, as she let Roy guide her from the chair. Conrad gave both of them a long, hard look and then shrugged his shoulders. He couldn't believe that his brother had even got her to go along with him, but then again, he picked up unsuspecting women all the time. I can't save them all, he thought to himself.

Roy and she walked towards the main door of the bar, dodging a brawl that was about to take place. Roy only had one thing on his mind. He was about to get laid. Holding on to her hand as if not to let her get away, he began rushing her out the door. When they were outside, he forced a kiss upon her.

Not really wanting to kiss him back, she allowed his wet, nasty tongue to go down her throat. She should've just bitten it off. But she allowed it to happen, feeling his hand touch her backside without notice. She pulled herself away from him.

"My van is right over there." She smiled and pointed in the direction. She had parked it on the side of the building in a desolate area, making sure it wasn't visible to the road—just in case the real owners had called the police.

"Lead the way," he eagerly replied.

She heard a familiar voice calling her name, stopping her in her tracks. Thank God, Roy nor Conrad had heard her actually call out her real name. Maybe it was her vampiric hearing, why she heard it clear as day. She turned around to see Victoria with her hand on her hip as she angrily faced her.

"I told you to leave me alone," she scorned.

"Don't do this!" Victoria sternly said.

"Go away!"

She grabbed Roy's hand as she watched Victoria throw her hands up in the air and walk off.

"Who was that?" he eagerly questioned. "Does she want to join?"

"No," Amara disgustedly replied as she turned her nose up at him when he wasn't looking. She pulled him towards the outside. Bastard. She couldn't stand how cocky his attitude was. He deserved everything she was about to do to him. Rid the world of this filth.

She heard his heart beat faster as they approached the van and sensed his body becoming aroused. Instead of just killing him immediately, she was going to have a little fun of her own first. Why not get satisfied in the process? After all, the mere thought of taking his life had turned her on.

Opening the back of the van, they both hopped in and shut the double back doors. Roy grabbed her and kissed her neck. She pushed him back. Then he raised her dress, and she in return, grabbed the back of his head, forcing it in between her legs.

He moved her silk underwear to the side and licked her sweet spot. Moaning at the action of his tongue, she enjoyed herself. She dropped her head back on the inside of the van. She felt every movement, and it was intense.

Her first sexual experience as a vampire and she was loving it. Up and down, side to side, she had to admit, the man had skills. Smelling the sweet aroma of his hair, she smelled his blood as well. She clenched her jaw and tried to focus on something else other than ripping his throat out. She had only been a vampire for a day, and fighting off her urges wasn't easy.

Fighting off the urge to take just a small bite, she stopped him. Pulling his head up, she gave him a long, engaging kiss, tasting her sweetness on his lips. His body reacted to her passionate kiss, feeling himself getting even more aroused. Before long, they intertwined.

While he thought she was enjoying his every move, she felt degraded. Rage filled every inch of her, and without warning, she felt her fangs emerge. The more he pumped in and out of her body, the more enraged she became.

She pulled herself away from him with one quick move. Then turned around and faced him. He was in shock seeing that the once beautiful woman that he was with was now some type of monster. She instantly grabbed his throat, sunk her teeth into his neck, and fed. He tried to yell, but her grip tightened around his neck, making it impossible for him. He scrabbled and gasped for air, but she would not release him.

The taste of his blood was more satisfying than the rat she had devoured. Human blood coursed through her body. An electrifying feeling came over her and that feeling raced through her like a jolt of electricity. His blood was beyond intoxicating. The total experience was exhilarating. Fulfilling.

Once she had enough, she retracted her fangs from his neck. Holding her head back and licking the blood from her lips–taking in the moment of pure pleasure. After about ten seconds, she looked back at Roy, who was holding his neck and gasping for air. She sensed pure fear.

He screamed again. She knew she had to shut him up quickly before anyone heard his cries for help. She took her sharp nails, dug them in the front of his throat, and pulled out his esophagus, crushing it in her hands. She watched as his lifeless body dropped. The whole action didn't even phase her at all. She was glad that she could shut him up as quickly as she did.

"Not bad for my first kill," she said out loud, watching as he bled out onto the van.

The human part of her had gone. There was no compassion for him, nor any form of sympathetic emotions. He deserved this! This is what she had planned to do to any man that viewed a woman the way he did. He wouldn't hurt anyone else.

She was pleased with the way she had attacked him. She wanted it to be ruthless and horrid. There was no niceness in her, and she was his worst nightmare. The look on his face before she killed him, made her sadistically smile. I'll never forget this, she thought. She ripped his shirt and began using it to wipe the blood off of her hands. She was more upset about getting blood on her than killing him.

While she was cleaning herself off, the van doors swung wide open. She was in shock as she looked into Conrad's horrified eyes. Not even an entire week as a vampire and someone was onto her this soon. He stood there, gazing in terror at his brother's mangled body, and instantly looked back up at her, only to see a monstrous face. He quickly pulled his gun from his waistband… BANG!

CHAPTER THIRTY

Conrad ran from the van as fast as he could, not looking back until he turned the corner. Once he felt he was far enough from the van, he pulled out his phone and dialed 911. His hands were uncontrollably shaking, and his mind was racing.

Horrified at what he had seen, he fell to the ground and wept for his brother. Roy! He couldn't get the image out of his head. His mind was all over the place and realizing that he was still holding his gun, he dropped it on the ground. He couldn't believe he shot her.

He looked toward the corner where the van was located. Swaying his head, he couldn't bring himself to walk around the building and looked. Two dead bodies lay in that van, and he didn't want to witness the scene again.

Eagerly waiting for the police to show up, his body quivered in panic and fright. It seemed like forever. Finally, two police cars pulled up. He got to his feet and waved them down. Once they got closer, he put his hands down and rushed over to them.

"Officer, I'm the one who called." His voice trembled.

He backed up from the officer's door as the officer stepped out of his vehicle. The other officer stepped out of his car as well and came around to where they were standing.

They looked at Roy, the sweat that was dripping from his body, and his nervous reactions.

"You called in a shooting?" the first officer spoke.

"Yes, my brother… this girl… let me show you." He couldn't get his words to make sense. It was easier for him to show them, instead of trying to explain.

They stayed a couple of feet back with their hands on their guns as they followed Conrad around the corner towards the van. He stopped and pointed towards it, not wanting to go anywhere near it.

The officers moved in slowly, creeping towards the back of the van. Once they were in position, with their guns now drawn, they nodded at each other and opened it up. They stood there in confusion, looking inside the back of the van.

He eagerly waited for them to respond, knowing it was a shocking scene. He would explain what needed to be done, especially the gunshot wound to Amara's head. Biting his nails and waiting to hear what the officers were going to do, he moved in a little closer.

"Come here, son." The second officer waved him over.

As bad as he didn't want to look at the scene, he did what the officer asked him to do. He drifted toward them until he finally reached the van. The door was blocking his view, and he was grateful for that.

"Is this some kind of joke?" the first officer sternly said, pointing at the inside of the van.

"What?" Conrad responded. A joke? How can two dead bodies be a joke?

As bad as he didn't want to look, he went around from the door that was blocking his view and looked inside. What the hell? The van was normal and there were no bodies, not even a bloodstain.

"I'm telling you, I shot a woman, because she killed my brother!" He touched the inside of the van, frantically looking around. "I know what I saw, and I know what I did." He was just as confused as the officers. "They were right here!" he yelled, once again pointing at the surface.

Both officers looked at each other, and the officer closest to him could smell the whiskey coming out of his breath. He shook his head and motioned at the bar, thinking that Conrad had too much to drink and was fabricating the story.

"Okay son," the officer said while putting his arm around Conrad. "Walk with me."

They walked back to their vehicles. Conrad glanced over his shoulder to see the second officer closing the doors to the van. They don't believe me, he thought as he turned back around.

"You got to believe me!" he yelled once again.

They eventually reached the officer's vehicle, and he took his arm from around him.

"What I believe is you had way too much to drink," the officer said sadly to him. "Go in, call a cab, and go home."

"But officer…" he tried to say before being cut off by officer number two.

"Go home, so we don't have to arrest you." He wasn't as compassionate as officer number one.

He knew he was getting nowhere with the officers and, for the sake of not being arrested, agreed to their terms. He turned his back towards them and walked back into the bar.

"Wait," he heard one of them yell.

He turned around to see officer number one holding his gun. He started heading back towards them when officer number two spoke up.

"Is this yours?" he said, holding up the revolver.

"Yes."

"We're going to hold on to this. You can have it back when you sober up," officer number one replied.

"It will be down at the station," officer number two said. "We are giving you a warning this time, but next time we will have to haul you in. Go in and call a cab."

He knew his hands were tied. He'd only had one drink. He wasn't drunk, but knew that they would not believe him. He nodded his head yes, turned around, and walked back into the bar.

He waited for about thirty minutes until the officers were completely gone. The thought of what had just transpired made him want to get drunk, but he had to find out what happened to his brother and that woman.

Once the coast was clear, he walked back outside. The officers were gone, his gun was gone, and no one was in sight. Just a bunch of parked cars, including his brother's, and him. Having no protection, he crept slowly towards the corner where the van was located.

He looked around at his surroundings once more and headed towards it. Opening it back up, he couldn't believe that it was empty, nor did it have any sign of blood. This was crazy. Could he have imagined it all? Smelling his hand, the scent of gunpowder on it still lingered. He knew it. This happened, and it wasn't a figment of his imagination. He needed to find out what had happened and wouldn't stop until he did.

He knew he had shot her. He knew his brother was bleeding on the surface of the van floor, but where did they go? And who cleaned the mess up? It was too quick to have done all that before the officers had arrived and as bad as he wanted to know, he had to figure out more information. Starting with who owned the van and who that woman was.

Closing the back door to the van, he went around to the side and opened it up. Searching for any sign, he went through the glove compartment. Nothing. Then he noticed a parking sticker that was in the corner of the front window.

Printed on the sticker was the name of the apartments, along with an address that was in the city. It was a start. He had to try. Hopping out of the van and roaming the area, he looked for any signs of their bodies. Nothing. He felt defeated and confused.

Walking towards his car, he looked at his brother's as well. Roy. He would find out what happened to him. Tears filled his eyes as he quickly wiped them from his face. There was no time for this. Pulling out his keys and sitting down in the driver's seat, he pulled out his cellphone and put the address in his GPS.

He was going to find his brother.

CHAPTER THIRTY-ONE

Rushing through and slamming her front door, Amara was finally home. Damn, she should've killed him. Why didn't she kill him? After all, he shot her directly in the head. She rushed over to the kitchen sink and scrubbed the dry blood from her hands and arms.

She questioned herself and her actions. She knew Conrad had seen her. Why did she let him get away? She shook her head in disbelief and turned off the faucet. Then focused on the bullet wound and pushed the bullet out of her head. The bullet shell dropped in the sink and bounced around.

She picked it up and twisted it around with her finger. She had every right to kill Roy. He was a jerk. But right now, Roy wasn't the one that was bothering her. It was Conrad and what he possibly knew and saw.

She went to her mirror in the bathroom and glared at herself ... Dried blood was still on parts of her face. Even though she was still glamorous, she looked like a mess. Her hair had branches, small sticks, and leaves stuck in it from dragging Roy's body deep in the woods.

It's a good thing she had her vampiric speed and strength. Because that was the only way she could move the body and clean up the mess before the police had arrived.

She reminisced about how she hid out of sight, listening to their conversation, how Conrad was certain of what he saw, and how the officers presumed he was drunk.

She touched the middle of her forehead. No mark, nothing. The perks of being a vampire saved her life. She should've removed the bullet and thrown it in the woods along with Roy, but now it was just a keepsake that reminded her of her first human kill.

She thought about how she quickly busted into a side bathroom that was outside the bar, finding a bottle of bleach, other cleaning supplies, and dirty rags sitting under the sink. The whole thing could've gone wrong. It was sloppy, but in the end; She could hide the body and get the job done.

But while burying Roy's body out in the woods behind the bar, she had sensed another presence. One that was much stronger than herself. Of course, it wasn't a human presence, but assumed it was another vampire. She had frantically looked around. Someone had been there, and even with her vampiric eyes, she noticed nobody.

She had homed in on the surrounding woods. For a second, she thought she saw a silhouette of a figure moving from behind the tree. She had studied the area but saw nothing. At that moment she wondered if it had been Victoria, Lou, or maybe even *The Order*, but after a couple of minutes of stillness and no sounds of dry leaves or fallen branches cracking underneath footsteps, she had ignored the notion and continued disposing of Roy.

Reaching over to turn the knob in the shower, she noticed she didn't have one mark of the struggle on her. Everything had healed. Even when she was running in the woods, she had snagged her arm on a branch that stuck out, splitting it open.

But all her battle scars had healed, and other than the dirt and blood on her face and in her hair, she looked normal. She took off the rest of her clothes and admired her body, then climbed into the shower.

After watching Conrad leave in his car, she'd rushed back over to the van, got in it, and drove it back to the city. She knew the owners would never know what happened. She chuckled to herself.

The night had been crazy, but still satisfying with the fact that she had her first successful kill of a human. The feeling and excitement were more than enough. Knowing that she could do such a thing without a blink of an eye was rather surprising and this wouldn't be her last time. She had felt no remorse for her victim.

Daylight was around the corner. She turned off the shower and dried herself off, peeking at herself in the mirror once again. She realized that the person she was gazing at was someone different from who she once was. The old Amara was gone, and her new self was something she couldn't yet describe.

Cutting off the light and heading towards the bed, her curtains were still closed. She hadn't opened them since this journey down this dark path began and as she climbed into bed, closing her eyes, she now knew what she was capable of — grinning before dozing off like a newborn baby.

It was the next day when she woke, but night again. Her nights were now her days, losing all concept of time. Her entire existence had changed. She wasn't a human anymore, but a part of a family of the undead–immortal.

She grabbed her cell phone, and there were ten missed calls, all from Mariam. She hadn't talked to her since the night Lou had stayed over. There was so much she wanted to tell her best friend about, but part of her knew she couldn't and didn't quite understand the concept of why. She knew that *The Order* was something she should fear, but Lou had trusted her when she was human to tell him about being a vampire. Why couldn't she do the same with Mariam?

Calling her back, she picked up the phone immediately.

"Where have you been?" she yelled.

"I'm sorry… I've been a little busy."

"Yeah… with that hot guy you brought home," Mariam teased. "But that is still no reason to abandon your friend… Best friend at that—"

As Mariam rambled on, she couldn't help but think about Lou. She was already missing him. But she'd concluded that trying to look for him was impossible. Her only chance was through Victoria.

"Yeah… I was with him," she hesitantly replied. She didn't want to lie to her, but she did anyway. She couldn't tell her all that was going on. Not Yet.

"Well, I was planning on stopping by your house today," she said.

She had to think of something quick. She didn't want her coming by, not until she understood more about being a vampire and, by all means, she didn't want to hurt her. Being a *newborn*, the way she could suppress some of her urges impressed her, but she just figured she was strong like Lou. She had only had one incident and after that, she was okay. But being new to this life, she didn't know how long that would last.

"Umm… I have plans." She lied again.

"You're brushing me off for Mr. Hottie?"

"Don't look at it like that," she said. She didn't mind Mariam thinking that she was with Lou. At least she would understand why her best friend didn't want to hang out without her.

"Well, okay…" She sounded disappointed. "But tomorrow, you're all mine."

"Agreed," she responded. At least this would buy her some time, knowing that Mariam would notice all of her changes, including her facial features. She had to come up with some excuse.

They said their goodbyes, and she hung up the phone. Then she heard a knock at her door. Who was that? Having people come over was rare for her. She hoped it had nothing to do with last night. Did someone recognize her? Or maybe it was Lou?

She hurried towards the door and took a minute to make herself look presentable for him if it was Lou. There was so much she needed to tell him if he had returned. She quietly peeped out the peephole. What the hell!

Conrad shook his head. He worried about Roy and his decisions, seeing that he was going down the same path as his parents did. No, Roy didn't bother with drugs, but women were his drug, and just like their parents, it ultimately led to his death. Or did it? Conrad still wasn't sure what had happened to his brother or the woman in that van.

It was raining, and he turned on his windshield wipers. He needed to find the address that was on the sticker—quickly. If his brother wasn't dead, did someone kidnap him? Either way, Conrad felt like time was ticking.

Not having much of a plan, he just needed to find the address and he would go from there. It was the only lead he had, and it was a start.

Looking down at the GPS, he had a couple of miles left to go. Trying to block out images of his brother's cold, dead body in the van, he turned on the car radio. A sad country song about death came across the radio and he turned it off. No, I'm not listening to this! He was trying his best not to think about his brother being dead, nor the way his body looked.

Then he remembered her face. The veins stuck out, the dark, cold, piercing, black eyes, and her teeth. Sharp points like fangs. She looked nothing like she had in the bar. She looked like a demon, leaning over his brother's body, with blood dripping from her mouth. What the hell was that? he thought.

There's no way that she looked like that. Maybe the shock of seeing his brother ripped to shreds somehow messed with his vision. All he knew was that he needed to find him, both of them. Something was going on, and he was determined to understand it all.

Finally pulling up at the address, he turned off the headlights and parked on the side. It was a locked gate, needing a code to get inside. He sat there and waited. Not knowing what he was waiting for, he sat at the door and just watched the building. He needed a plan.

While sitting there, he could get the image of her out of his head. Her face, her horrible face, continued to flash in his like an old black and white movie, stuck on repeat. He would never forget it and the way she had looked at him when he opened up the van doors.

He continued to watch the building. Every time a car pulled in or someone walked into the building, he jumped up and was on alert.

His heart beat out of his chest as he made sure he looked closely at each individual. It was a long shot, but he had to see if this was where she was located.

I killed her. What am I doing here? Someone had moved their bodies, and this was the only clue he had. If he could find out more about who she was, then maybe it would lead to their bodies in time.

Then he shook his head again. Maybe it will lead me to my brother, he thought. He didn't want to think of him as a body but kept hoping he was still alive.

Closing his eyes for a brief second, he needed to breathe. So many things played in his head, emotionally and physically drained. He opened his eyes, stuck the keys in the ignition, and started the car. It was no use. He didn't even know who he was looking for.

He put the car in gear, thinking he would go back to Inferno and see if his brother's car was still there. He didn't know what else to do. Glancing over at the building one more time before pulling off, he saw a woman walking on the sidewalk.

He turned the car off and sat there for a couple seconds more. He watched as she got closer to the building. "I can't keep doing this," he spoke aloud to himself. He started the car back up once again, and looking over one last time, he saw the woman's face.

He had found her.

CHAPTER THIRTY-THREE

Amara opened up the front door with a look of annoyance on her face.

"What are you doing here?" she questioned.

Without saying a word, Victoria nonchalantly pushed past her and escorted her inside. As she glanced around, she could tell that she was pleased with her taste in decor. But that still didn't answer her question on why she was there.

"Nice place," Victoria said as she turned around to gaze at her.

She closed the door. Victoria was here for a reason. Probably something to do with Lou. At least she could hear her out. She had come to her place unannounced. But how did she even know where she lived?

"Nope… well, sort of," Victoria said as she sat down on the stool in front of the kitchen counter and then glared at a bowl of apples. "And Lou told me, duh."

"Did you just read my thoughts?"

"Yep." She grabbed a red apple from the fruit bowl, wiped it clean on her shirt, and took a bite of it.

"How?" she said curiously. She couldn't read her mind. How was she able to read hers? She stood there as still as a statue, waiting for a response.

In better lighting, she could see how beautiful Victoria was. Her eyes were of a glorious ice-blue color that seemed to sparkle with a hint of brown. Very unusual, but the blend of both colors could mesmerize anyone that looked into them.

Her brownish-blonde hair against her pale skin made her features pop out, and she was very well endowed. With a big bosom and her perfect cleavage, she caught herself from being turned on by just her presence.

Victoria grinned. She knew exactly what she was thinking and was honored that she had found her sexually attractive.

"How can you read my mind and I can't read yours?"

"It's my gift," Victoria smugly responded as she rested the half-eaten apple on the countertop. "We all have one, you just have to figure yours out. There's so much you need to learn."

"I told you, I don't need yours nor Lou's help!" They were becoming a nuisance and a thorn in her side.

"I guess you think murdering a man and getting caught is how we do things?" Victoria peered at her with a stern look. "I saw you leave with that man. I was hoping you would heal him, and he would come back, but apparently no." She shook her head.

"You saw that?" She was in shock. How did she not notice her? Had she been that careless? She didn't even know she was being followed; however, she did think it earlier. Mistake number one.

"Usually, I'm better at being aware of my surroundings, but I didn't notice Conrad until it was too late, but you can handle your own," she said while twirling her finger around and pointing it at me. "Poor guy… you killed his brother… now that's a no-go."

She rolled her eyes at Victoria. She couldn't care less about Roy. What she wanted was for her to answer her questions. She knew Victoria was intentionally avoiding them. And she was becoming even more agitated.

"Were you in the woods watching me?"

"What? No. I left after the man shot you in the head." She giggled. "Now that was funny."

With a blink of an eye, she moved from the stool next to Amara, twirling a piece of her hair around her finger. She took a long sniff alongside her face, catching the scent of the sweet-smelling conditioner she had used to wash her hair.

"What is that?" Victoria said, referring to the conditioner. "Is it apples?"

She slightly moved away from her, not knowing what to think about her. She differed completely from the woman that sat before her at Inferno. This version of her was more forward and demanding. Deep down, she liked it. But she had to be serious and figure out what she wanted.

As she walked away from her with her back turned, she quickly grabbed the same piece of hair she smelled and sniffed it herself, feeling insecure. She wasn't sure if Victoria liked the smell of her conditioner or thought it stunk.

She glanced at her once again and couldn't help but look at her breasts again. She blushed and turned away, hoping Victoria didn't catch her gazing at them.

"Lou was right, sex stays on your mind." She giggled as she watched how uncomfortable she was around her.

"No, it doesn't," she snapped. Stop reading me! she thought, trying not to think of anything at the moment.

She watched as Victoria looked down at her chest, nodding towards it and smiling. She hadn't realized that her nipples had hardened through her nightgown. Using her vampiric speed, she grabbed her robe and quickly put it around herself.

"Hey, I'm glad I turned you on." Victoria tipped her head to the side and brushed her hair off her shoulder. "I still got it."

"Stop playing around," she snapped. She didn't know how to respond. She just needed Victoria to stay on her side of the room, and nowhere near her. "Tell me what you want or leave."

She straightened her stance as if she was tough, but she was nothing compared to Victoria and was no match. She didn't want to show any sign of vulnerability, so she kept a straight face and wondered if Lou had sex with her, too. The thought of that made her doubt the night she had with him.

"He wishes," Victoria said, rolling her eyes. "Lou is too manly for me… Not my type, if you know what I mean."

Victoria winked at her from the kitchen as Amara sat down on her bed. Then she quickly got up. She didn't want Victoria to think she sat down on the bed for a reason. Definitely not for sex.

She moved towards the couch instead and had a seat cautiously as she walked over and sat beside her. Damn, she smelled good… Shit! By the grin on Victoria's face, she knew she had read her thoughts once again.

"Tell me where Lou is? Or get out."

CHAPTER THIRTY-FOUR

"He roams around...place to place...always going back home," Victoria said while grabbing the nail file that was on the table beside her.

"Where's home?" Amara said, while observing her eagerly as she filed her sharp nails. "New Orleans, of course." Victoria continued filing. "That's where our roots are."

"Our?"

"Vampires," she responded. "You need to know this."

"Why?" She watched as Victoria instantly stopped filing her nails.

"There are things you need to know, like rules, and the way of living this life," she said. "Lou didn't change you just for you to die, anyway."

"What do you mean by that?" She knew some things, but not all. She watched Victoria cross one of her legs over the other.

Her movements distracted her; she was extremely attractive. She had never felt sexually attracted to a woman before, but something about Victoria and the way she moved turned her on.

"You do," Victoria said. Giving her that same seductive grin as before.

"Do what?" She had forgotten what she had even said.

"Need to listen... There are other things you need to take seriously, other than reflecting about my body and Lou's." She giggled. "Maybe I can satisfy your sexual needs later." She winked at her.

She blushed. She needed to stop considering Victoria in that way. The offer, however, did sound nice to her ears.

"What can you tell me I can't pick up my phone and Google?" she said, arching one of her eyebrows.

"A lot!" she spoke as sternly as she could. "I was observing you without you even knowing and others will watch you too. Like *The Order*… they will come after you if you don't stop your reckless behavior."

But she didn't care what Victoria was talking about. She was still a little frustrated that it was Victoria here and not Lou. She heard what she said. But apparently, no one saw her because she had gotten away with her crime.

After all, she was a vampire and unstoppable. She could just kill them in an instant and that would be that. But then she quickly thought about Conrad. He popped into her head and how he had gotten away.

She wasn't able to stop him, but then again, he shot her in her head. She had no time to worry about killing him. He had run off to call the police. But even the police thought he was a drunken fool, so she felt she had nothing to worry about with him.

She continued to stare as Victoria stood from the couch, then began pacing the floor, back and forth. If only she could read her mind as well. She gazed into Victoria's eyes and tried to focus, but it was no use.

She couldn't read her thoughts, and all she could do was wait for Victoria to speak. For a brief second, she thought about Victoria's perfect body, but knowing that Victoria was probably reading her thoughts, she focused on what she was saying.

"I know what you're thinking?" Victoria said in a sarcastic, upbeat tone.

Oh no! Not sex again. Victoria shook her head no. Good, she thought. Because this time, she had tried to focus on the words coming out of Victoria's mouth and not on her body. Hell, she only thought about it for a brief second. After all, it was hard not to notice her. She turned her cheek up to one corner of her mouth as Victoria paced the floor and waited for her to speak.

"You can't just go around killing innocent people," Victoria said as she stopped pacing and looked at me.

"You're talking about those assholes!" she yelled back at her. She felt her anger rising again.

"Call them what you want, you can't do it."

"Who's going to stop me?" she snapped back.

"Amara, there are rules, and you have to have some compassion," she pleaded. "Some form of heart." She walked closer to her. "You've got to think about *The Order*," Victoria said.

But she didn't listen and hastily jumped up from the couch, furious. She couldn't believe that Victoria would even try to stop her from killing the men that degraded women. She was a woman herself and should understand that she was doing the world great justice by getting rid of them.

"I don't care about *The Order*, and I don't care about your opinion," she barked. "That man was awful, and he deserved what he got."

"That may be so, but you cannot go around playing vigilante," she barked back. "And *The Order* is something you should care about. You leave bodies lying around... well, that's considered a threat to exposing our existence, something they don't take lightly."

She could tell that Victoria wasn't the type to let someone talk to her any old type of way and, as far as she was concerned, she was only helping her out of respect for Lou. She watched as Victoria tried to calm her nerves by taking a deep breath and closing her eyes.

"I know you are upset about Lou. But he didn't use you as you think. And being a *newborn,* your emotions are all over the place. You will learn to control them, but don't take your anger out on everybody else. Lou is someone you have fun with but trying to be his girl… that's never going to happen," Victoria tried to explain.

"Get out!" Amara yelled, pointing towards the door. The words that came out of her mouth reminded her of when she said the same thing to Lou. But she didn't care. Victoria had to go, and she was done listening to her.

Victoria headed towards the door as requested.

"Did Lou tell you how his *creator* died?" she turned and asked.

"No, and I don't care," she argued.

Why should she care about what happened to Lou's *creator?* He didn't even bother showing up to tell her himself. She was over the fact that Victoria was a messenger between the two. If he was so worried about her and what she was doing, wouldn't he be here?

She was done with the entire conversation and upset at the fact that she was arguing with someone she didn't even know, only meeting her at a random bar once with a brief conversation. She felt like Victoria was trying to tell her what to do—how to be a vampire when she was doing just fine.

She didn't care about rules, or what anyone thought about her. Killing these men made her happy, and she wasn't about to stop. She walked toward Victoria, opened up the door, and pushed her into the hall.

"They will come for you," Victoria said.

CHAPTER THIRTY-FIVE

Who the hell did she think she was? She looked out the peephole, making sure Victoria was gone. The frustration of her showing up angered her all over. Why the hell won't they just leave her alone? She was going to feed on the undeserving, and that was what she had precisely planned to do.

Shaking her head, she was feeling famished. It was time for her to feed once again, knowing the only thing that would quench her thirst–blood. Knowing that she needed to go out to hunt, she quickly got dressed and roamed the alleys.

While looking for her next meal, she couldn't help but think about what Victoria said. Who would come for her? Who are they? And who was *The Order*? After all, nobody had gone into details about them. But to be fair, she had kicked both of them out. Her emotions had been all over the place since she had changed. With *The Order*, she knew she was only supposed to fear them. At first, she didn't worry about it, but after a couple of seconds, it sunk in. She had only killed one man. It's not as if she had slaughtered an entire village.

Vampires feed on humans, so she didn't feel as if she'd done wrong. Part of her wished that she had never met Lou, Victoria, or Roy. After being lost in her thoughts, she noticed a man sitting alone at a secluded bus stop. She moved in closer and sat down beside him. He glanced at her, giving her a small smile. She smiled back at him and watched as he turned his head in the opposite direction, looking to see if the bus was coming. No bus was in sight, and then he looked down at his cell phone.

Of course, she saw an opportunity when he looked down. She had said that she would only feed on the undeserving, but her thirst outweighed her judgment and she grabbed him by the neck, pulling him closer to her. She felt a sense of shock come across him by her actions. He tried to fight her off, but her strength overpowered him. Her canines emerged and before she bit down, she glanced up to see a figure in the distance.

It was a woman standing there by a light post, just watching. She could see her face, but then the woman backed away, fading into the darkness of the night. The woman was another vampire, but why was she watching her? Maybe just out of curiosity because after the woman disappeared in a flash, everything was back to normal. She focused back on the man and quickly sank her fangs into his neck.

He tried to call out for help, but it was no use. No one was in sight, and no one could hear him. The more she drank from him, he had lost energy in screaming, and before long, he collapsed.

But she did not stop and continued to drain him until his death. After she finished, she dropped her head back once again, relishing in the delight of the feed as it replenished her.

She licked her blood-stained lips and looked over at the man that now lay lifeless beside her. Still, she had no remorse and cared less about taking a human life. Another favorable moment to add to her list of favorable acts.

But little did she know someone was watching and had seen the complete act take place. Victoria tried to warn her about *The Order*, but besides them, another person was lurking and silently watching. Conrad…

She murdered three other men after she killed the one at the bus stop, bringing her total for the night to four. No vampire needed to feed that much within a couple of hours. What she was doing was for pure fun.

One man tried to assault her in the bathroom of a club, but she swiftly pulled him in, locking the door, and ripping his heart out, leaving him on the toilet in the stall and closing it. She escaped through a window, taking his heart with her.

Later on, she passed a small lake and discarded it, only to find another suitor approaching. She could smell the alcohol on his breath. Reading his mind, he had just come back from sleeping with his mistress, leaving his wife and children at home to fend for themselves.

Of course, this infuriated her, and once again, she went on a rampage. This one she'd tortured for a little when he pleaded with her to stop because of his family. She broke all his fingers, gouged one of his eyes out, and taunted him before she ended his unbearable pain.

Each man had a different way of dying. The more she murdered, the more creative she tried to become. Some she drank from and others she just didn't like. Destroying these men was more to her than just feeding but getting vengeance for every woman they had hurt.

Picking up their bodies once she had killed them and trying to find a place to put it was the hardest part. There had to be an easier way, she thought. The only body she didn't hide was the man that tried to assault her. She left him in that stall on purpose, to be exposed for the world to see.

For the first time, she could do what she wanted and to whom she wanted to do it too. Nothing could stop her. She knew that there was so much to learn, but she had an eternity to figure it out. For now, she was just going to have a little fun.

After her massacre of men, which she deemed unworthy, she returned to her apartment and cleaned up. She opened the door and was shocked to see Victoria spread out on her couch.

"How did you get in here?" she retorted.

"You don't lock your door," she replied, shrugging her shoulders.

"Well, you might as well leave the way you came."

She heard a noise coming from her bathroom. Someone else was there. Victoria sat up on the couch, and she moved toward the bathroom to see where the noise came from. Looking in, she couldn't believe her eyes… Lou!

"Hello, beautiful," he politely said. He gave her a warm smile, watching the gaze on her face.

"It's you?" She jumped to give him a long hug, and he returned the favor.

After embracing each other for a couple of minutes, Lou pulled her from him. She soon found out that him being there wasn't for a reunion but more like an intervention on how she had been carrying herself as a new vampire.

"I'm not here for long," he said. "I'm here to get you to listen."

Her smile turned into a frown. She looked back at Victoria and then at Lou again. Is this a joke? Here, both of them were trying to tell her what to do again, as if she was weak. She had proven to be tough for a *newbie*.

"Look, I'm okay," she said. "You left me, and I figured out how to live this life on my own." She turned her back to him and walked away.

"I didn't leave you. Why do you think Victoria is here? And being tough doesn't mean you're rational."

"Now you're reading my thoughts as well. I just can't get a break, huh?"

"Since you all won't leave…" she interrupted him. "I will."

She stomped to her front door, and right before she opened it, Lou spoke.

"Stop and have a seat," he demanded.

Still trying to leave, she realized she couldn't. As much as she wanted to fight it, she turned and headed towards Victoria, doing what he had told her to do. Feeling trapped in a body that she could not control, she walked over to the couch and sat down. What just happened?

"I don't want to control you; But I'm your sire and any demand or action I tell you to do, you will do it."

Victoria giggled as she looked at the anger coming across her face. She stopped when Lou stared back at her. She cleared her throat, picked up a magazine, and pretended to read it.

"This is one reason I said I couldn't be with you," he explained. "You would never have free will around me. I would always have control over you, and that's not what I want."

She was understanding what he meant by that. After all, he demanded that she sit, and she did. She held her head down in shame. She knew he had a reason for leaving her, but she never gave him the chance to explain himself. Now she had no choice but to listen to what he had to say; it wasn't like she could get up freely and leave. She was a puppet, and

Lou controlled the strings. She watched him as he came over to have a seat opposite them. He gazed into her eyes.

"Let me tell you about the man that created me."

CHAPTER THIRTY-SIX

His name was Victor, and he was a powerful Omega. The part he had left out was that Victor had returned in the dead of night to get Lou to feed on his wrist, completely transforming him.

He explained to him that being a *sire* meant he would have control over him. Victor wanted Lou to run free for a while, but he told him that one day he would return.

Running into him years later, Victor had been watching over Lou ever since the night he'd attacked him in the alley. He had never truly left him. He let him live his life with Katherine freely, without being under his control.

Once she died, he consoled him, and they became close. And his *sire* taught him the authentic ways of vampiric life. Victor told Lou what and how they should live, even explaining *The Order*. But with that being said, Victor didn't follow the complete ways of the vampiric life and was the type to defy the rules.

Victor loved to kill. It didn't matter who they were. Young, old, rich, poor, it didn't matter. Anyone in his path. It was like a sport; it was entertaining for him and nothing more. Others warned him. Vampires didn't like this behavior. They needed to live discreetly for their survival.

Once they were part of the world of the undead, they had become enemies to the living. They were the monsters that went bump in the night, and once someone jeopardized their entire existence, they became the target. Vampires or not, they would destroy anything that could expose them.

Still, his *sire* did whatever he wanted. The other vampires trapped him and took him to a cell underneath an old cemetery to torture him. After decapitating him, they lit a torch and burned his body.

In doing so, the memories of him disappeared from their minds and they vowed not to touch a vampire stronger than him or ones that an *Omega* had transformed personally — naming them, The *Untouchables.* They gave them a rare tanzanite stone ring for all vampires to identify them. Under no circumstances were they to be killed for breaking any vampiric rules—in fear the history of their race would cease to exist.

These same vampires formed a small council, spreading from city to city, monitoring as many vampires as they could. They called themselves, *The Order.* Nobody knew how they chose their members or who they were, but they were always there.

—⟋⟍—

Lou didn't want this to be Amara's end. He saw so much potential in her and was only trying to help her live a better life as a vampire. And trying to keep *The Order* from figuring her out.

"Even a vampire with a thousand times normal strength can't fight off an army," he said. "You're going through what we know as a *blood-thirst* stage, unstoppable and uncontrollable hunger.… Don't worry, most *newborns* go through it. It's very hard to resist blood smells or even the sight of blood. It will pass, but I need you to fight your feelings of rage."

"But I could resist it. The first night just like you. I didn't attack a human, but fed on rodents just like you did."

Victoria cleared her throat loudly. Part of that statement was true. Amara fed on rodents, but she almost fed on a human as well. Knowing if it hadn't been for her, the human woman would've been a snack immediately after Amara's change. But the fact that her urges were far more suppressed than normal *newborns* was quite astounding. Considering most *newbies* right off the bat would've ripped the heads off of every human they had smelled.

"Okay, maybe I did have one slight slip up… but regardless, I still didn't feed. And at the bar, I could control my urges," Amara said, eyeing Victoria. "I was around many people then."

Lou paused for a second. It was impressive to know that she didn't just attack the first human she saw. But he frowned at the notion that she was just killing to be killing. He didn't bring that part up in fear she would shut down and kick them out again. "We need to figure out your gift. I'm curious to know what it is. Normal *newborns* wouldn't be so composed with their thirst."

"We haven't figured that out yet," Victoria jumped in. "But we will."

"Good," he said, addressing her. "But for now, I want you to stick around. Can you promise me you will work with Victoria and not be so reckless? I do care for you."

She held her head down in shame. By Lou telling his story, she wondered about the vampire woman watching her. Both Victoria and he mentioned *The Order*, but hearing what happened to Lou's creator made her realize how serious this could be for her. *The Order* wasn't just a myth, and these vampires existed; it was like law and order for vampires. The last thing she wanted to do was die such a horrible death.

"Even if I have people I would love to kill," Victoria jumped in, "I can't!"

"Amara, you can't live with this hate in your heart," Lou interjected. "But that's a journey you will have to take on your own… we are here to guide you, but you have to have willpower."

"And you need to learn how to kill and heal," Victoria said.

"Kill and heal?" she questioned. There was so much she was realizing, and she needed guidance. She felt embarrassed about her actions, but in some sense still felt justified. But she assured them she would stop.

"Victoria will teach you everything you need to know," Lou said. "I'll be returning to my home. Maybe one day you can join me," he said, smiling and releasing her from his command. He, without warning, used vampiric speed to open the front door.

"Until then," he said and left the apartment.

"Well, it's just me and you now," Victoria said.

"I guess so."

"I'm impressed," Victoria said with a look of amusement.

"For what?"

"That Lou could convince you so easily." She giggled. "Lou and his charm."

"More like, I don't want to be decapitated." She lightly shrugged.

She was sad that Lou had left again, but she understood his reasoning. The hurt that she felt from him was gone and instead, she was glad that he was still looking out for her, even if he wasn't physically around. He cared, and that's all that mattered to her. Smiling to herself, she looked over at Victoria.

"I'm glad you understand now," Victoria said as she read Amara's thoughts. "Lou is not a love interest. He is a loner and always has been ever since Katherine. But he is a good guy. And he doesn't want to see harm come to you and neither do I."

Instantly Victoria wrapped her arms around her, giving her a giant hug, knowing that she had gotten her closer to him. She didn't think she would get through to her, but she knew Lou would. Thanks, Lou, Victoria thought.

"Do you have faith in anything?" Victoria said as she released her from the hug.

"I once believed in a higher power, but that did nothing for me," she sadly said.

"Just because we are undead doesn't mean you can't have a fulfilling life. You're going to have to find something to believe in."

"Why?" she replied.

"Because even though we may have a lifetime, having faith in something can give us a purpose." Victoria gently grabbed her chin and turned her face towards her. "Maybe love?" She smiled.

She knew that was all she'd ever wanted, and she tried reminding her of that. Victoria got up and headed towards the door. "Well, training day is tomorrow."

"Tomorrow?"

"Yep, tomorrow." Victoria grinned.

Nodding her head, she rose on the couch to escort Victoria to the door. She was shocked at how easy it was for her to get up. When Lou had commanded her to sit, she couldn't move at all, feeling like a ton of bricks was holding her in place.

"Until the next time," Victoria said, turning towards her. She grabbed her by the back of the neck, jerking her head down, and planted a long hard kiss on her lips, smiling as she took off into the night.

"Wow! What had she gotten herself into?"

CHAPTER THIRTY-SEVEN

Conrad had sat outside the entire night, waiting for her to come back out, but it was pointless. When he saw her walk into the building, he couldn't believe his eyes, knowing that he had shot her. She should be dead. But that was her, clear as day, walking as if nothing had happened. If she was alive, maybe his brother was too.

After he saw her, he waited, but daylight had come, and for hours now, there was no sight of her. He had assumed she had gone in for the night and more than likely went to sleep. So, he left and came back at night, to continue to watch and wait on her.

Hopefully, she would lead him to his brother. Pulling off and thinking about Roy, he had headed back to Inferno to check on his brother's car. The sun had completely risen by now and deep down, he was exhausted. But when he had seen Amara, whom he still knew as Anna, it had given him an adrenaline rush.

After the long drive, finally, he was back at Inferno and it was quite different in the daylight than it was at night. It looked like an abandoned building that was about to collapse. He hadn't noticed that before, but then again it had been night.

The bar was closed, and there was no sign of life. There was nothing but pure silence and isolation, making it seem like he was in an old horror movie.

When it was open, the neon sign was flashing, and there were people all around, making the place more inviting. If he had noticed how the place looked, he probably would've never stepped inside. Then he realized that only one car sat in the dirt parking lot. It was the gray Chevy that his brother loved so much.

Conrad didn't stop and get out, instead driving around to the side of the building, noticing that the van had gone. Just like his brother, it had vanished. He didn't bother to investigate any further. He didn't want to touch or look inside his brother's car. His exhaustion had completely set in, and sleep was evading him.

Besides, he knew she had something to do with his brother's disappearance or death. So, he headed home. He needed a fresh mind to approach the situation again. When he got to the house, even though thoughts of his brother stayed on his mind, he had gotten a couple of hours of rest. As soon as nightfall hit, he headed back out to start his investigation again.

Finding himself back in front of her apartment building, he pulled up alongside the same curb, then parked the car, turned off his headlights, and waited. She had to come back out. He was going to be right there when she did.

After a couple of hours, he finally saw her. It was her; he would never forget her face. She walked a couple of blocks and turned towards a dark corner. Slowly following behind her, he parked on the side. Getting out, he trailed her on foot. He peered around the corner where she had turned.

The area was dimly lit, and the only thing down this street was a bus stop. Conrad watched her as she sat down alongside the man that had already been there. The distance was some feet away from him, but he still could see the silhouette of them.

Looking like she was leaning over to kiss him, he couldn't quite tell from where he was standing. HELP! the man screamed. He tried to rush over to help him, but he was too far away. He stopped in the street when he saw she had bitten him, backing up and ducking in between two buildings. She hadn't seen him.

Trying to stay hidden and look, he watched as the man dropped from the bench onto the ground. She had appeared to be licking her lips, but he couldn't quite tell. His heart was beating out of his chest. What the hell? He took another look. She and the man had both gone.

None of this could be real! He kept repeating it over and over in his head. Once he felt the coast was clear, he walked over to the bench where the man was, and all he saw was a pool of blood. It was real! Looking around in fright, he rushed back to the car as quickly as he could.

Jumping in, his heart was still pounding, and he was out of breath. During his nervousness, he dropped his keys as he tried to put the keys in the ignition. Damn it. Feeling for them under his seat, he finally picked them up, started his car, and took off, squealing his tires.

He was going to stop her. She had killed his brother and now this innocent man. What type of woman had that type of strength and that speed? Something was off about her. What she was doing was inhumane, unnatural, and monstrous.

After pulling up to his house, he went inside to clear his head. He needed to think, to process what he had just witnessed. Knowing that the police were useless, he had to figure this out on his own.

He pulled out a cigarette, lit it, and continued to pace the floor. Her eyes, her face, her teeth, and her biting that man—none of it made sense. She was a monster. She was acting like a vampire. A vampire? Were they real? What he saw was real! And he reminded himself, by remembering.

There was no other explanation for the events that had taken place. Conrad didn't believe in monsters, but this one was authentic. Even if the woman was one, he would kill her and avenge his brother.

CHAPTER THIRTY-EIGHT

Mariam wished it was easier to support her friend, but Amara had been distant for the past couple of days. As she sat across the dining table from Noah, she saw the look of concern on his face as well. They had met up at an outside restaurant named Rino's. This was a place that she and Amara loved to go to when the weather was nice.

Mariam played with her food, trying to replay the events that happened when she and Amara had gone to Inferno. And when her friend had met the mysterious man named Lou.

She still wasn't sure how she got home and why she would leave Amara to fend for herself with a strange man that neither one of them knew. That wasn't like her at all. Her memories of the night were still foggy, and she felt like she was under someone else's control.

All she could remember was that her friend would be safe as the blonde server from the bar escorted her home. Another person she felt she shouldn't be so eager to leave with. The reasoning behind her actions that night still baffled her.

Noah looked at Mariam with concern and deep down, he was worried about Amara as well. But not for the same reasons as Mariam. He was worried that he was going to lose her because of some random playboy and that he would never have a chance with the girl of his dreams.

"I'm sure she's fine," he said. "It's only been a couple of days and you have talked to her on the phone. A lot more than I can say for myself."

"Yeah, but something feels off." Mariam shook her head as she replied. "She's being awfully secretive and brushing me off. Like she's hiding something."

"Or maybe she's just really into this new guy?" Noah's voice sounded hurt by his statement.

"Oh, Noah." Mariam looked up at him. "I still have faith in the two of you."

"I've been in love with her ever since she stopped my father from beating me to death." He sighed. "I've never had someone defend me like that. The way she pushed him and started hitting him back... not even my mother had come to my defense. And just that alone... I would give her the world. I just don't understand why she can't see that."

"She's always been good at defending the ones she cares for," Mariam said. "And I know she has feelings for you, too. After all, you two did share that kiss."

"Yeah, I thought the same thing before she left me hanging over another man's phone call. A guy that ended up cheating on her and disrespecting her. I will never understand women."

Mariam watched as he took a bite of his broccoli and shook his head at that notion. "Amara doesn't have the best track record with men. You know this. But I can tell you that with you, you're different from her and I think that she's scared."

"Scared of what?" he questioned. "I would never hurt her."

"Scared that if you two don't work out, she'll lose you as a friend as well."

"She mentioned that, but that would never happen," he said and then took a sip of his water. "But she's not even giving us a chance."

"Sometimes when the same type of men has hurt a female so much, they get stuck in a cycle that they can't get out of. Repeating themselves with the same type of dogs over and over. She can't seem to get out of her way. Deep down, she knows you're a good guy, but part of her is scared, as I said. Scared of change or love. She's not used to it, but give her time. She'll come around. I'm sure of it."

"If you say so," he said. "Women are so confusing."

Mariam giggled. She looked up and saw a blonde-haired woman getting up from another table. She couldn't see her face because the woman's back was turned to her. But by her stance and physique, she felt like she knew the woman. Mariam stood up.

"Where are you going?" Noah asked.

"I think I know that woman." She paused. "I think she may be the woman at Inferno that night."

"What woman?" he questioned.

"The one that escorted me home… I'll be back," she said as she walked off from the table and towards the woman.

When she got closer to her, she elevated her voice. "Hey!" she said, but the woman paid her no mind, nor did she turn around. The woman rushed from her table and hit a corner, blocking Mariam's view of her. As Mariam quickly rushed around the corner, the woman had vanished.

Mariam stood there for a moment contemplating where the woman might have gone so fast and if that was even the woman who she'd thought it was. She sighed, gave up, and headed back over to Noah.

"Was it her?" Noah questioned.

"I guess not," she said slowly, taking a seat. "I was hoping it was. Maybe she could tell me what's going on with our friend. And what exactly happened that night?"

"I'm going to do something special for her," Noah said.

"What?" Mariam questioned as he broke her train of thought on the mysterious blonde.

"For Amara. I want to do something special."

Mariam sighed. "I think that's a good idea."

CHAPTER THIRTY-NINE

Another night had come and gone. Mariam had called her. But she had brushed her off once again. It had been four days since she had been born into this life of darkness. It was time for Victoria to arrive and show her the ways of her alternative lifestyle. Not knowing what to expect, she threw on some workout clothes and tennis shoes, waiting until Victoria finally showed up.

"Sorry I was late… Had to keep my eyes on someone. Anyway, I have someplace I want to take you." She smiled. Her demeanor was bubbly.

Knowing Victoria, no telling what she was up to and where they were about to go. She still followed Victoria out of the building to her car. When she saw Victoria's car, her mouth dropped. She was shocked and not shocked at the same time. The red convertible fit Victoria and her personality.

Jumping into her small red convertible, she was excited about riding in a car this nice. She had never been in a car like this, and it tickled her pink that she was in it. She put on her seatbelt and watched as Victoria started the car and smiled. Then they headed out of town.

Victoria hadn't said a word about where they were going. Listening to a rock band as the wind blew through their hair, she thought about her life. The things that had changed since she had become a vampire.

That she was feeding on humans now registered in her head. If someone had told her she would do such things a year ago, she would have laughed in their faces. But this was now a reality. She was immortal. She grinned. This was something that people didn't even believe existed, but now was her world.

And here she was, riding in a convertible with another vampire. The whole thought of it was funny. Her life had truly changed. Looking over at Victoria, she couldn't help but wonder how she'd felt when she was changed. She watched as Victoria smiled but was still focused on the road. She figured she had been reading her thoughts, but at this moment, she didn't mind. The breeze flowed through her hair as she enjoyed the ride.

Getting away from her apartment was nice. She glanced over at Victoria again, watching as she had one hand on the driver's wheel and felt the wind with the other. The silhouette of the moonlight across her face made her even more gorgeous. She was stunning. Flawless.

She wondered what Victoria had looked like before her change. Probably already gorgeous. Being a vampire brings features out and makes someone look even better than before, but Victoria was an exception because she seemed to be above the norm.

She envisioned Victoria sitting at a table with plenty of male suitors gawking over her as she sipped on her wine and giggled. It broke her vision when Victoria instantly swerved the car.

"What the hell, are you trying to kill us?" Amara shouted.

"No!" Victoria glanced over at her with a look of curiosity. "What the hell was that?"

"What was what?" She looked around, not focusing on Victoria anymore, but on whatever she was dodging with the car. "I see nothing."

"Oh, I just did," Victoria stated. "Me!"

"What do you mean, you?"

"I just saw myself sitting at a table with a bunch of men around me sipping wine. It flashed right before my eyes… as if I was there."

"Wait, I just visualized that about you."

Victoria went silent. She glanced over at her and didn't say a word. The silence was deafening. But Victoria didn't speak.

"What?" she said, forcing her to say something. Anything about what just happened.

"I think I just figured out your gift."

"Well… what is it?" she eagerly questioned.

Victoria didn't respond and while she waited for an answer, she realized she didn't recognize her surroundings anymore. She thought she knew her city, but never had she been this far out. Going down a winding dirt road, she watched as they passed horses and then cows. It was peaceful; she wondered why she hadn't moved to the outskirts of the city.

"We're almost there," Victoria said.

She could tell Victoria took pleasure in reading her thoughts or now seeing them.

Victoria had forgotten how it felt to be a *newborn* vampire, looking at the world for the first time with a unique set of eyes. Sometimes she caught herself wanting to smile, especially when she was praising her for her looks.

When she finally turned off onto a side road. Amara looked and saw a large building that almost looked like a factory. The outside of the building looked abandoned, with several broken windows.

"We're here," Victoria said as she parked the car.

"Here?" she questioned.

"Yep, this is home," Victoria said as she jumped from the car seat to the ground.

She opened her door and stepped out. Looking around, there was nothing but darkness for miles. And a building that seemed to be out of place for its location. It was a great place if you wanted to be away from everyone.

"Follow me," Victoria said joyfully.

Victoria bounced around in excitement for a brief second and then continued to walk forward. Amara figured she got little company by the way she was acting and how she was excited someone was here with her.

She followed Victoria to a door on the side of the building and watched as she opened it, then hit a switch on the sidewall. The long industrial lights came on one by one, and she was amazed at what she saw.

It was marvelous. Victoria had taken the old warehouse building and turned it into a fantastic living space with fencing swords and ancient artifacts. She couldn't believe her eyes. Victoria's place made her place look loathsome.

"This is where you live?" she said, astonished by the beautiful paintings lined across the walls.

"Yep, I designed it myself," Victoria said proudly.

She walked around, looking at the antique mask that Victoria had hanging up and the elegant oriental rugs that were below her feet. Remarkable. For a brief second, she felt as if she was in a historical museum, with stands that held historical items on display—each surrounded by protective glass.

"Over here," Victoria yelled at her; the place was enormous.

She walked over to her, where she stood at another metal door and waited eagerly as Victoria opened it and turned on another light. Looking inside, once again, the beauty of it all threw her back.

The room had mirrors that covered most of the wall and the middle of the floor was a wide-open space, almost like a dance studio without bars. The room was gigantic, with all different medieval weapons lining the walls.

"This is my training room," Victoria said.

"Training?" she replied. "What could you be training for with these types of weapons?"

"You have to be prepared for anything." She smiled.

"I see."

Victoria went over to the corner of the room. She opened up a chest and grabbed something out of it. She watched as Victoria turned towards her, holding a small knightly dagger. Confused, she watched as Victoria held it in her hands for a second, then quickly launched it towards her as the blade spiraled towards her head...

CHAPTER-FORTY

It was inches away from her face as she grabbed the dagger between both hands before she realized. She felt her cheeks flush as the anger came across her. She couldn't believe Victoria had just done that.

"What the hell!" she angrily yelled. "Are you trying to kill me?"

"A bullet didn't. Why would that?" She laughed.

She dropped the knife and scoffed at Victoria's sense of humor. She beamed at her. This was pissing her off already.

"Chill out, don't get your panties in a bunch," Victoria said, reading her thoughts. "I had to see how quick you were."

Newer vampires moved at a slower pace than older ones. But from how quickly she stopped the dagger, Victoria knew that her speed was better than most *newbies.* The quickness she possessed had impressed her. Turning the sides of her lips up, she formed a smile.

"I hope that thrilled you," she said, rolling her eyes.

"You're quick, but not quick enough to stop a bullet." Victoria giggled. "But now I know exactly what your gift is… Oh, Lou is going to be pleased to hear this."

She snarled at Victoria. Now she was just picking with her. Feeling like she was making fun of her because of what happened, she walked away. She wasn't about to stand by while Victoria cracked jokes.

"I'm not joking; I'm serious." Her voice was solemn. "Your speed for a *newborn* is unusual, your being able to control urges, and what I saw in the car… it's all making sense."

What she said made her stop and turn around. What was making sense and what was her gift? Of course, the thought of that piqued her interest. She wanted to know more and if she really could stop a bullet, how?

"Yes, you can stop a bullet, but with training," she said, capturing her attention even more. "You have the gift of perception."

"What is that?"

"You can project visions in others' minds. With and without touching them. Just as long as you're close enough. You can manipulate what others see and can even blind them temporarily. Both humans and vampires. Also, you are faster than normal vampires and your strength is slightly above average… quicker than a *newbie*."

"Really?" She was shocked she had that ability.

"Yeah… really… And it's rare," Victoria responded, and, with no effort, Victoria jumped from one side of the room to the other. The height of the jump was incredible. She landed with elegance on the ground with one knee bent and her hands touching the floor.

Then she darted back and forth across the room like a beam of light. Even for her vampire's eyes, Victoria's speed was so fast that it was hard for her to catch. It was almost like she was teleporting, then she stopped beside her.

This amazed her. Amara didn't know a vampire could move so fast, and she wanted to do the same. She wondered if she could move that fast and if she couldn't, how could she get to that point? She paid close attention to Victoria.

"See," Victoria said, giving her a quick kiss on the cheek before darting back across the room. "You are this fast, if not faster."

"Teach me," she eagerly said.

"In due time… little ladybug," she replied. "With age, you will become faster."

"How old are you?" she questioned.

"Just a couple hundred years old," Victoria confidently responded, as if her age was a badge of honor.

She raised her eyebrows in surprise. Wow! Looking at her, she didn't look a day over twenty-five. She was curious if that was the age when Victoria was changed. She also wondered how many things Victoria had experienced throughout her lifetime. It was crazy to think someone had lived that long. But then again, they were vampires, and time was not an issue.

"What's your gift?"

"Now that… a lady never tells." She waved her finger at her.

Victoria grabbed a sword out of the scabbard that hung on the wall. She tossed it to her and pulled out one for herself. The weight from the blade should have been heavy, but to Amara, it was light. She began swinging it around like an animated cartoon, then giggled out loud. For once, she was having fun and was eager to learn something new. But Victoria interrupted her playfulness.

"Attack me." Victoria motioned one of her hands at her.

"What?" she replied.

"Attack me!"

Looking at the seriousness on Victoria's face, she knew she wasn't playing. After all, this was training. She took a deep breath, and at vampiric speed, she rushed towards her.

She wasn't sure how to use a sword and mimicked what she had seen in an old movie.

She lunged forward, trying to stab Victoria with the sword, but each time she tried striking her, she missed. Victoria seemed to bounce around her at her vampiric speed, dodging each one of her attacks. She was too fast for her, and she couldn't keep up. Finally, she just stopped and gave up.

"Come on, stab me!" she encouraged her. She made a swift move and, with the sword, sliced open her arm.

She screamed out in pain, dropping the sword and grabbing her arm, and looked at Victoria waving her hand as if she was saying come on—-this pissed her off even more. She picked up the sword and raised herself back up, glaring at Victoria, the smirk on her face enraging her.

But Victoria continued to smile and taunt her, as she knew her actions would make her even madder. She wanted her to attack her and not go easy on her. She watched her actions.

A look of surprise came to her face as Amara rushed towards her with force and slid through her legs. She came up from underneath her and sliced open her leg. Damn. Victoria screamed out in agony. She backed up, looked at her leg, and smiled.

"Nice job." Victoria looked up at her as she held her leg.

After a couple of minutes of them going back and forth attacking each other, their blood painted the surface of the floor. Victoria figured it was enough for the day and she agreed. They both dropped their swords.

She looked horrified around the room at the blood. She didn't understand why it shocked her so much, being a vampire and all. But maybe it was because the blood was hers and Victoria's this time.

"Who's going to clean up this mess?" she questioned.

"Don't worry about it," Victoria replied. "I'll compel someone to clean it."

"Compel?"

Victoria didn't answer her. She figured she would explain that in due time. She realized that both Victoria and Lou had a method of their madness in explaining things to her.

"I want you to try one more thing." Victoria said, gazing at her. "Blind me."

"What?"

"Blind me… just focus on taking my vision."

She locked eyes with her and focused. But nothing happened as Victoria stood there with a questioning look.

"Maybe you're not focusing hard enough, but with your gift, you should be able to do it," Victoria disappointingly said.

"Sorry," Amara replied.

"Don't worry, you will be able to do it soon enough."

Regardless of what she still didn't know, she had picked up some moves from Victoria and found out about her gift—that was a start. She already felt a little stronger than she once was and was grateful for that. She could see that Victoria was pleased with her fighting skills and that made her even more confident about herself.

Looking around again at the blood that draped the floor, her face went paler than usual. She couldn't even imagine what their bodies looked like with the damage that was done to them by swinging around the swords.

Had they been human, they would have been mangled and dead.

CHAPTER FORTY-ONE

"Don't worry about it. You're already healed," Victoria said, pointing at her arms and legs. She was reading her thoughts and knew what she was already thinking.

She anxiously looked over her body. She was right. There wasn't a mark anywhere on her. If it weren't for her bloodstained clothes, nothing would show there was even a fight. Humph. She knew vampires healed themselves, but that was quick.

"The only thing you can't heal is decapitation." Victoria laughed, but she was serious at the same time. "Come on, let's have a drink."

"Decapitation…" she said as her body shivered. Just thinking about that made her cringe.

She watched as Victoria grabbed both swords, took out a cloth to wipe them down, and put them back in the scabbards. It fascinated her that even with the blood that draped across Victoria's face, she was reserved and still as radiant as ever.

They walked back into the next room, and Victoria went around to the bar area. The stools in in front of the bar were elegantly made, and they added style to the room. Victoria motioned for her to sit down on one of them in front of her. She watched Victoria wipe her face off and then pour two shots of whiskey.

Victoria then handed her a wet towel to wipe off her face as well. She couldn't help but look at Victoria's bosom. It had ripped in the front while they were training. Her cleavage stood out in her black lacy bra, making it hard for her to turn away. Everything about her screamed sexy. She drank her shot, trying not to get aroused, and set it down on the bar top.

Victoria smiled and topped off her drink as well. She slammed her shot glass down and began pouring them another one.

"Don't worry," she said. "I may let you touch."

Blushing, she remembered how Victoria could read her thoughts–something she kept forgetting and sensed how her body was feeling towards her. Deep down, she imagined touching Victoria's breasts, but did Victoria have to catch every thought she was thinking? She rolled her eyes at her.

"Can you stop doing that?" she snapped at her.

"Doing what?" Victoria smiled at her, knowing exactly what she was talking about.

"Reading my thoughts," she said. Even though it annoyed her, she wanted to know how Victoria could read her thoughts, but she couldn't read hers.

"We all have a gift, an ability that differs from one another," Victoria said as she took her shot of whiskey.

"What is your story? What about your *maker*?"

"That's a story for another day," she said, "A tragic story… For now, let's just drink."

She didn't push it. Victoria would tell her in her own time, so she switched topics. "Why do vampires drink so much?"

"It helps us suppress urges, kinda like taking an anxiety pill," Victoria responded. "And because it's fun."

As they drank shot after shot, she realized it took a lot of liquor for a vampire to get drunk. But, after finishing the whiskey bottle, she felt buzzed. That didn't stop Victoria from pulling out another one.

She told her about the vampire rules. She started with basic instructions. Such as, don't go out in direct sunlight, only being out at dusk till dawn, sleeping during the day, and only feeding when needed.

Then Victoria explained that hunting humans wasn't always necessary. She told her about *feeders*. People who offered their blood to vampires hoping one day they, in exchange, would be changed into one as well.

It shocked her to learn that *feeders* would give up their blood to them. She told her she would introduce her to a couple, to prevent her from feeding on random people.

"You know you really need to stop hiding bodies," Victoria expressed. "All you have to do is bite yourself and apply your blood on a bite wound. That will heal a human."

"Ahhh," Amara mumbled. She felt stupid. She didn't have to kill anyone if she didn't want to. But then again, those men that she did—she wanted them to suffer.

"Also, you need to see if you can compel them first, before doing this. Compelling a human is hypnotizing them. Something that I like to do, but Lou hates it." She giggled. "All you have to do is look them in their eyes and tell them what to do."

"Really?" Amara questioned.

"Yes, really," Victoria replied. "Like any other vampire, you need to make sure that you can compel the person first, then you can feed on them. You should be able to sense if they are susceptible to compulsion. If they aren't, you need to find another victim. And to remember that you can't compel all humans. By doing this, after you feed on them, you can make them forget about what happened and not expose them to what you were doing and what you are. A vampire. Remember that our entire existence depends on it."

"Interesting. I'm liking being a vampire." Amara laughed. "These rules aren't so bad."

"Well, there are stricter rules." Victoria's face changed into a serious look. "Such as not killing your own kind, meaning vampires, and never going without feeding. Without proper nourishment, it can cause you to become weak and more susceptible to being attacked by both humans and vampires. It can also cause you to attack someone you didn't want to because your urge will be uncontrollable. Remember that."

"Got it. Don't kill vampires and feed."

"And never underestimate your opponent. Just because they are humans does not mean that they cannot kill us. There have been stories upon stories of humans killing our kind. Never underestimate the power of someone else… And one more thing. And you might not like this one, but it is what it is," Victoria said.

"What is it?" Amara put her hand on her hip.

"Obey your sire… In your case, Lou. Even if he doesn't demand you to do something. It's a respect thing. If he commanded you, you could not go against it, anyway. It would be impossible for you not to do what he told you to do because he has control over it. There's no way around that. So, just obey."

Amara grit her teeth at the thought of obeying any man. But if that's what she had to do, then she had no choice. She would play along for now. She studied Victoria as she came from around the bar and stood next to her. As Victoria put her shirt over her head, she was staring as hard as she could. And watched as she exposed her perky breasts and perfect abs.

She had been curious how perfect they would look, and now she was seeing them. She blushed as she felt her body respond with excitement. Deep down, all she wanted to do was touch them. Victoria gave her a seductive look. And she knew she had been reading her thoughts again.

"Are you ready?" Victoria walked closer to her.

"I've never done this before," she said shyly, holding her head down.

She knew she wanted her badly. But she had never been with another woman. She also sensed that Victoria was way more experienced than her when it came down to that, but she was ready to experience it. This was going to be exciting and new. "I'm ready," she said as she reached across the bar with her eyes closed. But nothing was happening. She opened them back up.

"To go?" Victoria replied in confusion.

This time, she hadn't been reading her mind. She grabbed a clean shirt that was next to her and put it on. Victoria paused for a second and realized what she had been thinking. She laughed as she grabbed her keys.

"Calm down, ladybug," she jokingly said. "Not just yet." She gave her a wink, as she headed out the door.

She stood there, dumbfounded and embarrassed. Damn. Then she giggled slightly to herself and followed her. Taking one last look inside Victoria's home, she cut off the lights and shut the door.

As they headed back to her apartment, Amara thought about Victoria telling her to blind her. She thought so hard about it she felt Victoria instantly swerve the car.

"Okay, stop it," Victoria yelled out. "I'm driving!"

"I'm not doing anything," Amara quickly yelled back as she noticed the car was all over the road.

"You're blinding me!"

The car swerved again, and Amara panicked. She didn't know how to give Victoria back her vision and a couple of seconds later, Victoria was screaming out her name again.

"Amara! Give me back my vision now!"

The car swerved as Victoria tried to blindly drive. They swerved off the road, into some grass as the car bounced all over the place. Amara braced herself against the dash and squinched her eyes in the moment of panic. She did the only thing she could do. In the same way she had blinded her, by just thinking about it, she did the same to stop it. She stopped focusing on Victoria being blind and on the tree they were about to hit head-on.

"Dammit," Victoria yelled out as her vision came back. And right before the collision, she immediately hit the brakes only inches from the tree and glared at it.

"I'm sorry," Amara said softly as she watched Victoria try to gain her composure.

"I know we're vampires and all but hitting a tree… that would've hurt. And my car, I'm believing you're trying to get me to wreck her… My poor baby." Victoria shook her head as she patted the dashboard. "You're going to have to get your gift in control. You definitely need more training. But at least now I know you can do it."

Amara's heart was still pounding out of her chest and she couldn't believe that she just physically blinded someone without even touching them. She looked at Victoria and then back at the tree. "Yeah, I agree… more training is needed."

CHAPTER FORTY-TWO

Conrad had been staking out her apartment. He was taking pictures of her and the people whom she was hanging around. After he watched her go inside, he figured she was in for the night. He took off and headed back to his house.

It had been a week, and he needed to know what he had to do to stop her. He hadn't quite come to terms with the fact that she could be a vampire, but what other explanation did he have? All he knew about vampires was what he had watched on television. He couldn't believe he was even entertaining the idea that this was possible. But he knew what he had seen.

The next morning, he called a local priest, hoping that he would know something. After all, vampires were evil. The priest he was calling was a little unorthodox and believed in things out of the norm. Conrad had read about him in the local paper.

The priest made the local news because of his different beliefs. Not only did he believe in God and the Devil, but other supernatural beings as well. The priest tried to warn people, but no one believed him, and he was relieved from his duties because of it. He had heard about him years ago and about his different practices.

He knew reaching out to him was a long shot. Maybe this priest would listen to him and not think that he was a lunatic. It wouldn't hurt to try, he thought. He picked up the phone, and to his surprise, Father Borman answered.

"Hello?" a man on the other end answered.

"Is this Father Borman?" Conrad replied

"Yes, it is," he said. "May I ask who's calling?"

"You don't know me; my name is Conrad," he told him. "And I'm in desperate need of your help."

"What is this about?" the priest replied.

"Something I can't explain over the phone," Conrad replied. "But something I know you have experience in."

There was a long awkward silence and Father Borman gave him his address to come and meet him in person. Deep down Conrad felt the priest knew it had to be serious and something that probably dealt with the supernatural. But Conrad didn't hesitate; he wrote his address down, thanked him, and hung up the phone.

Yes, Father Borman had his unconventional ways of preaching. But the fact he believed in the underworld caused Conrad to believe he could help him. To Conrad, this was a blessing that Father Borman was not the average priest. Of course, he believed in Heaven and Hell, but he also believed in things of the underworld, such as demons, spirits, and witches.

A lot of other priests had shunned him as well as the community for spreading conspiracies about such things. But he did not let them sway him. He believed a higher power had given him the ability to see the evil that others didn't.

Even though he no longer had a large congregation, he did still had some people that believed in him and followed his word. For that very reason, he continued with his preaching and his practices.

He had moved out of the city onto some farmland, and from his barn, he created his church. The people that still followed him didn't mind the hour's drive to hear his word.

Conrad knew that Father Borman would listen to him and hopefully give him some advice on how to stop Amara. Someone that wouldn't think he was insane. He decided he would drive to his farm and try to get him to help. Conrad grabbed his keys and hopped in his car.

Driving out of the city and towards Father Borman's home, he thought about all the events that had taken place. How he was a simple, hard-working member of society a week ago, and now he was some type of vampire hunter. This was crazy. But what choice did he have? His brother was gone, and he needed to stop her.

While in his car, He had made another call ahead of time, letting the priest know he was close. Finally, he pulled up to the small white farmhouse, and he parked his vehicle. Taking a minute to collect his thoughts, he sat there.

He watched as Father Borman opened up the screen door and stepped out onto the porch. He waved at Conrad with a welcoming smile on his face. The priest was an oddly shaped man with an enormous belly and a long scruffy beard. Not exactly what he thought he would look like. Conrad opened his car door and stepped out. He smiled back and began walking towards him.

"Hey, welcome," the priest said as he held his hand out.

"Hello," Conrad replied, shaking his hand.

"I'm Father Borman, and you must be Conrad." He smiled.

"Yes, sir," he responded.

Father Borman invited Conrad into his home. He took one look around outside and then shut the front door.

"So, what can I help you with?" he asked as he motioned for Conrad to have a seat on the couch.

"I think I have a problem." He gazed at the priest. "And I think you're the only one that can help me."

Father Borman gave him a questioning look. Walking over to his kitchen, he took the top off of a glass bottle filled with brown liquid. Opening the cabinet, he pulled out two glasses and poured into them. He grabbed them and walked back over to Conrad.

"This must be serious. Come to me." He handed Conrad the glass he held in his hand.

"Thank you," Conrad said as he took the glass. Whiskey? I didn't know priests drink, he thought to himself. "You might think I'm a little crazy. I haven't quite wrapped my head around it." He tossed back the glass and took a drink.

"Well, that lets me know you're not dealing with something you feel comfortable asking anyone else." Father Borman took a sip from his glass. "Just spit it out, son."

"I think I have a vampire problem." He tried not to look at the priest. Embarrassed by what he had just said, he turned his head.

"You're not the only one." The priest rose from his seat and walked over to the kitchen. This time, he grabbed the whole glass bottle and brought it back over to where they were sitting.

"You don't think I'm crazy?" he questioned him. Surprised by the Father's reaction, he didn't know what to think.

"Listen, you're not the first that has come to me and probably won't be the last," he said, pouring more whiskey into Conrad's drink.

Father Borman explained to Conrad that over the years, people had come to him about vampires. At first, they questioned him about the whole situation until he had witnessed the evil for himself.

He took another drink from his glass. With the look on his face, what he had seen shook him to his core. It took him a minute to even speak. He just continued to shake his head as if he was trying to erase the memory.

Then he spoke. Told Conrad about the time he had stayed late in the church to finish some paperwork. After cutting off the lights and locking the doors, he heard what he thought was a woman yelling.

He walked around the side of the church to see a man biting a woman's neck. He tried to stop the man, but when he looked up, his face was something that he had never seen before. It stopped him in his tracks. Frightened, the beast glared at him and continued to take another bite out of the woman's neck.

He ran towards the entrance of the church, almost dropping his keys from his shaken hands. Terrified, he unlocked the door just in time. He tripped inside the door as the beast headed toward him.

Watching him, he saw his face. Those demonic jet-black eyes, the veins that bulged from his face, and his bloody sharp teeth, the image painted in his head. He was monstrous.

The demon, as Father Borman put it, was trying his best to get inside the church. But every time he tried to enter, he had been thrown back as if there was an invisible force field stopping him.

He let out a roar, mad that he couldn't reach him. He could tell in the beast's eyes that he wanted to kill him, but, for whatever reason, he couldn't get past the door. After attempting to get in, he finally stopped, looked at him, and then darted off into the night.

At that moment, Father Borman realized that there were things beyond him. He tried to explain to the church's council what he saw, but they didn't believe him. After that incident, he looked for others that had experienced what he had.

Once he had found a small group of believers and victims of the beast, he preached about it. Of course, the church council didn't like it, and they shunned him. They fired him from his position and ran him out of town.

One man from the group was determined to stop the beast that roamed in the night. Over the years, they learned different tricks and ways to stop being attacked. But vampires were very cunning and weren't as easy to come across.

The man's name was Levy Hafner and Father Borman decided he was going to introduce Conrad to him. He had more experience in dealing with vampires and could teach Conrad a couple of maneuvers when dealing with them.

"She killed my brother," Conrad cried. Realizing that they were real, he knew his brother was dead. "I witnessed it."

Father Borman walked over to Conrad, putting his hand on his shoulder. He knew that there was nothing he could say that would ease his pain. All he could do was let him know he was there for him.

"You will get your vengeance, my son," he solemnly told him. "Hopefully, that will ease your pain."

"I wish I could get my brother back," he said as he wiped the tears from his face.

"He's at peace now."

CHAPTER FORTY-THREE

Conrad watched as he walked over to the black phone that hung on the wall. He dialed a number and began talking on the phone. Watching him walk out of the room, he could no longer make out what he was saying.

Conrad then finished the little whiskey that was left in his glass and then reached over, grabbed the bottle, and poured more into his cup. Vampires were real. Taking a drink, he shook his head that this was even possible.

Father Borman finally appeared back in the room and hung up the phone. He looked at Conrad and smiled.

"He's on his way," he said.

Conrad nodded his head. Being emotionally and physically drained, everything that had been going on the past couple of days wore him down. But there was no time to become weary.

About an hour later, the night was settling in. Conrad heard a truck pull up from outside. Father Borman walked to the front door, opened it, and greeted the person who was on the front porch. They exchanged some words and then the man finally came into the house.

He was a middle-aged, tall, slender man. Not someone that seemed to fight off vampires. He had shaggy brown hair and wore a baseball cap. His tattoos showed on both arms from the cut-off shirt he was wearing.

"This is Levy," Father Borman said as he walked in the door after him.

"Nice to meet you. My name is Conrad." He stood up to shake his hand.

"So, I hear you have a vamp problem," Levy said as he looked him in the eyes.

"Yes, sir, I do," Conrad replied.

"Well, let's get started," he responded.

Levy headed back out the door and towards his truck. Both Conrad and Father Borman followed in behind him. Once they reached the back of the truck, Levy began handing them items to hold.

"We will need these," he explained.

He handed Conrad something that looked like a bow and arrow. It looked altered to shoot something other than what it intended to. He gave them a couple of oak stakes sharpened to a point.

Conrad looked at the items and couldn't believe his eyes. He had seen similar things in the movies with vampires in them. Do they use these in real life? he thought as Levy grabbed a heavy black bag and put it over his shoulder.

"Where do you want to do this?" Levy asked the priest.

"We can go to the barn; there's more space," he replied.

They all headed towards the back of the farmhouse. A couple of feet away, there was a red barn that sat out in the field. Walking towards it, Conrad watched the priest pull a wooden board from the front of the doors and place it to the side.

Opening up the doors, they walked into a wide-open space. There were no animals inside, only bales of hay for the horses. They walked over to a wide wooden table, and Levy placed the black bag on top of it.

"There are some things you need to know first," he told Conrad as he pulled out items such as a bag of rice and a bottle of liquid with a cross on it. Conrad assumed this must be holy water.

Levy explained to him that vampires had incredible speed and that there were things that could weaken them. It would make them vulnerable to human attacks.

He showed Conrad the bottle with liquid. Holding it up, he explained what Conrad already assumed was holy water, stating that it wouldn't stop the vampire, but it would burn one. If thrown in the eyes, it would temporarily blind them.

It was an excellent thing to have if one was close enough to him or was running at him, about to attack. He said that vampires couldn't enter a home without being invited; however, a barn or an outdoor building would not stop them.

The next thing he told him was that if rice was spilled, a vampire would have to stop and count each grain, which would give him enough time to run and find some place to hide. He said that their senses, being heightened, would make it easy for them to find him. So, make sure when hiding, it was some place they couldn't enter.

He explained the general stuff such as they couldn't be in the sunlight, and only stakes made of oak, through the heart, would kill them. They needed to be decapitated and burned to stay dead.

Then he held up a broken necklace with an amulet hanging from it. It was in the shape of a cross with a red stone in the center. Levy told him that this was his prize possession for fighting off a vampire.

With this amulet, a vampire couldn't attack him. From generation to generation, this amulet had a spell placed on it for protection. When a vampire came near it, it immediately disabled the vampire, taking away its speed and strength. It also caused the vampire to be in pain, giving someone just enough time to do what they needed to kill it.

Conrad watched as Levy held the necklace, swaying from side to side. He wondered what Levy had been through to know about these things and if he had ever fought off a vampire. The thought of all this was insane; he hadn't quite accepted the fact that they were real.

Levy continued to pull out various items and explain to Conrad what they were and how to use them. Father Borman stood by, taking notes inside his head, just in case he ran across another one.

As they were in the middle of their conversation, the barn doors flew open with enough force to knock them off the hinges, flying in opposite directions. They all jumped in fear. The dust flew in the air, choking them, as they held their arms across their face. When it somewhat settled, they could see a tall woman with high heels walking in.

"What?" she said, throwing her hands up in the air. "Nobody invited me to the party?"

CHAPTER FORTY-FOUR

Victoria stood there with a stone-cold look on her face as the men scrambled to grab items, but she was too fast for them. She took Levy and picked him up by the neck, right before he could pick up the amulet. Flinging him across the room, he hit the wall with such force that it knocked him out.

She then went after the priest, who tried to grab the holy water, and with one swift move, she snapped his neck like a twig. Hearing his neck-breaking, Conrad stood stone still. Pure fright ran through his body, paralyzing him.

Noticing that Levy was trying to get up, she moved quickly over towards him and bit him on the neck. He screamed out in pain as she drank his blood. Using all of his strength to pull her off him, none of his efforts worked.

Conrad saw a moment of opportunity to grab the amulet and run off. He ran as fast as he could to Father Borman's house. Conrad could barely see before him in the dark. His heart was beating like a drum, but he didn't turn around. Run, run!

Only seconds behind him, he fell into the front door, just in time, and onto the ground. Victoria stopped right before entering, looking at the perimeter of the doorway. She knew she couldn't enter. Unknown to Conrad, the priest had a spell put on the door to keep vampires out, and she could sense that. The priest knew that contrary to belief, some vampires could come into a home uninvited. Victoria was *a warrior* and she was one of the vampires that could.

"Next time," she said, smiling at him right before she hurried off.

Conrad took a deep breath and dropped his whole body back. While lying flat on the floor, he gazed at the ceiling, trying to catch his breath. What the hell just happened? Seeing firsthand the abilities of a vampire questioned his whole competence of being able to kill one.

He knew he was not safe at night, deciding at that moment that he would wait until daylight before leaving the house. Thinking about what had happened to Levy and Father Borman, he was no match. The beast could still be out there, he thought.

Once he felt safe enough to even approach the door, he shut it and locked it behind him. He looked over and grabbed a blanket that was draped over the couch and a couch pillow. Conrad looked around the room and found a corner to lie in. He made sure he could face the door.

Then he held the amulet that he had grabbed and gripped it close to his chest. Part of him was still shaken and fearful that she would return. He watched the door until his eyes grew heavy and he finally dozed off…

—⟋⟍—

After attacking the two men, Victoria had gone home to clean up the bloodstains on her clothes and body. Then she had to get ready to head towards Amara's house. She had been monitoring Conrad's every move since Amara killed his brother. She had noticed him watching both of them the night she dropped her off in front of her apartment. Victoria had always been vigilant about her surroundings.

Victoria had already planned to meet up with Amara but hunting Conrad down was just an extra thing she had planned on the side. But the night's sole purpose was to continue assisting Amara. She had so much to teach her about being a *newborn* vampire. She needed to figure out a way to help Amara control her gift and how to conduct herself out in public. There was a lot that Amara didn't know.

Victoria had planned to take Amara to an underground costume party. The people that attended this event usually dress up as various monsters, including vampires. Perfect disguise. It was no special occasion or holiday, but these parties gave vampires a way of hiding in plain sight. It was exclusive and by invitation only. Victoria, however, had an invitation and a plus one.

The parties changed to a different location every other week, and no one knew who threw the parties. But the vampires that attended it were grateful for it. It was a tranquil place to feed and be themselves, and as a plus, donors always seemed to attend the parties as well. Perfect setup.

This party would give Amara the chance to be herself and possibly meet others of her kind. Victoria wanted her to know that she wasn't alone and how other vampires handled themselves. Hopefully, being around other vampires would calm Amara's impulse to kill everything in sight.

After Victoria finished perfecting herself, she hopped in her red convertible and drove over to Amara's place. Conrad was still on her mind. She knew he was going to be a problem, and until she could handle him, Amara needed to watch her back.

She parked her car out front, glancing over at where Conrad once watched them. But his car was not there tonight. She figured she had scared him off from what she had done earlier, but that didn't mean he wouldn't come back.

CHAPTER FORTY-FIVE

Amara appeared at the front of the apartment with a bright smile on her face. She was ready to go. There was never a dull moment hanging out with Victoria, and she knew tonight was going to be fun.

"Hey, girl," she said as she opened up the car door and got in. Her first instinct was to put on a seat belt. But then she giggled and unbuckled it.

"Hey," Victoria responded.

Victoria started up the vehicle. She could tell that something was on her mind, but she wasn't sure what. After all, she didn't have the luxury of reading another vampire's mind.

"What is it?" she said as Victoria pulled off.

"Remember the guy's brother of the man you killed?" she said.

She wasn't sure whom she was talking about. She had since killed several men, she thought, looking at Victoria with a confused face.

"The one you called your first kill." Victoria glanced over at her with an aggressive look. "At Inferno?"

"Oh yeah." She laughed. "Raunchy Roy, what about him?"

"Well, his brother is after you," she told her. "But I handled his friends for you… he got away."

"I'm not worried about him," she smugly responded.

"You need to take my warnings seriously. I've told you before, don't underestimate him because he is human. If I'm worried, you should be too."

"Okay... Okay," Amara sarcastically replied. "Fear the human."

Victoria secretly hated how nonchalant she acted. Even though Conrad was human, it didn't mean that he wouldn't be a threat. But she wasn't about to argue with her. She would have to learn for herself.

"Good," Victoria told her as she shook her head. "I warned you."

Amara still rolled her eyes. The last thing she was worried about was a weak human. She was more concerned about tonight and fitting in with other vampires. The party was her opportunity to meet other members of the undead.

"I need to take a detour real quick," Victoria said.

"Okay, where are we going?"

"You'll see."

Victoria pulled up to a side street. Amara looked at her with confusion on why they were even there when they were supposed to be training. But before she could speak, Victoria shushed her by putting up her finger to her mouth and slowly lowering it.

"Look," Victoria said, pointing straight ahead of them.

Amara's heart dropped when she saw Noah walking her way. "Are you crazy?" Amara shouted. "He is going to see me!"

"Not if you blind him."

"What?!" Amara said in a panic. "You know I can't control it."

"You better hurry, he is getting in our eyesight."

Sweat dripped off Amara as she concentrated hard as she could on Noah going blind. Not in a million years did she ever think that she would use her gifts on her friends. The people she cared for were loved. But it had to be done or risk getting exposed.

Suddenly, Noah stopped in his tracks and began rubbing his eyes. Just by his reaction, she could tell that her gift was working. Victoria put the car in gear, and they drove past him. Amara broke her focus on Noah and saw him confusingly continue to walk down the street. What was he even doing? Why was he still in the city? She pivoted her focus back on Victoria, who was now grinning ear to ear.

"That's not funny. He could've seen me!" Amara angrily snapped.

"If I didn't put you in a high-stakes situation, then you wouldn't have used your gift," Victoria replied. "And that's payback for almost hurting my baby." She patted her dashboard while giggling.

"How did you know about Noah, anyway?"

"I told you I'm always watching, and I did a little research on you."

"What do you mean, research?"

"Well, I saw your redheaded friend and him were out together eating and I thought I would listen in for a little while. Now that man is a looker. Good choice. He would've been a great boyfriend," Victoria teased.

Amara felt herself blushing. "What did you hear?"

"Well, your friend, she was worried about you and so was he. I wouldn't be surprised if they showed up at your door," Victoria said while taking one hand off the wheel to flip her hair. "And did you know he has a crush on you? The way he talks about you, clearly, he's in love."

"We're just old friends." Amara glanced out the car window. "Maybe one day I'll give him a shot."

Victoria immediately slammed the brakes, causing Amara to almost hit her head on the dash.

"What the hell!" she yelled as they came to a screeching halt in the middle of the empty street. Amara quickly looked around, making sure no one had seen what Victoria had just done.

"No, you won't!" Victoria snapped at her. "You listen to me. No human relationships. You got it! I'm trying to keep both you and me alive."

Some of the tension had worn off after another long drive out of the city. She thought about Victoria and how stern she was with her not having human relationships. It was another warning from Victoria and her warnings were adding up.

She watched as they pulled up to what looked like an abandoned warehouse. She couldn't hear anything from the outside, and she wondered if they were even at the right location.

"Are you sure this is the right place?" she questioned her as she looked around.

"Don't you trust me?" Victoria smiled as she walked past her.

She had never thought about that question before. She guessed she did. Victoria and Lou had been the only people consistent in her life since he'd changed her. She was considering Victoria as a friend, and she was contemplating taking Victoria up on the offer to stay with her. After all, she no longer had a job and would eventually have to give her apartment up as well.

Following Victoria to the back of the building, she saw a single shed that seemed to be out of place. On the side of the door, there was an engraved snake in a circle, as if the mouth was eating the tail.

"What is this?" she said as she touched the engraved symbol.

"That's a *Glyph*… It's a symbol that's meant to mark vampires' safe spaces, houses, or locations where we hang out at."

"Cool," she said as Victoria opened the door. "Umm, where are we going?"

"I said it was underground."

She stepped into the shed with Victoria realizing that it was a secret elevator. Who made this place? Not thinking too hard about that question, she watched as Victoria hit a button, and the elevator went down.

"Cool, huh?" Victoria said.

The elevator finally stopped, and the door opened. The rave music blazed throughout the room, and she looked in awe. There were so many types of people. Some of them had on neon jewelry, from necklaces to bracelets. Some of them held glow sticks and waved them around.

Some of them wore costumes with fake vampire teeth. When she saw them wearing their teeth, it tickled her. If they only knew. Victoria grabbed her hand as she bounced up and down with the crowd, following the beat of the music.

The room was like a club with flashing lights, tables, and booths. It had a dance floor and at least four bars with servers. Nice. She hadn't expected the place to look the way it did, mainly since it was located underground.

The scenery reminded her of her old job that Victoria had advised her to call and tell them she was quitting. She was going to miss her old life. She loved the bar scene, but it was nice being on the opposite side for a change. Meaning not working, nor did she have to.

Victoria led her to a bar and ordered two drinks for them. Surveying the room, she tried to figure out who was a vampire and who was not. But she wasn't having any success in trying to spot them.

"If you want to spot them, watch their movement," Victoria yelled over the music.

Once again, she was reading her mind. However, she didn't mind this time because she legitimately wanted to know.

"See?" Victoria said as she pointed at a woman across the room. She handed her a martini and began sipping on hers.

She paid close attention to the woman. For a brief second, she could have sworn she saw red glowing eyes on the woman. It was something the naked eye could not have seen. The woman moved differently from the circling people.

She seemed to be almost floating and moving with such elegance, as if she wasn't touching any of them. She moved through the crowd like a spirit hovering over the living.

"Come on," Victoria said as she moved through the crowd.

"Wait," she said as she pointed. "I've seen her before."

"Who?" Victoria questioned

"Her…"

Victoria looked over towards the large booth she was pointing at. There sat a sophisticated man and two dainty-looking women. They dressed as if they were from another time. She didn't know if it was their costumes or real clothes.

"Well, they saw us now." Victoria sighed. "We have to go speak to them. They are like royalty, older vampires, and it's disrespectful if we don't acknowledge them… but follow my lead with talking and don't mention that you have seen her."

She nodded. They headed towards the table and once they reached it, the three vampires looked her up and down, analyzing every aspect of her.

The woman she saw sat there with a slight smirk on her face. She was a beautiful woman with blonde hair and greenish-gray slanted eyes. The woman sitting next to her was equally gorgeous, with jet black hair, dark brown eyes, and heart-shaped lips.

The gentlemen sitting in between them had shoulder-length black hair, devilish reddish- blue eyes, and long black claws that he tapped against the table. He was not at all inviting. She wished she had Victoria's gift of reading their minds. All she could do was stand there like a log.

"Awww, Victoria," he said as he extended his speech. "I was wondering if you were coming to say hello… and here I thought you were still mad at me after all these years."

Victoria clenched her teeth. "This is Celeste, Lilith, and Silas," Victoria said, pointing each one out as she introduced them. "And this is our newest member, Amara."

"My pleasure," Silas spoke as he grabbed her hand and kissed it.

While he was holding her hand, she visualized him in the 1900s. She could see him being a true gentleman that greeted the ladies by tipping his hat and taking off his jacket for a woman to walk across a puddle.

"Wow, what a wonderful sight," he said as he let go of her hand. He smiled at her with delight and looked toward Victoria. By the look on his face, she had already impressed him. "Only if it were true."

"What?" she replied, shockingly, not meaning to use her gift at all. And definitely not on him. Something about his demeanor creeped her out.

"You visualized me tipping my hat to women and throwing my jacket over puddles for them to walk across," Silas said. "Because I was holding your hand, I saw it as well."

"How wonderful," Celeste said. "Do me." She held out her hand for her to grab.

They all stared at her as they waited for her to grab her hand. Noticing that all eyes were on her, she held her hand. Still confused about what she was supposed to do, she closed her eyes and visualized her apartment.

Celeste began describing the apartment to each of them. They listened with delight as she spoke. She finally opened her eyes and let go of Celeste's hand, and all of them clapped with amusement.

"What a wonderful gift," Lilith replied.

"We all have gifts," Victoria interrupted. "And be careful when touching someone."

"Yes, we all have gifts. I have the gift of debility," Celeste said proudly. "I can paralyze you by just looking at you… but I would never do that."

"You will do it if I say," Silas spoke up and said, glaring at Celeste. He looked back towards Amara.

He laughed. She looked towards Victoria and knew that she was not happy but didn't speak a word. And she also knew that when Victoria told her something, it was for her own good and something she needed to know.

The way Victoria was so submissive to Silas's demands and rude remarks, without snapping back at him, let her know he was not someone to be played with. Victoria seemed threatened by these vampires, and, because of that reason, she trod with caution.

"Who is your *creator*?" Silas questioned her.

She looked over at Victoria to see if it was okay to answer his question. Victoria nodded her head, letting her know it was all right.

"His name is Lou," she responded.

"Aww, Luciano," Celeste said with a smile.

She could tell that Silas didn't like the way she responded, as if she had secretly fantasized about him. He gave her a sharp look that could have slit her throat. Celeste immediately took the smile off of her face.

"He is rather a fine gentleman," Silas said, trying not to show any more of his jealousy. "It's rare for him to change someone, especially since what happened to his *creator*."

She paused at his sly remark. "What does Lou's *creator* have to do with anything?"

CHAPTER FORTY-SEVEN

Victoria grabbed her arm from underneath the table and when she turned to glance at her, she shook her head no. She snarled up her nose, rolled her eyes, and shut up. She didn't know what the big deal was, but by the look on everyone's faces, she was not about to question Silas anymore. Fear briefly came over her. After all, she knew nothing about vampire politics or what should be or should not be said to Silas.

Even though she knew nothing about him, something was already rubbing her the wrong way. She no longer had the impression of him being the gentleman that she had visualized. She turned towards Victoria as she heard her break the awkward silence.

"Well, she's special," Victoria said, putting her arm around her and squeezing. "And still learning,"

"Must be," Lilith said, gawking at her.

"Well, how about a round of drinks?" Silas said, changing the conversation and clearing his throat.

They all watched as he held his hand up, and a server approached them. He told her to bring them their finest bottle of champagne and some more wine for the table. The server took his order, and as she turned around, she noticed two small bite marks on her neck.

"She's a feeder," Victoria said, knowing what she had been thinking. "She willingly let us feed on her, but because of the party, she wanted to keep the marks on her neck without us healing her."

"There's a room in the back, just in case you need to feed," Celeste spoke up and said. "There are plenty of donors there, waiting."

She couldn't believe her ears, but then again, nothing surprised her anymore. She was part of a whole new world, and there was so much she didn't know. Still trying to process the moment that she and Silas had, she looked around the room, stopping when someone caught her eye.

It was a man that was standing across the room. For some odd reason, goosebumps formed all over her body. The way she was feeling towards him seemed more intense than she ever had as a human and, for her, being a vampire, she seemed magically drawn to the person, but it was something about him.

She looked him up and down, staring at every inch of his body. Watching his muscular arms, boldly standing out from his tight-fitted t-shirt. His muscles flexed with each movement he made, and she could even see the sweat dripping off the back of his neck from the warm temperature in the room.

His strong stance made the spot in between her legs beat like a tiny heartbeat as she looked at every inch of him, to his nicely built legs. If only she had X-ray vision, she thought. He turned halfway, not fully exposing his face, and she tried staring in between his legs. She could see the bulge in his pants from where she was sitting. Damn.

He was having a conversation with another guy whom she assumed was a friend of his. She decided she was going to introduce herself to him.

"Excuse me," she said to Victoria, motioning for her to let her up from her seat.

"Where are you going?" Victoria questioned while reading her mind.

"To powder my nose." Amara winked and shot Victoria a slight grin. Annoyance came over Victoria's face. She didn't want her to leave.

Victoria turned her nose up and squinched her eyes, knowing that was not what she was planning to do, but stayed silent. She got the feeling that she did that because of Silas and the others at the table. She moved out from the booth, letting her out.

She walked across the room. The closer she got, the more attractive and familiar he became. He was tall and when he turned his head, his smile was languorous, sexy, contagious… and big.

Noah. What the hell? When did he get here? This was the first time since he'd left her apartment that she had seen him up close and personal. Using her gift on him earlier that night didn't count. She had been more focused on getting away without him seeing her.

She couldn't help but notice his clean-cut beard surrounded the curves of his plump, juicy lips. He looked even better than before. He was perfect, even down to the mole that sat on the right of his lower face. Why hadn't she seen him like this before? Maybe she was looking at him differently because of her vampiric eyes and her feelings towards him. Only being a friend seemed to fade away.

She continued to analyze him in her new vampiric state. It was like going from regular colored television to HD when looking at him now. His long sun-kissed brown hair that he had pulled up in a man bun seemed to have more definition to it and she thought about him letting it down and running her fingers through his hair.

He mesmerized her at this moment. She realized her feelings toward him differed from before. As they locked eyes, the attraction was instant. She couldn't hold back her actual feelings for him and brush him off this time.

"Hey, what are you doing here?" she said as she gave him a hug. He was strong, yet manly.

"Just hanging out with a couple of friends... what are you doing here?" He grinned as he released from the embrace, eyeing her. "Wow, you look great. And different... but in a good way."

"Just makeup, that's all," she was quick to reply. It wasn't like she could tell him her looks changed because she was a vampire now. "I'm with friends as well."

"Mariam's here?"

"No, different friends."

"Oh," he curiously responded. "Is everything okay?"

This was an awkward moment. She knew he was wondering why she wasn't with Mariam when they had always stuck together. Especially when going out. They looked out for each other in that way, and he knew it.

She gazed as he placed his hands on her shoulders. Just his touch did something to her body, making her instantly want to rip off his clothes. She visualized it and instantly he grinned. Did he see that? She remembered what Victoria had said about watching out for who touched her and who she touches. She immediately backed up, causing him to remove his hands from her shoulders. But at least this cleared up the awkwardness of not having to explain why Mariam wasn't with her.

Then another whiff of his scent invaded her nostrils. Not only did his cologne smell delightful but also the scent of his sweet blood. It smelled so… enticing. It was hard for her to fight back the urge to taste him.

CHAPTER FORTY-EIGHT

She closed her eyes, suppressed her urges, and opened them back up. Noah should not be in a place like this, surrounded by a bunch of vampires. And to make matters worse, she was now a threat to him. He had to go and now.

"Ummm, Amara," he calmly replied, breaking her train of thought.

"Noah, listen to me," she said. "I want you to leave this place."

She sensed worry and confusion coming from him, but she couldn't tell him anything and at that moment, it didn't matter. She was more worried about his well-being than anything and tried not to show her worries across her face but looked at him with a steady eye.

"Well, can we have a drink?... Before I go," he questioned her with a smile.

He was gorgeous with his perfect white teeth. His smile seemed to light up the room. Looking down at the glass he had in his hand, she took it.

"Thank you," she sighed quickly, gulping it back. "You need to go now... Did you drive?"

"Yes." His brows furrowed in concern. "Can you tell me what's going on?"

"I will later… Just leave your friends and go now, please," she anxiously said, not knowing if his friends were actually vampires.

"Okay?" he responded. He didn't like that idea, but with the panic that she was in, he did as she had asked. "I'll go."

"Just tell them you had an emergency."

For some odd reason, he was now someone that she could see herself in a relationship with. Of course, maybe her feelings had always been there. As a vampire, her emotions were heightened. Vampire and human—she wondered how that would work. They could be like Lou and Katherine. Noah was a good guy. Even Mariam had always wanted them to be a couple, and she didn't need her vampire abilities to know this. After all, she had known him all of her life. But breaking her thoughts once again, the smell of his blood was overwhelming her.

She tried turning her head away from him, but it wasn't working. Afraid that her fangs would emerge, she knew she had to end this conversation quickly.

"Are you okay?" Noah questioned. He noticed the distress coming from her face before she turned away from him.

"I have to go," she replied.

"Wait," he responded as he grabbed a napkin from the bar. He grabbed a pen and wrote. "This is my new number. I still want to tell you about my surprise."

He handed her the napkin, and she grabbed it, nodding her head and now covering her mouth. She desperately needed to get away from him. Why couldn't she control this? When she was talking to Roy, she could. Why was this time different?

Leaving his side, she rushed over to the table with Victoria and the others. They watched as she struggled to sit down, holding her mouth in frustration. It embarrassed her that her fangs wanted to come out, talking to Noah.

"You need to feed," Victoria told her. "Let's find you a feeder."

She glanced in Noah's direction. He was heading towards the door, and she was happy that he was leaving. Victoria got up from the booth, and she followed her to a room at the back of the club. Continuing to hold her mouth, she watched as Victoria opened a door and then another one after that.

When she looked in, she couldn't believe her eyes. So many vampires were feeding off of humans that would give up their blood. These humans were not in any distress or pain but enjoyed the fact that they were the food.

She read some of their thoughts. Some wanted to be vampires, some got sexual pleasure out of it, and some just wanted to help. It was an extraordinary scene, and she couldn't believe that a place like this existed.

Victoria guided her over to a black leather couch, and she took a seat, Victoria sitting beside her. Both of them looked around the room at the various humans that were without a vampire.

"Pick which one," Victoria told her. "Not all humans will be to your taste."

"What do you mean?" she responded.

"Have you ever been close to a human, and their smell was repulsive?" Victoria said.

She thought about the night when she was at Inferno. The bartender had smelled so horrible that it made her nose turn up. She wasn't sure what it was.

"Yes," she responded

"Well, that person was not for you," Victoria explained. "It could've been a toxin in their blood, like drugs, or their personality altogether."

"Personality?" she questioned.

"Yeah," Victoria replied. "Evil-doers taste sweeter to me; however, the good ones may taste better to you."

She was shocked to find out that unique humans may taste a different way. But Victoria told her to look at it like alcohol; top shelf tastes better than cheaper liquor. But yet, there is a variety to choose from in the world. It's the same for human blood.

Victoria called two females towards us. She took a whiff of both of them. They weren't as sweet-smelling as Noah was, but their scent wasn't bad either. They must be the cheaper liquor, she thought to herself as she giggled.

The entire atmosphere was much better than hunting a human down. Having a feeder was more manageable and less chaotic. However, it took away from the thrill of the hunt. Doing it this way was more convenient.

Both of the women sat on each side of Victoria and her. Pulling back their hair, they exposed their necks, waiting for them to feed. Both Victoria and her bit down on their necks and drank their blood.

Once they had finished, they both raised and licked their lips. It surprised her that her feeder looked her in the face and smiled at her. They really do like this. The women stayed seated.

"Now, heal them," Victoria said.

She watched as Victoria took her sharp nail, slit her wrist, and placed some of her blood on the woman's neck, where she had bitten her. Before her eyes, she watched as the woman's puncture wounds healed.

She repeated the same actions that Victoria did. She used her nail to make a slit on her wrist, gather some of her blood, and heal the woman's neck. Wow! She thought about the times she had bitten someone, killed them, and then hid their body.

"Now you don't have to be a serial killer," Victoria giggled.

A serial killer? She had never thought of herself like that before. The entire purpose of killing those men was because they had bad intentions toward women. But she felt like she had moved on from being vindictive.

She watched as both women got up from the couch and moved toward the other vampires. There were so many of her kind, vampires, out in the world. She thought about her human life and how she hadn't ever run into one before Lou. It was only a matter of time. She was truly living life with blinders on.

Victoria got up and headed back towards the club area, and she followed her. She felt better and was not hungry anymore. Thinking about Noah, she wondered if he was still by the bar, but when she looked, he was gone. She could relax.

"Well, leave it alone." Victoria turned and scolded her. "You are no longer part of their world."

She once again realized Victoria had been reading her thoughts. When she did that, she hated it. Regardless, she thought, if she could control herself around him, he would never have to know about her.

"It will not work," Victoria said again, interrupting her thoughts.

"Can you stop that?" she replied, rolling her eyes. "Stop reading my thoughts."

Victoria continued to laugh until they reached the table with the others. Silas, Celeste, and Lilith watched in confusion at why Victoria was laughing. Then they looked over at Amara to see that she wasn't at all amused.

She scanned the room, looking for Noah, but he had left. He had written his number on a napkin that she'd placed in her pocket before rushing off. She would call him later.

"Don't call him," Victoria whispered, reading her thoughts once again.

"I told you to stop doing that," Amara scolded her.

"Sorry, it's a habit," Victoria replied, holding her hands halfway up as if to say, don't shoot me. "But don't."

"Call who?" Silas spoke up, reading Amara's thoughts because he couldn't read Victoria's.

"As you know, Amara is a *newbie* and is still letting go of her human attachments," Victoria said. Looking toward her, Victoria quickly shut up when she saw her angry face.

Sila's face turned from somewhat delightful to disgusted. The thought of a human disturbed him. Everyone turned to watch the anger that had come over his face, and she looked at him in confusion.

"It's despicable for a vampire and a human to have any form of relationship!" he scorned her, almost yelling.

"He is a friend," she snapped back, defending myself from his tone. "And I told him to leave."

"Amara, chill." Victoria's voice sounded like a warning.

Silas raised his hand and Victoria went silent.

"Vampires that cross that line deserve the consequence they get." He kept his now stone-cold eyes on her. Then he shot a nasty look at Celeste. "You will face judgment if you cross that line."

CHAPTER FORTY-NINE

Victoria could see that Silas was no longer at peace with her and needed to lighten the tension that was now in the room. After all, Silas was a Ruler, and she hadn't gotten the chance to explain any of this to Amara or how powerful he was.

"Okay, let's just calm down," Victoria said. "We're just having a conversation here."

"Who are you to demand anything of me?" Silas quickly scorned her.

"Silas... I was just..."

"Hush child," he interrupted her, dismissing Victoria as a child. Anger grew in her face but yet she didn't say another word.

Silas stopped for a moment and looked at everyone sitting around the table. Each one of them was staring at him. He calmed down and formed a small smile on his face. He looked over at Celeste, who was looking back at him with fear.

"This is the tale of your tale," Silas said to Celeste, looking at her as if she was a disgrace. Victoria nor Amara liked the way Silas's attitude came across.

She sensed Celeste didn't like the fact that Silas had brought her up. Celeste held her head down in shame, not knowing what to say. Of Course, Amara being Amara wanted to know what had happened with her and her human encounter.

"Do tell them." Silas smirked at Celeste as he gestured towards her. He was slightly giggling and seemed to get pleasure from her pain as he tipped his champagne glass up and drank. His mood had changed so quickly. From rage to arrogance.

Even though she wanted to know, she could tell in Celeste's eyes that it scorned her for whatever had happened. She felt bad and looked at Silas more like a foe instead of a friend. He was becoming a bully in her eyes instead of the gentleman that she had first thought. She wondered why Victoria even introduced her to him, but she was sure Victoria would tell her later.

"She doesn't have to if she doesn't want to," she spoke up.

Silas's pushy way was getting underneath her skin. Silas looked at her with a menacing grin. He held up the palm of his hand at her words just like he had done with Victoria, and she sank into her seat.

"It's okay," Celeste quickly spoke up. She once again looked at Silas and then looked at her. She took a deep breath and told her tale.

"It started when I met a man named Daniel. He changed my world upside down. It was love at first sight, and I knew he was the one for me, despite our circumstances. Yes, I was a vampire, and he was human, but none of this mattered to me."

She glanced over at Silas who was snarling his nose up at her. The disgusted look on his face let everyone know how he truly felt about her story. He despised human and vampire relationships and felt that any vampire that would engage in one was a disgrace to their kind. But she continued despite his attitude.

"I vowed never to reveal what I was to him in fear of his reaction and *The Order*. He loved me dearly, and I loved him. There were no secrets in between us except that one. Never speaking about what I was, I tried my best to conceal it."

"You shouldn't have even started this despicable relationship. You are lucky *the Order* spared you," Silas barked.

Celeste held her head down in shame. She wouldn't dare challenge Silas. All she could do was to continue with her story. Amara eyed Silas with disgust. She hated the way he was speaking to Celeste and the way he was looking at her as if she was nothing more than a piece of trash. And as bad as she wanted to speak, she stayed quiet.

"I told him only things from my previous life when I was human, not of my new one as a vampire. After never being introduced to my family, I told him they had died. Even with the lies, I hoped everything would work out."

"Did it?" Amara finally broke her silence. But by the looks on everyone's faces, she quickly realized that the question was foolish. She sunk in her seat and waited for Celeste to continue.

Celeste took a deep breath, holding back her emotions. "Of course, once I told one lie, it forced me to keep up with several of them. Deceiving him made my life with him miserable. The first significant lie began when he wanted to start a family with me. Of course, vampires cannot have children, but I led him to believe that I wanted children with him. We moved to the countryside to start a fake family.

"He constantly talked about how he wanted a boy and a girl. I stirred the pot by telling him what a noble father he would be. But this secret was weighing on me. I knew how badly he wanted children, and the guilt ate away at me.

"Lies upon lies, I told him. Why I couldn't go out in the sunlight, of course, I blamed this on a rare blood disorder. Daniel accepted that, and he still stood by my side, feeling sorry for me, not being able to enjoy the beauty of the sun.

"Then came the lies about why I would have to go off in the middle of the night alone. I knew I needed to feed, but to him, I needed some space. Feeding from the animals on the land didn't entirely satisfy me, and I was starving," she said and then paused as if she was holding back tears on what was to come next.

But Silas showed no sympathy for her. He wanted Amara to know what would happen if she was ever as deceitful as Celeste. He discarded Celeste's emotions by rolling his eyes and scoffing at certain words she said.

"By all means, don't stop," he said sarcastically. "We are finally getting to the good part."

Amara wanted to speak up so badly and defend Celeste, but Victoria squeezed her leg underneath the table. She looked over at her and Victoria slightly shook her head. Amara squinched her lips together and continued to listen to Celeste.

"Consistently being weak because of the lack of human blood," Celeste said, "my instinct for it overwhelmed me. I mostly fought off my urge not to attack him. But his scent was everywhere, and it became harder for me to fight." Celeste shifted in her seat.

"I isolated myself and stayed away from him as much as I could. I could barely look at him in fear my face would change before him. Not loving him the way he deserved ate away at me. I loved him and didn't want to be away from him. My options were becoming limited.

"Because of his love for me, he was determined not to give up on our relationship. Daniel had to figure out what was wrong with me. He tried talking to me and showing more affection, but none of his actions were working. His heart seemed broken, and he couldn't figure out what he had done for me to hate him so much.

"I knew what he was thinking, and I tried to reassure him it was a personal issue that I was having. Despite my better judgment, I let him hold me one night, when my urges had fully emerged.

"He only wanted to hold me for the night, and because of that, I lay beside him. I laid there without even feeding on an animal. I suffered in silence as he kissed me back and put his arm around me.

"The smell of his blood was so intense, and I tried to fight against it. He whispered to me that he loved me and he wanted us to work out. He even apologized for things that I knew weren't his fault." She sighed. Her voice was quivering, and a single tear dropped from her face.

"It's okay," Amara said, trying to console her. She didn't care what Silas thought at the moment. He was getting amusement out of her reliving this story. And it was cruel. "You don't have to finish if you don't want to."

"I tell her what to do, not you *newbie*," Silas barked. "Continue."

Amara grew angry, but Victoria squeezed her leg again. She eyed Celeste, waiting for her response.

"It's okay," she told Amara. "Before I knew it, his limp body was in my hands. I had attacked him, draining him till his death. My hunger had taken over my mind and body to the point I wasn't able to stop before killing him." She sobbed as she continued her story, wiping her tears with a napkin off the table.

"I cried out in horror when I realized what I had done. The love of my life was gone, and I was the reason for his death. I vowed never to fall in love again, and the thought of Daniel still haunts me to this day."

Amara watched as a tear trickled down her face. Celeste wiped it off quickly and looked over at Silas, who showed no sympathy for her. What an asshole, Amara thought. Then she realized the whole reason she was with Silas.

Celeste was punishing herself. She didn't feel as if she deserved love. After all, she had killed the one thing in her life that was good. Silas wasn't kind to Celeste or Lilith, and before the night was over, she realized they were nothing more than his play toys.

His uncaring way angered her, and she despised men like that, and if she could kill him, she would. She visualized ripping his throat out and setting both the women free. She looked over at Victoria and realized she had projected her vision onto her. But Victoria didn't speak a word.

Victoria placed her hand on her shoulder to calm her down. After all, she would not win that fight. She shook her head no at her and she put her head down. She knew precisely what Victoria was trying to do. Silas would destroy her if she made a move toward him.

"I think it's time for us to go," Victoria stood up and said. She grabbed her arm and pulled her up to her feet. She could feel the rage building inside of her.

"Leaving so soon?" Silas smirked.

She said nothing. Being around him angered her but she as well didn't respond, only rolling her eyes.

"I need to educate my *newbie*," Victoria sarcastically spoke up.

"I suggest you do that," Silas said with a demanding voice. "Maybe we can get back together one day and talk about that gift of yours, Amara. I'm a connoisseur of those things, and Victoria refuses to join me. And her gift is wonderful. Did you tell your *newbie* that so desperately clings to your arm why she does that?"

Victoria gave him a sour look, and he shot her a look of deviancy. He nodded towards Lilith to speak up, but she seemed just as evil as him.

"Victoria has *the gift of Allies*," Lilith said. "It is hard to dislike them and easy to become attached to. Of course, other vampires can't read their minds. Their strength and speed are remarkable. She is such a little warrior. Weaker than Lou but yet stronger than a *newborn*."

"Yes, *a warrior* indeed," Silas said, looking at her. "Such a shame she won't join our little family… You and your *newbie* would be perfect additions to my wonderful collection."

CHAPTER FIFTY

Amara looked at him crossly. She knew there was more of a story behind him and Victoria. And she didn't know if he meant her joining him or the both of them, but at this moment, no way in hell was that going to happen.

Victoria quickly rushed her from the table before she could say anything else and out of the club. Once they were outside in the car, Victoria spoke.

"You're going to have to control yourself," Victoria scorned.

"He's a jerk, and he treats them like they're nothing," she yelled back.

"That's their business," Victoria yelled back. "He is way older than you and me; he would have killed us both."

"I hate men like that," I replied. "I could feel his attitude towards them."

"I understand, but you have to pick your battles." She opened the car door. "Silas is an asshole, but also royalty in our world… he is to be respected. Do you think I wanted to go over to that table… with you? No, but in the presence of a *Ruler* we must greet them, or it's a sign of disrespect… punishable."

"I can tell you don't like him," she said as they both got in the car and headed towards her apartment.

"You're right, I don't, but he can't read my mind as he can yours," Victoria snapped. "Lilith and Celeste are his *blood puppets*, and he is a *Ruler*. They are the eyes and ears for him."

"Okay… What is a *blood puppet* and a *Ruler*?" she questioned.

"Minions that follow and obey the *Rulers* out of deficit or as a punishment for breaking a vampiric rule… They are eyes and ears for the *Rulers* and *Rulers* watch of the *Primus*, the very first vampires, but I have seen none."

"Okay… that's not confusing," she said sarcastically. "So they don't follow him because they want to?"

"No, they follow him because they have to… or face death," she said as she stared at the road. "I want him dead… and once I have enough *newbies* under my wing… maybe one day."

"So, is that why you wanted me as a *companion*?" she questioned. "You're not even in a *comate stage*, are you?"

"No, I just need people to believe that, and partially I needed you and because I like you. You're sort of like me, of course. I'm not as hardheaded as you. You were single with no kids, still young, and a badass with disrespectful men." Victoria giggled. "And I want to build an army against Silas."

"Against that asshole!" Amara snarled her nose up at the thought of him. But she couldn't help but think about how powerful he must be for Victoria to need an army to go against him. Someone needed to do it. "I'm down for that."

Victoria took a long sigh. "Lou must know nothing about what I am planning. He knows Silas very well… they used to be *companions* until Lou left him. I don't want him a part of this. If Lou found out…" She broke off.

"I won't say a word, I promise, but Lou and Silas? What an odd match," she said, glaring out the window as they drove. "What happened to them?"

"If we all were characters in a fiction series… their story would need to be part of a whole sequel." She giggled. "Right after mine, of course."

"Well… what's your story?" she questioned. "Since we are sidekicks now."

Victoria smiled at the thought of them being sidekicks and then her smile faded into a frown as she told her story.

It was 1868 in the Smithsonian era, just like Lou, only fifty years later. Victoria was a twenty-five-year-old dazzling woman. Even though men pursued her heavily, her taste was not for the pickle that dangled in between their legs. But of course, back in those days, being openly gay wasn't tolerated. It was funny how her sexual preference didn't matter as a vampire.

She grew fond of another woman. They secretly snuck around and fell for one another. They decided they would live in a cabin in the woods far from the townspeople for them to have privacy and for no one to find out. But their secret didn't stay a secret for long.

Victoria had always acted like a man. Hunting, gambling, partying, and outdrinking them. Looking back on it, that was probably what gave her away and her not having a suitor for her age. Of course, the men became jealous of a woman outshining them. Women were only supposed to bear babies, clean up, and look after them—nothing more.

One man followed her and found out about her little secret. That night they came back and assaulted both of them and then buried her lover to death on a stake right in front of her. They claimed what they had been doing was evil, went against their beliefs, and for that, she would have to live with the death of her lover. But really, it was over jealousy. They wanted to weaken Victoria and put her in her place. Not to act like a man but be a woman and do as she was told.

Lou heard her cries and came to her side. He could relate to her pain and took her under his wing. Come to find out, it had been Silas—that was the man that followed her and told her secret. Of course, he was a blood drinker at this point and the only reason he told was that he admired her strength and attitude. She was relentless in his eyes. He felt she would be an excellent *blood puppet* by his side. He could've just changed her, but he wanted to break her spirit so that he would seem like a savior, so the townspeople were told instead.

After the townspeople had left her alone in her misery and before Lou heard her cries, another vampire approached her. She had slit her wrist in front of Victoria and said, "This is to protect you. Drink my blood… one day I will return." Victoria did it because something about the woman seemed more like a friend trying to help instead of a foe. And because she felt she had nothing to live for… why not? Afterward, the woman sped off in the dead of night. Then Lou found her in her transitional state—that was where the cries were coming from.

Later in life, Lou had told her that her creator was a powerful witch hybrid and someone Silas kept close and as a secret to him. But it was pointless to search for her and she went on believing that her *maker* would return… one day.

"A witch hybrid?" Amara questioned.

"Yes, witches that are transformed into a vampire making them half-mortal and half immortal."

"So there are witches, too," she asked. "What else is out there?"

"That's part of a sequel," Victoria teased. "I think we have had enough history lessons for the night."

Amara nodded and quietly thought about Silas, Celeste, and Lilith. Victoria and Lou had been attached to him. A part of his sadistic world, and it made her cringe. Silas was a monster and not in the vampire sense. He got off on people's pain and Silas's attitude about humans made her wonder if he wasn't secretly part of *The Order* that no one knew who they were.

She realized this was the very reason Victoria needed her to stop Silas and his narcissistic behavior. But with her, there were only two in this army that Victoria wanted to build so badly.

"Am I your first?"

"First what?" Victoria questioned.

"The first person who was changed for this army."

"Yes. But I will add more: it takes time to find the right people that could give Silas a run for his money." She sighed. "I can put any human through the *transformation* to become what we are. However, like all other things, there are rules. I needed Lou to change you. I needed him as my shield. That way, if you act up or get out of control, I wouldn't get punished for your actions."

"Shield?"

"Yes. An *Untouchable*. They are protected from being harmed by *The Order* or *a Ruler*, like Silas. They can break as many rules as they want."

"Can I put someone through the *transformation*?"

"You're *a lesser*, but then again, Lou changed you. I don't know, maybe. But I don't think you should explore that option any time soon. Training a *newbie* is a lot of responsibility, with a lot of consequences riding on their behavior."

Amara glanced over at Victoria, feeling guilty. Her destructive behavior and not being willing to follow any vampiric rules had put Victoria's life in jeopardy. Maybe even Lou's. Even though Victoria had stated he couldn't be harmed.

She secretly questioned herself why Victoria hadn't told her this before. But then she quickly realized that it had been her own fault for not knowing. Being angry with Lou and feeling discarded by every man in her life was the only thing she had focused on, and the reason why she hadn't taken the time to listen in the first place.

She began thinking about Silas again. She could tell that she had been reading her thoughts and something about Victoria's face made her wonder if she was wondering about Silas as well. This whole time she only thought he was a *Ruler*, but could it be possible that he was part of *The Order* as well? Then she quickly removed that thought from her head and just gazed out the window.

It was a long, quiet drive until Victoria broke the silence. She needed Amara to understand that all the connections and relationships that she once had with the human world died the day she was reborn.

"You need to make new friendships and relationships of your kind. Your attachments to humans cannot be like before," Victoria stated. She could tell that she understood she wanted to keep parts of her old self, but it would only lead the people that she loved to their death. "I know you don't like that notion and all of us don't think the way Silas does or *The Order*. But we have all faced pain over human relationships and it's not worth it… not if you care about them. You will meet others like us, and don't mention human relationships around a vampire."

At that moment, Amara's cell phone rang. She looked down to see who it was. Mariam. She had forgotten all about her. Letting it ring until it stopped, she didn't answer. How was she going to leave her best friend alone? They had been through so many trials. Mariam was the only one that had been there for her all of her life.

"You've got to let her go."

CHAPTER FIFTY-ONE

Regardless of what Victoria or anyone else thought, she was not about to turn her back on Mariam. She would have to find a way. Mariam was her best friend/sister, and they had been through all the good times and bad times together. She would never hurt her. She loved her, and letting her go was not an option.

Victoria pulled up at her apartment building. She stepped out of the car and shut the door.

"Thank you for the night out… despite Silas." She giggled. Victoria nodded her head and smiled.

"Do nothing stupid?" Victoria said as she glared at her. "And watch your back."

She watched as Victoria drove off into the dead of night. Once she was out of sight, she looked down at her phone and took a deep breath. She needed to call her back. She was feeling guilty.

Once she stepped into her apartment, she placed her purse down and hit the redial button on her cell phone. Listening as the phone rang, she didn't know what she was going to say when Mariam answered.

After two rings, she heard Mariam's voice come across the phone. She prepared herself for what she would say.

"I am so mad at you," Mariam said on the other end. Not even a hello. She could tell that she was furious.

"I'm sorry, I've been so—" she said, but Mariam interrupted her.

"It doesn't matter. I haven't seen you in days. Do you even answer your phone anymore?" Mariam yelled.

"I know. I promise I will make it up to you," she mumbled.

She secretly wished that she could tell her what had happened, but she couldn't. The only thing she wanted to do was find out how to make this friendship work without harming Mariam.

"Make it up to me by telling me what's going on," Mariam said. "We can get breakfast in the morning and talk about it."

There was a long pause. In the morning? She knew she could not be out in the sunlight. She had to make up some lie about why she couldn't. This was going to be harder than she thought. This was the first lie she had to tell her friend. Someone she cared for. Just like Celeste. She thought about how many more she would have to tell after this one.

"Hello?" Mariam said after noticing the long pause on her end.

"I've had a long night and a hangover. Maybe you can come over tomorrow night?" she quickly replied.

"But you love breakfast." Mariam took a long pause. "Okay, I guess I'll see you tomorrow night."

After hanging up the phone with Mariam, she could tell by the disappointment in her voice that Mariam felt as if she was brushing her off.

Even though that thought was far from the truth, she needed time to think and how she was going to make all this work. There had to be a way. No matter what, she would not destroy their relationship. Mariam was family, a sister, and a bond that she wouldn't break.

She knew the sun would rise soon. She took a shower and got dressed for bed. As she lay there, she thought about Celeste and Victoria's past. What a tragic end. She didn't want her life to go or her friends to end like that.

Even though she was a vampire, she still wanted a healthy life. She wanted to have a relationship with Mariam and Noah. It was just two humans. How hard could that be? If she stayed fed and possibly explained her situation, maybe it wouldn't be that bad. And she would just pay more attention to her surroundings.

Then she thought about what Victoria said about *The Order*. How they could not speak about what they were. But how would they know? She was pretty sure if she told Mariam what was going on that she wouldn't say a word. So many thoughts ran through her head.

Thinking that the only friends she could have would be vampires made her very nervous. If they were anything like Silas, she could do without them. She remembered Lou had fallen in love with a human, and they were okay until the day she died. So, was it possible? If only she could get ahold of Lou and find out what he had done.

But Lou had gone back to New Orleans, and if she asked Victoria, she already knew what her response would be. Victoria was big on rules and keeping her in line. There would be no way that she would agree with her on any form of human relationship.

She tried closing her eyes and shutting her mind off. So many thoughts flashed through her head like a primitive black and white movie. She knew it would all work out. She wasn't losing anyone she loved in her life. Finally, she could doze off in a deep slumber.

It was the next night. She had slept through the day. She woke up from her slumber. Stretching her arms as she rose, she looked around at her empty apartment. She draped her legs off the end of the bed and swung them back and forth.

She thought about Mariam and Noah. Knowing that she had hurt Mariam's feelings the night before, she knew that she would have to make it up to her. Then she thought about Noah and grabbed the napkin with his number on it from the nightstand. She was determined to call him.

There was something about him that drew her to him. She had felt him: his genuine emotions, intentions, and his spirit. Being a vampire gave her an advantage over human mindsets.

She only wished that she had given him the time of day before her *transformation*, but then again, maybe this was the way things were supposed to have gone. Everything happens for a reason. He now had her full attention, and she was going to act on it.

She knew the rules; she knew about *The Order* and the consequences. But again, she felt as if she could take on the situation and had already done so.

She picked up her cell phone and dialed Noah's number. There was no nervousness about her actions. She was quite confident in calling him. The phone rang.

"Hello?"

"This is Amara…"

"Hey," Noah said. "I was waiting for your call."

"I had a little hangover, so I slept in," she jokingly replied.

"I see, it's night again." He giggled. "You want to tell me what happened last night?"

She could sense his delight in her calling, and this made her even more excited to get to know him as a lover, not just a friend. They continued their conversation, catching up on old times, which lasted about two hours. They had so much in common. After all, it was she that convinced Mariam to sneak him into the house late at night when his father and mother argued. That situation took a toll on him.

Noah knew all about her. Her favorite color. The music she liked. Even about her family. Never had a man been so interested in her. How could she have been so blind? She was used to the assholes that only wanted to get in her pants.

They laughed and giggled at each other, like two children playing. The entire conversation was friendly and comfortable. And familiar. She didn't have to hide anything from him other than being a vampire. She told him she wanted him to leave the club because that wasn't a good place to hang out and he agreed while making light of the weird characters that occupied the place. He hadn't talked to the friends that he had recently met since then. Amara listened as it felt nice to feel normal, more like a human.

When she hung up the phone, there was a knock at her door. The loud noise still startled her. Mariam. Getting up and heading towards the door, she opened it. She had forgotten all about her coming over.

"Mariam!"

CHAPTER FIFTY-TWO

That morning while Amara was sleeping, the same morning that she suggested for them to hang out, Mariam was out having breakfast alone. Mariam missed her friend and didn't know what was going on with her. But she knew it was something.

Mariam had known her long enough to know when Amara was avoiding her. But for what? The scene in her apartment didn't feel like another rejection from a man. She knew Amara would cry her eyes out if it was. So, what was it?

They kept no secrets from each other, and when Amara's parents got into a tragic car accident and had passed away, it was Mariam's family that took her in. She had held her that night and begged her parents to take her. Amara's other family members didn't come around——- estranged and druggies.

Mariam's parents got custody of Amara to make her a permanent member of their family. Amara loved it, as well as Mariam. They were already best friends, and now they were going to be a family.

As little girls, they had become sisters and had formed a truly unbreakable bond. Even though Amara's parents' tragic end took a toll on her, at least she had Mariam, and that was all she ever needed from then on.

Mariam took a sip of her orange juice, replaying their moments as friends over and over in her head. There was no way that Amara would choose any man before her. So, what was it? She was going to understand it no matter what it took.

Mariam felt they were beginning to become estranged from one another and she didn't like that thought at all. She thought about how much Amara had changed since she met Lou. Was he the one behind her strange actions? Mariam thought about how she could only get hold of Amara at night. Amara slept during the day, and she used to be a morning person when she didn't have to work.

Mariam could barely get her to answer her phone, and every time she planned to do something with her, she was busy. Maybe it was depression? Or maybe Lou was controlling her actions? That's how mental abuse started. Mariam thought of many things and worried even more about Amara.

She continued to eat her breakfast. With her fork, she pushed parts of her scrambled eggs onto her plate from one side to the other. Her appetite had come and gone. It was a beautiful day, and she wished Amara was enjoying it with her.

She held up her hand and called the server over to her table. She asked her for the bill and watched as the server looked down at her uneaten plate in confusion. The woman removed the plate before her and walked off to get the bill.

Mariam knew Amara was asleep, but as soon as it became night, she was determined to see her friend. They had agreed on it. And no matter what, she was showing up at her door.

The server returned with the bill. She looked at the receipt, pulled out her credit card, and handed it back to her. She watched as the lady walked off. The woman had features that reminded her of Amara. Taking that as a sign, she was going to help her friend with whatever she had going on.

As she got up and left, a blonde-haired woman that she had noticed sitting alone seemed to watch her. She was holding a newspaper to cover her face, but she had caught her several times, removing the paper and glaring at her. She didn't even eat, thinking to herself. And she wondered if this was the same woman she had seen when she was eating out with Noah.

But she couldn't focus on her. She was more worried about her friend and as she quickly left, she glanced back one last time, just to make sure the suspicious woman wasn't following her.

She wasn't.

CHAPTER FIFTY-THREE

"Shocked to see me?" Mariam said as she pushed her way inside and looked around.

"Sort of. You usually call before you come," she softly replied as she shut the door. "What are you doing here?"

"Ummm, you didn't want to have breakfast, remember?" Mariam placed her hand on her hip. "I'm confused why you have been dodging me?"

"I'm so sorry—"

Mariam interrupted her before she could finish her sentence.

"I'm tired of hearing I'm sorry," Mariam snapped. "What is going on? I am your best friend, and you have never treated me this way."

"Whaddaya mean?" She knew what she meant, but she couldn't find the words to come out of her mouth. She needed to come up with something quickly.

Mariam sat down on the couch and placed her purse to the side of her. There was no way she was leaving until she got answers.

"We are always together. I gave you your space because of that hunk of a man you liked so much, but enough is enough. Is he the reason you don't want to be around me anymore?"

She stood there, powerless. It hurt Mariam, she could tell. She could feel her emotions. Hurting her was the last thing she would ever want to do to her. It wasn't as if she could just blurt out, "Hey, I'm a vampire," and that Lou had changed her into one. That was something that she would have to work up to.

"So much has gone on since that night, and I am going to tell you everything, I promise, but in due time." She looked at her sadly.

"Who are you right now? What do you mean in due time? When have we ever had secrets between us? You don't even look the same."

Mariam jumped up from the couch in fury, mad at the fact that she was acting as if she could not trust her. This was going to end now. She demanded to know what she wasn't telling her.

"Calm down," she said in a sharp tone.

When she looked at Mariam's face, she could tell that the tone of her voice outraged her even more. Speaking to Mariam like this was not going at all the way she had planned. But no time like the present. She thought about just blurting it out, but she knew Mariam wouldn't believe her. And then she would have to show her.

"Okay, I'll tell you everything," she finally broke.

She couldn't lie to her. This was her friend, her sister, and she knew Mariam was right. There had been no secrets between them. So why start now? Regardless of how the truth was going to sound, she deserved to know.

Mariam sat back down on the couch, waiting for her to respond. She watched as she walked over to the kitchen and grabbed two glasses and a whiskey bottle. The simple fact that she was pouring whiskey confused Mariam a little because she didn't drink like that, and she could sense that from her. This action seemed to repeat itself with drinking, but this was a way to suppress a vampire's craving.

Just as she was about to carry both drinks over to Mariam, there was another knock on her door. She placed the glasses down and went to answer the door. To her surprise, Victoria stood before her.

What are you doing here? She said in her head. She knew Victoria could read her thoughts, and she didn't want to alarm Mariam.

"Stopping you," Victoria said smugly. "I knew how you felt when I dropped you off the other night."

She pushed past her just like Mariam had done. Tonight was the night everyone was overpowering her. Once again, she shut the door and glared at both of her friends.

She threw her hands up in the air as if to say she gave up and went back to the kitchen, grabbed another glass, and poured another drink, this one for Victoria. She would not let her stop her. Mariam needed to know the truth.

Victoria walked over to Mariam and held out her hand to introduce herself. She watched them closely.

"Hi, I'm Victoria. You must be Mariam?" She formed a smile on her face.

"Yes. Don't I know you?" Mariam replied, shaking Victoria's hand. "I do. You are the girl from the bar... that was with Lou."

"Ummm, yeah," Victoria hesitantly responded. She knew she had compelled her to forget about her driving her home, but she should've compelled her to forget them. And right now she wanted to compel her to forget about all the weirdness coming off of Amara lately. But she was going to let Amara handle that.

Thank God for perfect timing, she thought as Amara walked over to both of them, handing each one a glass. Victoria grabbed hers and took a swig.

"Since when do you drink this stuff?" Mariam questioned Amara while looking into her glass.

"A lot has changed," she explained until Victoria interrupted her.

"Until she met me." Victoria glared at her.

She knew what Victoria was trying to do. Mariam deserves to know. She spoke in her head once again, knowing that Victoria would pick it up, and switched her eyes towards her, glaring. Victoria was supposed to see that she was serious. She understood it might be dangerous for Mariam, but they didn't keep secrets from each other.

"Who are you?" Mariam replied.

"A friend. More like a friend of a friend." Victoria once again smiled. She was looking over at her to see the look of disgust on her face. But she shrugged her off.

Mariam looked at both Victoria and Amara. Not knowing what was going on between them, she was becoming frustrated. She didn't care about Victoria; she only wanted to know what was going on with Amara.

"Okay, stop this!" Mariam yelled as she placed her glass down. "Enough is enough; both of you are hiding something, and I want to know what it is."

Once again, Mariam jumped off the couch, but this time a pointed quill from the couch snagged her arm. It scratched her just enough to make her bleed.

"Ow, shoot," Mariam said as she grabbed her arm. "Damn, that hurts, and I'm bleeding." She angrily looked up at her, but then a look of shock came across her face.

Amara's black veins had formed on her face and her canines emerged.

And she couldn't stop herself.

"Amara, Stop!" Victoria yelled as she jumped up, ready to stop her.

Victoria knew what was about to happen and could smell the blood from Mariam's arm throughout the air. There was no way that Amara was going to stop herself. Friend or no friend, the smell of her blood was too strong.

Mariam stood there in shock, and her body froze. She couldn't move and didn't know what to do. What the hell? Was this her friend standing before her, not looking like herself, but like a monster? Chills ran down Mariam's spine. She backed up slightly, almost tripping over her two feet.

Victoria quickly jumped into action. She grabbed Amara just in time before she attacked Mariam, throwing her across the room. But Amara was still in attack mode. She lunged towards Victoria, and with one swift move, Victoria put her on the ground. Using all of her strength, Victoria held her down as Amara struggled to get up.

"Get off me!" Amara yelled. Her fangs had emerged, and her hunger took over. She tried to raise her, but Victoria was too strong for her.

"Remember who she is!" Victoria yelled back. "Mariam, your friend!"

It took a minute for it to register, but Amara stopped struggling once she heard her name. Mariam, oh my God! Her face went back to normal, as she became calmer.

"Control yourself," Victoria told her. She wasn't about to let her up until she was for sure Amara could do just that.

Taking a couple of deep breaths, Amara closed her eyes. After a couple of seconds, she seemed to be back to normal. She slowly rose as Victoria let her up. What just happened?

"You almost killed your friend," Victoria said as she rose off the ground. She dusted herself off and shot Amara an angry look.

Amara looked over at Mariam, who had crouched down in a corner. Tears ran down her face, and she was profusely shaking. Amara felt her sense of terror and fear; she couldn't move. Not even to console her friend. What have I done? She had never seen Mariam so frightened in her life.

"You haven't fed, leave… go feed," Victoria sternly said as she pointed towards the front door. "Now! I've got her."

Amara looked at Victoria and then over at Mariam again. Getting up and standing on her feet, the only thing she could do was trust Victoria. Amara wasted no time, and with vampiric speed, she rushed out the front door.

Once Amara was gone, Victoria looked over at Mariam. She was still frightened, scared to look up, and shaking. Victoria felt sorry for her. She forgot how it felt to be a human and to witness such a thing. She walked over to her and stood there.

"Please don't hurt me." Mariam put her hands over her head, trying to protect herself.

"I will not hurt you," she breathed.

Victoria reached down and grabbed both of Mariam's shoulders. Helping her as she stood up, she saw the fear in her eyes. Sympathy ran through Victoria. She could feel every emotion that Mariam was feeling. Her confusion, fear, hurt, and pain were all over it, Victoria felt it.

Mariam finally stood up and looked at her like a helpless child. She was still fearful of her and didn't know what to expect. But she let Victoria guide her to the couch to have a seat. Victoria then headed towards the bathroom and retrieved a first aid kit to bandage Mariam up.

Once Victoria returned, she kneeled in front of Mariam. Then she slowly grabbed her arm and treated the wound. She knew Mariam was watching her closely, so she did not make any sudden moves that might frighten her further.

"It's okay," Victoria said, trying to console her.

"What just happened?" Mariam responded. Her voice was still trembling.

"Something that I was trying to stop Amara from doing."

"And what's that? Killing me?"

Tears streamed down Mariam's face. She was so confused but knew that the friend that'd been there all of her life was not the same person. What was that? Who was that? She questioned herself. Her face? She wasn't able to shake the image out of her head.

"A vampire," Victoria replied.

She had been reading her thoughts, and she couldn't believe she allowed those words to even come from her mouth. She had always been strict in the rules of being a vampire. But at this moment, against all her beliefs, she broke all her rules.

And now here she was, doing what she was trying to stop Amara from doing. Telling the truth about what they were. She couldn't help herself, and some part of her felt bad that all this had happened.

Mariam seemed nice and only wanted to look out for Amara. The same thing she had been doing since Amara became a vampire.

Mariam didn't speak. It took her a moment to collect her thoughts. Had Amara come out and said she was a vampire, she would have laughed in her face. But after the events that just happened and what she had witnessed, the situation wasn't funny at all.

"A vampire?" She shook her head in disbelief, but she knew Victoria was serious.

"Yes," Victoria replied. She finished bandaging up Mariam's arm. "All done" She smiled at her and then stood up.

Mariam looked down at her arm and then back up at Victoria. She had so many questions and calmed down enough to listen to whatever Victoria had to say and needed to understand. She was grateful for Victoria at that moment. I need to thank her for saving my life; she thought to herself. Mariam couldn't wrap her mind around the thought that her best friend was about to attack her.

"No problem," Victoria proudly said. She was reading Mariam's thoughts. She was pleased that she could save her life. Yeah, I'm a hero, Victoria thought, putting a big grin on her face. Hearing that made her feel good inside.

Victoria then walked over to the kitchen and grabbed the bottle of whiskey and two more glasses. She poured the liquor into them, filling them up to the rim. When she finished pouring, she walked back over to Mariam and handed her the drink.

"You're going to need this," she told Mariam, watching her grab the glass from her hand.

Mariam didn't like to drink, but at this moment she knew Victoria was right. She needed to calm her nerves and hope that Amara didn't return the way she'd left. Taking a big gulp of whiskey, she turned her face up as she swallowed it and almost threw up at the taste.

"Lightweight, huh?" Victoria giggled.

"Yeah, something like that," Mariam replied as she shook her head in disgust. She looked over at the door. "Is she—"

"She will be fine; she just needs to feed." Victoria took a drink of whiskey. "You were almost her dinner."

Victoria laughed until she looked over at Mariam, who looked horrified at that thought. She realized it was way too soon to be joking. She straightened her face, looked away, and took another drink of whiskey. Damn, that was a poor joke. She set her glass down on the coffee table.

"I'm sorry," she said. "Sometimes, when we are hungry, we can't control ourselves when we smell blood." She pointed at Mariam's bandaged-up arm.

"Have you fed?" she wearily replied.

Victoria picked up her glass. Giggling, she smiled at her and headed towards the kitchen again. Victoria was already liking Mariam. Just by her reply, she could tell she had a little sense of humor about herself.

"Of course. Besides, I'm older, and I can control myself."

Victoria poured herself another drink. This time, she grabbed the bottle and headed back to the couch to have a seat. She looked at Mariam's half-empty glass and filled it back up.

"Fed? On humans? Because that's what vampires feed on," Mariam nervously said.

"Sometimes but not always." Victoria took another sip of whiskey. She pointed at Mariam's glass for her to take a drink as well.

Mariam saw Victoria pointing and grabbed her glass again, taking another drink; this time, it wasn't as bad going down.

"How? When?" Mariam had so many questions to ask and her head was spinning with them. She wanted to know when Amara had turned from being her best friend to a vampire.

"Okay, none of that matters. Just know that I'm a vampire, and so is Amara. We are not the only ones, and usually, humans never know about us." Victoria glared at her.

"Who am I going to tell?" Mariam questioned. She already knew what Victoria's look meant.

"Hopefully, no one," she harshly replied. Victoria's face turned from friendly to questioning. Victoria had decided to not compel her over the information she had just said.

Mariam felt a knot in her throat and swallowed hard. She could tell that Victoria was not joking anymore. By the look on Victoria's face, Mariam knew she meant business. I hate to find out what would happen if I did tell some-one, Mariam thought to herself. She took another sip of her drink. Just how quickly Victoria switched her mood made Mariam feel nervous all over again.

"I told you I will not hurt you," Victoria softened her voice.

She could hear Mariam's heart speeding up, and she wanted her to stay calm. "You just need to understand that if you do, mine and Amara's life would be in danger."

Mariam said nothing. She just shook her head up and down, agreeing that she wouldn't say a word. There was a long, awkward silence, and then they both heard the door. Mariam hurried towards the end of the couch, frightened.

She knew it had to be Amara.

CHAPTER FIFTY-FIVE

Amara walked in the door without looking at Mariam or Victoria. She turned her back towards them, slowly shutting the door. She wasn't sure what Mariam was going to say and how to apologize to her for her actions.

After closing the front door, she stood there for a brief second, taking a deep breath and finally turning around. She first looked at Victoria, who smiled at her and then at Mariam, who was staring at her fearfully. No one said anything. Then finally, Mariam broke the silence.

"Did you feed?" she stuttered.

Her question threw her off guard. "Umm... yeah." The fact that those words came out of Mariam's mouth shocked her.

She didn't even think Mariam would still be here or asking her if she had fed. What did Victoria tell her? And why wasn't Mariam frightened to death of her? After all, she tried to attack her. She watched as Victoria grabbed her glass of whiskey, got up, and walked toward her.

"Yes... I told her," Victoria said while handing her the glass. "As you can see by her questions."

She looked at her in shock. Victoria was the last person she'd expected to break a vampire rule. But she was relieved that she did. She grabbed the glass from Victoria and took a drink.

"You told her?" she replied.

"Nah, the boogeyman." Victoria threw up her hands, shook her head, and walked back towards the couch to have a seat. She felt as if she had no faith in her at all, and this made her a little upset.

"Are you okay?" she questioned Mariam.

"As long as I will not be your meal." Mariam wasn't as fearful anymore and noticed the liquor was taking effect.

Victoria laughed. She has a sense of humor, she thought to herself after hearing Mariam's response. Victoria liked her and understood why Amara was so fond of her. "Maybe humans aren't so bad."

"So, you got her drunk and told her what we are?" She glanced at Victoria.

"To be fair, I told her and then got her drunk." Victoria gave her a big grin and giggled.

"Let's lay you down," she said to Mariam as she walked to her.

The whiskey had taken full effect, and Mariam was no longer capable of holding her head up or being fearful. The room was spinning, and she just wanted to lie down.

"I hope you know I will never hurt you. I never meant to put you in this situation," Amara whispered. "I hope you will forgive me."

Mariam said nothing in response and Amara could only sense her drunkenness coming off her. Nothing she could immediately read. She would have to wait until she woke up to see how Mariam truly felt about the situation.

She wasn't a vampire at this moment, but a friend that was helping her. Mariam allowed her to pick her up and put her in the bed.

She grabbed her cover and placed it over her. "I love you, Mariam," Amara whispered. Mariam mumbled something, but she couldn't understand her drunken slur. She just rubbed her head until Mariam closed her eyes and fell asleep.

Once she knew Mariam was sound asleep, she headed towards the couch where Victoria was sitting. She dropped next to her and then dropped her head back. She was so glad that Mariam didn't get hurt. Thank God for Victoria. Raising her head again, she grabbed Mariam's whiskey glass and finished it.

"You're welcome." Victoria gave her a smug smile.

"You knew, huh?"

"I didn't know it was going to happen like this, but there was a high possibility that your friend would have become a snack," Victoria replied.

"I thought I could handle it. Had she not cut herself, I would've been fine," she defended herself.

"The thing is, you didn't, and so it's not good to be friends with humans," Victoria scorned her. "We are now the predator, and they are the prey."

"Why are you upset?"

"You still don't understand!" Victoria jumped up, "I just broke a vampire rule, and now we could be in danger because of your stubborn actions… again."

"I never asked you to come over," she yelled back. She projected her pent-up anger over what had happened to Victoria.

"Thank God I did, or you would've had one dead friend." Victoria got angry. "When I tell you to do something, just do it."

"You are not my boss!" She stood up. "Are you Silas now?"

"You're right, I'm not!" Victoria yelled. "I'm only trying to help you, but you don't want it. You are a *newborn* and know nothing of this world. Stop thinking only of yourself." Victoria stomped towards the door.

"Like you? You only want me for your stupid army of *newbies*."

She stood there glaring at Victoria. She could feel the anger coming off of her, and even though she didn't want to admit it, Victoria was right. Ever since she had become a vampire, she had been making foolish moves, and this time it almost cost Mariam her life and now she had offended Victoria.

She took a glance over at Mariam sleeping. Their yelling was causing her to toss and turn. The last thing she wanted was for her to wake up. She knew she needed to calm down and think about her actions, for once.

"Wait," she spoke up and said. "Don't leave… I'm sorry."

She sat back down on the couch and held her head in her hands. The entire night was a big mess, and she couldn't lose Victoria. Not now, not ever. She knew she needed her and was grateful she was even here.

"Maybe we should compel her not to remember?" Victoria said as she walked back towards the couch.

"No, I want her to know." She kept her head down. "She deserves to know the truth." Finally, looking up at Victoria, she had formed tears in her eyes. She knew Victoria would never understand their relationship, but this was one person who needed to know everything that had happened to her.

"Okay, I'm going to stay and make sure you don't devour your friend," Victoria sarcastically said. She hated to see anyone cry around her. "But you better make sure she says nothing to anyone."

"I will," she quickly replied as she wiped the tears from her face.

"And no more human friends," Victoria replied. "She will be the only one."

Victoria still didn't feel this was a good idea, but she was going to let her have her way this time. In the back of her mind, she still didn't trust Mariam not to say anything. She secretly worried about *The Order* and what they would do if they found out.

Amara shook her head in agreement. Then she remembered Noah; she had set up a date with him. He was a friend, and she liked him. She tried not to think about him, or the date that she had planned with him. Knowing that Victoria was probably reading her thoughts, she thought about something else. But by the look on Victoria's face, it was too late.

"Absolutely not!"

CHAPTER FIFTY-SIX

Conrad had waited until daylight before walking outside of Father Borman's home. He barely slept the whole night. Continuously jumping at every noise, he was fearful she would return. Thoughts of the female vampire ripping the priest and Levy apart played over and over in his head.

Feeling guilty that he had just left them behind, he struggled with that thought. What could he have done? She would have killed him, too. She was way too fast and strong. He shook his head in misery, as he felt he was the reason that they were no longer alive.

He knew he needed to check on the bodies. Dreading the scene, he finally mustered up the nerve to go outside and head toward the barn. Not only was he emotionally drained, but physically drained as well.

Slowly heading towards the barn, he glanced at the sun that stung his eyes. At that moment, he was grateful to see it and that it was daylight. He knew as long as it shined, the sun protected him from the creatures of the night.

The closer he got to the barn, the more he sweated. The doors no longer stood as they once did, for the female vampire had knocked them off their hinges. He had seen nothing like that, only in the movies. Conrad paused for a minute before he moved any closer. He debated with himself whether he even wanted to see it. What lay ahead?

He took a deep breath and moved closer to the entrance. The full scene of what happened was visible to him. He saw Levy's body lying to the left of him. It was bloody and mangled, and Father Borman's dead body was a couple of feet in front of him, in the same condition.

Conrad turned his head in horror at the sight of both bodies. He couldn't believe the damage that she had done to them. The destruction that she'd left behind was unimaginable. None of their planning had worked. She had ambushed them, and at that moment, the vampire had killed them with no effort. What went wrong? he thought to himself. He was sure Levy knew how to defend himself against such an attack.

Then visions of his brother flashed in his head. Tears streamed down Conrad's face. He couldn't save him, and he couldn't save them, he said to himself. Then he balled up his fists and cursed at God for not being there. A wave of anger he had never felt before rose in him.

After all, if vampires were real, then there had to be a God. But where was he? Conrad dropped to his knees and sobbed even harder. He pounded his fists on the ground. He had so much rage in him he didn't know what to do.

While feeling sorry for himself, he heard a car pull up out front. He quickly wiped his tears and looked back over at the bodies. The feeling of rage quickly turned to fear. He hoped they didn't think he did this. Nobody would believe the truth! He panicked and hurried from the barn.

The man getting out of the car hadn't noticed which direction Conrad came from. He was too busy pulling out bags of groceries. When he saw Conrad, he gave him a quick smile and continued to pull out bags, placing them on the ground.

"Hey, can you give me a hand?" the gentleman spoke.

Conrad was still in shock from the night before, and the dead bodies that were still lying in the barn. He didn't know if he should just tell the man or help him with his groceries. He stood there in a trance.

"Hey buddy, did you hear me?" The man looked up and saw Conrad's face this time.

The man saw the distressed look all over Conrad's face. He stopped what he was doing and rushed over to him. The man put his hand on his shoulder. He noticed Conrad seemed paralyzed in fear and could do nothing but look forward without saying a word.

"Are you okay?" the man said. But Conrad still did not respond. The man became concerned. "Where is Father Borman?"

Moving past Conrad, he ran into the priest's home. It took him a minute before he returned from outside the home. With a confused look on his face, he noticed Conrad was still standing in the same place he had left him.

He walked towards Conrad, and this time he grabbed him by the shoulders and shook him. Snapping him out of the trance that he was in, Conrad could finally look the man in the face.

"Where is Father Borman?" the man repeated.

CHAPTER FIFTY-SEVEN

I'm a friend of Father Borman," the man said. "Now where is he?"

Conrad's eyes filled with tears. He pointed towards the barn in the back. The man looked at Conrad and then the barn before he took off running towards it. He stopped short of entering when he noticed someone had knocked both doors off.

He sauntered towards the entrance. Once he walked in, he noticed Levy's body and then Father Borman's body. He ran to Levy first and checked his pulse. Dead. Then he stood up, looked over at the priest, and slowly walked towards him.

As he approached his body, he held his head down and knelt beside him. He touched his arms, feeling for a pulse, but deep down, he already knew that he was dead. He screamed out in anguish.

Conrad heard the scream and ran towards the barn. He knew what the man probably thought when he saw the dead bodies, but he had to explain what had taken place. Running into the barn, he stopped as he watched the man crouching over Father Borman's body.

"I didn't do this," Conrad cried out. He got nervous. He didn't know what the man was thinking or what he was about to do.

The man did not respond to what Conrad had said. He just looked at the priest lying before him. He drifted Father Borman's head to the side to see the chunk of his neck ripped off.

Finally, standing up, he slowly turned around and gazed at Conrad. His face turned red, and anger filled his body. He looked back over at Levy and clenched his fist, then he looked back at Conrad.

"I didn't do this," Conrad repeated.

"I know," the man replied.

"It was the woman," Conrad tried to explain, but the man interrupted him.

Then it registered inside Conrad's head that the man had believed him. He looked at him in confusion. He couldn't believe that he believed him and didn't expect this response at all.

"Help me with their bodies," the man said.

Conrad was shocked. Did he just say help him with the bodies?

"Who are you?" he questioned, but the man ignored him. He watched the man walk past him and to the outside of the barn. Conrad was still stuck in a state of confusion.

After a couple of minutes, the man returned with an ax and a shovel. Conrad was more focused on the shovel in his hand. The man looked over at Conrad with a blank face. Conrad wasn't sure what the man was about to do. Was he going to attack him? Conrad backed away from him.

The man walked past him and headed towards Levy's body. Conrad took a deep breath. He was sure that the man was about to strike him, but apparently, that wasn't his intention.

"Come on!" the man yelled, dropping the shovel beside the body but still holding the ax in his hand.

Snapping out of his state of confusion, Conrad wasn't sure what he was supposed to do, but he hurried towards the man and Levy's body. He watched as the man swung the ax over his shoulder and then swung it down towards Levy's neck. Decapitating him.

"Oh, my God!" Conrad yelled as he turned his head from the horrid sight. "What the hell is wrong with you?"

"There's no time for this," the man replied. He touched Conrad on the shoulder, causing him to jump. "Start a fire," he said and handed him a lighter.

"Do what?" Conrad was so confused.

"Start a fire!" the man yelled again. "Use the metal barrel and some hay, start it now!" He pointed towards the barrel that was in the barn's corner.

Conrad had no clue what to do, other than what the man had asked him. He rushed towards it, grabbed a handful of hay, and began stuffing the barrel. Once finished, he lit the hay on fire and watched the flames blaze.

He heard another grunt and looked at the man. This time, he was over Father Borman's body. Taking another swing, he decapitated his head as well. This man is crazy, Conrad thought. He didn't know whether to run away or stay.

"Get over here!" the man yelled at him again.

Conrad's decision didn't matter; the man decided for him. He guessed he was staying. Walking towards him cautiously, looking at the blood splattered all over his face, and his clothes, he watched as the man pointed at Levy's head.

"Grab it and throw it in the fire," he told him. He watched as Conrad hesitated. "Get out of your feelings and do it now."

Conrad swallowed hard before he walked closer to the head. He wanted to throw up but kept it together. With two fingers, he bent down and pinched a piece of hair, pulling it up off the ground.

He turned his head as he kept the decapitated body part at arm's length. Then he strolled to the fire pit and dropped his head in. The fire blazed even harder, and Conrad looked away from the sight of it.

When he turned his head, the man was right behind him with Father Borman's head in his hands, and with no problem, he tossed the head into the fire as well. Is this happening? Conrad thought. Then the blood from the head flew all over Conrad, as the man threw it, and when Conrad realized blood was on him, he freaked out.

"Calm down," the man told him. "We're almost finished; we have to bury the bodies."

The man rushed back towards Levy's body. Grabbing the shovel, he dug a hole in the ground.

"Are you going to help me?" He stopped what he was doing and looked toward Conrad. "There's another shovel on the side of the barn."

Conrad felt disgusted because he had blood from a decapitated head on him. But once again, he followed the man's commands. Trying to wipe the blood off of him, he headed out of the barn in the same way that the man had previously gone. When he reached the side, he saw a shovel sticking from the ground.

He walked over towards it and pulled it out of the ground. What the hell was he doing? Decapitation and burying bodies? Conrad tried to take a minute just to process it all, but he heard the man yelling for him inside the barn.

He rushed back in with the shovel in his hand. The man pointed at a spot on the ground next to Father Borman's body. Conrad knew that the man wanted him to dig, and that's what he did.

"Make it deep enough to cover the whole body," the man said. "We need to finish this before dark."

Dark!

CHAPTER FIFTY-EIGHT

The thought of the sun going down terrorized Conrad all over again. The last thing he wanted to be was outside for the woman to come back and kill them both. He dug faster. He wanted to finish this and get into the house as soon as possible.

It took them quite a while to finish digging the graves. Once finished, they pushed both bodies into the holes and covered them up. Then they went to trash the groceries that were ruined by the man's car.

The sun was going down, and they quickly rushed into Father Borman's house for their safety for the night. Conrad had a seat on the couch, and the man went to the kitchen to look for something to eat.

"Are you hungry?" the man said.

He grabbed a loaf of bread and set it down on the counter. Then he went to the refrigerator to pull out items to make sandwiches. He cut up a tomato and spread mayo on the slices of bread before him.

"What?" Conrad responded.

"Are you hungry?" the man repeated himself.

Conrad looked at him, confused. He couldn't believe this man was fixing sandwiches after he had just decapitated two men and buried their bodies. Who was he? Conrad was still trying to process everything that they had done and yet didn't know the reason they had.

Then Conrad looked at his blood-stained clothes and looked at the bloodstains on the man as well. Who could think about food? All Conrad wanted to do was wash the dried-up blood off of him.

"Who are you, and what was that?" Conrad asked.

"My name is Tyler," he responded without stopping what he was doing.

"Well, Tyler, what the hell did we just do out there?"

Tyler finished making the sandwiches and walked over at Conrad. He handed him a plate with a sandwich and chips. Then Tyler sat down in Father Borman's chair. Conrad watched him as he took a bite and chewed his food. The blood had dried on his hands and Conrad couldn't believe that he was still eating. It took a moment before he responded.

"That was a vampire attack out there, and from the items that I saw, I'm sure Levy was trying to train you in his simple way."

"You know about them?"

"I sure do. What we couldn't have was Father Borman or Levy turning into one of those things. That vampire could've easily given them her blood without us knowing. It's just better to be safe than sorry."

Tyler continued to eat his sandwich. Then he set his plate down, got up, and headed towards the kitchen once again.

"What do you mean, turn?" Conrad responded while looking down at his sandwich. Turning up his nose at it, he had no appetite to eat.

"I've seen them kill men, and the same men become them; there is one way to make sure they don't come back, and that's what we did out there."

Tyler grabbed two glasses and began pouring water into them. He walked back over to Conrad and sat back down. He handed him a glass of water and ate again. How was this not bothering him? Conrad had so many questions.

Conrad looked towards the screen door. It was now night. The main door wasn't closed, and it made him nervous. He got up from the couch, shut it, and locked it. He wasn't taking any chances with the woman that attacked them.

"You're a part of this world now, whether you like it or not," Tyler told him. He took a sip of water and set his cup back down. "Now that you know they exist, they will come for you."

Tyler's words echoed in Conrad's head. Come for me? Cold chills ran through his body. He backed up from the door and sat back down. He couldn't understand why Tyler was so relaxed and collected about the whole situation.

Everything was moving so fast. Tyler's reactions and ways confused Conrad, but he was grateful that he was there. Conrad didn't know what he was going to do or how he was going to handle the situation of the dead bodies that were in the barn.

Conrad continually looked at Tyler as he watched him eat. All he could think about was the dried-up blood still on his hands as Tyler took bite after bite. This made Conrad's stomach turn and knot up. But he still kept watching him like some dreadful accident he couldn't turn away from. He looked Tyler up and down, analyzing him.

Tyler was a built man that seemed confident and well disciplined. He was brave but appeared to be a little arrogant at the same time. The structure of his body and his muscles told of a man that continuously worked out. Possibly military? Conrad thought.

He could tell this man was no stranger to vampires. To Conrad, he seemed to know a lot about them. Levy knew about vampires, but Tyler was more confident with them. It didn't faze him at all to spring into action and do what he had to do to the bodies of his friends.

"Who are you?" Conrad repeated the same question that he had asked twice before.

"I'm a vampire hunter."

Holy shit!

CHAPTER FIFTY-NINE

Conrad sat there, stunned. What the hell is a vampire hunter? He didn't know what to think about Tyler. Who in the world would attempt to hunt those monsters? But then again, he was trying to kill the one that had killed his brother.

"What do you mean?"

"Exactly what I said," Tyler replied.

"Like Levy?"

"Nothing like them." Tyler finally finished his sandwich. "Father Borman and Levy only wanted to have the means to protect themselves; however, I destroy as many as I can."

"So, you hunt them?" Conrad questioned.

"Yes," Tyler replied with a straight face.

"How? They're so strong and vicious."

"That may be so." Tyler leaned in closer. "We have to be fearless. Just because they are undead does not mean that we can't stop them."

"Have you killed any?"

"Of course!"

It shocked Conrad to hear this, but by the look on Tyler's face, he knew he was telling the truth. Levy had shown him items to help protect himself, just in case they encountered a vampire, but that didn't work out too well.

Father Borman had told him that there were others out there that knew vampires existed and looking at Tyler, it was now confirmed. Conrad wondered if there were other vampire hunters as well.

Thinking to himself, he thought about how many vampires were out in the world. How many times had he passed one? Were they that common? Then he thought about what Tyler had said earlier.

"What did you mean when you said they would look for me?"

"Vampires don't like anyone knowing they exist; they try to hide in the shadows of the night. If they ever found out that you know they exist, they will try to take you out. Kill you."

"So, I need to be worried."

"Very much so, my friend." Tyler gave him a slight smirk. "Don't worry; I'll train you properly."

Looking at his blood-stained clothes again and thinking about what had happened before, Conrad didn't know if he wanted to be part of what Tyler was a part of or be a vampire hunter. He couldn't see himself chasing down vampires and killing them. Just being terrified of the vampire woman, he didn't have any confidence in himself.

Tyler looked like he could take one of them on. Conrad gave him a "yeah, right" look. Even if Tyler was to train him, that didn't mean he could go through with it. Hunting vampires? That was something he needed to think about.

The sight of his brother flashed in his head. Conrad thought about the entire purpose of following the one that killed him and the reason he ended up here. Why do all of this if he did not avenge his brother's killer? He knew he didn't go through all of this for nothing. He nodded his head at Tyler in agreement.

Tyler had been noticing Conrad consistently looking down at his clothes since the moment they had come in. He wanted Conrad to get used to the sight of blood. That was the whole reason he hadn't washed his hands off while eating. He knew what he was doing, and he was trying to break Conrad in.

"Go take a shower and get some rest," Tyler said to him. "Training will begin in the morning."

He wasn't looking forward to him training him to kill vampires, but what else could he do? Conrad was in too deep.

Conrad didn't reply; he just got up and headed down the hallway. It was weird being in someone else's house that had just died. But he had to stay in it another night until it was safe to leave in the morning.

He looked around at each door until he finally found a bathroom. He had stayed in the front room the whole night before, too terrified to move. He hadn't eaten, slept, or attempted to use the bathroom.

He felt better since Tyler was there. He could relax some. Looking down at his bloody clothes for what seemed like the hundredth time, he replayed the events that had happened earlier. His stomach knotted up. He didn't know if it was because of hunger or because it sickened him by what he had done.

Conrad looked around the bathroom and found a clean shirt hanging up. He guessed this would do. Then he looked in the closet and found a towel and a washcloth. Moving towards the sink, he took a minute just to look at himself.

The bags under his eyes were heavy. His hair was all over the place, and splatters of blood were on his face. He looked like how he felt. He shook his head and turned on the faucet. Wiping his face-off, he couldn't believe that he had thrown a human head in a fire pit. Who am I? he thought to himself.

He took a deep breath and took off his bloody clothes. His life had changed drastically since the night his brother had died. Leave it to Roy to introduce him to the world of vampires. The thought of that made him giggle briefly. His brother always seemed to get him into some form of mess.

Then the thought of vampires and vampire hunters made him giggle even more. He still hadn't accepted that fact. But he was part of this new world now, and he had to prepare for whatever lay ahead.

While Conrad was cleaning himself off, Tyler prepared a cot on the floor for him to sleep. By the way Conrad freaked out, he knew he wouldn't feel comfortable sleeping in Father Borman's bed. He didn't mind giving him the couch and sleeping on the floor.

He knew deep down that Conrad had what it took to be a vampire hunter. Not everyone could handle such a thing, but the fact he'd helped him instead of running off told him a lot about his character.

After about an hour, a fresh Conrad appeared from the hallway. He looked a lot better than he did when he went in. Conrad saw the corners of Tyler's mouth form into a smile. Then he noticed the cot on the floor and the couch made into somewhat of a bed. His sandwich and glass of water were still sitting on the end table.

"Eat and get your rest," Tyler said before heading down the hallway to clean up as well. "You're going to need it."

CHAPTER SIXTY

Conrad laid down on the couch. He was exhausted and didn't even want to think about anything that had taken place the night before or earlier that day. As he heard the shower running, he looked at the ceiling. He closed his eyes and dozed off.

Conrad couldn't believe that he had even fallen asleep. He had such a hard time sleeping before Tyler showed up. Maybe the presence of Tyler being there put him somewhat at ease and made him feel safe. If it weren't for the smell of eggs and bacon waking him up, he probably would still be sleeping.

"Good morning, sunshine,. Tyler giggled as he placed scrambled eggs from the skillet onto a plate. "Hope you like your eggs scrambled."

Conrad wiped his eyes and sat up on the couch. Stretching his arms, he was glad that he could get some rest and see the sunlight coming through the blinds.

"Yeah, that's fine," he replied. "What time is it?"

"Seven am," Tyler said. He walked over to Conrad with a plate of food in his hand. "Eat up; you're going to need your strength."

The food smelled great, and Conrad was hungry. He ate while thinking about what Tyler had in store for him. He knew he wasn't physically fit, but for some odd reason, he felt his situation was about to change.

Tyler handed Conrad a t-shirt and a pair of shorts. Conrad stopped eating for a second and looked at them.

"Don't worry, they're my clothes." Tyler smiled. "I went out to my car to get them while you were asleep."

That was a relief to Conrad's ears. After all, he was still wearing a dead man's shirt. Just the thought of that sent more chills down his spine. He continued eating his food. He knew Tyler had a big day planned for him.

After they had finished breakfast, Tyler walked toward the barn. Conrad followed closely behind him. He wished they would just leave the property altogether, but that's not what Tyler had in mind.

Once they were inside, Conrad looked at the barrel and the two fresh graves on the ground. It didn't bother him as bad as it did before, maybe because they'd covered the bodies this time.

"There's space in here to train and the weapons that Levy left behind," Tyler told him. "First off, we have to get you in shape, and show you how to use this correctly." He had grabbed the stake that was on the ground and began tossing it in the air.

He watched as Tyler held the stake, did a forward roll on the ground, and launched it into a bale of hay. Damn, he's good, Conrad thought. He watched Tyler get up from the ground, walk over to the stake, and pull it out.

"Straight in the heart," Tyler said. "It won't kill them, but it will stop them in their tracks."

"Levy told me something."

"Forget what Levy told you; I'm going to tell you what you need to know and show you how to do it… right."

Some things that Tyler touched on showed that Levy had been right, but other things like the bag of rice weren't. Tyler explained to him it was always good to have holy water, but garlic would protect him if it were a sudden attack.

He asked Conrad precisely what happened when the woman vampire came through the barn, and Conrad gave him a play-by-play of the incident. Tyler told him that if they had garlic on their necks or even on them, the smell alone would have kept her from biting them. Vampires can't stand the smell of garlic, and it acts as a repellent with them.

Tyler paused for a minute and told Conrad to come over and have a seat beside him. He then walked over to a bale of hay and sat upon it. He watched as Conrad did what he asked him to do.

"Before we start with the physical stuff, let me give you some background on the monsters that we are dealing with," Tyler said.

"Vampires can walk among the living during the day. There are very few of them that can. They are much older, stronger, and faster than the ones that hide in the shadows. I wouldn't attempt to kill one of them, not unless they tried to attack me first.

"They can walk in the sunlight?" Conrad questioned. His eyes were wide open, and this didn't make Conrad feel comfortable at all.

"Yes, some of them can and witches," Tyler responded.

"Witches?" Conrad questioned. First vampires, now witches? At that moment, he realized how clueless he was, but nothing surprised him anymore.

"There are more things out there than just vampires."

CHAPTER SIXTY-ONE

Tyler explained to him that in the world they live in, some people go their whole lives without knowing that these supernatural beings exist. Some people, like them, run into them, and then they are part of their world.

Conrad listened as Tyler told him that witches dislike helping vampires; they are their enemies. Centuries ago, they worked together, and they cast a spell on a vampire to walk in the sunlight. From that one vampire, he created others, and those of his *sire* line could do the same.

"How do you know all of this?" Conrad said.

"That's for another time." Tyler smiled.

He went back to telling Conrad more basic but essential information that he needed to know. If he even attempted to explain the whole vampire history, it would be night again.

"How do you know who a vampire is and who is not?" Conrad quickly said.

"Great question."

He used garlic as an example. Garlic was the one thing that may save his life with no training. He told Conrad that wearing garlic in a crowd of people, even a small amount on the neck, can draw them out and cause them to notice the person wearing it.

"Even if humans can't smell the scent of garlic, the vampire sure can, and they will turn their noses in disgust, trying to get away from it. Pay attention to people's reactions; the vampires will hold their noses and do certain things that are noticeable. It's horrific to them, almost like the smell of a dead body to us, but times ten," Tyler continued.

"Be ready because they will follow you. A human doesn't just go around wearing garlic. So, if you are, then odds are you know about them, and like I told you before—"

"They will come for me," Conrad interrupted.

"Correct." Tyler patted Conrad on the shoulder. "You're a quick learner. That's good."

Then Tyler talked about mirrors and their impact on them. He told Conrad to carry a small compact mirror as a woman has in her purse, and that this minor item would help him out more than ever.

"Mirrors work well, so carry one," he proclaimed. "Vampires sometimes flicker in them. If you suspect someone to be a vampire, see if their reflection flickers. However, make sure it doesn't reflect some kind of light towards them. Then they will know you are watching them." Tyler wagged his finger at him before continuing.

"The point is to be invisible, for them not to be aware of you," he warned. "Catching them off guard can be a lifesaver."

Tyler wasn't sure about the whole mirror thing, for he had never attempted it himself, but it was something he wanted to try, and even though he seemed like an expert on vampires, not everything he knew was right, but he wanted to sound bold in front of Conrad. After all, he had killed several vampires and Conrad wouldn't have known what was right or wrong. He took pride in the way Conrad listened to his every word.

Tyler explained little things like vampires casting no shadows, and how having a gun with real silver bullets could slow them down. But just like everything else, Conrad would need to be trained on pulling a weapon fast enough.

Tyler told him to carry a small knife. He pulled it from his pocket and showed Conrad. Mimicking cutting his palm, he said to him that making a slight cut in his hand would be beneficial. Tyler told him that vampires would pick up the smell of fresh blood and their faces would change before him. And that once he did that, it would put him in a dangerous situation, so be prepared to fight.

He also told him about their pale skin tone and the perfection in their looks. However, he told him that looks are not always reliable for knowing who a vampire was, but despite that, to try to notice certain features about them. They were beautiful creatures and very cunning in their ways. They would try to lure him in.

"The trick is to watch people's reactions after you do these things. Vampires are the only ones that would take notice of such small actions." Tyler closed his knife and put it back in his pocket. "Your eyes will have to be trained to spot them."

"It's a lot of training." Conrad giggled.

"It will keep you alive," Tyler replied. "Tell me why you were here?"

"My brother," Conrad softly said as he held his head down.

"They killed him?"

"Yes," Conrad replied.

He told Tyler about his brother, the woman at the bar, what he had seen opening the van doors, and how he'd tracked the woman down. His eyes filled up with tears, but he quickly sucked up any emotions that he had.

"So, you want revenge?" Tyler spoke.

"Yes!" Conrad replied.

"It can't only be about revenge. That will take a toll on you, making you weak and vulnerable." Tyler placed his hand back on Conrad's shoulder. "Those that seek these monsters for revenge always lose."

"So, I just let her get away with it?" Conrad angrily said.

"I'm not telling you that and in due time, we will trap her." He took a deep breath. "It won't bring your brother back, and you won't feel any better, trust me."

Conrad knew Tyler was right. He would have to be patient and trained correctly to destroy the vampire that killed his brother. He couldn't just go on a rampage and end up getting killed. Be patient, and the time will come, Conrad tried to remind himself. After all, Tyler knew when and what to do with vampires.

"We will get her, my friend, but I'm giving you a purpose to continue, even after that."

Tyler knew deep down that they might never catch the vampire that killed Conrad's brother, but he wanted to give him hope and a reason to train harder. Then he stood up.

"You will be a great vampire hunter, trust me," Tyler told him.

"I don't know about hunting vampires. I'm not built for that type of work."

"You said that you wanted to take down the one that killed your brother, right?"

"Yes, of course," Conrad said. "But not make it a habit."

"You kill one of them, you need to kill them all. It's not a one and done thing and other vampires will seek vengeance for the one you killed."

He did not completely sell Conrad on the whole idea of hunting down vampires, but any skill that Tyler could teach him would only help him in the long run. He thought about catching the vampire that killed his brother. Then he stood up as well and was ready to train further.

They spent hours working out and getting Conrad used to building muscle strength and speed. By the time they finished working out, Conrad was exhausted. He looked over at Tyler. None of the workouts seemed to have fazed him at all.

"Go home, eat, get dressed, and I'll call you to let you know where to meet me," Tyler said. "It will be night," Conrad hesitated.

"I know." Tyler smiled.

"I'm confused?" Conrad had no clue what Tyler meant.

Why would they go out at night? His body was sore, he was hungry, and all he wanted to do was sleep. He hadn't even completed his training. It has only been one day, he thought. Giving Tyler a confused look, he stared at him. Tyler kept a grin on his face until he finally spoke.

Even though Conrad only had one day of training, Tyler knew the only way for him to learn was to throw him in it. "We're going to find a vampire to kill!"

CHAPTER SIXTY-TWO

After staying awake until daylight, she was getting tired. She would have already been asleep. Her days were now her nights, and her nights were now her days. It was only natural for her to feel exhausted.

She looked over at Victoria, who was wide awake. Nothing ever seemed to bother her. Deep down, she secretly admired Victoria. Her toughness, the way she carried herself, her distinct taste in food, clothing, decorations, and even alcoholic drinks. She also admired her personality, down to the way she looked and dressed

Victoria looked up from the magazine she was reading and gave her a slight smile before turning a page. Once again, she had been reading her thoughts. And she continued reading them. She had stayed with her the complete night to make sure she didn't attack Mariam.

A sudden thought then came to her. Mariam was still here! She immediately looked over towards the bed. There she was, sleeping like a baby. What will she say when she wakes up? Not wanting to bother her while she still slept, she stayed silent partially because she didn't want to face what Mariam had to say.

She was glad that Mariam could get any sleep at all, considering the night she had. Thank God for alcohol and

Victoria. Putting both her hands on her face and wiping her eyes, she looked over at Victoria again. She watched as Victoria set her magazine down on the end table and hopped to her feet.

"You're right, the alcohol did help." Victoria shrugged her shoulders. "And again, you're welcome," she smirked.

Amara didn't care about Victoria reading her thoughts this time. At least, Victoria knew how grateful she was for her being here and saving her friend's life.

"I'm going to fix her a divine breakfast," Victoria said as she got excited about the whole idea. "I'm a superb cook."

She knew Victoria had something on her mind by the way she had hopped out of the chair. She shook her head at her, smiling as Victoria proudly headed towards the kitchen. Is there anything this woman couldn't do? She giggled to herself.

She was glad that Victoria admired Mariam. A human? That was a shock! The two friends she had in her life could get along. Even though she knew that the one thing they had in common was both a problem—her.

Listening to Victoria humming, she watched as she danced around the kitchen to her tune. All she could do was shake her head. She wished she had that much energy—her silly friend.

Their relationship had flourished so much since she had first met her. They had their arguments and disagreements, but regardless, they had each other's back. Maybe one day she could show her she had her back as well, she thought. Creek. She heard a movement coming from the bed.

"Oh, my head—"

She looked over at Mariam; she had woken up.

"What happened?"

"You don't remember?" she answered her question with another question.

As soon as Mariam heard her voice, it was as if someone opened a floodgate. Oh, she remembered! Mariam thought. She shot her a nasty look. Vampire. How could her best friend attack her like that? Why hadn't she warned her of what danger she was in by just being around her? She should've been honest as soon as she had become a vampire. So many thoughts ran through her head.

Mariam held her forehead, dropping her head down and closing her eyes. Just thinking caused her headache to pound even more. It was killing her. She would have never drunk as much as she did had it been under different circumstances.

Victoria saw the pain that she was in and sprang into action. With vampiric speed, she grabbed two aspirin, and a glass of water, and was handing the items to Mariam at no time. She giggled as Mariam jumped at how fast she sat down beside her.

Vampire speed, Mariam thought while grabbing the things out of her hands. She didn't know if she would ever get used to the abilities they had. But then again, she didn't even know vampires existed till last night.

"Thanks," she said, while looking cautiously at Victoria. Mariam put the two pills in her mouth and drank her water.

"You're welcome," Victoria replied, and with a blink of an eye, she was back in the kitchen preparing the food she was cooking.

Mariam shook her head as she watched how quick Victoria was. She then thought that vampire speed could be useful for some good, other than attacking someone. But she still was trying to see some good at being one. Victoria didn't seem so bad, but what would happen if she was hungry? Mariam thought. For some odd reason, she liked her anyway.

She looked back over at her. She looked like her friend, but a different person at the same time.

Mariam didn't even want to look at Amara. After all, she did almost end her life. She was still angry and didn't know what to say. All she knew was the person she once knew was gone, and an imposter sat before her.

"Oh, I remember," Mariam harshly replied.

Amara knew Mariam was angry with her, but she hadn't seen her this upset. After all, she did almost kill her. It was never her intention to hurt her, and she knew, at that moment, that maybe she should've listened to Victoria from the start. Maybe she could've controlled herself if only she had eaten.

"I'm sorry."

"Save it!" she yelled back. "I told you, I'm tired of your apologies."

"Okay, ladies, ya'll are friends," Victoria said, interrupting the both of them and trying to lighten the mood. "Food is done!"

They both turned to look at her, holding up plates of food and smiling back at them. She walked over and handed both of them a plate.

Mariam was still upset but calmed down to a certain extent. She still knew that she was in a room with two vampires and didn't want to pick an argument. After all, she figured that if one of them got mad, it wouldn't be the food on the plate they would try to eat. She looked towards Victoria and the plates of food.

"Vampires eat food?" Mariam asked.

"Of course, silly." Victoria chuckled. "It doesn't fill us up, but we still eat it. Besides, with our heightened abilities, we can taste every flavor."

"Hm." Mariam grabbed her fork and ate, thinking about the woman that was watching her when she had breakfast alone.

Without reading her thoughts, Amara could tell that Mariam didn't know what to think of what Victoria just said. She didn't like the fact that regular food didn't fill us up and she knew what did. But, despite what Victoria said, Mariam tried not to show any fear and just ate what Victoria had made.

She could tell that Mariam was friendlier to Victoria because she was the hero in the current situation. But she knew her friend. She just needed to give her some space, and then they would be back to normal. It was a good sign that Mariam hadn't rushed out after waking up and the fact she was sitting here eating among them gave her hope.

"After she's done, I'm going to take her home," Victoria said, breaking the silence.

"What? How? It's daylight!" She was confused.

"Oh, I'm special," she replied, tossing her hair back like she always did when she was proud of herself or her abilities. "Some of us can do that."

"Every time I think I'm finally figuring out this lifestyle, I find out something new," she expressed. "Can I go out in the sunlight as well?"

"I wouldn't suggest you do that!" Victoria glanced at her before taking another bite. "Not unless you want to become a pillar of salt."

Listening to our conversation, Mariam was taking everything we were talking about in. Once again, she didn't like the words coming out of Victoria's mouth. Vampires walking among the living in the day gave her a feeling of uneasiness. But regardless, this was a perfect time to make a smart remark towards her, almost killing her.

"Or maybe she should," Mariam spoke up and said, rolling her eyes at her. "Maybe she needs to know how it feels… to almost die!"

"I told you I was sorry. I couldn't control that!" she pleaded.

"Okay girls, this is a conversation for another day." Once again, Victoria tried to change the subject. "Eat, enjoy the wonderful meal I prepared." Victoria understood why Mariam was more than pissed, but she didn't want them arguing.

"You know what? I think I'm done." Mariam put down her plate and rose from the bed. "I'm ready to go home now!"

"You're done?" Victoria said, looking at Mariam's half-eaten plate.

"Yes… done with everything!"

CHAPTER SIXTY-THREE

Watching Mariam's reactions and listening to her sly comments, Amara knew Mariam was more upset than she had originally thought. This was a different Mariam from the kind and forgiving one. It made her wonder if they could save their friendship.

"Wait a minute," she yelled. "We need to talk about this."

Victoria sat her plate down and walked toward Mariam. She tried to follow behind her, but Victoria held up her hand for her not to take another step. She knew she wanted to address the situation and make everything okay, but now wasn't the time.

"Mariam?" she cried out. Tears filled her eyes. But Mariam did not show any form of emotion towards her.

"Get some rest, Amara," Victoria whispered. She could tell that Mariam was upset with her.

She watched as Victoria held the door open for Mariam, but before she walked entirely out the door, she repeated herself.

"Mariam!"

Mariam stopped for a minute, took a deep breath, and turned around. She looked into her eyes as a tear ran down her cheek.

"I'm sorry, but this friendship is over." She turned around and headed down the hallway.

Victoria motioned an "I'm sorry" with her mouth as she turned her back towards her as well and headed out the door.

She watched as the door slammed behind her. She dropped to the ground and cried. Mariam was serious, and this time she wasn't coming back. Even without feeling Mariam's emotions or reading her thoughts, the tears that had fallen down Mariam's face let her know all that she needed to know. She had lost her best friend, and she wasn't coming back.

Her cell phone rang, breaking her from the emotional state she was in. Who could this be? She wasn't in the mood to talk to anyone right now. But she got up and grabbed it, anyway. Looking down at her screen, she read the name that popped up. Noah!

She had forgotten all about him, and he was calling her now, with perfect timing. She needed some good news and something to lighten her mood. Before she answered the phone, she wiped the tears from her face.

"Hey," she said, trying to act upbeat.

"Are you ready for our date tonight, beautiful?"

"Of course," she responded without thinking first.

Damn, The date! She debated with herself whether this was the right thing to do. What if she attacked him? She couldn't lose him like she'd just lost Mariam.

"Great! I have a special place I would like to take you. It's part of that secret I told you I have." She could hear him smiling through the phone.

"Sounds wonderful," she responded, still trying to sound excited. But deep down, she ached about Mariam and was now worried about him.

"A special place for a special woman," he said. "I'll be there at nine!"

"Wonderful!" she replied as she hung up the phone. Her sadness crept back in, and she couldn't even get excited about Noah wanting to take her out.

She looked at the phone for a moment. What was she doing? She questioned herself. After what happened with Mariam, how was she ever going to face him? Going back and forth with herself, finally, she came up with a solution. I'll just feed before we go. She smiled to herself.

Defying once again what Victoria told her not to do, she felt as if she could handle the situation. After all, she would've been fine had she fed before Mariam showed up at her door. Victoria didn't have to know, and she wasn't about to tell her. She blocked her mind and thought about something else.

Noah was a good man, and she could tell it. There was no way she was about to pass up this opportunity. Maybe she could find love, she thought as she came up with reasons. This was the right thing to do.

Still feeling exhausted, she stretched her arms and yawned. The bed was calling her name, and she needed to get some rest. Not only did she need the rest, but she also knew that she needed to feed her hunger before Noah arrived. Walking over to her king-sized bed, she dropped on the mattress face first and fell asleep.

———∽∽———

She woke up feeling refreshed and hungry. The feeling in her stomach reminded her of that. She did what she always did when she had to quench her thirst—go to the alley beside the apartments, and feed on the rats that roamed around.

When she made it to the outside and the alley, she noticed a drunk man was peeing in the dark. She was going to take advantage of the opportunity. It was dark, and no one could see what she was about to do from the street.

She approached the drunken man that was both shocked and pleased to see a beautiful woman in a dark alley. He pulled his zipper up and even attempted to flirt with her. She smiled as she listened to his drunken babble.

Then she made her move, biting the man on the neck and drinking his blood. It energized her body like a lightning bolt. He didn't taste as well as she had hoped. But it would have to do for now. The alcohol in his blood wasn't a mix. It was better than the rats.

He was so drunk he could barely scream out for help, and after a minute of struggling, he just gave up on fighting back. When she finished, she bit her hand and dabbed her blood on his neck. Then she grabbed him by his shoulders, looked him in his eyes, and compelled him to forget about her, the attack, and to go straight home.

She remembered what Victoria had said. *Compulsion* didn't work on some humans and to make sure it did before attacking them. Oh well, she didn't go step by step, she thought. But It worked! The man acted like he didn't even see her. Walking zombie-like past her, she watched the man until he turned the corner onto the street.

Proudly heading back to the apartment, it impressed her with what she had done. No killing and hypnotizing humans. Good Job! She felt invincible. At that moment, no one could tell her anything.

Her stomach was full, and she felt even more confident about being around Noah for their date. Still upset by what happened with Mariam, she needed this night to go well. She had to prove to herself that she could make it work, just like Lou did.

Finally, back in her apartment, she looked over at the clock on the wall. She had about an hour and a half before Noah would arrive. Hopefully, Victoria wouldn't pop up tonight nor follow her. Going out with him had to stay a secret. Just until she could prove to Victoria that she could maintain a vampire-human relationship.

She walked to her closet and couldn't decide what to wear. She wished she had Mariam for this and tried not to think about Mariam at this moment because she knew it would bring her down. The task was at hand, and she focused on it. Being indecisive had never happened to her before, at least not since she had changed into a vampire. The one thing about being a creature of the night was that everything looked great on her.

But she was nervous. Noah was different, and she wanted to impress him. He didn't tell her where they were going, only to a special place. Dress, no dress? Heels or tennis shoes? It was wrecking her brain just trying to figure something so simple out.

She went with the dress, and it had not failed her yet. Looking at her reflection in the mirror, she knew she looked cute in it. Wearing this dress hadn't been the first time for her. It was the one she wore when she had first met Lou.

She hoped wearing it would bring her some form of good luck. Before putting it on, she took a quick shower and pampered herself. When she finished, it was almost time for Noah to arrive.

She kept a positive attitude while putting on her outfit and trying to block any negativity that tried to cloud her mind. Doubts and the thought of Mariam would come through now and then, but she quickly focused on Noah and their date.

She remembered when she had first set her vampiric eyes on him and the thought of that made her smile. The attraction had been so strong with him; she knew he differed from all the rest.

There was a slight knock at the door. She wanted to rush over and answer it with her heightened speed, but she took a couple of deep breaths, collected herself, and calmly walked over to open it.

When she opened it, he was in a suit and tie. He was even more attractive, all dressed up. All she could think about was pulling him inside and ripping his clothes off. No... calm down. She gave him a flirty smile instead.

"Hello, beautiful." His smile sparkled. "Are you ready?" He held out his arm for her to grab hold of it, like a true gentleman.

"Yes, I am."

CHAPTER SIXTY-FOUR

They walked hand in hand down the hallway and out to his car—a Mercedes Benz S Class, beautiful.

"Wow, Noah. Look who is making the big bucks now." She laughed while swaying towards him and slightly bumping against him.

"Yeah, I got a raise," he teased. "Being a business owner of a tech company has its benefits."

"Noah. Congratulations." She gave him a quick hug and released him. She knew he had always wanted to own his own business, but she never thought to this extent. "I'm so proud of you."

She had to give Noah credit; the man had determination. He walked to the car door and opened it for her, then got in the driver's seat.

Once they were in the vehicle, she wondered what he had planned for their first date. Their date. That felt weird considering she'd never thought this would happen. She looked over at him and admired his facial features. He was so handsome. Feeling like the luckiest woman in the world, she put a smile on her face as he pulled off.

"You look wonderful tonight," Noah said.

"Thank you." She could feel herself blushing. Could vampires blush? She tried not to show it and blurted, "Where are we going?"

"It's a surprise." He glanced towards her, the corner of his lips turning upwards.

They continued to drive through the city. As he drove, she watched out the window. She was still curious about where he was taking her. She tried to read his mind, but he was one that she couldn't read. This pleased her and made being with him even more interesting.

They finally reached their destination and Noah pulled up to a large brick building. No signs were on the building, only the address number. This isn't a restaurant, she thought to herself. Wondering what the place could be, she watched as Noah turned the key to shut the car off.

Then he hopped out of the car, rushed over to her side of the door, and once again, he opened it for her. She loved the fact that he was rolling out the red carpet and trying to impress her. She stepped out and looked up at the tall building. Still confused about what was inside, she grabbed his hand and followed his lead.

Pulling a key from his pocket, he unlocked the door, and then stepped inside. Noah flicked on a light, and she could finally see.

She tried entering the door, but a force stopped her in her tracks. She had forgotten she couldn't walk into a home without being invited in. Noah looked at her in confusion.

"Well, come on in," he said giggling. He thought she was playing with him.

Thank God, she thought to herself. Without him saying those words, she could never go inside and how would she explain to him that she couldn't walk through his door.

"Is this your place?" she questioned.

"Yeah, that was my surprise for you and Mariam," he said excitedly. "I've moved back to the city."

Her mouth dropped to the floor. Noah had turned his loft into a beautiful art studio. Victoria's place was impressive, but this was ten times better. She giggled to herself. She knew if Victoria had heard her say that, she would have thrown a fit. It's a good thing she's not around. For various reasons.

"Is this your artwork?" she said as her eyes were wide with excitement.

"Yes," Noah replied as he watched her reactions.

"Wow, I'm speechless. I mean, I knew you had talent, but this is amazing."

She walked around the room, looking at the amazing paintings. The people he had painted and the beauty of each painting surrounded her. The images were powerful, and he had captured every detail. He had an excellent eye for beauty, and it showed.

Then, she noticed a small dining table in the middle of the floor. He had it set up beautifully. She watched him as he walked over to a chair and pulled it out for her. Walking over and taking her seat, she smelled a pleasant aroma coming from the kitchen area.

"This place is very special to me. These paintings are my heart and soul… like you," Noah said as he grabbed the bottle of wine off the table and poured it into her glass. "I thought I would invite you to be the first one I showed them to. I love Mariam, but your opinion means so much more."

She was stunned by the thought of what he had said and could tell he put time and effort into setting up the perfect night for just the two of them. She watched as he filled her glass up halfway with red wine. No man had ever taken the time to do anything like this for her.

"Instead of going to a restaurant I wanted to cook for you. I hope you don't mind," Noah said.

"This is amazing," she replied.

She liked the idea that he wanted to do something different for her. Him bringing her here and cooking for her was way better than any fancy restaurant. He cared for her enough to invite her into his home and his world. Just those simple actions spoke volumes.

He walked over and continued preparing the meal that he had planned for the two of them. She smiled when she saw him put on the apron over his suit. A man that could cook. She couldn't think of a better date. Noah had grown from the quirky little boy that they once played with to this well-rounded and successful man.

He walked back over with a large wooden salad bowl in his hand. He placed it down in the middle of the table.

"I hope you like lamb."

She nodded her head in agreement. He could have made a simple sandwich, and she still would consider this her best date ever. She could sense his emotions, and that she was in his presence made him happy.

Once they finished eating their dinner, Noah and she then moved over to the chaise and had a seat. The night was going well, and she could tell that Noah genuinely enjoyed her company. She could feel it because of her vampire abilities.

Their personalities were so different, but it seemed to balance both of them out. She was more stubborn and ruthless, damaged by emotional scars. He was caring and humble—the type of man that put other people first.

There was no logic in fate. Noah and her. This was unbelievable and if Mariam wasn't mad at her, she would love the notion they were together. Was she moving too fast? Was she falling too soon?

Noah had always been a part of their lives. He was a very close childhood friend. She knew him, and he knew her. It seemed like the perfect situation. Something a romance novel would be about. Childhood friend moves away, comes back improved. Sweeps old crush off her feet and they live happily ever after. That sounded perfect to her besides the whole vampire part.

Time seemed to leap, and they spent the rest of the night laughing and joking with each other, catching up on old times. The energy was high between them, and the passion for one another was present.

"Can I ask you a question?" Noah asked. He took his finger and moved a strand of her hair that was hanging down across her face and put it around her ear.

"Yes?"

"Will you stay the night with me?"

CHAPTER SIXTY-FIVE

The question shocked her, and she had to think about it. It wasn't the fact that sex was more than likely going to take place, but because she couldn't trust herself not to wake up hungry and make Noah a snack.

The other thing that bothered her was the fact that she couldn't walk in the daylight like Victoria, and she had to be hidden from the sun.

She analyzed the room closely, trying to find a solution. She could always sneak out to feed while he slept. In her mind, that solved one problem. Then she thought about the sun again. Maybe she could close the curtains and block out the sun. Then she could make up an excuse why she couldn't leave until nightfall. She knew Noah wouldn't mind as long as she was with him.

She looked around the room. He had tall windows with no blinds or curtains to block the sun when it came out. Something so simple as spending the night was now a big deal. There was no way that she could stay the night, not here.

"Ummm," she hesitated, still trying to think of what to say. But Noah interrupted when he saw the worried look on her face.

"It's okay, I don't want to rush this," he said, smiling at her. "I don't want you to feel like I'm pressuring you because I'm not. And I don't want this to be a one-night thing. I've dreamed of this night with you. I think you're wonderful, always have. And I can see a future with you if you would like to pursue one."

She just looked at him and placed one finger across his lips. No words could form in her mouth at that moment. It felt like it had been a lifetime. She had waited for only one man to say those words, and that man had been underneath her nose all this time. She could feel what he was feeling, and he was sincere.

This wasn't about sex, and he did like her for her. And she sensed he meant every word that he spoke. Another smile came across her face as she looked him in the eyes. Holding back her tears, the only thing she wanted to do was show him how much she appreciated him.

Leaning over, she gave him a passionate kiss. He put his hand on her back and pulled her closer. His smell was intoxicating, but at that moment, she could hold back the thought of his blood. She focused on his soft lips against hers instead.

She stood up, facing him, and slowly removed her dress. He watched in surprise as he saw the silhouette of her body through the silky, red slip. Grabbing her hand, he guided her to his bedroom, where she sat down on the bed.

"Are you sure you want to do this?" he asked.

"I'm sure."

CHAPTER SIXTY-SIX

"You know we don't have to," he said, but she put her finger on his lips to silence him and then stepped back.

She motioned for him to remove his clothes. Then she watched as he removed his shirt and pants, stripping down to nothing but his boxers. His chest was smooth, sculpted, and hard. Just looking at his body made her giddy on the inside.

He moved towards the bed and sat behind her. Massaging her shoulders, he felt how tense her muscles were. She relaxed as she felt his warm palms moving on her shoulders. His hands felt magical, and they pleased her body as he gently ran his finger down the side of her arm.

He took one hand and pulled down the strap on her silk slip. Then he slowly kissed her on her neck, down to her shoulder. She closed her eyes as she took in the feeling of his soft lips touching her skin.

With each kiss, she let out a soft moan. The feeling that was running through her body was euphoric. She could feel his warm breath going down her spine as he kissed her on the back of her neck.

Her senses awakened, and even the wind coming from his mouth sent an inviting frigid chill through her. Her fangs wanted to protrude because of the seductive feelings she was having, but she held them back.

Then he took his hand and gently pulled down the other strap, causing it to fall to her lap. Her breasts were now exposed, and she cried out to be touched, but he didn't turn her around.

Taking his hands, he moved each one under her arms and lightly pinched each erect nipple simultaneously. She moaned even harder. Her body shivered as he teased her with his soft touch.

He continued and rubbed the tips of his fingers across her chest. As he did, her sweet spot pulsated like a tiny heartbeat in between her legs. It screamed out for him to touch it as well. Touch me. Touch me, please. Her body called out for him.

He slowly continued to rub both of her breasts, exploring and feeling each curve. Releasing one, he moved his hand slowly down her body and across her stomach until he reached her sweet spot.

She gasped at the excitement of his touch. Feeling his finger rubbing across it, she held back her urge to let go. Too soon, she told herself. His hands felt so enchanting in between her legs, and she felt herself wanting to explode.

Noah could feel her excitement on his fingertip from the wetness that soaked it. He smiled as he removed his finger, teasing her body. His manhood was rock hard, but he continued to explore her body.

She rose and faced him. She wanted him to look at her, all of her. Gazing at him, wanting him to see her beautiful figure in its naked form. Watching his eyes gaze upon her perfection, she could tell he liked everything he was seeing, and this made her smile.

She moved towards him as she put her hands on his chest and pushed him back onto the bed. As he laid there, she moved in between his legs, grabbing his manhood and taking it into her mouth.

His body stiffened as she moved her head up and down. He yelled out in intense pleasure. He could feel her tongue motioning around his rod. With every motion, she could feel him wanting to let go.

She raised her head and seductively crawled up his body, but to her surprise, he grabbed her by the waist and flipped her on her back. He was now on top of her and, wanting to return the favor, he spread her legs and placed his head between them.

Feeling the suction of his wet lips on her, she gripped the pillow. She moaned out loud, feeling his tongue licking her and teasing her woman part. Trying her best not to climax, she couldn't hold back anymore. She loudly moaned as she reached her breaking point.

He raised and smiled at her. Leaning in, he placed his rod inside of her. Gasping once again, she could feel every inch of him. She put her arms around his back as he pumped in and out. Even though it felt good, she tried to hold back her strength. She didn't want to hurt him. She stayed focused and made sure she didn't lose herself in the moment.

She could feel his tiny heartbeat coming from his chest pressed against hers. She could also feel his body shiver from her cold skin. But he didn't seem to mind. She buried her face in his shoulder. The scent of his sweet blood made her want to bite him. She fought the urge back. He smelled so appealing; she just wanted to taste him.

Thinking about Mariam and the thought that she might not hold back, she resisted, but there was no way that she would ever forget his scent. She focused on his motions and how good each stroke felt inside of her.

Holding him even tighter, she could feel his pace speeding up. She could feel herself coming to another climax. Holding back the feeling, they both moaned at every movement. She could tell he was about to release, and at that moment, she let herself go with him.

They both screamed out in pleasure at the same time. The feeling was electrifying and exhilarating. Noah slowly removed himself from her. Falling beside her on the bed, he tried to catch his breath.

He turned to look at her. Watching as she turned her head towards him, he smiled.

"You're amazing," he whispered.

She smiled back at him. She wanted to stay in this moment forever. Feeling the emotions coming from his body, she could tell he wanted the same thing. They looked at each other for a moment without saying a word.

Then Noah grabbed the blanket and placed it over the top of her. She knew he thought she was chilly. He had felt the coldness of her skin. She was glad that he thought that instead of something else. She tried to play it off.

"Thank you," she pretended. "I was cold."

She smiled, and he smiled back. Then she realized it was only a couple of hours before daylight, and she knew she couldn't stay any longer. She felt disappointed, so she raised and sat on the corner of the bed. Knowing that she would have to disappear at certain times, was a part of the problem she had to figure out. She had to leave. Shaking her head, she put her face in her hands.

"Are you okay?" he asked.

"Yeah," she quickly responded. "I just need to get home."

"Okay," he sadly replied. She knew he was wondering if he had done something wrong.

But when they both went to his bathroom, they teased each other, and horse played. Having fun like old times assured him that everything was okay and that he hadn't disappointed her.

"I hate the fact that the night has to end," he said.

"Me too," she responded as she gave him a long, loving kiss. "Next time, you can stay with me."

"I would love that," he said, then smiled in agreement, knowing that he would see her again. He was disappointed she didn't want to stay, but he would not force her to do anything she didn't want to do. After all, he had waited many years for them to reach this point

It had indeed been an amazing night. She finally felt like she had found the one. Noah was a man that loved her for her. And he was standing right here beside her.

After cleaning themselves and getting dressed, they walked out to his car. They held each other's hands and giggled like high school kids. The night couldn't have been more splendid.

He opened the door for her as he patted her playfully on her butt. She shot him a flirtatious look as he shut the door. He laughed as he ran around to his side of the car and hopped in.

CHAPTER SIXTY-SEVEN

Conrad and Tyler were preparing to hunt and kill their first vampire. Tyler wanted Conrad to see how vampires operate in ordinary settings.

Conrad had gone and done what Tyler had told him to do. He had gone home, ate, and got dressed. Then he waited until later that night for Tyler to come and pick him up. He was still hesitant about the idea of being a vampire hunter, but to kill the vampire that caused his brother's life to end, he needed him.

While getting dressed, he pulled the amulet from his pocket. He hadn't told Tyler that he had it and figured he would just hold on to it. When the time was right, he would use it, but until then, he wanted to learn everything that he could without it.

He placed it in a drawer with a lock. It will be safe here, he thought. Hopefully, Levy was right about how it worked. He remembered him saying that if a vampire was close enough to him, this would strip away all of their powers. He put the key in the drawer keyhole and locked it.

Then he heard a knock on his door, and he went to answer it. There stood Tyler with a snarky grin on his face. Conrad held the door open for him to come inside.

"Nice place," Tyler said as he walked around the room. "Do you have anything to drink?"

Conrad looked him up and down, noticing the black book bag he was wearing. He didn't even acknowledge it. He figured Tyler would explain what was in it when the time was right.

"Yeah, in the kitchen," Conrad responded as he shut the door and pointed towards the dining area.

Tyler walked into the kitchen and opened up several cabinets. After searching each one, he finally found what he was looking for—a bottle of dark liquor. Grabbing a glass, he poured himself a small drink.

"That was my brother's," Conrad said as he walked into the room. Roy was the real drinker in the household and always kept a bottle of whiskey in the cabinets.

"Well, let's toast to him," Tyler said as he grabbed another glass and poured a drink for Conrad.

Conrad took a deep breath and grabbed the glass. Why not? he thought as he tipped the glass up to his mouth and took a drink. Besides, he knew there was no arguing with Tyler, and it was best to just go with the flow.

"So, what's the plan?" Conrad asked.

"Well, we're going to a club." Tyler took another drink. "That's their favorite hangout. It's dark, a lot of drunk people, and easier for them to stalk their victims."

Thinking about what Tyler just said to him made sense. After all, if he were a vampire wanting to be among humans, then a club would be the perfect place to hide in plain sight. No one would even hear someone screaming for help if they were getting attacked.

He looked down at his clothes and then at Tyler. They dressed the same. T-shirts, blue jeans, and tennis shoes.

"Glad I dressed for the occasion?" Conrad said as he looked down at his outfit.

"Yep, you're fine," Tyler replied.

Tyler took the black backpack off his shoulders. He then placed it down on the kitchen table. He pulled out a small perfume bottle and set it before them.

"What is that?" Conrad asked.

"Something we need for the night." Tyler turned to him. "Here you go."

Conrad choked as Tyler sprayed the contents of the bottle on him.

"What the hell? Is that garlic?" he said as he fanned the air.

"Yep." Tyler laughed. "Don't worry, the smell won't be as strong by the time we reach the club."

While Tyler sprayed some on himself, Conrad pulled a part of his own shirt to take a whiff. It was strong, and he turned his nose up. He knew that this was essential to their safety and to draw the vampires out. But damn, it smelled horrible, he thought. The smell of garlic filled the air.

He was still curious about what else Tyler had in the bag, but he didn't question him. Looking at Tyler placing the item back in the backpack, he pulled nothing else out. Still watching him, he zipped up the bag and tossed it back over his shoulder.

"Are you ready to go?" Tyler asked as he walked past Conrad and headed towards the front door.

Conrad walked towards the bottle of whiskey that Tyler left sitting on the countertop. He poured himself a shot and quickly tossed it down his throat. He scrunched his eyes at the taste of it. One more shot, he said to himself.

"Yep," he replied as he slammed the shot glass down on the table.

Liquid courage, he thought. He was probably going to need more than that. He walked over to Tyler and grabbed his jacket from off the coat hanger.

He would face the demons without turning back.

CHAPTER SIXTY-EIGHT

The thought of the amulet came across his mind. Part of him wanted to rush and grab it, but he didn't. He reminded himself that he needed to train without it first. The more he could fight these creatures off without it, it would be better.

Taking another glance around his home, he cut off the lights and shut the door. It might be the last time he ever returned. Once he was outside, he hesitated before taking another step. Never would he have thought that he would fear the night.

But that was before he realized that the things that go bump in the night existed. Being with Tyler made him feel more comfortable, but that he was about to hunt a vampire down seemed unbelievable.

"Come on!" Tyler yelled out to him. He had reached the car and was watching Conrad debate with himself.

Conrad took another deep breath. No turning back now. He finally stepped off the porch and headed towards Tyler's car. While getting in the car and putting on his seat belt, he couldn't shake the feeling that tonight was the night his life would genuinely change forever.

They both sat in the car, not saying a word. Tyler turned on the radio and the sound of rock music blazed in the air. The music wasn't Conrad's cup of tea, but it wasn't his car either. He had no choice but to listen to it. He watched as Tyler shook his head at the music and started singing part of the words.

With his slicked-back hair, black leather jacket, and a cigarette hanging from his mouth, he pounded on his steering wheel to the beat of the music. The life of being a vampire hunter seemed to fit him. Tyler reminded him a lot of his brother and the way he acted when he was alive.

Conrad dropped his hand back on the car seat and closed his eyes. He tried taking small breaths as he felt the wind blowing on his face. The night air was fresh and helped to relax his nervousness. He knew he needed to focus.

Finally, they pulled up to a building with a line of people standing outside. Conrad looked at the sign about it. The Pink Pigeon? Who would name a club that? He thought to himself. He shook his head and watched as Tyler drove around the building and parked in the back.

He noticed there was very little light out in the parking lot, and at that moment, Conrad understood why it was the perfect hunting ground for vampires. It would be easy for a vampire to follow someone out of the club, heading to the dark parking lot to get in their car.

"You ready?" Tyler said as he turned off the engine.

Tyler was excited and pumped up about hunting vampires. However, Conrad wasn't sure if he was doing the right thing. After all, they were going to look for trouble. He had always been used to avoiding it.

"As ready as I'm ever going to be," Conrad replied as he took a long breath.

Tyler reached in the back and grabbed his backpack. Whatever he had in it, it would help assist them on their mission. Conrad wondered how he was going to get inside with it being on his back. After all, clubs around the area were very cautious of people that carried large bags. It was because of security measures.

"Are they going to let you in with that?" Conrad questioned him.

"The doorman is one of us." He smiled as he walked through the parking lot.

Conrad shut the car door and rushed to catch up with Tyler. Finally reaching him, he thought about what Tyler had just said. He wondered what he meant by that. Closed mouths don't get fed, he thought and spoke up.

"What do you mean?" Conrad asked.

"I told you there are more of us out there." He continued to walk. "We still have regular jobs."

Conrad felt stupid after Tyler's response. Of course, they worked. He had in his head that vampire hunters did nothing else but that. They weren't just sitting around somewhere training for hours. He giggled to himself when he realized that in today's society, that made little sense.

Tyler walked past the people standing in line and straight to a big, husky man that stood at the door. Conrad followed closely behind him as he watched his interactions with the man. Tyler gave the man a handshake and then pulled him in for a half hug.

"This is Conrad," Tyler told the man as he placed his hand on his shoulder.

"I'm Aaron." He held his hand out.

When Conrad shook his hand, the man firmly squeezed his, and it felt like the man damn near broke it off. He was firm. At that moment, Conrad realized how weak he was. He pulled his hand back and rubbed it with the other one.

"Nice to meet you," he said, looking at his hand and then back up at him.

"Glad to see someone joining the club." He winked at Conrad as he waved both him and Tyler inside the club.

CHAPTER SIXTY-NINE

He's not afraid a vampire could read his thoughts or sense he is a vampire hunter?" Conrad whispered in Tyler's ear.

"Nah, he found out a long time ago that they can't read his mind… and Aaron knows what he's doing. He's a loyal soldier."

Conrad wondered what it took to be a soldier in their line of work as he looked around at the tons of people that were dancing. They were jumping up and down to the rhythm of the loud music that came from the DJ booth. There was a mixed crowd inside the place, with both older and younger people enjoying themselves. No one was under the age of twenty-one; however, that was because of the alcohol that the club served. The age limit made Conrad feel a little better about being inside there.

"Let's get a drink," Tyler yelled at him, over the music that was blasting.

Conrad nodded his head and waited for Tyler to lead the way. Once they reached the bar, he could hear him telling the server to give him two beers. He was shocked Tyler had not ordered a stronger drink.

The bartender handed Tyler two bottles of beer, and he gave one to Conrad. He motioned with his head to follow him over into a corner that had little people around. Taking a sip of his beer, he glanced around the crowded club.

"No whiskey?" Conrad jokingly said.

"Not when we're working." He took another sip. "Got to stay focused."

Conrad tipped the nozzle of the beer toward Tyler for a toast and took a sip as well. He looked at the people dancing and drinking around him.

"Tell me what you see?" Tyler asked him.

"Ummm, people dancing," he replied.

Nothing seemed out of the ordinary for him—just a bunch of people enjoying themselves. Of course, he had never seen a vampire. He tried to see anything that stood out differently, but he had no luck. They all looked the same to him.

He looked at Tyler and shrugged his shoulders. He saw nothing. Then a tall, mysterious man walked past them. The man turned up his nose at them and gave them an angry look. The man stepped back as far as he could to walk past them.

Conrad noticed his reaction and then glanced over at Tyler. Tyler hadn't budged and continued to look into the crowd.

"Did you see that?" Conrad excitedly questioned him. "Did you see his reaction?"

He raised his hand and started to point in the man's direction, but Tyler pushed his arm down before he could.

"Calm down and don't make yourself obvious," Tyler said as he kept his head straight. He took a sip of his beer. "He's now watching us play it off."

The thought that a vampire now focused on their every move made Conrad uneasy. He tried to mimic Tyler and play it cool. Looking out in the crowded room, he tried his best not to look over in the man's direction that had just passed.

He must have picked up the scent of the garlic, Conrad thought to himself. To his human nose, he couldn't smell anything anymore, but to a vampire, the smell was overwhelming. Now he knew what Tyler had meant when he said they couldn't stand the smell. The man had shown him all he needed to know.

Confused that Tyler hadn't made a move yet, Conrad was sure that this man wasn't a man but a vampire. But he knew Tyler had his reasons for his current nonchalant behavior.

Tyler noticed that Conrad was getting antsy, so he spoke up to calm him down.

"Not yet," Tyler said. "Let him try to figure us out. He will follow us; be patient."

Tyler didn't look towards the man or Conrad. Still focusing on the crowd, he leaned his back up against the wall and propped his leg up, taking another sip of his beer.

Conrad was anxious and somewhat frightened at the same time. Was this happening? He veered off into the crowd, trying to see what else he could pick up. This time he focused more on the people he was watching.

Finally, after about an hour of just watching, Tyler finished with his beer. Conrad's had already gotten warm, but he understood it was just a prop to use as if they were part of the crowd.

"Let's go."

CHAPTER SEVENTY

Conrad noticed that Tyler never looked back in the man's direction but avoided it. Since he didn't, Conrad didn't either. From what Tyler had told him, the vampire would follow them. Tyler was flirting with some girls as he headed towards the entrance. He's good, Conrad thought as he formed a smile on his face. He liked the fact that Tyler showed no signs of nervousness.

While they walked, Tyler had slipped his backpack off his arm and opened it up. He grabbed a glass bottle with some clear liquid inside of it. Without turning around, he moved the bottle to Conrad.

Feeling Tyler trying to hand him something, Conrad grabbed it and looked down. He held it in his hand, only assuming that it was some holy water. Finally, they had made it out of the club. Tyler said goodbye to the doorman and walked around the corner into the dark parking lot.

Tyler still had said nothing about the bottle at this point. Walking towards his car, Tyler stayed a couple of steps ahead of Conrad, and Conrad followed behind, asking no questions. Conrad wanted to look back, knowing that a vampire was following them, but he kept his head straight and once again sped up to keep up with Tyler. He didn't want to be the one the vampire attacked.

Tyler had moved the backpack slowly in front of him. Conrad watched as he dragged a stake out of the bag. Something was about to happen, and Conrad could feel it. He pulled the nozzle from the bottle he was carrying, his heart pounding out of his chest.

Just as his heart pounded, an arm grabbed Tyler by the shoulder and spun him around. Conrad jumped when he realized it was the same man that was in the club. He didn't even hear him behind them.

The man backed up as he caught a whiff of the garlic on him. From the look on his face, the man became angry. He shook his head in disgust and moved toward Tyler once again.

"Now!" Tyler yelled at Conrad, looking at the bottle in his hand.

Conrad rushed into action without thinking and threw the liquid in the man's face. The man grabbed his face and screamed out in agony. The sound from his mouth was deafening. Conrad watched in horror as the liquid acted like acid. He could see his face burning and smoke in front of him.

Tyler wasted no time. The vampire was blinded and in pain. Rushing towards him, Tyler quickly stabbed the stake directly in his heart. The man dropped to his knees, screaming, and then fell over, hitting the ground, face first.

"Come on," Tyler said as he grabbed the vampire's arm. "We don't have a lot of time."

Conrad rushed over to Tyler, and he helped him drag the vampire to the back of his car. Tyler then rushed to the driver's side, hit a button, and popped the trunk. Conrad saw a bunch of items, but only the ax stood out. He grabbed it quickly and tossed it to Tyler.

Catching the ax, Tyler made one swift move and decapitated the vampire's head. Conrad watched as the head bounced on the ground and landed on his foot. He looked in horror as the eyes were still open.

Tyler then grabbed a sizable brown burlap bag from the truck. Picking up the vampire's head and placing it in it, he suddenly grabbed large pieces of plastic from his trunk and covered his back seat.

Tyler was moving so quickly that Conrad stood there not knowing what to do. He watched as Tyler grabbed the bag, tossed it in the back seat, and walked back around towards the body. Tyler then took a glance around to make sure no one was watching and told Conrad to help get the body in the car.

Conrad followed his instructions and helped him put the decapitated body in the back seat. Tyler then shut the door and grabbed a large bottle of water from his backpack. He took a drink of it and then poured the rest of it on the blood that had stained the ground.

"That's not enough water to clean that up," Conrad told him.

"Don't worry, it's supposed to rain." He giggled as he got in the car and started the engine.

As they pulled off from the scene, Tyler told him they had to burn the body just like before. Because of what they did with the priest and Levy, Conrad understood what came next. The whole decapitation thing didn't bother him this time. Maybe it was because it wasn't a human but a beast. One of them had killed his brother.

Tyler had driven to an empty field. They pulled the body out, formed a small fire, and disposed of the vampire remains. After they burned the body, Tyler pulled out a cigarette and lit it. He made a small circle in the air with the smoke that came out of his mouth. He wiped his forehead off with a rag he had grabbed out of his trunk and tossed it towards Conrad.

"It's not always that easy," Tyler told him as he took another puff of his cigarette. "But it was still a victory for us. Good job."

Conrad felt great as he wiped the spots of blood off his face. His adrenaline was still pumping through his veins. Even though Tyler had done most of the work, Conrad felt as if he had done something. He tossed the rag back to Tyler as he hopped into the driver's seat.

"Toss me the keys," Conrad said. He saw the look of confusion on Tyler's face. "Come on. We still have time."

Tyler had no clue what Conrad was talking about. He flicked his cigarette in the air and threw Conrad the keys. He let no one drive his car, but since Conrad was still excited about killing a vampire, he didn't want to spoil his mood.

Conrad said nothing to him as he drove. Tyler turned on the music and relaxed in the seat. It felt nice that someone else was driving for a change and disposing of a body was exhausting. Tyler sat back and relaxed. He closed his eyes and dozed off.

He woke up when he felt the car stop. Feeling like he had just closed his eyes, he looked at the time and realized he had been asleep for about thirty minutes. He looked around at the area and was confused.

"Where are we?" he asked Conrad.

"I've been watching her for a while; she will show."

CHAPTER SEVENTY-ONE

Conrad and Tyler were sitting outside of Amara's apartment, waiting and watching, Conrad wanted to approach her. He knew Tyler didn't think this was the right time to make a move against her and tried to talk him out of it.

"You can't go after her now. We need to plan and prepare," Tyler told him.

"I know, I just want you to see her," Conrad replied as he anxiously looked at every person who walked on the sidewalk.

"I don't understand your reasoning behind this," Tyler annoyingly replied. "You are not prepared to take her on."

Conrad said nothing and continued to watch. He knew he wasn't prepared to take her on just yet, but he hoped Tyler would step in and do the work for him. He kept watching the area like a hawk. He knew she would eventually show up.

"We can't attack her with all these people around," Tyler argued as he shook his head in anger.

Just as Tyler said that, Conrad perked up and quickly opened his door.

"I know," he replied, as he slammed the door.

Conrad had spotted the murderer of his brother, the woman known to him as Anna, and a man walking down the sidewalk. He jumped out and approached her.

"Wait!" Tyler yelled as he jumped out, following behind him. Conrad, thinking that he could confront her with minimal training, was reckless to him.

Conrad had his eyes on her and a gentleman holding hands and walking towards her apartment complex. He quickly stepped in front of them, stopping them in their tracks. Tyler stepped in behind him, grabbing his arm and pulling him back.

But Conrad jerked his arm from him and angrily stood face to face with her.

CHAPTER SEVENTY-TWO

"Do you remember me?" he retorted.

He watched as she turned up her face. But she didn't make a move. By the look on her face, he knew she knew who he was. There was no fear in him this time; he had waited so long to confront her.

Tyler once again grabbed his arm and pulled him back. This time, he put more strength into doing it.

"I'm sorry, ma'am," Tyler spoke up and said. He tipped his head towards her and the gentleman, then harshly pulled Conrad towards the car to get away from them.

"What are you doing?" Conrad yelled.

"Saving your life, idiot!"

CHAPTER SEVENTY-THREE

Victoria had warned her about him, and she couldn't believe he had been bold enough to step up to her. She wanted to rip his head off. But Noah had been beside her, and others were out on the street. Killing him had to wait. But it didn't stop her from thinking about it. She tried to play it cool and not allow herself to get upset. But what was she to do?

Noah had questioned who he was, but she had pretended not to know the man and convinced him he was nothing but another random weird person out and about on the streets.

"Must have mistaken me for someone else," she had told him.

"Must have," Noah had responded, still glancing back to make sure the men had disappeared. He hadn't been comfortable with how the man approached her, but if she said she didn't know him and it all was a misunderstanding, then he had no choice but to let it go.

Noah had safely walked her to the front of the apartment complex door.

"Do you want me to come up?"

"No, I can make it the rest of the way, thank you," she responded.

She held back from giggling at the thought of Noah trying to protect her. Little did he know she was a full vampire, and that she didn't need his protection. However, she respected the fact that he cared and that it was a cute gesture. He kissed her softly on the forehead before turning to leave.

She headed down her hallway, trying to wrap her mind around the events that had just unfolded. Who does he think he is? She should've ripped his head off. She was furious. Thinking about Conrad, she knew he was going to be a problem.

Victoria had warned her about him, but she didn't listen, and now he was bold enough to approach her on the street. If Noah hadn't been there, she would have killed both men. She had to do something about him.

How was she going to have a relationship with Noah when Conrad lurked in the shadows? No longer did she feel like the predator, but more like the prey, and she didn't like that at all. Then she thought about Noah. What if he tells him about her and what she is? That made her worry even more. There was no way that she could risk that.

As she walked down her hallway, she was almost to her door when someone grabbed her and quickly pulled her into a dark corner, slamming her head up against the wall. Being a vampire didn't help with the pure force of the attack and, at the moment, it damn near knocked her out.

"You're treading on thin ice, newbie," the woman's voice said. "You know the rules."

Amara shook her head and could finally see the woman. It was Celeste.

"Celeste?"

"You were kind to me in Silas's presence, but don't get it wrong, I will kill you over your indiscretions," Celeste snapped. "Human and vampire relationships are forbidden."

Amara jerked away from Celeste in anger. She didn't understand why Celeste wanted to be Silas's puppet in the first place, or why she was standing before her now, acting as if she was *The Order*.

"Of all people I thought you would understand and besides, I'm breaking it off with him," Amara said.

"I do understand, and that's why I'm giving you a warning instead of reporting you back to Silas, who would be less talkative than I am now." Her voice grew stern. "But rules are rules, and consequences are consequences. Vampiric laws are to be followed."

Celeste stepped up to her, causing Amara to press up against the wall. Then Celeste took her finger and pointed it directly in her face. "Again, this is your warning."

Before Amara could respond, Celeste took off in vampiric speed down the hall and Amara stood there by herself, panting. Celeste was by far stronger than her and she could have easily taken her life. No matter how nasty he was with her, Celeste was a true puppet of her Ruler, Silas.

Celeste gave her a warning, and she was grateful for it. She was right. Had this been Silas, she probably wouldn't be alive at the moment. She couldn't even reach out to Victoria to tell her what happened because she shouldn't have been with Noah. This incident she would have to keep to herself. She walked to her apartment door, checking for any signs of Celeste, but she was long gone. Amara went inside and shut the door.

Negative thoughts followed, thinking about the two human relationships she had in her life. She lay on her bed and thought about Mariam and hated what had happened between them. She missed her.

But there was nothing she could do to get her to come around ever again. After all, she did almost kill her, and that was Mariam's breaking point. That would be anyone's breaking point. She understood that, but it was still heartbreaking.

She thought about Noah again. Was being with Noah actually going to work? She wanted to be with him, but Conrad had made her reconsider the whole situation. Of all voices that would come across her mind, Victoria ran through her head like a wild tornado. *Maybe she's right*, she thought.

Then she thought about *The Order* and Celeste. Who were they, and were they watching her? After all, it was easy for Conrad to find her and Celeste. If they were watching her; then not only her but Mariam, Noah, and Victoria could be in danger. She was playing Russian roulette with all of her friends, putting them at risk. Tears filled her eyes, and a small tear fell down the side of her cheek.

At that moment, she only wanted her normal life back. Nothing was going the way she had planned, and it was all because of her actions. She wiped the tears from her eyes. Becoming a vampire wasn't feeling like a blessing anymore, but more like a curse.

There was so much she needed to know about this new life, but she had walked around as if she was untouchable. Now her past actions were biting her in the ass. *When are you going to grow up, Amara?* she asked herself. More tears flowed down her face.

All she'd ever wanted in life was a partner—someone to grow old and be happy with. Money and material things never mattered to her. She only wanted love and to have someone that truly loved her. It hurt just to think about it.

For years, men had used her for nothing but her body, instead of seeing her for who she was. Still, she would bend over backward just to have someone in her life. Skipping through different men, hoping that each one would be different, but they weren't.

Now Noah and she could finally be a couple and she knew he was the one for her. He was perfect in every way, and he truly loved her back. Not just for her body, but for her. He looked at her differently and not like the suitors before him. She could see herself living happily and growing old with him.

Why? Why was she cursed? What had she done so wrong to deserve this? Why was everything taken away from her? She grew angry. She felt as if she was right back where she had started, only lying in her bed crying, not in the shower this time.

Deep down, she knew she couldn't be with Noah the way she wanted to, and for the first time, she was going to be mature and do the right thing. She couldn't risk any harm coming to him.

She needed to change her ways, listen more, and care about someone other than herself, but she debated all those thoughts. She needed to turn this situation around.

She had to let him go.

She reflected on her life as a vampire. At first, she was immature, reckless, and unpredictable. Revenge and hatred filled her heart. She took the gift that Lou had given her and turned it into a nightmare. It had hardly been a week, and she had learned that being a vampire was much more than being a monster.

She hadn't cared about other people, nor what people thought. She didn't care about her actions or their effect on them. But things were different now. Many people she cared about were being affected. No longer did she have the desire to cause any pain to anyone that she came across.

After crying her eyes out, she was finally out of tears. She rolled over and grabbed her pillow. Burying her head in it, she knew that she would have to talk to Victoria about Conrad and Noah. She knew Victoria would be angry with her, but she needed advice and how to protect Noah. She was going to break it off with Noah, but that would not make Conrad go away.

Closing her eyes, she tried to shut her mind off. She was mentally exhausted. Instead of thinking about the beautiful night Noah and she had, Conrad and heartbreak filled her mind. She took a deep breath and, after a couple of minutes, finally dozed off.

When she woke up, she didn't feel any better. She dreamed of Conrad and Roy and how she killed him. In her dream, Conrad had found her and killed her. This dream disturbed her deeply.

She needed to talk to Victoria. She reached for her cell phone off the nightstand and called her. As always, Victoria was upbeat and ready to spend time with her. She didn't want to tell her the reason she needed her to come over, only the fact that she needed to talk to her.

Once they hung up the phone, she knew that she would have to make another phone call, and that was to Noah. But for right now, she needed to feed. She got dressed and headed out the door. She needed to be back before Victoria arrived.

She found small prey in the alleyway she always went to. The thought of feeding on a human held no interest to her. After returning home and fully fed, she knew it wouldn't be long before Victoria showed up. She replayed everything in her mind like a little black and white movie. She remembered clearly the moment Conrad walked up to her, the look in his eyes, and how concerned Noah had been.

She was grateful that Noah didn't go into detail about why Conrad would approach her like that. He only asked her if she knew him, to which he told him no. Another lie. It seemed like lies were piling up. But after tonight, she wouldn't have to worry about it because she was determined to break it off with him.

Hearing a pounding noise at her door, she knew it must be Victoria. She strolled to the door and opened it. After giving it some thought, she had decided that she would not speak about Noah. It was probably for the best that she didn't, and she would have to come up with a way to make sure Conrad didn't get anywhere near him.

Knowing that Victoria could read her mind, she solely focused on Conrad and not on Noah. As always, Victoria was bubbly as she walked past her and headed straight to the kitchen. Pulling out a bottle of whiskey from the cabinet, she made herself at home and poured a drink.

"Okay, what is it?" Victoria said as she sipped her drink.

"Conrad," she replied. She had already decided not to speak about Celeste at all.

Victoria turned her eyebrows up. She was clueless about what she was talking about. Walking towards the couch, with her drink in hand, Victoria had a seat and looked at her. She shrugged her shoulders and shook her head.

"The guy that was plotting against me," she responded.

"Ahh, yeah, the barn guy, the brother of the man you killed." Victoria took another drink as she giggled. "I told you he was going to be a problem. What did he do?"

"He was bold enough to approach me." She decided she needed a drink as well.

"Did you rip his head off?" Victoria laughed.

"No," she responded.

She couldn't tell Victoria the real reason she didn't. Noah being there had to remain a secret for now. Victoria had a mean streak, so she had to come up with a reason Conrad was still alive. Why hadn't she taken him out right then?

She watched as Victoria looked at her with confusion. Trying to focus only on Conrad, she didn't want Victoria reading her mind. She had gotten good at keeping her mind clear from her being able to pick up what she was thinking.

"And why not?"

"There was another man with him," she quickly responded.

Victoria scooted to the edge of the couch. She had all of her attention, and she needed to know more about this mysterious man. Victoria knew that she had killed everyone he was with the night at the barn. Who had he teamed up with now? she thought.

"Describe this man," Victoria intriguingly asked.

"I don't know," she replied. "Military type guy, muscular build, and dark hair."

She walked to the kitchen and fixed herself another drink. She didn't care about his friend, only Conrad, and his bold move against her.

"Are you sure?" Victoria said as her voice cracked.

She glanced over at Victoria. She could hear the nervousness in her voice, and this was unusual for her. Victoria had always been fearless. Why did this seem to be a problem? She watched as Victoria held her head down and fiddled with her fingers. Worry was all over her face.

"What's wrong?" she seriously questioned her.

"I've told you before that we are not invincible." She looked up at me. "And if this is who I think it is, we have a big problem."

"Okay?" she replied as she went to have a seat next to Victoria.

"Not only do we have *The Order*, but there is another group that we need to be worried about, and they are human."

"What group?"

"Vampire hunters!"

This shocked her. There were vampire hunters? She didn't know why she was so stunned by this information. Vampires existed, so it made sense for vampire hunters to exist, as well. If someone had asked her a year ago if vampires exist, she would have laughed in their face. But, with all jokes aside, the thought of vampire hunters wasn't funny but a serious threat.

"So, what do I do?" she asked.

"Run!"

CHAPTER SEVENTY-FIVE

She couldn't believe that Victoria just said that. Run? By the look on her face, she could tell that she was serious. Frightened, this was the first time she had seen the face of uneasiness in Victoria.

"He knows what you are and the fact that he approaches you without fear lets me know he is ready to kill you and knows how," she said, "Be careful, that's all I'm trying to tell you."

She took in all of Victoria's words. However, she was more worried about Noah than she was about herself. She wasn't worried about Conrad hurting him, but more about if he would tell him about her.

"Should we kill him?" she questioned

"If he is with a vampire hunter, the odds are he's training to become one. For now, no, but if he continues to become a problem, then we will have to."

In her mind, he was already a problem. A threat. She couldn't risk him telling Noah that she was a vampire or worse, try to recruit Noah to be a vampire hunter. But Victoria was right. She needed to watch her back and let him be for now.

There was a knock at the door. She wasn't expecting anybody and wondered who it could be. She looked at

Victoria with a baffled look on her face and walked to the door. Looking out her peephole, her whole world had just turned upside down. Oh, no!

Putting her back against the door and looking toward Victoria, she didn't know what to do. Her heart sank to her stomach as she once again looked back through the peephole. No, no, no! What are you doing here? She had no choice but to open the door.

"Hey, beautiful." Noah smiled while hugging her.

She didn't say a word. Following Noah's lead, she embraced him. The secret was now out of the bag, and she could feel Victoria's eyes all on her. There was nothing she could do at this point.

"Well, well, well," Victoria spoke sarcastically

Victoria shot her an annoyed look as she held out her hand to Noah. She remembered him from the night they had gone out. She had thought that Amara learned her lesson with Mariam, but she guessed not.

"I'm Noah." He smiled as he shook her hand.

At that moment, she tried not to think about Victoria. She knew what her facial expressions meant. She invited Noah inside and told him to have a seat. Watching him walk over to the couch, he was just as handsome as the night she'd met him.

But she wouldn't let his looks distract her and needed to stay focused. She couldn't break it off with him in front of Victoria. That would have to wait. Noah didn't deserve to be embarrassed, and she needed to explain herself to him.

"I'm sorry just to show up," he said. "I called several times, but you didn't answer."

Walking over and grabbing her cell phone, she looked. He was right. It was on silent mode, and she didn't even realize it. Secretly, she wished she had answered the phone. It could have prevented him from coming over.

"My phone was on silent," she said, putting a frown on her face. She held up her phone to show him.

"It's okay; I was only making sure you were okay," he replied. "I was worried about that creepy man and his friend approaching you like that."

The thought of him checking on her made her heart melt. No guy had been that concerned. She blushed at his response and turned her phone off silent. When she looked back up, she could feel Victoria's eyes gazing at her.

"So, how long have you all been seeing each other?" Victoria said without taking her eyes off of her.

"We had our first date last night." Noah smiled.

She knew that Victoria's questions were to figure out how long she had been hiding the fact that she was talking to Noah. She knew Victoria didn't trust her with humans, and that she told her to leave them alone seemed to not be registering in her brain.

"Oh?" Victoria eyeballed her. "Last night."

I'm sorry. She knew Victoria was reading her mind at this point. Victoria squinted one eye slightly in disapproval. She didn't care what Noah had to say, only the fact that she was once again not listening to her.

She shook her head in displeasure. The more humans she brought into her life, the more *The Order* would be on their radar. Victoria was getting fed up with her and her ways.

"Do you work with her?" Noah spoke up and said, trying to break the awkward silence. He wondered where Mariam was.

"No, just a friend," Victoria responded with a stone-cold face.

Noah could tell that there was some tension in the room, but he had no clue why. He looked up at her and then towards her glass on the end table. Maybe it was the wrong time to come over. But he had to make sure she was alright. The way the guy had approached her the night before worried him.

"Would you like something to drink?" She quickly jumped up to prepare him one.

"Sure," he responded.

"Me too," Victoria said while she held up her empty glass.

No one said a word as she prepared the drinks. The silence was deafening, and if a pin dropped at that moment, it would echo. She knew Noah was confused, and that Victoria was pissed, but there was nothing she could do or say to make either of them feel less uncomfortable.

She handed them both their drinks and sat down beside Noah. She ran her finger across the rim of her glass. Feeling ashamed, she knew that she would have to break it off with him.

Victoria had been reading her thoughts. Even though she went against her better judgment, she realized she was attempting to correct it by breaking it off with Noah. She was relieved to know that was her intention. She guzzled down her drink and put it on the table beside her.

"Well, I guess I'll be on my way," Victoria said as she looked at both of them.

She wanted her to do what she had to do and break it off with him. The longer she was in the room, the more time wasted. Leaving now, while it was on her mind, was the best thing she could do.

"Let me walk you to the door," Amara replied.

Jumping off the couch, she followed Victoria to the door. Once Victoria was in the hallway, she held up her finger at Noah, and he nodded. She walked into the hall and shut the door behind her.

"I was going to tell you," she whispered to Victoria.

"Just break it off."

CHAPTER SEVENTY-SIX

She watched as Victoria turned her back and headed down the hallway. Once she was no longer in sight, she took a deep breath, looked at the door, and walked inside. There Noah sat with his drink in hand, looking at her.

"Is everything okay?" he asked.

"Yeah, she's just in one of her moods." She threw up her hands and uncomfortably let out a giggle as she walked over towards him.

"Are you okay?" He placed his hand on her back and slowly rubbed it.

His touch made her want to throw the whole idea of breaking up out the window, but she needed to stay focused. This decision was to keep him safe, and then maybe once the threat of Conrad was gone, they could pick up where they had left off.

She removed his hand from her back and placed it in hers. Looking him in his eyes, she could feel his nervousness and his concern for her. Facing him made it even harder. She didn't want to hurt him. He was too good of a person for that. She took another deep breath and slowly opened and closed her eyes. Tears formed, regardless of her trying to hold them back.

"Noah, you are a great man," Tears rolled down her face. "But we can't continue this."

He was in shock, and she saw that this hurt him. But why? he thought. He tried to figure out what went wrong and why she was doing this. Their connection was perfect for each other, and he knew she liked him. Then he spoke up.

"Is it because of her?" He pointed towards the door. Thinking that Victoria had something to do with this sudden action of hers, he got angry.

"No." She cried harder.

"Then tell me what it is?" He grabbed her chin and gently raised her head. "I know you well enough to know you don't want to do this."

She couldn't bear to face him, and she didn't know how to explain any of this. All she knew was that it had to be done. Her hand trembled when she looked him in his eyes. She could feel his pain.

"I can't." She put her head down and looked at the ground. "This is for the best."

"We can't talk about this?" The sadness in his voice came through. "I don't want this to end."

"It has to," she sadly replied.

Noah set his glass down. None of this made any sense to him. She had always been the woman of his dreams, and it ended as quickly as it had started. He stared at her for a moment and realized that whatever reason she had, she wasn't willing to speak about it.

"You need to leave," she said.

Finally, looking him in the eyes, she had to let him know she was serious. Watching him look at her, he looked towards the ground and nodded his head. She continued to watch him as he grabbed his jacket without saying a word.

She didn't get up to walk him to the door. Instead, she held her head down and tried to wipe the tears from her eyes. She knew if she took one glance at that moment, she might change her mind.

When Noah reached the door, he put his hand on the doorknob and slowly turned it. He looked at her once again, but she made no eye contact with him. He shook his head in disappointment, having one last thing to say to her.

"I have something to say, and I'm serious when I say this." He watched as she raised her face to look at him. With a tear in his eye, she heard the words she had been waiting to hear her whole life.

"I'm in love with you."

CHAPTER SEVENTY-SEVEN

Conrad felt emboldened and full of life. For the first time in a long time, he felt as if he was the one in control. He knew Tyler was upset about his actions, but he didn't care. He finally got to face the vampire that killed his brother, and that felt liberating.

He felt more energetic and less afraid and was ready to take on the world. His attitude had changed drastically, and the doubt about being a vampire hunter had gone away. This was precisely what he wanted to do. He couldn't wait to become stronger, to be more like Tyler, and to take every one of those creatures on.

Sitting in Conrad's house, Tyler was outraged. Conrad watched him jump up, pace the floor, and then sit down again. No words came from his mouth. One minute he looked as if he was going to speak, but then he would shake his head and say nothing. Conrad knew he had acted recklessly and had put both of their lives in jeopardy. Finally, he heard Tyler speak up.

"What were you thinking!" Tyler yelled as he put both of his hands on top of his head. "Do you know what you did?"

"I just wanted to let her know that I'm not afraid of her," Conrad replied. He watched as Tyler began clapping and then stopped.

"Congratulations, superman. What you did put her on notice," Tyler barked. "Now, how do you think we will ever be able to kill her?"

Conrad held his head down. He never wanted to interfere with any plans of taking out the vampire that murdered his brother. The rush of them killing the vampire at the club still ran through him the moment they approached her. He wasn't thinking beyond that.

"What do we do now?" Conrad asked.

"I don't know, Sherlock; you just put her on alert," Tyler scoffed at him and rolled his eyes. Anger was written all over his face.

"We can come up with a plan," he said. Conrad wasn't willing to give up just yet.

"What plan?" Tyler looked at him. "The one thing we had as an advantage was the element of surprise, and you ruined that."

Conrad knew that he had messed up. But there had to be a way. Tyler didn't want to go after her anymore, but Conrad wasn't willing to accept that. He owed it to his brother to get justice for him, and that's what he was still going to do.

"You're lucky she didn't kill us both." Tyler shook his head once again.

Replaying the moment, Conrad thought about what Tyler just said. Why didn't she kill us? She had let him yell in her face and do nothing at all. Then he remembered the man that was standing beside her. Could it have been because of him? Conrad felt the wheels in his brain turning.

"The man!" Conrad jumped up.

"What about him?" Tyler replied.

"She didn't attack us because of him." Conrad was now pacing the floor as he held his chin. He felt like he was onto something.

"So what? It's a good thing she didn't," Tyler replied. "We were defenseless."

Conrad knew Tyler was right and that the night could've gone wrong. But it didn't, and that's all that mattered. There was something about the man that caused her to hold back, and he felt he needed to understand it.

Tyler moved over to the couch and leaned back. He was exhausted, both mentally and physically. Thinking about Conrad, he couldn't have a vampire hunter going rogue. Like everything in life, there were rules they must follow.

Tyler knew that being smart and not letting the vampire world know who they are had kept him and others alive all these years. He wasn't about to let Conrad ruin that because of his vengeful ways. Tyler understood Conrad sought revenge, but he was going about it the wrong way.

Closing his eyes, he could still hear the patter of Conrad's feet as he paced the floor. He knew he was trying to think of a plan. But the vampire had seen both their faces and would be on alert.

Tyler also understood that Conrad only wanted to get justice for his brother, and he understood how he felt. He had been in his shoes long ago when a vampire killed his sister. But regardless of how much rage he felt, he had to be patient, and Conrad needed to learn that as well.

He hadn't trained Conrad enough yet for him to be a vigilante or some kind of superhero. Once Tyler taught him accurately, then they could kill the vampire that had killed his brother. But not before then. Thinking about Conrad's actions was causing him to have a headache.

Tyler no longer heard Conrad pacing the floor anymore. The room had become completely silent. He opened his eyes to see what was going on. Conrad had left the room, and he could hear him in the back.

When Conrad reappeared, he saw a gold necklace that was dangling in his hand. He focused on what he was holding and realized what it was. The amulet of la sorcière Isabella, a witch from the French Quarter of New Orleans.

"Where did you get that?" Tyler questioned him, sitting up in amazement.

"Levy had it." Conrad shrugged.

Tyler got up from the couch and walked toward Conrad. He took the amulet from his hand and studied every inch. This amulet was the most powerful weapon that they had against the vampires, and Conrad had it the whole time.

"Do you know what this is?" Tyler asked.

"I know it strips a vampire of its power." Conrad shrugged again. He knew what Levy had told him, but he didn't understand why Tyler was so amazed by it.

Tyler walked back over to the couch with the amulet in his hand. He cradled it as if it was a baby. Conrad watched him eyeballing every inch of the necklace. He could tell that it fascinated even Tyler to see it.

"What is it?" Conrad asked again.

"Something to remind you that there are more supernatural beings in the world than just vampires." Tyler smiled. "Let me tell you the folk tale behind this."

CHAPTER SEVENTY-EIGHT

Tyler told him of a woman named Isabelle. She wasn't just a woman, but a well-known powerful witch of the French Quarter. Even though people feared her, she was kind and, from what he had heard, extremely beautiful.

"A witch?" Conrad questioned. He remembered Tyler mentioning them while he had been training him.

"Yes, an actual witch," Tyler replied. "I told you before, vampires are not the only things that walk among us." Tyler continued with the story.

Isabelle had no lover or partner in her life. From what he had heard, she was saving herself for the right man to come around. She vowed to stay a virgin until then, and instead of finding a husband, she devoted her time to her magic.

But a man never came into her life. No human man. It was a vampire's eye that she had caught, and he wanted her for himself. He was in awe of her and secretly protected her from any danger that she wasn't aware of herself.

He knew she was a witch and had the power to destroy him, but his love and infatuation with her overpowered any notion of him staying out of harm's way. The more he watched her, the more he learned about her, and the more he fell for her.

Until one day, a man tried to attack her. No one was around to save her, only the vampire that hid in the shadows watching her. He couldn't stand by and watch this drunken man take advantage of her. At that moment, he took action, regardless of whether she saw what he was.

Without hesitation, he came to her rescue. He killed the man in front of her, ripping him limb from limb, showing her his true self. After he had killed him, he turned to look at Isabelle. Finally, he was face to face with the woman he loved, and instead of her running away in fear, or worse, she sauntered over to him. Putting her hand on his monstrous face, she didn't see him as a demon of the night, but as her savior.

From that night on, they were inseparable. She taught him simple spells, and he told her about vampire ways. They were perfect together and in love as well. He had made the woman of his dreams a reality in his life.

He had stopped feeding on humans for her and starved himself, only feeding on animals that dwelled in the woods and alleys. He would do anything for Isabelle, and she knew it.

Eventually, they married. They held a private wedding with a couple of vampires and humans, bringing witches and vampires together in harmony for the first time. They gathered together in their home and instead of inviting every vampire in, one by one, Isabelle had cast a spell for them to walk freely in and out of their home.

She felt safe with him. With his vampiric abilities and her witchcraft, they were unstoppable. Her fellow witch friends knew he was a vampire but accepted their unity. But Isabelle made them vow to keep it a secret, and they never spoke about it again.

His friends, however, tried to warn him about being in a relationship with a human. Not only would she be a distraction, but they also informed him that his blood lust might be a problem for him, but he didn't listen. He had fought off the urge a dozen times and had been okay with being around her.

But his thirst for human blood only lay dormant for so long. The day Isabelle cut her arm, she realized that the monster in him was more powerful than the love he had for her. Because of her witch abilities, she could stop him before he attacked her.

The idea of hurting her saddened him deeply, for he knew he would never intentionally harm her. He loved her and only wanted to protect her. He packed his bags and kept her safe by leaving. But she had other plans.

Even though he had almost killed her, she still didn't see a monster in him. She loved him to the moon and back. Because of this love, she would not allow him to leave and created a spell that would enable him to stay.

She worked tirelessly on it until the day it was finally complete. Using a red stone and a pure gold necklace, she created an amulet that she could wear around her neck. With this, his vampiric powers wouldn't work when he was close to her. It would make him powerless, as if he was human. It also included any other vampire that was around it.

Knowing that her life wasn't at risk thrilled him, and no longer were they in fear of his thirst for human blood. They could be together as long as her human heart beat. She had protection from the amulet and her hero for all other things. Their world was now perfect in their eyes, and their love grew even more profound.

They lived in utter bliss until the day other vampires got word of the amulet and their relationship. Vampires do not agree with relationships with humans and especially not one with a powerful witch, such as Isabelle.

Witches, like some humans, were a threat to their existence. They were not their allies, but their enemies, and the thought of one of their kind marrying one was treason. They could not allow this to go on and would have to destroy both of them, also knowing that his love for Isabelle had caused him to let down his guard and that would be a perfect way to strike at him.

One night as Isabelle slept, she was suddenly awakened by screaming and shouting. This was the night she regretted casting a spell for any vampire to enter her home. Vampires had come, but none of them had been their friends.

She watched as two unfriendly enemies held her lover in each of his arms. She knew they were vampires as well because her lover could not break free from them. Trying to use her magic to stop them quickly, she felt an arm grab her from behind. He grabbed both her arms and prevented her from doing what she needed to do to save him.

The vampire that held her down realized that in the amulet's presence, he had no power. He knew that the physical amulet couldn't be touched but he could touch the chain. So, he ripped it off her neck and tossed it across the room. He bit down on her neck, sinking his sharp fangs into her. She screamed out in agony.

Her lover heard her cries, but he could not escape. He watched in horror as she tried to escape his grasp, but he was too powerful for her. Her lover continued to watch with tears in his eyes as the vampire grabbed her neck. Then he pulled her head upwards, so that she was looking toward him.

She watched as he motioned his lips to tell her he loved her. Tears ran down her face as she watched them break his neck and rip his head from his body. She cried out as she watched in horror. Then the vampire holding her sank his teeth into her throat once again. She slowly closed her eyes as he drained every bit of life from her. She died alongside him.

The other vampires buried both of their bodies together, and their gravestone served as a reminder to future vampires that death would be their fate for such treason. They killed them and told other vampires of the story, spreading fear in those that ever dared to have a human relationship. Those vampires took the necklace and hid it in a safe place, so they would not use it as a weapon against them.

However, karma has a way of coming back around, and the vampire that killed them and took the necklace faced death as well. A human had staked the vampire as he slept in his bed. The vampire kept the necklace beside him as he slumbered, not realizing the power of the necklace had stripped away his vampiric abilities, being that close to him.

Tyler took a deep breath and then looked at Conrad. He then told him he believed that the human that killed the vampire, as he slept, was one of the very first vampire hunters. And he believed that the vampire hunter then took the necklace and passed it down from generation to generation.

The only thing Tyler couldn't figure out was why Levy had it? Sure, he was a vampire hunter, but he wasn't the brightest bulb in the bunch when it came down to it all. He must have had it in his family for years, waiting for the day he had a child that he could pass it on to.

He realized Levy had kept the amulet the whole time and never shared this information with anyone, which surprised him. Now that Levy was dead, Tyler was glad that it ended up in another vampire hunter's hand, instead of an actual vampire.

Tyler watched as Conrad pondered the story that he had told him. It startled him when he heard Conrad yell out.

"Love!" Conrad jumped from his seat. Tyler looked at him in confusion. "The vampire and the witch were in love."

"Okay? So what?" Tyler questioned. He continued to admire the amulet in his hand. "The creation of this is the point. Not love."

"You're wrong," Conrad said excitedly. "Love distracted the vampire. That's how we get her."

CHAPTER SEVENTY-NINE

Tyler turned up his face. Conrad was still getting revenge and he couldn't believe it. He had thought they had moved past that point. He had no clue what Conrad was talking about, with the whole love thing, and wished he would forget about the vampire he had confronted. They needed a proper plan and love wasn't it. But the amulet could hold the key to all their problems.

"That's the only thing you got?" Tyler giggled. "Love?"

"Don't worry about it. I know what to do."

"If you say so."

Tyler shrugged him off and stuffed the amulet on the couch pillow. He laid his head down and closed his eyes. It was late, and Tyler was tired. Dealing with Conrad and whatever crazy idea he had come up with would have to wait.

A couple of days passed, and Conrad never told Tyler what he was up to. He needed to monitor Amara without him. He gave the amulet to Tyler to hold for safekeeping just in case a vampire came for it.

In the meantime, he had been watching Amara come and go. He hadn't seen the gentleman that she was with that night, but he soon found out where he was. All of her late-night strolls weren't only to feed but to watch Noah…

CHAPTER EIGHTY

She was the one that had ended it with Noah, and now her heart ached from it. Breaking it off with him was the hardest thing that she had to do. Fighting with herself, she wondered if she did the right thing. She loved him. She thought about the night she broke it off with him over and over.

Hope and happiness had left her body the night he did, and she saw no reason to keep going. Night after night, Noah stayed on her mind as she would leave her apartment, only to feed on the rodents and squirrels that scurried in the alleyways and then return. His scent wouldn't go away, and she smelled him in every room of her apartment.

She had lost him and Mariam. Victoria was her only friend, but she was angry with her, *The Order*, Lou, and everyone else. She needed someone to blame for all of this, and even though she knew Victoria told her the right thing to do, it angered her even more because she was right. Not to mention Celeste giving her a warning that she was not about to take lightly.

Her cell phone rang, and she picked it up and looked at it. Victoria. She hit the decline button and set it back down. She didn't feel like talking to her or anyone else. Victoria had been trying to get hold of her for six months now.

Even when Victoria came to her apartment, she stood by the door without answering it. Victoria read her thoughts outside of it and understood her pain. She gave her words of encouragement and told her things like it would be okay, but eventually, she stopped dropping by and gave her space for the moment. But that wouldn't stop her from keeping an eye on her.

What was the purpose of being a vampire or having this gift if she had to turn away the ones she loved? None of it made sense to her, and she wished she wasn't a vampire... so that she could die.

They were perfect together. She would put her life in danger just for their relationship and keep him safe. But none of it mattered now because it all had to end because of vampirism. She thought again about how being a vampire was feeling more like a curse than a gift.

She couldn't stand by and let him go like that. Someone had to pay. She started thinking about Conrad and grew angry. Someone had to end this. If he had not approached her that night, she could still have possibly been with Noah. He caused this. The thought of killing him ran across her mind, and for the first time in weeks, she smiled.

The walls were closing in, and she needed to get out of the house. The only thing that was on her mind was Noah and the hurt in his eyes when he had left. She decided she needed some air.

After riding around the city, she found herself in front of his door again. She turned off her car lights and got out. Walking up to his window, she heard laughter. She ducked down low, taking a peek inside, and her heart sank.

There he was, the man of her dreams, entertaining another woman. He had on the same apron that he had worn the night he had cooked for her. The aroma coming from the inside smelled great. She knew he had prepared that meal for the woman that was now attempting to take her place.

Her anger rose. She knew six months had passed since she had broken it off with him, but she didn't expect him to move on just like that. It should hurt him as well. Did he ever really love her? She knew it was selfish to think that way. He'd tried to reach out, even coming over to her apartment several times, like Victoria. But she had expunged him from her life. What else could he do but move on with a woman that looked like a knock-off version of her?

She gritted her teeth. She should be that woman with him, and as she continued watching him, he smiled and kissed the woman on the cheek. He held a wooden spoon up to his mouth, blew off the steam, and then let the woman taste the food from it. That woman was supposed to be her. Tears filled her eyes once again.

She didn't know why she kept doing this to herself. Since the day he left, she had been following him. At first, he walked around, sad, and stayed by himself. But then one day he met the woman that he was now with, and she could tell that she made him happy.

She had ignored all his phone calls but listened to each message he had left, pleading with her just to return to him. She even listened to his message that he was going to move on, but if she ever returned, he would be there. But she couldn't return. Not then, not now, not ever. She knew it was best not even to answer his calls. She had done the one thing she didn't want to do even before she had become a vampire.

And that was to hurt him.

What was she to do now? He was happy and had moved on, but she was miserable and lonely. She knew she couldn't continue to stalk him night after night and looking at him with another woman only made her rage grow.

She convinced herself that he was just like all the rest. It was easier for her to think that way. It gave her a reason to hate him, to be angry and not care. Even though, deep down, she knew it wasn't true. Keeping this mindset was better than the truth, which caused her nothing but pain.

Walking away from his window, she got back in her car and screamed. She was done with doing what was right! There was no pleasure in it, and she was determined to at least do something that made her feel better.

Killing without remorse.

In the six months Conrad had been training with Tyler and watching Amara watching Noah, he assumed they had broken up. She had been secretly watching him and the new woman he was with. And by the way she was stalking him, she cared for him. He could use this to his advantage when the time was right.

He had watched her on one particular night. Darting in and out of the shadows, she followed her love interest. The man had no clue that she was there, but he knew. What was she doing? he thought as he stayed in his car, observing her through binoculars. She was so worried about this man that she didn't even notice him.

Watching closely, he saw the man approach another woman, kiss her on the cheek, and hug her. Conrad then looked at his brother's killer, who was not happy with the situation at all. She looked as if she was about to attack. Noah and the woman didn't even notice as they walked into a restaurant together.

Knowing that she was miserable made him happy. He felt no remorse for her, and she deserved whatever was coming to her after killing his brother.

Conrad watched as she wiped her face as if she was crying and then disappeared into the night. That was all the confirmation that he needed. She was in love with this man, and for whatever reason, they had broken up.

Every night she would leave her apartment to feed and then watch him, and he was grateful that she wasn't feeding on humans like he had seen her do before. He knew everything that he needed to know. A vampire's love for someone is strong, and it was difficult to let go.

She had led him straight to her lover, and that was what he had been hoping. He couldn't approach her again, but he could talk to him alone. He could see that this man was her weakness, and he needed him on his side.

He waited a couple more days before making any moves. He trained with Tyler from dusk till dawn, day after day. His skills were getting better, and he even impressed Tyler with how quickly he was catching on.

They had hunted down a couple more vampires, killing them and then declaring victory. Even he had successfully staked his first one, decapitated the head, and burned the body. It was becoming second nature to him.

Still in the back of his head, he thought about her and the man. She wasn't off the hook, and he was yet determined to talk to him. He hadn't spoken a word about her to Tyler, and Tyler never brought her up. It was as if the night he had approached her had never happened.

Once he was comfortable enough in his training, he decided he was going to approach the vampire's lover. Even though he had moved on, she hadn't, and Conrad knew she was still watching him, night after night.

He waited till morning and headed over to the man's house. He knew she was asleep during this time and that she would be nowhere around to attack him. The good thing about most vampires was the fact that they couldn't be out when the sun was out. Daylight was his friend.

He parked his car and headed up towards the door while playing in his head over and over what he was going to say to him. Hopefully, the man would listen and understand. He took a deep breath and rang the doorbell. After what seemed like a lifetime, Noah answered the door.

"Can I help you?"

Conrad said nothing at first. He could tell that he was processing the fact that he had seen him before, and once he realized it, his face went from friendly to concerned.

Noah knew he was the man that had approached him the night of his and Amara's first, and only, date.

"What are you doing here?" Noah asked. He looked at the man with anger.

"We need to talk."

CHAPTER EIGHTY-TWO

When night fell, Amara drove around the city hopelessly. She ended up at the bar where she had met Roy. She went inside and ordered a drink from the bartender. The music blazed in the air, and after about five shots of whiskey, she had become tipsy.

She scanned the room, looking for a victim, a man. Trying to find one that only wanted one thing from her–sex. Finally, he approached her. She smiled as she read his mind, and the thoughts that were running through his brain were unimaginable.

Smelling like a brewery, he was perfect. He whispered in her ear all the nasty things that he wanted to do. She should kill him right now, dropping him dead where he stood, but she continued to keep a grin on her face and flirted back with him.

She placed her hand on his shoulder and visualized them having sex out in the parking lot and him enjoying it. The man's face was stunned. He didn't know what had happened and didn't care. He had seen everything that she needed to show him. She sensed eagerness and excitement coming from him, and she knew she had him hooked.

Finally, after a couple more drinks, she got up from her seat and headed toward the bar entrance. As expected, he followed behind her, thinking that tonight was his lucky night. She walked outside, and he came out right after her.

Looking around the parking lot, no one was in sight. Grabbing him by the collar of his shirt, she pulled him close to her and gave him a long passionate kiss. His lips felt cold and lifeless. Nothing compared to Noah, but it didn't matter. She was going to kill him, anyway.

The taste of him disgusted her, and she turned her face up as he pulled away from her. Reading his thoughts, she knew he liked nothing that remotely seemed romantic. His only interest was to get inside of her pants and leave after the act was over.

She lured him into the back of the building, and he quickly unbuttoned his pants, waiting for her to take action. Glancing around one last time, the night was quiet, and no one was around. She smirked at him, and her face changed before his eyes, fangs protruding from her mouth.

Pure horror came across his face. He was speechless and tried to take off running, but she was too quick for him. She grabbed him by his shirt, and he yelled out as she sank her teeth into him.

She then bit down harder and pulled her head up with such force that it ripped his jugular vein from his neck. Spitting it out, she watched as blood shot out of his neck. He tried to hold his wound, but it was no use, and the blood he was losing caused him to drop to the ground.

She laughed as he struggled to stay alive, blinding him a time or two just to see him squirm around in pure terror. He clawed at the ground before him, trying to lift himself up and then dropping back down to the ground. After a couple of minutes of struggle, he had given up and died.

Looking at his lifeless body, she giggled to herself. Killing him brought her some type of joy. She knew she was not supposed to kill anyone just because she wanted to and to heal them after feeding, but she needed this. This action reminded her of who she was before. The Killer. The beast she had become before Victoria had tried to change her and before Noah.

She didn't care anymore. Going back to her old vampire ways was easier. She had been heartless, and nothing bothered her. The feeling of superiority was what she wanted again, and she was determined to be her old self.

Hearing a noise, she glanced over to the side of the building. She saw a silhouette of a shadow. It was watching her. She used her vampiric speed to move toward the shadow, but when she had gotten close, it had disappeared into the night.

She looked around, but no one was there. Who was that? Someone had been there, and as quickly as they had left, she knew it had to be a vampire. One that was much faster than her. She looked back over at the man's lifeless body and then back in the shadow's direction.

Turning back around and heading towards the dead body, she stopped in her tracks. Victoria! There she stood before her with her arms crossed, giving her a nasty look. Victoria had crossed her arms and was tapping her foot. She wasn't in the mood for her and pushed her out of her way.

"Why are you stalking me?" she angrily yelled as she stomped towards the dead man's body. "I thought you were giving me my space."

"What do you think you're doing?" Victoria scolded her.

She stopped walking and turned around, looking her directly in her eyes. She pointed her finger towards the corner of the building, where she had seen the shadow figure watching her.

"Was that you?" she asked.

"What? No!" Victoria replied in confusion. She looked at the area where she was pointing. "I don't know what you're talking about."

"That wasn't you, watching me." She gazed at her.

"Don't you think I would have stopped you from doing this?" Victoria waved her hand at the dead body. "You know me better."

She knew Victoria was right. There was no way she would stand by and let her kill a human for no reason. At least not in front of her and leave a corpse on the ground. She stood there for a second, pondering on who was watching her. It had to be Celeste like before. Then she thought about *The Order* for a brief second, and then no longer cared.

"What are you doing?" Victoria harshly asked again. "Are you trying to commit suicide?"

She reached down, looking at the man for a brief second, admiring her kill. Then she grabbed his lifeless body, picking it up and tossing it over her shoulder. She gave Victoria a cursory look and a smirk.

"Trying to dispose of this body," she replied, trying to be smart with her, and then shook her head as if it wasn't a big deal.

"You know what I mean," Victoria replied. "Was someone watching you?"

They walked into the woods behind the bar without saying a word to each other, Amara kept walking until she felt she was deep enough in and dropped the body to the ground.

"You wouldn't believe how heavy he was." She giggled.

Victoria was getting pissed off by her laid-back attitude. She knew that breaking up with Noah had hurt her, but that was no excuse for her actions, and it was serious because someone had been watching her. What she was doing was beyond reckless, and they had been over this time after time.

"Was someone watching you?" Victoria questioned again.

"Maybe Celeste, but I frankly don't care… Let *The Order* come for me. Let them all come for me." She laughed. "I will just blind them and rip them to shreds."

"None of this is funny, Amara," Victoria yelled. "I know you're upset about Noah—"

"Don't!" she yelled back, cutting her off. "Don't you dare speak his name!"

Her anger rose. She still felt that Victoria was part of the reason they were no longer together and the fact that she would even bring him up enraged her. Listening to her, she had not only lost Mariam, but Noah as well.

"You must have a death wish," Victoria shouted. "Remember… I'm not the enemy here."

"Oh?" She got in Victoria's face. "You're the reason I'm losing the people I love."

"If it weren't because of me, you would have killed the people you loved," Victoria snapped back. She was pissing her off.

"If it wasn't because of you, I would never have been a vampire."

"No, you would've been bleeding to death in the back of that rinky-dink club you worked at."

Amara grew angrier and pushed Victoria back with such force she almost knocked her off her feet. She watched as Victoria slowly looked up at her, and without warning, she charged.

"You ungrateful little bitch!" she yelled as she pushed her back, causing her to stumble and fall.

"Ah!" she yelled. "I'm sick of this. I'm sick of you, Conrad, and being a vampire." Letting all her rage consume her, she got back up and charged back at Victoria.

But Victoria was too fast for her, and when she got close to her, Victoria grabbed one of her arms and swung her around, letting her go in mid-air. She slammed up against a tree. The bark shattered when she hit it, and the leaves fell from it.

"You want to fight me?" Victoria yelled. "Go ahead! But you will not win."

She looked up at Victoria with fury in her eyes and knew she couldn't beat Victoria in a battle. Victoria was just too strong. She flung the piece of hair that hung down in front of her face.

"I don't need you, and I never did!" she screamed. "You wanted me, to transform me. You are the one that caused all of this!"

"Fine." Victoria threw both of her hands up in the air. "You never have to worry about me anymore. Good luck with *The Order*. You're on your own!"

CHAPTER EIGHTY-THREE

Victoria quickly vanished into the dead of the night as she watched. She had never seen her so upset and, frankly, she didn't care. Let her go. Let them all go. She rose from the ground and dusted herself off.

Feeling like she had already lost everyone in her life, one more didn't seem like such a big deal. She looked at the body and dug a grave with her sharp nails. With her vampiric speed, she finished in no time. She dropped the body in the hole and covered him up.

She was annoyed. Hiding bodies was something she could do without. Besides, it was time-consuming for a vampire. It had been a long time since she'd had to. She had been doing it the proper way and healing the individuals that she had attacked.

Raising her head and looking at the dark sky, the full moon glowed. This night had been a disaster. She had been just fine until then and happy that she had killed a man without thinking twice about it.

She finally reached her car in the parking lot. Looking around for the last time, she was still the only one outside. It was funny that she had killed a whole man, and no one even noticed… at least no one that was human.

Starting her car, she thought about Noah once again. Why couldn't she get him out of her head? She started driving out of the parking lot and soon was on the road. Covered in blood, she didn't even bother to clean herself up with the rag that lay in the back seat.

So much was running through her mind. She couldn't turn off her thoughts, and before she knew it, she was in front of Noah's place once again. Cutting off her headlights, she sat there for a second with her eyes closed. Why was she here? She opened her eyes and looked towards his place.

She noticed his lights were still on. Stepping out of her car and creeping to the window, she saw no one inside. The lights being on and him not being in bed was unusual for Noah, especially this late. She had been watching him night after night and had gotten used to his schedule.

He wasn't a night owl, not unless he went to a bar with his friends, and even when he did, he still left early to go home and be in bed. He was predictable in the things he did. Even when they were children. She smiled at the thought of his small habits.

The smile turned into a frown when she thought about where he might be. Probably with her. She tried to shake off that thought. The thought of him lying next to her made her skin crawl.

She took another look inside his place. No one. The only thing that confused her about him not being home was the fact that he had left on all of his lights. Why wouldn't he cut them off? Figuring that he probably left them on to deter a burglar, she shrugged it off.

She headed back to her car and got in. It was getting late, and the sun would soon be rising. There was nothing left for her to do but head to the house and try to get some rest. The night had been long, and she was ready to go home and drown herself in her sorrows.

When she finally reached her apartment, it brought her no relief. The door was open when she went inside. She looked around and the silence spoke louder than anything. She was alone and miserable.

She thought about Victoria. Feeling a little guilty about the way she'd acted, she went to the kitchen to fix a quick drink. Victoria had now left her for good, just like everyone else. The one person she had left, she had pushed away. She didn't care. She tried to convince herself that Victoria was her enemy now, but she still liked her. Damn Victoria's gift of Allies. Taking a drink, she slammed her glass down on the countertop.

Looking down at her hands, stained with blood and dirt, she chuckled to herself at the thought that she tried to fight Victoria. She would have never won that fight, and she knew it. The thought tickled her enough to form a smile on her face.

But when she looked up at her lonely apartment, the smile left as quickly as it had come. What was wrong with her? Why had her whole life been a mistake? It wasn't possible to be a vampire correctly, she cried out. She was getting used to crying out in her times of depression. This was becoming a bad habit.

No matter how much she hollered, she knew she would never get an answer. But it was worth a shot. She poured herself one more drink, and when she finished, she tossed the glass in the sink.

Walking over to her nightstand, she grabbed her cell phone. There was no missed call or any texts. She felt like no one cared about her anymore. She scrolled down her contact list. Mariam's name came across the screen, and she stopped for a moment to gaze at it.

She nervously dialed the number and listened as it rang in her ear. Her heart pounded against her chest. What if she answered? What was she going to say, after all this time? She hadn't spoken with her since that night. She listened anxiously and waited, but after the fourth ring, it went straight to voicemail.

Damn it! She hates her! She took her phone and tossed it across the room. It hit the wall and shattered into pieces. Then she knocked the light off the nightstand, watching it fall to the floor and breaking as well.

Tears flowed down her eyes as she dropped to the ground. She lay on the cold hardwood floor, curled up in a ball. Wishing she was dead, she realized that this time she was indeed by herself.

After a while, she cried herself to sleep. But as she slept, she dreamed of several vampires coming to get her for not following the vampiric rules. In her dream, she ran as fast as she could, passing everyone she loved.

First, she ran past Mariam, who turned her back to her. Then she ran past Lou, and he did the same. Then came Noah and after him, Victoria. They all turned away from her as she screamed for help.

Then the vampires that were chasing her blocked her off, forming a circle around her. She looked at every one of them as she pleaded for her life. They were chanting something that she couldn't understand, and when they were just about to rip her head off, she woke up.

Regardless of her nightmare, she had gotten some sleep throughout the night; it was now daylight outside. She raised herself off the floor and headed toward her bed. Looking around the room, she saw a white piece of paper in front of her door.

She slowly walked over to it. In her confused state, she looked around her apartment once again as if someone had entered without her knowledge. But it was still just her. Someone must have slid it under the door while she was asleep, she thought as she bent down and picked it up.

It was a piece of plain white paper, folded up. She opened it up and read the words written inside.

IF YOU EVER WANT TO SEE YOUR LOVER AGAIN...COME TO THIS ADDRESS AT SUNDOWN, OR HE'S DEAD!!!

CHAPTER EIGHTY-FOUR

Noah! She gazed at the note once again. There was nothing she could do at this point. It was daylight outside, and she couldn't go out. She was stuck. Waiting was not her strong suit. But in this case, she had no choice.

When she had seen that Noah wasn't home, but his lights were on, that was the moment she realized that something wasn't right. Now, she had confirmed someone had kidnapped him and was using him against her. She thought for a second about who it could be. *The Order* would've killed him or changed him, so she highly doubted them. Then one name came to mind. Conrad. He was the only one that hated her enough to want to hurt her.

She wished she could call Victoria and get some advice, but she had ruined their relationship, and there was no way that Victoria would help her now. She had to do this on her own and save Noah. She was not going to let anyone hurt him. There was nothing she could do until the sun went down. She had to wait…

Conrad nervously paced the floor. What did he do? He had done the unthinkable and questioned himself about his actions. Kidnapping someone was never in his plans, but he had no choice. Noah would have gone back and told the very vampire he was trying to kill.

He looked over at Noah, who was struggling to get out of the chair. Conrad had wrapped a rope around his arms and tied him down. With a piece of cloth covering his mouth, Noah tried to yell, but his screams were muffled.

When Conrad talked to Noah about Amara, he had invited him inside his home. He fixed Conrad some tea, and they sat down at the kitchen table. Noah wasn't sure why Conrad was there, but he had told him he needed to talk to him about Amara.

Even though he and Amara were not together anymore, Noah still loved her, and if she was in trouble, he was going to be there. He watched as Conrad sipped his tea and didn't say a word. Finally, after a couple of minutes, he spoke.

"You date the woman I approached?"

"Amara?" Noah held his head down.

"So her name is not Anna?" he snapped. "And what happened to you all?"

"No… What? What does that matter?" he replied. He looked at Conrad and he seemed unhinged, so he answered. "She broke it off with me, but I'm not sure why."

Conrad stared at him for a moment and then took another sip of his tea. For the first time, he knew the vampire's actual name, and it wasn't the same name that she had told his brother at the bar that night.

He already knew that he and Amara had broken up, but he tried to play it off. He had been following her and watching her watch him, but he would not let him know that information at all. Noah was clueless about her being a vampire.

"Who are you to her?" Noah asked. "Are you a friend?"

"Far from it," Conrad sharply replied.

Conrad's reaction put Noah on notice. If he wasn't her friend, then who was he? Grabbing the empty teacup that sat in front of him, Noah turned his back and headed towards the kitchen sink. He washed the remaining dishes that were left.

"So, what is your business with Amara?" he asked. Keeping his back turned towards Conrad, he continued to clean the dirty plates.

Conrad got up and sneaked up on Noah while his back was towards him. He pulled out a small syringe and placed it in his neck. Noah turned around and tried to fight him off, but the medicine inside was taking effect.

Backing up and watching Noah slowly drop to the floor, he looked around Noah's home, making sure no one else was around. He heard a thud, and it was Noah, ultimately hitting the ground.

He walked over to him and nudged him with his foot. Noah didn't budge and was out of it. The tranquilizer was running through his system, and Conrad knew he wasn't waking up for a while.

His intentions were not to kidnap him. He honestly wanted to explain to Noah what Amara was, but he could tell by the looks Noah was giving him that he was becoming defensive of her.

Conrad tried to think quickly. How was he going to get Noah to his car? Then Conrad noticed that there was a garage around the back of Noah's house. He rushed out to his car, drove it around to the end, and pulled in.

When he got back inside, Noah was still lying in the same spot, sleeping like a baby. He pulled out some rope that he had grabbed from the front seat of his car and tied Noah's legs together. Then Conrad grabbed his arms and dragged him to the trunk of his car. Noah was massive, but he'd gotten him in the trunk. Thanks to Tyler and all the training he had put Conrad through, he was a lot stronger than he thought.

Once he was in the trunk, he tied Noah's hands and gagged his mouth. Conrad shut the trunk and rushed over to the driver's seat. He wiped the sweat from his forehead and tried to slow down his breathing.

He quickly collected himself and pulled out of the garage. While driving, he realized he had no actual plan. The only thing he wanted to do was to get Amara alone and destroy her, just like she did his brother.

Now that he had Noah in the trunk of his car, Conrad did not know what to do or where to take him. Conrad drove around for a little and then thought about what Tyler's reaction would be.

It was time to take him to Tyler's place.

The place where Tyler had trained him was perfect and Conrad headed there.

Once Conrad got to Tyler's abandoned building, he pulled Noah out of the trunk and inside. No one was around, and there was a small metal chair in the corner that was welded to the ground. Conrad moved Noah over to the chair, sat him up, and secured him to it.

He looked at Noah sitting there. With his head dropped downward, bound, and gagged. He'd kidnapped someone. It was an unbelievable sight, even to Conrad. But there was no time for him to panic.

He looked at Noah once again and walked over to him. He slapped Noah hard in the face to awaken him. As Noah slowly came to, he struggled when he realized he was tied up. He tried screaming, but it was no use. With his mouth covered, he looked up at Conrad with anger.

"I will not hurt you," Conrad spoke. "I'm going to remove the gag so you can speak."

After Noah nodded, Conrad did what he said he was going to do and removed the gag from his mouth.

"What is this?" Noah said as he struggled to break free.

"I'm sorry… I had to," Conrad replied. "I need you."

"For what?" Noah yelled.

"As bait." Conrad shot him a nasty look.

"I don't understand?" Noah pleaded.

"You will soon enough. I slipped a note under the monster's door right before I came to you," Conrad replied. "I wasn't planning on kidnapping you, just talking to you, but I'll explain everything later."

"Why? To hurt her?" Noah yelled once again.

"Trust me, I'm more at risk of being hurt than she is," he replied. "I need her to come to us."

"Look what you did to me!" Noah shouted. "Don't you touch her, or I'll kill you myself."

"I will not hurt her," Conrad said as he rolled his eyes. "I promise." But deep down, he knew he was lying. He only needed to make Noah feel more comfortable and trust him.

Noah didn't know what Conrad had in mind, but if he kept him talking, it was a better chance for him to break free and stop him from doing whatever it was he had planned.

Noah quietly struggled to break free. Conrad walked over to the small refrigerator and grabbed a cold-water bottle. Pulling down the gag, he gave him several drinks of it.

"Thank you," Noah said after he finished drinking. "Now tell me what's going on?"

"You will not believe me when I do, but okay," Conrad replied as he set the bottle of water down on the floor.

Conrad grabbed another chair and set it down in front of Noah. Looking at him face to face he began telling him how he first met Amara. Conrad told Noah about how he first met her and what she had done to his brother and how he still hadn't recovered his body.

Noah looked at him with a straight face. If all this had happened, why was Amara still alive? None of it made sense, and he thought Conrad was crazier than he imagine.

"I know you don't believe me." Conrad stood from his chair. "I was like that at first."

"You're telling me she ate your brother, and you shot her in the head?"

"Yes!" Conrad responded. "She's a vampire!"

CHAPTER EIGHTY-SIX

Noah could no longer hold his laughter back. This man was delusional. He had gotten himself kidnapped by a man that thinks vampires, and probably werewolves, exist.

"Let me go," Noah said to him as he continued to laugh. "I've known her all my life… Trust me, she's no vampire."

"None of this is funny!" Conrad yelled at him. "And you will see."

Noah stopped laughing as he saw the anger rising in Conrad. Amara is a vampire, he thought. He tried to consider some of her behavior when they had gone out together, but nothing seemed out of the norm. Other than her cold skin and flawless features. But still, he wasn't quite sold on the idea of vampires. But regardless, as hard as it was to believe him, he had to pretend he did, at least. He wasn't sure what Conrad could do at this point.

"Okay, if she's a vampire, then you're going to kill her?" Noah questioned.

"Yes," Conrad responded.

"Wouldn't that be impossible?"

"I thought that at first." Conrad stopped pacing the floor and sat back down. "But now I know it is achievable, and I'm using you to lure her in."

"Why would she fall for that?" Noah said.

"Because she's in love with you."

It shocked Noah to hear those words coming from Conrad's mouth. Amara had answered none of his calls, and she had disappeared from his life. Why would he think she was in love with him? Noah deep down wished that had been true, but by her actions, it was more the other way around.

"Since you know so much, then you should know I haven't talked to her in months," Noah told him.

"I know more than you," Conrad smirked. "She has been following you and your little female companion every night."

Noah was speechless. He couldn't believe what Conrad had just said. Had Amara been following them? He dropped his head in shame. If she had, Noah didn't want her to think that he didn't love her, nor wanted to be with her. He was still in love with only her. The woman was only a co-worker. He had told Amara he was moving on, hoping she would reach out to him. But she had and would always be the woman he wanted.

They both jumped when the doors of the warehouse slammed open. Tyler looked at Noah tied up, and then he looked at Conrad. His face became bloodshot red. Conrad jumped out of his chair and rushed towards Tyler.

"What the hell is going on?" Tyler yelled.

"Listen to me before you get upset."

"Untie this man; you have lost your mind."

Conrad pushed Tyler back before he got close to Noah. Tyler stopped and shot Conrad a look. Whatever was going on, Tyler didn't want to be a part of it.

"Listen, I have a plan," Conrad pleaded.

"What plan?" Tyler barked at him.

"To catch the vampire that killed my brother."

"By kidnapping a human?" Tyler walked forward, but Conrad stopped him once again. "Move, so I can untie him."

"Wait, this is the one she loves, and she will come for him," Conrad cried out.

Tyler stopped trying to push Conrad. He looked at Noah struggling in the chair and then back at Conrad. This man was being held hostage and, clearly, Conrad had already set things in motion. The only thing that Tyler could do was let it play out.

"What if she doesn't come?" Tyler took a deep breath and ran his fingers through his hair in frustration.

"She will."

Noah was looking at both of them, confused. He couldn't believe what he was hearing. Talk about vampires and Amara being in love with him all seemed a bit too crazy. He just wanted to be let go and nothing else.

Tyler looked at Noah. He walked over to where Conrad had once sat and had a seat. He looked Noah in the eyes for a second and sized him up. Neither one of them said anything and only stared at each other. Finally, Tyler broke the silence.

"I'm sorry about my friend," he said. "He is obsessed with killing this vampire."

"You believe in them, too?" Noah questioned him. Now I'm dealing with two crazy people, he thought to himself.

"They're real, and you're about to see that firsthand." Tyler picked up the bottled water beside Noah and gave him another drink. "I know you don't believe us, but you will."

CHAPTER EIGHTY-SEVEN

As soon as the sun went down, she was ready to take action. No one was going to hurt Noah. Conrad was going to have his head ripped off. She already knew that this was a trap, but she would risk it all for him. She headed out the door and then to the address that was on the note.

When she got close to the address, she parked her car on a side road and walked the rest of the way. She didn't want them to hear her pull up and from behind a nearby tree, she watched the building. The lights were on, and she knew they were waiting for her.

She used her vampiric speed and looked inside of a side window. Conrad and Tyler were pacing the floor, and then she saw Noah tied to a chair. She looked around the room and realized there was only one way in and one way out. The front door was her only option, and Conrad was continuously watching it.

She had no choice but to face them head-on and headed towards the front of the building. Taking a minute before opening it, she took a deep breath. Here goes nothing. She kicked open the door with so much force it flew across the room and the loud sound of it was like lightning striking, making all of them jump.

Both of them backed away from her, not knowing what she was about to do. She slowly walked in and looked at Noah. He looked back at her as their eyes met and shook his head. He was trying to warn her that this was all a trap.

"I'm here," she said as she held up her hands. "Now, let him go."

"I'm glad you showed," Conrad replied.

He was way more confident now and didn't fear her. He held a stake behind his back, waiting for the moment to strike, and moved closer to Noah, just in case she used her vampiric speed to untie him.

Tyler moved towards the right-hand side of her. He didn't have a stake, but he possessed the amulet. However, he wasn't close enough for it to work. Tyler was waiting for the right moment to move.

She observed both of them while reading their thoughts. She was not about to let them blindly attack her. Then she watched Tyler to the right of her, and she watched Conrad that stood in front of her. There was a significant amount of distance where she could see if they ran toward her.

Noah was still struggling in the chair. He had loosened the ties from around his hands. He just needed the right moment to bend down and untie his feet. Noah watched both Conrad and Tyler. As they focused on her, they didn't realize he was almost free. Bending down slowly, he could loosen the rope around his legs.

"Okay, now what?" She gave them an angry look, as she continuously glanced over at Tyler, watching his moves.

"You killed my brother," Conrad yelled. "And now it's time for you to pay."

"Your brother deserved it," she yelled back.

She moved closer to Conrad, and Conrad took a step toward her. Fury raged through his body as he gripped the stake tighter in his hands. Tyler moved closer and was now in range for the amulet to work.

She tried to make her fangs protrude but could not. A funny feeling came over her, and she felt as if she was just human. She looked over at Tyler to see him dangling a necklace as he moved in closer.

"Your powers are gone, evil one," Tyler said as he smiled at her, then he looked at Conrad and yelled. "Now!"

She watched as Conrad moved towards her and pulled out a stake. As he approached, Noah could escape and run past him. He stood in front of her, shielding her, just as Conrad plunged the stake forward.

Noah gasped as he looked down at his chest. Conrad had stabbed him. Noah grabbed it with both hands, trying to pull it from his chest, but it was no use. He looked at Conrad in shock, as he fell back, and she caught him in her arms.

"No!" she cried out.

Conrad was also in a state of shock when he noticed he had stabbed Noah instead of her. He looked horrified. He realized that he just killed an innocent man. What had he done? He had been in such a rage that he didn't even realize that Noah had broken free.

Tyler was stunned and paralyzed at the sight of what had taken place. He watched as she held Noah in her arms. He hadn't realized that another vampire had snuck up on him. Someone tapped him on his shoulder and Tyler jumped in fear. His eyes widened as he looked into the man's face. He knew it was over for him.

Lou had returned and as he smiled, he watched as Tyler nervously held the amulet in his hand. Even though the amulet stopped him from using his vampiric power, he still grabbed Tyler by his neck. Both of them struggled, and Tyler dropped the amulet. Then Lou took his foot and kicked it away from him.

Conrad rushed towards the amulet as Lou and Tyler fought. He grabbed it, then looked at Lou, holding Tyler in the air with one arm. And then he glanced over at her. She was still on her knees, holding Noah's lifeless body.

This was Conrad's chance. He knew he could not win this fight, and while both vampires focused their attention elsewhere, he ran out the door, hopped in his car, and drove off as fast as he could. He had escaped.

Lou held Tyler up in the air by the neck. He had been waiting to kill this vampire hunter for a long time. He laughed as Tyler struggled to break free, and with a quick twist of Lou's wrist, he broke Tyler's neck and dropped him to the ground.

She held Noah as he coughed up blood. He was still holding on, but his breathing was slowing down.

"I never stopped loving you." He looked up at her. He was fading away, and she could feel it.

"I love you too." she cried as tears flowed down her cheeks.

She watched as he coughed up more blood, and then he closed his eyes. Noah died in her arms and there was no bringing him back. Another tragic end in this life of darkness.

Lou walked over to her and put his hand on her back. He looked down at Noah's lifeless body. She looked up at him tearfully and then back down at Noah.

"I'm sorry that this happened to you," Lou sadly told her. "No one deserves this type of pain. Victoria and I know it all too well."

With everything she had been through, deep down, she knew that Lou's lover never died of old age. But now wasn't the time to question that. She only wished she had listened in the very beginning and hadn't been so stubborn. If only she had followed the rules, Noah would still be alive. A single tear ran down her cheek.

"I understand now," she breathed. She slowly raised, still holding Noah's head. Then she placed it gently down on the ground and kissed him on his forehead. She took a pause and turned away from him.

"You didn't abandon me."

"No, I didn't. I'm always around."

"Me too," she heard a woman's voice say out loud.

They both looked towards the door to see Victoria standing there, smiling. She saved her as well.

Lou put his arm around her, and they slowly walked toward Victoria. Both of them had only wanted to protect her from herself, and now she understood why vampires and humans could not have a relationship.

"I think it's time for a vacation," Victoria said as she put her arm around her as well.

"You don't hate me?" she said as she sniffed her nose. "I am so sorry for the shitty way that I treated you. I should've listened when you told me human and vampire relationships would never work. You were only trying to prevent this from happening."

"It's all water underneath the bridge. You're family and we love you," Victoria replied. "But you get on my nerves… *newbie*."

It saddened her at the thought of Noah's untimely death and the fact her actions had caused it. But there was no more she could do. He was gone forever. All she ever wanted was for someone to love her and accept her. Noah did just that.

But she was going to follow all the vampiric rules… Until it was time to go after Silas but just like Victoria would say…

That's part of a sequel.

EPILOGUE

Celeste pushed open the tall wooden doors that led into the dining area. The décor was grim, and the lighting was dim. The only lighting was from the candles that flickered in the room. She walked over to the table where Silas and Lilith sat.

She watched as they sipped human blood out of elegant wine glasses. Once she reached Silas, she bowed down before him. He looked down at her and slowly set his glass on the wooden table.

"Rise, my child," he said as he took a deep breath. Just the presence of Celeste annoyed him, and she knew it. "What do you want?"

"I have information to tell you, my lord," she said as she kept her head facing the ground.

"What information?" he harshly asked. He looked over at Lilith, rolled his eyes, and then looked back at Celeste. She was weak and pathetic to him.

"The *newbie…* Amara. I've been watching her since I heard Lou had transformed her."

"Yes, go on," he said. Anything that involved his old *companion* always piqued his interest.

Celeste slowly looked up at Silas and told him all the things that she had witnessed. She could tell that he was eager for what she had to say, for he leaned in closer to her. She told him about Amara and her human relationships with Noah and Mariam and even told him she believes Mariam knew what they were.

She also told him about the times she witnessed Amara killing innocent men. She said she saw her burying their bodies without healing them on two occasions, and that she was out of control, refusing to follow any vampire rules.

"As you can see, she has broken many vampiric rules, my lord."

"What! How dare they!" Silas screamed, his voice echoing in the room. His face went from normal to its vampire state, exposing all of his teeth. "And you're just now coming forth with this?"

"I apologize to you, my lord… I wanted to make sure," she nervously said in fear he would decapitate her where she stood. She had seen it happen before. "And Victoria has been helping her."

"They choose to defy me! *The Order*? They will not make me a fool, nor will I allow this treason to continue. Where are they?"

"They have taken off. All three of them… Lou, Victoria, and the *newborn*."

With his monstrous face, he glared at both Celeste and Lilith in anger. They were terrified of him at that moment. He'd killed loyal subjects in an instant, because of pure anger.

They watched as he closed his eyes for a moment. He took in deep breaths and didn't say a word. His face slowly changed back to normal. Then he opened his eyes and sat back down. Celeste watched as he grabbed his glass and took a sip. Once she knew he was calm, she spoke up once more.

"My lord?" Celeste said as her voice trembled.

"What?" he sternly replied. He was still trying to remain calm. "Haven't you said enough?"

"I'm sorry to report that there is also a new *vampire slayer* among us," she said as she squinted her eyes in fear of his reaction.

But he remained seated and calm. What was he to do about Lou—an *untouchable*? And the *Vampire Slayer*? He took a couple more sips of blood, looking at Celeste. then finally spoke.

"This will not go unpunished. We will do something about all of them," he replied. "Go retrieve the human girl, Mariam, and bring her to me."

Celeste nodded her head and bowed once more. She headed towards the door, but quickly stopped in her tracks when she heard him speak and turned to face him.

"I see you are trying to work on your indiscretion. You're showing *The Order* that you are trying to amend your treasonous act… by throwing others under the bus. I pity anyone that ever trusts such a foul immoral." He laughed. "Nevertheless, well done… Now, bring me the human girl."

"Yes, my lord." Celeste nodded as she formed a slight grin on her face and, with vampiric speed, she left the room.

"Yes," Silas said out loud while holding his wineglass in the air. "This is war."

ABOUT THE AUTHOR

T.L Sturgis (Tyeshia Sturgis)

Driven by a fiery passion and a solid predilection to hook her audience through exciting content, T.L Sturgis writes relatable stories that resonate well with young and adult readers. She is an ardent and veteran author who uses writing to escape reality and explore the creative world, giving her a chance to carry her audience to momentous exhilaration full of lessons and reflections.

Sturgis has comprehensively written on different genres and themes in a rich and full-time writing journey that spans more than 10 years now, the most outstanding among them being psychological thrillers, poetry, and fantasy. She has several titles under her bosom, making her one of the household names in the current American book readership.

Sturgis lives in Kentucky, and through her writing talent, she firmly believes that she will consistently stir the creative world with more exciting and engaging books that will
keep her audience reading for life.